ALSO BY NICHELLE GIRALDES

No Child of Mine

THE FOREST OF MISSING GIRLS

THE FOREST OF MISSING GIRLS

NICHELLE GIRALDES

Copyright © 2025 by Nichelle Giraldes
Cover and internal design © 2025 by Sourcebooks
Cover design by Caroline Johnson
Cover images © Melchior van Nigtevecht/Stocksy, PeopleImages.com - Yuri A/Shutterstock

Sourcebooks, Poisoned Pen Press, and the colophon are registered trademarks of Sourcebooks.

All rights reserved. No part of this book may be reproduced in any form or by any electronic or mechanical means including information storage and retrieval systems—except in the case of brief quotations embodied in critical articles or reviews—without permission in writing from its publisher, Sourcebooks.

No part of this book may be used or reproduced in any manner for the purpose of training artificial intelligence technologies or systems.

The characters and events portrayed in this book are fictitious or are used fictitiously. Any similarity to real persons, living or dead, is purely coincidental and not intended by the author.

All brand names and product names used in this book are trademarks, registered trademarks, or trade names of their respective holders. Sourcebooks is not associated with any product or vendor in this book.

Published by Poisoned Pen Press, an imprint of Sourcebooks
1935 Brookdale RD, Naperville, IL 60563-2773
(630) 961-3900
sourcebooks.com

Cataloging-in-Publication Data is on file with the Library of Congress.

Printed and bound in Canada.
MBP 10 9 8 7 6 5 4 3 2 1

For C & K
My sisters, whose roots are forever tangled with mine.

CHAPTER 1

No one ever warned me how much of my life would feel like playing pretend. Pretending I knew what I was doing, where I was going, what I wanted. Pretending I was happy.

When I was a child, make-believe was fun, the sort of game I could lose myself in for hours in the forest behind my house. That forest seemed to possess a magic of its own, plucked straight from a fairy tale. Not the sanitized kind we were fed in children's movies where princes fell in love with young maidens without voices or shoes but rather the darker, bloodier kind. Where toes were chopped off, eyes carved out of their sockets, and children were eaten. Those stories, where danger and magic danced, were as familiar to me as my own pillow.

I suspect I felt the way most children feel about their own imagined worlds, the line between reality and the impossible so blurry that it was difficult to tell the difference. But even now, when I no longer believed in fairies or witches, something about those trees still made me shiver. The forest was the kind of place Hansel and Gretel got lost in, filled with trees plucked straight from Snow White's race through the haunted woods. Trees that whispered through the night. Branches that reached down low to brush their leaves across my cheeks. The trees that surrounded my childhood home for miles on each side felt alive. It was a place that I played in during the day and refused to turn my back on once it got dark.

As I got older, it became easy to forget the dark magic of the trees, to tuck the memories in a back corner of my mind where they'd collect dust. Especially when I moved away. Especially when I moved to a place where hot cement and incessant sunshine blotted out any secret shadows where magic might hide.

Even as I forgot the trees, part of me still believed that life contained its own sort of magic, that things would work out like in a storybook, the next chapters unfurling without much effort. A beginning of a life that led seamlessly toward a middle, then continued in a clean, straight line to an ending—if I was lucky, a happy one. That eventually, all my pretending would become something real. But so far, my life hadn't worked out that way.

I unhooked my key from my key ring and set it on the kitchen counter, a wide swath of black quartz that I had learned how to perfectly wipe so there wouldn't be any streaks. This place, Tom's place, was the kind of home I had always imagined for myself—a beautiful modern apartment with big picture windows and pale hardwood floors. I walked through the kitchen again, pretending to do one last check despite the fact that all my belongings were already packed into my car. It's funny how little you accumulate when you live your life tucked into the corner of someone else's.

I opened the fridge one last time and took in the rows of perfectly arranged bottles and cans on the top shelf, giving way to the mismatched take-out containers below. A familiar desire sprang up in my stomach. I wished I felt at home here. I never had, even when this had technically been my address. In the months I lived here, I never felt like more than a houseguest who had slightly overstayed their welcome.

I had lived in a studio apartment when I first moved to LA, fresh out of college. It was tiny and never felt clean, even after a full day scrubbing at the grout in the bathroom with a toothbrush. I hated it. When my lease was up, Tom, who at that point was my boyfriend of nine months, asked me to move in with him. I assume he felt bad for me, or maybe he was tired of driving twenty minutes out of the way to pick me up when we went to dinner. I had already taken to spending most nights at his place anyway, much preferring the double marble sinks in his bathroom to my tiny sink with an impossible-to-clean orange ring around the drain.

When he'd broken up with me less than two weeks ago over a candlelit dinner, I wasn't completely surprised. I had felt it coming. He had grown bored with me. But I hadn't expected it so soon. I hoped for another few months with him. While our relationship wasn't exhilarating, it wasn't bad. I was happy to endure conversations that never went past small talk and evenings out that felt like obligations to keep my beautiful apartment and enviable boyfriend. But the illusion of my perfectly composed life was fragile. Everything collapsed the moment he didn't want me anymore.

He explained that he wasn't ready to settle down. It didn't

matter that I wasn't ready either. My novelty had worn off. He had already memorized the exact weight of my breasts. The birthmark inside the slight dip in my left hip bone was familiar. The way my skin broke out in goose bumps when he whispered my name in my ear no longer reminded him of his power over my body. These things, the parts of me that only he possessed, had become mundane and unexciting. They had lost their magic.

"You're incredible, Lia," he said. "But I'm not ready to take the next step right now. I wish we'd met a few years from now when I'd be prepared for all that."

I nodded through his explanation while I picked at dinner. When he wanted to settle down in a decade or so, I would no longer be a candidate because he would want the twenty-three-year-old version of me with my tits high and forehead unwrinkled. He wanted to put this version of me on ice until a wife and a baby seemed more palatable.

I knew that I shouldn't blame myself for his waning interest. I shouldn't be required to reinvent myself into something new every full moon to keep him from growing bored. But I still felt like I'd failed because I couldn't keep him entertained, as if I were a movie he had walked out on because there weren't enough car chases.

He would have kept you if you were prettier...if you were just a little better, a small voice whispered in my ear. I tried to shoo it away like a fly at a summer picnic, but it was persistent. I should have pretended that I didn't hear it or, at the very least, didn't believe it. But it felt true. I had worked so hard to shape myself into the sort of girl who belonged in this city with Tom.

It was an expensive regime. The workout classes. The salads. The bimonthly highlights. And skin-care routines. I had carved out new ways of dressing, talking, and moving through the world. But it hadn't been enough. The glass slipper didn't fit, even when I cut off my toes.

The morning after the breakup, I called my mom. I couldn't justify living in LA on my current salary. I didn't want to find another crusty studio in a part of town so far from the ocean that it might as well have been Nebraska. "Come home," she told me, when I explained that Tom had ended things. Maybe she asked me, but regardless of whether it was a demand or a request, I agreed without hesitation.

I hadn't been happy in LA. Not in a long time. It was a low-grade discontent that lingered in the background most days, a quiet melancholy that I could have lived with for a while. There had been something undeniably tempting about leaving the seasonless city for the comfort of my childhood bedroom. The endless sun had started to grate on me. I dreamed of rainy days and trees under whose branches it was easy to forget the color of the sky.

Twelve days later, my car was packed, and I was headed back to my home in the trees.

CHAPTER 2

I had forgotten just how frightening these woods were at night. My memories of them had become tinged with the candy-coated layers of nostalgia that painted my childhood in Technicolor. Even during the day, the forest was dangerous. It was deep, stretching for miles and miles on all sides, trees clustered so tightly together the house disappeared after just a few steps past the first branches. It was the kind of place it was too easy to get lost in.

But at night, it was worse. The tree trunks looked white in the glare of car headlights, cutting through the darkness like sharp teeth, the forest an endless mouth. As I made the familiar turn into the winding driveway, I felt like a thousand eyes were watching me from the darkness, their stares raising the hair on the back of my neck. The forest felt alive, like a wild animal—unpredictable, uncontrollable, something that could kill me without a second thought but for the moment was curled up at my feet.

Yet, even given all that, it still was the place that I felt most at home. We had moved into this house just before my third birthday, a few years before my sister was born. Most of my childhood memories had taken place under these branches. Perhaps it was just the familiarity that felt comforting, even when it was tinged with fear. But there was something more, something that kept pulling me back. This place felt written into my bones.

Every time the driveway turned, my headlights illuminated a new section of trees, the bright light making the deep shadows more pronounced. It was only a two-minute drive. Less than a half mile separated the house from the main road, but it felt like it took longer, the minutes stretching lifetimes as I recalled every time I had driven down the winding path between tree trunks. My tires crunched against the gravel road, a siren song beckoning me home.

The noise always brought me back to my childhood, to the moments during long car rides when I knew that the trip was almost over. I would slow my breath and relax all the muscles in my body so my father would carry me to bed. My mom would carry my sister, who never failed to wake up when the car stopped, her tiny whines and babbles filling the space that the sound of the gravel had left behind.

The house wasn't visible until you rounded that last bend in the road. There was nothing but trees and darkness until you made the final turn, and then it appeared all at once. Golden light poured out from the windows, a lighthouse on a stormy night.

I pulled my car up against the house, the silence thick as I turned the key. My car was stuffed with everything I had acquired over the past year. White dresses and cutoff shorts, bikinis and oversize hats, blazers and barely scuffed heels, unlit candles, and books I'd never read.

I had gone to college a few states away on a campus with brick buildings and grassy quads. But I still spent my holiday breaks and summers here, each semester just a long trip away from home. The move to LA was different, though. It was supposed to be a clean break, the first chapter in a new part of my life. I hadn't planned on ever coming back.

But here I was again, staring at my childhood home and wondering if I'd made a mistake. I told myself I wouldn't stay forever—just a few months, until I figured out what came next. Yet, as I sat with the warm light from the front porch pushing back the darkness of the surrounding forest, I wasn't sure leaving would be so easy.

I could see the front room from my car, the lamp on the side table still on, a wedge of light cutting across the floor from the kitchen. At night, the house became a stage, every corner visible from one window or another. I slipped out of my car, grabbing only the tote bag I had tossed on the passenger seat. The rest of my belongings could wait until the morning. The air outside was cold. Winter was already here. Its icy breath cut right through my sweatshirt. I ran up the porch steps, eager to be locked inside, safe from the cavernous dark.

I kept my eyes fixed on that front window, waiting for someone to appear and notice me. It wasn't very late, but maybe everyone had already gone to bed, forgetting that I was arriving tonight. Perhaps I could slip inside without waking anyone, although that seemed unlikely.

I had tried to sneak out of my house only once, when I was in high school. Driving my own car was out of the question. There was no way I would make it down the long gravel driveway without the whole house hearing. You could hear cars on that driveway from every room. So, one night, after I had confirmed both of my parents were asleep, I snuck out the back door and made for the trees. My friends were supposed to meet me around the corner, their car idling on the street at the end of our driveway. But I never made it that far. The moment I was deep enough in the woods that the trees hid the light from the windows, I turned back and ran inside the house, feeling like something was chasing me. I was certain that, at any second, a hand would reach out and grab my ankle and pull me into the dark.

I was out of breath by the time I made it back to the house and slipped in the back door. I couldn't have been gone for more than a few minutes, but I found my mom leaning against the counter.

I waited for the reprimand. I didn't bother making excuses. Even in the dim light of the kitchen, she couldn't have missed my outfit: ripped jeans, a too-small tank top, and gray eyeshadow smudged halfway to my temples. Even then, I was practiced at pretending, trying on different versions of myself to find which girl would be the most appealing to the people around me.

My mother's eyes traced over me while I stood frozen, my hand still on the knob. She barely seemed to register that I was there, and then the slightest smile had lifted the corners of her mouth. "You shouldn't use that shade on your lips.

It really washes you out." To this day, I would think about that comment every time I tried on a new lipstick color. My mother's voice was never far away when I looked in a mirror to assess if my cheeks looked too pink or my skin too pale, always seeking her approval, even when she was hundreds of miles away.

The comment had been routine, just one of thousands of unspoken expectations. My mother had rules about everything from skin care to hair color. There were rules about what I needed to look like. Rules about what were acceptable methods to achieve that. Rules about what I wore. Rules about what I ate. Rules about how loud I laughed or talked. Rules about what I was allowed to talk about. Rules about what I should enjoy. The rules, her rules, were carved into the insides of my eyelids, little reminders every time I blinked. It wasn't like there was a handbook somewhere. Most of the time, the rules went unspoken, governed by disapproving glances and sighs. But still, they were always present, like walls moving in closer and closer until it was impossible to breathe, narrowing the acceptable circumstances I needed to exist within.

She pushed away from the counter, sparing me one more glance. "Lock the door," she said over her shoulder, then floated up the stairs. I had braced for my punishment to be doled out the following day at the breakfast table, but she'd never mentioned it again.

She was waiting for me in the kitchen tonight too. Her long blond hair was swept back in a twist, her posture perfect as she sat at the table. My mother, Elizabeth, was the kind of woman who would draw attention the moment she walked into a room. It wasn't just that she was beautiful, although that was certainly true with her perfect blond waves, pearly white smile, and bright blue eyes. It was something more than that. You didn't want to merely admire her; you wanted to *be* her. To peel off her skin and slip into it for a while. She exuded an effortlessness that felt possible only on the glossy pages of a magazine. If I had to choose a single word to describe my mom, it would be that one: effortless.

I looked nothing like her.

At a glance, you might not notice the differences between us—two women of roughly the same height, both with long blond hair. We looked the same in the way that a pet might begin to resemble its owner. Not a matter of genetics but of habit and preference. My eyes were smaller than hers, my nose wider, my chin softer, my dark roots clearly peeking out from my scalp, my face greasy after a few too many days spent in the car. It wasn't that I looked ugly, like some strange alien creature, but no one would ever call me effortless.

Her glasses were low on her nose, an empty wineglass sat to her left, and an artfully disordered stack of paper was on her right. The glasses were a new addition from a few years back, a little reminder that she was getting older too. Her face had softened some over the years, a few new faint lines appearing each time she added a candle to her birthday cake. But she had never so much as considered plastic surgery or any sort of injection. She said there was something unnatural about those sorts of procedures, and she wanted to age gracefully. It was easy to say that when you looked the way she did. She was already an *after* picture.

She looked up at the sound of my footsteps, the light from the laptop screen reflected in her lenses. "How was the drive?" she asked.

"Not too bad, but I'm grateful to be home," I said, as if the last two years in LA had been nothing but a bad vacation where my luggage had been lost and they had double-booked my hotel room.

The dogs heard my voice, and their claws clicked against the hardwood as they headed toward us. Poppy and Daisy, a pair of goldendoodles my parents had gotten while I was away at college. As soon as they spotted me, they pressed their noses into my palms. I scratched their heads, and their collars jingled in the quiet house.

"Are you hungry? I can heat something up for you," my mom offered. The gesture was almost obligatory, but it was comforting all the same. I couldn't remember the last time I'd had a home-cooked meal that I hadn't made myself.

The dogs had already grown bored of me, walking away in tandem to their matching beds in the living room. I shook my head. "I'm okay. I think I'll probably just head up to bed. I'm exhausted." It wasn't a lie, but more than that, I was eager to be alone in this space. To recalibrate myself into the version of Lia who would be expected here.

"You look tired." The words were innocent enough, but coming from her, they felt like judgment. She would have arrived looking perfect: clothes unwrinkled, hair freshly blown out, probably with fresh flowers and a handwritten thank-you note. I had been home for five minutes and was already falling short of her expectations. Her vague disappointment was familiar as it lingered in the air between us. "Get some sleep," she said, her eyes returning to her screen.

I watched her face for a second, illuminated by the kitchen light and the blue glow of her laptop. Even as a child, I had known my mom was not like other mothers. There was something almost otherworldly about her.

When I was in kindergarten, I told my classmates that my mom was a lost princess who had left her kingdom and could never find her way back home. It was the only explanation that felt feasible. It was the only way I could rationalize how she felt different, better somehow than the other parents. She would have been the heart of any fairy tale, either as the lost princess I imagined as a child or the evil queen. Someone as beautiful as her wouldn't be relegated to a side character.

Sometimes I wished she looked more like everyone else, with crooked teeth or a lopsided smile. The slight imperfections in ordinary faces were comforting. They gave you something to hold on to, to sink your nails into, a part of them to memorize and fall in love with. My mom was too perfect; her face was made of marble and silk, far too easy to slip through your fingers.

I turned and headed for the stairs as she tapped against the keys. I was almost out of sight before I heard her say, "Welcome home, Ophelia."

The sound of my name made me hesitate on the first step. Another signal that I was back home. My mother was the only person who called me that. No one in my life in California had ever called me by my full name. I had become Lia, a lighter version of myself, uncomplicated by the weight of a Shakespeare play. What kind of parent would give their daughter the name of a drowned girl, a name sure to lead to tragedy? But here I was, Ophelia again.

CHAPTER 3

I woke up to low chatter and plates being pulled from cabinets in the kitchen. My room was washed in a strange gray as cloudy morning light slipped past my curtains. It had looked practically the same since I went to college. A queen bed with crisp white linens sat in the middle of the room. The night before, after a hot shower, I had fallen asleep within minutes of crawling under the sheets, which still smelled of detergent and fabric softener.

I anticipated it being difficult to transition from the noises that had soothed me to sleep in Tom's apartment. His steady breathing from the other pillow. The echo of footsteps from the apartment above his. Car horns and sirens leaking in through the window. Constant little reminders that I wasn't alone. Instead, the silence here acted as a sort of balm, pressing against me until I was unconscious. I hadn't slept that well in months.

I pulled myself out of bed and headed downstairs, where

my dad and Evie, my younger sister, were sitting at the kitchen table. My mom was already dressed for the day, her hair falling in sleek waves just past her shoulders. I didn't know when she slept. She was always in the kitchen when we woke, making us breakfast in a full face of makeup with her hair freshly washed and styled. As a child, I hadn't ever thought twice about it. Only recently, now that I knew how long it took to look that polished, had I begun to question it. When did she have to drag herself out of bed to be ready by the time we stumbled down the stairs with sleep still in our eyes?

I leaned down to kiss my dad on the cheek. He didn't look up from the block of text he was reading on his phone, but he reached a hand up to pat my arm as I bent down. "It's good to see you, honey. Happy to have you home." I refrained from mentioning that he hadn't actually seen me because he hadn't looked up from his phone since I'd come downstairs.

My dad had always seemed a bit disinterested in us; it wasn't as if he didn't care about us—he just didn't care about the details. He attended every one of my sister's dance recitals and had even made a sign when I graduated from college, but I wasn't sure he could have named a single one of my high school friends. The specifics of our daily lives weren't his domain. My mother orchestrated every aspect, while he was just along for the ride.

Evie's face was also down in her phone, but I made no moves to interrupt her scrolling. She was still in high school, a little more than six years younger than me. That gap in our ages dictated every aspect of our relationship. We had never shared clothes or secrets. Still, growing up, she felt like an extension of me in a way, her presence laced through all my childhood memories. Our lives are braided together at the roots, impossible to untangle.

I remember being ten, eating cotton candy on our family's first trip to Disneyland, and when I wouldn't share, she bit me so hard, we both cried. I still have a faint half-moon scar on my upper arm. Or when I was twelve, and she broke her arm climbing a tree in the woods, and I carried her to the house on my back while her cheek was pressed against me, tears leaking into my hair. Or the day my family dropped me off at college. She spent the entire trip rolling her eyes, arms crossed over her chest, annoyed that I was the center of attention. But, as my mother fussed with the pillows on my narrow twin bed, I caught Evie wiping away tears with the back of her hand when she thought I wasn't looking. In the years since I had left home, she had transformed into a teenager—a full person in her own right. She was no longer an accessory to my story but the driving force in her own. And my presence here was merely an interruption to her life.

"Ophelia," my mom called, "do you want spinach in your eggs?"

"I can make my own breakfast," I said with a yawn, before wandering over to the elaborate espresso machine my father had gotten my mom four Christmases ago. Now she used it to have a cup of coffee waiting for him every morning before he came down the stairs.

"I know you can. But I'm already at the stove. Spinach?"

"Sure," I said. No more words were exchanged as the espresso machine whirred, and my mom hummed quietly as she shifted the eggs in the pan. I hadn't expected fanfare when I returned home, but it was strange how easily I fell back into the simple rhythms of mornings with my family.

"You'll be home for dinner?" my mom asked as Evie brushed past me to stack her breakfast dishes on the counter.

"Uhhh…" Evie paused.

My mother interrupted her before she had a chance to make an excuse. "It's Ophelia's first night home," she said, making it clear her words had been less of a question and more of an expectation.

Evie glanced in my direction with an eye roll. The annoyance wasn't directed at me but our mother, who was too busy cooking my eggs to catch the look. I'd missed this part of having a sister, these little moments of shared understanding that are only possible with someone you grew up alongside.

"Then I guess I'll be home," Evie said with a sigh, throwing her backpack over one shoulder. "Can I bring Maddie?"

"Of course. She is always welcome," my mother said as Evie headed for the front door.

My father exited the dining table soon after Evie did, pausing to kiss my mom before walking out the door with a single wave in my direction. I settled onto one of the stools at the counter while my mom started the morning dishes. A large picture window over the sink looked out into the woods around our house.

I had missed the bright reds and oranges that painted the trees each October. Most of the leaves had already fallen, and those that clung to the branches had long since been leeched of color. Now all that remained were bare trees that felt ominous even during the day. There was something unsettling about the way the shadows between them seemed to eat the light.

As a child, I had always loved being in the forest. Evie and I spent hours building forts, climbing trees, and crafting whole separate worlds under the branches. Our mom would take us on long walks on barely visible trails, packing picnics, spending entire days out there. Even when I was a teenager and had outgrown most of those games, I would wander through the forest, finding quiet spaces to listen to the wind whispering through the leaves. It seemed to calm me. The hum of nature quieted something restless in me. No matter the weather, there was rarely a day that I didn't spend at least a few minutes walking between tree trunks, until Krista went missing.

Krista McNeil wasn't the first. Girls had always disappeared in these woods. *Girls* might have been a condescending word to describe them. Young women went missing here—women who straddled the line between adolescence and adulthood.

There wasn't a pattern. No regular cadence to the disappearances. We could go years without one, and then three would vanish between the Fourth of July and Christmas. No clear connection between them—except that once the trees took them, they were never found.

Krista's disappearance hit me harder than the others because she was so young. She was only fifteen—the same age as me—and a sophomore at Saint Catherine's, the Catholic school in the neighboring town. She vanished while walking home from school, the same short walk she had taken every day for years, usually crowded with other students.

I didn't know her. I didn't recognize her in the pictures that populated every corner of our town for weeks with her wide smile and long red hair, but still, it felt too close. School buzzed with conversations about what had happened to her. The girls measured which one of them had gotten closest to tragedy and walked away unscathed:

"I used to go for runs on those trails."

"I almost went to Saint Catherine's."

"I walked home alone that day too."

It could have been me was an unspoken echo through all their stories.

I had stopped spending time in the woods after that.

"What are your plans for the day?" My mom had finished the dishes and was drying her hands on a towel.

"I've got some writing to do for work. And I've got to catch up on emails."

I was currently working as an assistant for a small lifestyle brand. It wasn't exactly what I had dreamed of, but it paid well enough and would be an excellent opportunity to network. Or at least that was what I told myself as my classmates went off to grad school and started prestigious fellowships while I wrote Instagram captions and blog posts about the next "life-changing" white T-shirt. When I'd started, the team was still working remotely, a holdover from the pandemic, but as months turned into years and Cerise finally let go of the lease on the office, it became clear that we were never going back to working in person.

My inbox was filled with an obscenely high number of unread emails, since I had ignored all but the most urgent over the last few days during my drive out here. "What about you?"

My mom had been a stay-at-home mom since I was born, and I didn't think she was planning on suddenly entering the workforce when Evie went to college, but she kept busy. Her calendar was likely more crowded with events and meetings than my own. "I've got Pilates and then lunch with Grace and Jane. And this afternoon, I have a meeting for the Christmas gala."

I nodded, taking another sip of my latte.

"I know it's been busy and you haven't had the time to work out lately," my mom continued after a long pause. From anyone else, I might have accepted it as an offhanded comment about my work schedule picking up over the last several months, but from my mother, it was more than that. "But I'd love to have you along for Pilates. Lucy is amazing. I think you'd love her." I didn't miss the way her eyes lingered on my arms, like she could tell I'd been trading my usual morning workouts for an extra hour in bed. They were hidden under my oversize T-shirt, but I knew she'd noticed. She always noticed.

"That sounds nice, but I don't think I can make it today." If I had my choice, I would avoid the process entirely, but I doubted that would be an option.

"Later this week, then," my mom said. "I'll send you her schedule at the studio."

I didn't see my mom again for the rest of the day. I spent most of it sitting at the desk in the corner of my room, answering emails and finalizing the next month's editorial calendar. At some point, both dogs had decided to join me and were stretched out across my carpet, their paws twitching as they dreamed. The house was quiet, and I had opened my window to let in the bright sunlight and the brisk breeze. The curtains moved with the chilly air, filling my room with the sound of the wind filtering through the trees. Even though I was working, it felt a bit like the beginning of a weekend getaway, the world outside my window crisp and serene.

I spent my lunch unloading my car. Poppy and Daisy followed me, bounding behind and chasing each other through the short grass between the house and the tree line as I moved boxes into the back corner of the garage. I had several suitcases full of clothes, which I would need to lug up to my bedroom, but the rest of my things could stay tucked in here for a few months.

Part of me wanted to move as few items upstairs as possible, to live out of a suitcase for my time here, as if lining up my stuff in the dresser drawers would be admitting failure. I didn't want to let myself get too comfortable and forget that this was temporary. It would be too easy to settle into the familiar rhythms of this place and forget to leave. When I was here, I was always defined by my relationship to my mother. I was Elizabeth's daughter, Ophelia. I didn't want to live my life as merely an extension of her. I would allow myself a few months here to rest and figure out what came next, but I wouldn't stay forever.

"Poppy, Daisy, let's go back inside," I called to the dogs as I grabbed the last suitcase and headed for the door. Neither dog returned to my side. "Poppy, Daisy," I said again. I couldn't see either of them from where I stood inside the garage. I set the suitcase down and walked out toward the driveway. The dogs were usually good about staying close, so it was strange that neither of them had appeared at the sound of their names. I wasn't eager to go tromping through the woods to find them if they had decided to wander off.

I saw Poppy as soon as I turned the corner. She was standing facing the woods, her ears pinned back against her head, a deep growl rumbling out of her chest. "Poppy?" I took a couple of steps hesitantly toward her. "Where's Daisy?" I asked, as if Poppy could have responded to me. Her eyes flicked in my direction before returning to the trees.

"Daisy, come," I called into the tree line, searching for a glimpse of a blond tail. Poppy continued to growl, the sound making my arms break out in goose bumps. "Daisy!" I took another couple of steps forward. The branches seemed to dip toward me, and the remaining dead leaves trembled as I passed. Poppy followed right next to me, still growling. I stood at the edge of the woods and repeated her name. This time, it came out as a whisper instead of a shout.

"Daisy," I said. My voice quivered as I tried to be louder this time. I turned to make sure I could still see the house behind me, even though I'd only taken a few steps into the woods. Poppy and the white pillars of my house were still visible through the branches. Something rustled to my left. I shrieked, then immediately clamped a hand over my mouth, afraid I'd just alerted whatever was in these trees to my presence. "Daisy, come on," I pleaded with the dog I couldn't yet see. "Let's go inside."

A glint of something gold shined from a spot near my feet. I reached down toward it, brushing aside a few leaves and dirt that had blown over it. Then I pulled a gold chain from the ground. Four letters dangled from the bracelet: *JELK*. I read them back and forth, trying to make a word, but if they held any sort of meaning, I couldn't decode it. Despite where I'd found it, the metal didn't look tarnished at all. Someone must have lost it recently. I slipped it into my pocket. Maybe it was my mom's or my sister's. I'd ask about it when they got home.

A breeze moved through the dying leaves on the trees, filling the air with a whispered crackling. Then I spotted a blond tail bobbing in my direction from deeper in the forest. Daisy trotted toward me, her tail wagging and her tongue hanging loose out of the side of her mouth.

I exhaled. "Daisy, where have you been?" I grabbed her collar and led her back to where Poppy was still waiting. I resisted the impulse to run, but I moved as fast as I could, unable to shake the unsettling feeling that someone was watching me from the shadows. I released Daisy once we were clear of the trees. Poppy immediately started sniffing at her but seemed to be soothed by her sister's presence.

"Let's go, ladies," I said, grabbing the suitcase again and shooing them inside the garage. I didn't inhale until all three of us were safely in the house with the door locked.

CHAPTER 4

When I came downstairs for dinner, everything about the scene in the kitchen was familiar. My mother stood at the stove, wearing a floral apron I had given her for Mother's Day years ago, while classical music played softly in the background. "Do you want a glass of wine? I have a bottle of white open." She gestured toward the half-full bottle sitting next to her on the counter.

"Sure," I said. I pulled a glass down from the cabinet without having to think about where they were stored. It was a level of muscle memory I had never quite mastered at Tom's place, always forgetting if it was the second or the third drawer where we kept the bottle opener.

I remembered the bracelet in my pocket and set it on the counter before taking a sip of my wine.

"What's that?" my mom asked.

I untangled the gold chain, the light overhead catching on the letters. "A charm bracelet, I think. I found it in the woods this morning," I said.

My mother leaned over the counter so she could get a closer look. "Oh, you know what. I think that might belong to a friend of mine. We were out on a walk the other day, and it must have fallen off. Thank you. I'm sure she'll be glad you found it." She smiled at me and then returned to her spot at the stove.

"Do you need help with anything?"

"Thank you, but no. Everything's nearly done. Go sit down. Keep your father company."

I hadn't even noticed him until my mom pointed him out, but my father was already seated at the head of the table. He was once again scrolling on his phone, but this time he at least looked up as I walked into the room.

"Are you all settled in?" he asked.

I nodded as I sat down at my usual spot at the table, which was already set with my mother's fall decor. "I unpacked my car this afternoon. I left a few bins of stuff in the corner of the garage. I don't think it's in the way, but let me know if you need me to move it."

"I didn't even notice it. I'm sure it's fine," he said. He was saved from further conversation by my sister thundering down the stairs, followed by Maddie.

Maddie and Evie had been best friends since they were toddlers in the same dance class. Their friendship had been instantaneous, and they had been inseparable ever since. If you found one of them, the other was rarely far behind.

Back when I was in high school, I had driven both girls to dance class every Monday and Wednesday. Despite how often I whined about it messing up my schedule, I didn't really mind the drive itself. I enjoyed the sound of the girls laughing over my music as they wrestled bobby pins into their buns and rushed to eat granola bars, leaving the back seat covered in crumbs. Maddie was always polite and made sure to thank me, even when my sister was already racing toward the door of the studio, her dance bag bouncing off her pink tights. The car had always felt too quiet after they'd piled out.

Evie walked through the kitchen, reached into the salad bowl, and plucked a cherry tomato off the top. "Evangeline," my mother scolded, catching Evie even though her back was turned. "Can you at least put the salad on the table if you're going to pick at it?"

Evie rolled her eyes but placed the blue bowl on the table before plopping down in her chair.

My mom followed her, carrying a tray with some sort of chicken-and-rice dish that she set in the middle of the table before settling into her own seat. "How was your day?" she asked in my direction. "Did you have enough space in your room? You're welcome to work in your father's study if you need to spread out. The internet tends to be stronger on the main level."

"I was fine."

"How are you feeling? Are you holding up okay?" she asked. She had loved Tom and might have been more upset about our breakup than I was. I hadn't thought about him all day.

"I'm fine." I felt like I should miss it more. Not just Tom, but everything I had built out there. I had lived in California for a year and a half, but I didn't have much to show for it.

Instead of carving a space for myself in the city, I'd found that just because I lived somewhere big and interesting didn't make my life feel any larger. My world had been small, made to feel even smaller by the potential of the city swirling around me. I didn't know what to do with the fact that I'd stepped into a future I once dreamed of, only to find it hollow.

"You're better off without him anyway," my mom assured me, mistaking my short answer for repressed sorrow. "And we're glad to have you home for a little while."

I wasn't ready to admit it, but I was relieved to no longer live in California. I was embarrassed that what I had wanted had made me miserable. And I was more embarrassed to admit my desire to move so far from home had been primarily motivated by my mother's hatred for the idea. But a weight had lifted off my chest the moment the traffic-packed highways were no longer visible in my rearview mirror.

"You seemed to like him well enough last month," I snapped back, though I would have agreed with her if pressed. Tom and I would never have worked in the long term, but I had an instinctive need to oppose my mother every time she critiqued any of my choices, even when I knew she was right.

"I never liked him," Evie announced between bites of salad. Everyone at the table turned toward her, surprised by her interjection.

"Really?" I asked. I had been under the impression that everyone loved Tom. He had come home with me for a few days over the summer to meet my family. The moment Tom left, my mom immediately started asking if I thought he would propose. She thought he was charming. While I didn't remember

Evie being particularly interested in him, if she'd had anything negative to say at the time, she'd kept it to herself.

"He spent the whole trip trying to impress Mom. It was weird."

I shrugged, but I knew what she was talking about. Tom had always been a little more over the top with his compliments and affection when people were around to witness it. But I had found it charming how much he cared about making a good impression. I was a little surprised Evie had picked up on it.

"Like I said," my mother added, "for the best." She turned to Evie and Maddie. "How was school today, ladies?"

"Fine," Evie said.

"Anything exciting happen?"

"Nope."

My mother let out a sigh and turned to Maddie. "Madison, how is dance team going this semester?"

"Pretty good. Things have been stressful with college applications and all the senior-year stuff, but it's a good group of girls this year."

"Where are you applying?" I asked.

Maddie turned toward me. "I'd really like to go to Vanderbilt, but my grades aren't quite as good as Evie's, so I'm applying to a couple of other places too." A pink blush stained her cheeks as she smiled nervously.

"But you have way better extracurriculars than me," Evie cut in. "You were dance team captain, and you spent all last summer as a camp counselor. It all balances out."

"What do your extracurriculars look like, Ev?" I asked. "You can't just do dance team. You need to look well rounded."

I didn't really know why I was offering advice; I hadn't so much as thought about college applications since I had filled out my own years ago.

"She volunteered with the library over the summer and helps at the food bank once a month. I tried to get her to join the planning team for the Childhood Cancer Walk, but she didn't want to do that," my mother said, shaking her head.

"Evie, I know it's annoying, but you have to make sure you have a really solid résumé. Colleges are getting even more competitive these days," I said.

"Thanks, *Mom*," Evie said, with a pointed glare in my direction. "But I think I've got it covered."

I didn't respond, instead looking down at a particularly interesting slice of cucumber in my salad. My sister was right. I was overstepping, echoing my mother without even realizing it.

"I'm sure you'll be fine, Evie," my dad interrupted, in a clear attempt to defuse the tension between me and my sister. "Colleges will be lucky to have you. You too, Maddie. You are both wonderful young women."

We let the topic move to something less sensitive. The girls were soon swept up in their conversation, featuring a cast of characters whose names I didn't recognize. It was a whirlwind I couldn't follow, but it was like they were back in my car, laughing before dance class.

"Are you going to see Kiera while you're in town?" my mom asked me. "She just started teaching at the elementary school."

I hadn't heard that name in a while, but Kiera Bradford had been one of my friends in high school. We had never been as close as Evie and Maddie, but I had spent many summer weekends hanging out at her pool with the rest of our friend group. "Probably not. I haven't talked to her in years." We had made an effort for the first few months of college, texting each other and getting lunch when we were both back in town, but things had quickly fallen off.

"You should reach out. I'm sure she'd love to catch up and grab a coffee," my mom said, standing and gathering a stack of dishes.

I tried to imagine what that might look like, what we would talk about after so long. She was a teacher now. She had wanted to be one for as long as I could remember. She would probably show me pictures of her classroom, decorated in some adorable theme. Maybe she'd share a few stories about her students. Then it would be my turn, and what would I tell her? That I'd moved to LA and hated it? That I had a job I liked well enough but wouldn't be anyone's dream job? That I had fallen headfirst into a mediocre relationship and neglected all my friendships along the way? No thank you. I'd rather skip that conversation if I could help it.

As soon as my mom cleared the table, the family dispersed. My father retreated upstairs. Evie and Maddie headed to a friend's house with a reminder from Mom about Evie's curfew. I lingered in the kitchen, helping with dishes as my mom told me about her day and asked me a few more questions about work. I was grateful she didn't bring up Tom again.

I was drying the last dish when I turned to find my mom pulling on a pair of tennis shoes. "Where are you going?" I asked, although I could have predicted the answer by the way the dogs danced around her ankles.

"I'm going to take the dogs for a walk."

"It's dark," I said, pointing toward the window, as if she might not have noticed. This wasn't the same as city dark, where the night was warmed by the glow of streetlights and storefronts. Beyond the reach of our porch lights, it was pure black.

My mom laughed. "You've been away for too long. I do this all the time. You used to love a nighttime walk in the trees." She walked past me toward the back door.

"Be careful," I said, anxiety clawing at me at the thought of her alone out there.

The door opened, and a cool breeze blew into the kitchen. She paused and looked back at me before she followed the dogs over the threshold. "Don't worry. I know these woods like the back of my hand."

As soon as the door clicked closed behind her, the house was quiet. The only noise was the low hum of the evening news from my parents' bedroom. I watched her as she walked down the gentle grassy slope that led from the back door to the trees, until she disappeared, the night swallowing her.

CHAPTER 5

Working from home felt lonelier without the constant noise of a city around me. My mother had disappeared again this morning, not long after Evie and my father, leaving me alone in the house. Beyond the sound of my keyboard, I could hear only the occasional birdsong drifting in through my window. I had gotten so used to the quiet that I jumped when I heard a car rumble down the gravel driveway in the late afternoon. The dogs jolted to their feet from where they had been stretched out in a patch of sunlight.

"Mom?" Evie shouted into the house a few moments later, as the front door swung open.

I shoved away from my desk and padded to the top of the stairs. Evie had her head stuck in the fridge, and Maddie had pulled up a stool at the counter. "Mom's not home," I said.

Both girls jumped as their heads swung in my direction, their ponytails swaying behind them. Evie's hair was a bright blond nearly identical to mine, and Maddie's hung in glossy brown waves. Neither of them had changed out of her spandex shorts and matching T-shirts from dance practice.

"When will she be back?" Evie said.

"I don't know. She said she had a meeting for some Christmas thing." I shrugged.

"Okay." Evie pulled a pair of water bottles from the fridge and tossed one in Maddie's direction.

I wasn't sure what my role in this situation should be. The girls hadn't needed a babysitter for years, but I still felt like I was supposed to be in charge. "I'll be in my room if you need anything."

Evie nodded and turned back to the still-open refrigerator.

I went back into my bedroom and closed the door. While, technically, we had a few hours until the end of the workday, I didn't have any more meetings, and there was nothing pressing left on my to-do list. Apparently, a quiet house was great for my productivity. I had accomplished more in the last two days than in a week in LA. I left my computer open in case anything urgent popped up and started unpacking the boxes and suitcases I had brought in from my car yesterday.

The closet and dresser contained remnants of a past life, another version of me. There were T-shirts from school fundraisers and charity runs, garment bags with brightly colored dresses from various school dances, and a few coats I hadn't taken when I moved, but most of the hangers and drawers were empty. I unloaded the majority of my clothes, although I left a suitcase packed with sundresses and bikinis and shoved it to the back of my closet; I wouldn't have any use for them here.

I was going through the handful of books I had brought

with me when my phone buzzed from my desk. A text from Mom, sent to Evie and me: **I'm meeting up with your dad for dinner in town. Feel free to order in!**

I headed downstairs to where Evie and Maddie were stretched across the living room floor. From the top of the stairs, the scene below could have been a still from a coming-of-age movie, books and notebooks open in a messy fan around them.

"Did you get Mom's text?" I asked, hollering over the railing.

"Yeah. We can do the Thai place or pizza, unless you want to pick something up. Those are the only places that deliver," Evie said, not bothering to look in my direction.

"Either is fine with me."

"Okay, let's do pizza, then. I'm starving, and the Thai place takes forever." Evie had already taken out her phone and was dialing. "Pepperoni?" she asked, turning to Maddie.

"Can you order me a salad too?" I asked.

"Why?" Evie asked.

"Because I want one," I said.

Evie rolled her eyes. "Their salads aren't good… Hi, I'd like to place an order for delivery." Her voice shifted to something more pleasant. "Yeah, can we get a large pepperoni pizza?"

"And a salad," I whispered at her. I wasn't expecting anything extraordinary; I just wanted something green.

"They're gross, Lia," Evie whispered, pulling the phone away from her mouth.

I didn't say anything back, just stared at her, until she said, "And the house salad," rolling her eyes.

"Thank you," I said after she hung up.

She rolled her eyes again, turning back to her homework without another glance in my direction.

I returned to my room, this time leaving my door open. The girls' conversation drifted up to me. It was nothing scandalous, just lengthy discussions of their classes filled with people I did not know, broken by short stretches of quiet where I assumed they were attempting to actually do their homework.

It didn't take long before I was completely unpacked. I flopped onto my bed, pulled out my phone, and scrolled through all the updates I had missed while working.

Over the last two years, my social media accounts had shifted from personal to professional, used almost entirely for work. My feeds rarely contained pictures of my friends or my family, their lives long ago relegated to the unseen bottom of an endless scroll. My own feed had turned into a portfolio for my personal brand, the curated version of myself that I wanted others to see. A version of my life composed of nights out and weekend trips, rather than a lackluster breakup and my childhood bedroom.

A loud burst of laughter came from downstairs. I smiled despite myself, grateful for the familiar sound of home. I couldn't tell if coming back felt like a pause, a vacation from my real life, or if my time in LA had been a blip. I could imagine those months I'd spent in the California sunshine fading into my memory as I settled back in here. It would be easy to stay, build a life here, and eventually get my very own house in the trees. But I wanted a more impressive life than just an echo of my mother's path. I reminded myself that this was a temporary escape, not a permanent move. But I knew that if I wasn't careful, this place would wrap its roots around me and hold me here.

It was dark out when the pizza arrived. I hadn't noticed the sun disappear while I mindlessly scrolled, stretched out across my bed. Back in LA, I would have been doing the same thing, lost in my phone while I waited for my food to arrive. "Lia!" Evie called from downstairs, a shout that would have gotten her a stern look from our mom if she had been home. "Pizza's here."

I rolled off the bed, catching my reflection in the black panes of glass. I pulled the curtains shut without looking too closely outside. The windows in this house looked out into the unbroken black expanse in a way that made my skin crawl. It wasn't so much the dark itself but rather the eerie feeling that there could be someone out there watching and I wouldn't be able to see them.

Evie and Maddie were already holding sodas and plates piled with two slices of pizza each when I made it down the stairs. "We're going to go eat outside," Evie told me as I walked into the kitchen.

"It's cold out." It had been chilly during the day, even with mostly blue skies. I was sure the temperature had dropped several more degrees now that night had fallen.

"It's not that cold, and we'll light the firepit," Evie said, balancing her soda under her chin as she pulled the back door open. Poppy and Daisy raced out behind her, eager to have company in the yard. Maddie followed Evie out, and the fire burst to life a few moments later.

I leaned over the counter to pull the Styrofoam container that I was sure held my salad toward me, then popped the lid open. I hadn't expected a gourmet salad experience, but the wilted lettuce topped with a pile of tomato wedges and limp peppers was worse than I could have imagined. The thought of eating those slimy leaves made me almost gag. I closed the lid and tossed the whole thing in the trash. Then I grabbed a plate from the cabinet and loaded two slices of pizza onto it.

Both girls were visible from the window. Evie's ponytail bobbed enthusiastically as she told a story. Maddie was turned toward Evie, and I could see the outline of her face against the fire. They both had blankets wrapped around their shoulders, and their plates of half-eaten pizza sat on a table between them. Beyond them, the woods loomed, only the first edges of the trees visible from the light cast by the firepit. But the dark trees felt less threatening framed between the girls, as if the forest itself had been made more hospitable by the warm glow of their friendship. A lump formed in my throat. I missed those friendships that could only grow in the pressure tank of high school.

I didn't have those sorts of friends anymore. The friendships where we would spend hours talking through every aspect of life had faded slowly in the months after I graduated from college. It was astonishing how the girls I had spent hours with every day were now relegated to a few occasional text messages. They weren't gone entirely. We would grab a coffee if they were in town. Maybe I'd even give them a phone call on their birthday. But I didn't have people who I was living life alongside anymore. I had never really established a new group in Los Angeles either. I started dating Tom within months of moving out there, before I had a chance to make any new friends of my own in the city. During our relationship, his friends had, by extension, become mine, but those friendships had been lost in the breakup too.

I would have loved to join Maddie and Evie, wrap a blanket around my own shoulders, and tiptoe into their world. I wanted to hear about the people they wanted to go to prom with, the teachers who gave too much homework, and the latest gossip from the dance team. But I knew I wasn't invited, so I took my pizza into the living room and turned on the TV.

I finished both slices and was contemplating another one when the door opened and closed behind me. I craned around to see Evie wandering in while carrying empty plates, followed by the dogs. "How was the salad?" Evie called from the kitchen. I was sure she had seen the Styrofoam container in the trash.

"Disgusting. You were right. I didn't actually eat it," I admitted, scratching Poppy under the chin.

Evie walked toward me, glancing up at the TV. "I told you," she said. I rolled my eyes. "What are you watching?"

I turned back to the screen, where two women in sparkling tops were talking at a rooftop bar. "I'm not totally sure," I said. Based on what I had seen, it mostly involved wealthy women bickering over glasses of wine, although I wasn't sure that description would really help narrow things down. "From what I've gathered so far, I think they're all sisters, or maybe they all married brothers? I don't know. Right now, they're fighting over whether to go to Spain or Greece for vacation."

"Sounds enthralling. I'll leave you to it." Evie turned and headed for the back door. The dogs didn't follow her this time, both curling up by my feet.

I had barely looked up toward the TV when the door crashed open. I turned around, ready to lecture Evie about slamming doors. The smirk she had been wearing less than a minute ago had vanished. Her face was white, and her eyes were wide. She looked a decade younger, the same face I had babysat when I was thirteen.

"Lia, did Maddie come inside?" she asked. Her voice was trembling.

I shook my head, even though we both knew there was no way Maddie could have slipped inside without Evie noticing. She had been inside for only a few minutes, and we would have heard the door if Maddie had come in.

Evie's arms were crossed over her chest as she stared at me. "She's gone."

CHAPTER 6
A MISSING GIRL

Something rustled in the leaves. A few weeks ago, the neighbor's cat had gotten out and wandered over here, and I wondered if it had happened again. I slowly crept toward the trees so I didn't spook him. If it was the cat, I had to get him inside. It was dangerous out here at night. There were all sorts of things that would love to have him as a snack.

The bushes were dark, but I looked for the distinctive glow of a cat's eyes somewhere amid the leaves. As I moved closer, the hairs rose on the back of my neck. I was alone in the yard, but the light from the house was still bright and warm behind me. I reached toward the branches as the trees seemed to bend down, beckoning me closer.

"Excuse me," someone called out from the foliage.

I stumbled back a few steps, almost falling over.

"So sorry. I didn't mean to scare you," a woman said.

She stepped closer, but I couldn't make out her face. She was still cloaked in the thick darkness of the forest, yet there was something familiar about her. I tried to take another step backward, but my jacket snagged on a tree branch, holding me in place.

"I was out for a walk, and I got turned around. And then it got dark," the woman continued. Her voice was light and nonthreatening. It made me feel a little silly for how terrified I was. My heart was racing in my chest, each beat seeming to whisper, *Run, run, run.*

"You're welcome to use my phone," I said, turning to gesture back at the house. I should have known better than to turn my back on the forest. Something pinched the back of my neck. "Ow," I said, reaching for the spot as the woman's hand pulled away, holding an empty syringe.

"What are you doing?" I tried to ask, but I couldn't get my lips to form the words. Everything felt too heavy. The world was softening around me.

My knees buckled, and the woman caught the weight of my body with a grunt. "Shh," she whispered, her breath hot against my ear. And then the world went black.

CHAPTER 7

"What do you mean, 'she's gone'?" I asked. I jumped to my feet and walked to where Evie stood just inside the door. Past her I could see the chairs where the girls had been sitting. The firepit was still roaring, casting flickering light on the blankets draped over two abandoned chairs.

"She's gone, Lia. I went back outside, and she wasn't there," Evie said.

"Maybe she went around front? Could she have left something in your car?" I asked. I pulled open the back door, and immediately goose bumps prickled across my bare arms. Evie didn't move. I stared out into the black. I could feel Evie behind me and see the warm kitchen light spilling out into the night, but the trees seemed to call, the wind rustling their leaves like a whisper.

"I don't think she would have walked around outside. She would have come through the house if she wanted to get something out front," Evie said.

My sister had only been inside for a few minutes. It was too soon to worry. There were a dozen reasonable explanations for where Maddie could have gone. But in my bones, I knew that whatever lurked in the trees had her, and they wouldn't give her back. Daisy brushed against my leg, sticking her head out the door alongside me. A growl rippled through her.

"Maddie," I called out. It was probably quieter than would have been helpful, but even that had felt too loud. I didn't want to announce my presence to whatever was out there.

"I'll check the front yard," Evie said.

I spun around, giving the trees my back against my better judgment. I could almost feel their long, spindly limbs reaching for my ankles. "Wait. Let me put on shoes. I don't think you should be out there by yourself."

Evie nodded. Neither of us said what we were both thinking: Maddie was out there by herself.

I ran upstairs, slipped on a sweatshirt and the first pair of shoes I could find, then rushed back down. Evie stood exactly where I had left her, fingers combing through Daisy's fur, the dogs flanking her on either side. I tossed Evie the extra sweatshirt I had grabbed. "It's cold out."

She nodded and slid the shirt over her head. It fit her loosely, hanging past the edges of her fingers, making her look even smaller than she already did.

I grabbed a flashlight from the closet. "Ready?" I asked, my hand already on the knob. Evie nodded and opened the door.

We took a couple of steps on the porch, pulling the front door closed behind us. *We shouldn't be out here.* Everything in my body told me to turn around and go back inside. "Maddie?"

I called out. We could see Evie's car from where we stood; nothing was moving. Evie went down the steps and I followed close behind her.

"Mads?" Evie's voice was tentative as she reached the cars and peered around the side. "This isn't funny. You're scaring me."

Evie crept around the house, glancing over her shoulder every few feet to make sure I was following. It was darker over here, the light from the windows not reaching around the corner to the deep shadows. I swung the flashlight in an arc to illuminate our path. "Wait, Evie," I said. She stopped as I pulled the light toward the tree line. The flashlight lit a small circle of tree trunks in yellow light, the rest even blacker in contrast. I took a few steps forward.

"You can't go in there," Evie whispered behind me.

"I'm not going to." I wasn't sure when we had moved from shouts to whispers, not wanting to wake whatever might be sleeping somewhere deep in the trees. "I just want to get a little closer."

Fallen leaves crunched underfoot as I took a few steps toward the trees. Evie followed me, and she curled her fingers into the material of my sweatshirt at my back. I could hear her breathing in short, shallow pants. "Maddie?" I called again. The trees seemed to swallow the sound. I swept my flashlight over the branches and low bushes, looking for anything that moved. I took another step along the edge of the forest, Evie's feet shuffling behind me. "Maddie?" My voice was even more hesitant this time.

"I don't think she would have gone into the woods," Evie whispered.

I didn't say what I was really thinking. I didn't think Maddie had ventured into the forest of her own accord, but that didn't mean she wasn't out there. I thought back to how the dogs had acted the day before. "I know. I just wanted to check," I said. I gave the trees around us another pass with my flashlight. The woods stretched for miles in all directions from here, broken only occasionally by another house. It would be next to impossible to spot someone if they didn't want to get found, especially at night. If someone or something had taken Maddie, they would want to stay hidden. We wouldn't find them.

"Do you have your phone with you?" I asked Evie. She didn't answer, but I saw the screen light up in her hand. "Try calling her."

Evie's fingers flew over the touch screen, and then we both froze as she held the phone in front of her, the blue glow illuminating her face. The phone rang once. Evie's eyes closed as she bit down on her bottom lip, and we both prayed that Maddie would answer on the second ring.

A faint buzz came from near the house. Our heads shot up, and Evie ran toward it. I followed right behind her, the flashlight beam bobbing against the ground in front of me. I could see the dogs waiting through the glass of the back door, watching us approach the house with their tails wagging. The firepit was still lit, flames dancing in the breeze. Tucked into the blanket discarded on one of the chairs was a glowing screen. On it, Evie's and Maddie's faces filled the frame, their cheeks pressed together, tongues sticking out of their mouths, their hair pulled into tight ponytails, and glitter coating their eyelids.

Their faces were too close to the camera to make out much of the background, but it looked like they were at a dance competition, their matching jackets just visible at the edges.

Evie's fingers reached toward it, but I grabbed her arm. "Don't touch it." I didn't need to explain; we both knew why. If Maddie was truly missing, we couldn't risk disturbing any evidence. Instead, we just stood there, staring at the phone until it went dark again.

Evie looked up at me, her phone hanging limply in her hand.

"Maybe she went inside while we were out here. We could have missed her," I said. I didn't really think that was possible, and Evie didn't either, but she silently followed me through the door.

The dogs jumped around our feet, their nails tapping on the hardwood, eager for attention after our short trip outside. "Maddie?" I shouted into the house. "Are you in here?"

I turned to see tears streaking down Evie's cheeks as she watched me, waiting for me to tell her what to do next. I didn't know. I was supposed to be the adult here, but it felt like a lie. I didn't want to be in charge. I felt as frightened as Evie looked, but we couldn't both fall apart. "You go check upstairs. I'll check the main floor and the basement."

She nodded and wiped her face with the sleeve of her sweatshirt before running up the stairs, Daisy and Poppy following her in what they likely assumed was some elaborate game. I began my search of the ground floor as Evie's shaky calls for Maddie echoed above me. There weren't many places where someone could hide here, so after a cursory sweep, I headed down to the basement. I knew the chances of finding Maddie were slim. Still, I shouted her name and opened every door, checking in closets and under furniture.

When I returned to the main floor, Evie was waiting for me in the kitchen. Her face was taut and colorless. As soon as our eyes met, she shook her head.

"She wasn't in the basement either," I whispered. We stood watching each other for a long moment, not sure what to do next.

Evie and I both turned at the sound of a car coming down the driveway. Evie rushed to the front window, and I followed, trying to see past the bright beams of the headlights. It was my mother's white SUV. I knew it was irrational, but for a second, I let myself hope. Maybe Maddie would walk through the door with my parents. Maybe she had wandered somewhere down the drive, and they'd pulled over to pick her up.

The dogs barked and ran to the door. I didn't know what would have possessed Maddie to wander off and not come back as we shouted for her. I had to assume it was some sort of terrible prank. The door opened, and where I hoped to see Maddie with her bare legs and bouncing ponytail, laughing at the joke she had pulled on us, was just our mom.

"What are you girls doing?" she asked. I was sure it was an odd sight—Evie and me standing in the kitchen, a flashlight still clutched in my hand, all the lights in the house turned on and blazing into the night.

"Did you see Maddie?" Evie asked. Her voice was softer than I had heard in years, all her teenage attitude stripped away. Once again, I felt like I was watching the version of my sister that she had left behind in elementary school.

My mother's smile faltered, and she raised her eyebrows, a faint pair of lines appearing between them for a moment. "On the way in? No. I thought she was coming with you after practice?"

"She's missing," I said. The words felt too small for the reality, an annoyance rather than something disastrous.

"What do you mean?"

"She and Evie were having dinner outside by the firepit. Evie came in to put their dishes away, and when she went back outside, Maddie was gone. We've looked everywhere," I explained.

Evie watched me, her teeth working away at her bottom lip again.

"I'm sure she just went home. Maybe she wasn't feeling well," my mom said, offering Evie a little smile.

"I drove us both," Evie explained. "Her car's still at school."

My mom kept her smile plastered to her face. She had always been able to hide her fear well. "Perhaps her mom…" she started with another excuse. Another possible way that this missing girl could be safe out there somewhere.

I interrupted. "No. Her phone is still sitting outside. Mom, she's gone." We didn't have time to pretend. We should be afraid. The girls who went missing in those woods never made it home again.

My mom's teeth closed over her bottom lip in a nervous tic that mirrored Evie's. Her eyes dropped to the floor, and I could practically hear the gears whirring in her head.

"Where's Dad?" I asked.

She didn't look up when she answered me, her eyes still tracing the swirls of the hardwood. "He needed to finish something up at the office, but he'll be home soon." She took a big inhale and looked over at Evie. "Let's call her mom before we do anything rash."

My mom tapped her phone screen a few times. "Can you go turn the firepit off?" she said as she raised the phone to her ear.

"Hi, Christie." I heard my mother's voice shift to the one she used around other adults. Something both lyrical and authoritative. I had listened to it so much as a child, repeating the cadence back to myself when I lay in bed. Even now, I could hear its echoes in my own voice when I entered stressful situations, like a job interview, an important phone call. I put on a little bit of my mom, wearing her as a second skin when I needed to be taken seriously.

I stepped away from my mom and sister, slipping out onto the back porch. As the door closed behind me, it muffled my mother's phone call, leaving me to the quiet rustle of the night. I turned off the firepit and waited as the flames shrank, then slowly vanished. The back porch light was still on, but it didn't feel like enough to cut through the dark. I stood in the rectangle of light that slipped through the windows, the shadows of Evie and my mom on either side of me.

My earliest memory of my sister was the time when I'd tried to leave her in the woods. Evie couldn't have been more than a few months old at the time. The three of us had just gotten back from a walk. Evie was asleep in a stroller, and our mom had run upstairs. It was one of the rare moments when

I was alone with my new sister, and I took the opportunity, pushing the stroller toward the back door before I even had time to fully consider a plan.

The stroller jostled as I went over the threshold, and I paused for a moment to make sure I hadn't woken Evie, but she didn't stir, so I kept going. I didn't want to hurt her. I imagined myself the hero of this story, returning this little creature back to the forest, where she'd be taken in by some family. Her life would be magical and wonderful, never having to go to school and instead spending her days playing on the forest floor, and my life would go back to the way it had been before. I wanted to be the sole object of my mother's affections again.

I didn't stop walking until the stroller was tucked behind a cluster of trunks and drooping branches. As soon as I was satisfied with my hiding spot, I turned and ran back to the house.

My mom was waiting for me, leaning against the open back door. She waited until I was close enough that she didn't need to raise her voice. "Where's Evangeline?" she asked.

I stumbled to find an answer that would be sufficient but couldn't think fast enough with her stare piercing through me.

My mother got tired of waiting for me to produce a lie. "Go get her," she said, an instruction that left no room for conversation.

Looking back, I wonder if she had panicked for a moment before she spotted me. If she had the wind knocked out of her with the terror of her children missing, both her daughters vanished in the few seconds she had left them alone. But, in my memory, she was eerily calm; if she had been afraid, she hid it well.

I turned around, trudging through the grass for the tree line where I had stowed the stroller. Evie had woken up. She wasn't crying, just looking around, transfixed by the canopy of leaves. The moment she saw me, her attention pulled to me as I crunched through the undergrowth, she smiled. A wide toothless grin that bore no malice toward the sister who had abandoned her in the woods a few minutes before.

I started back up the hill, Evie babbling happily at me as I shoved the stroller through the grass. Our mom met me halfway, her hand closing around the stroller the moment it was within reach. "She's your sister; you need to take care of each other," she said to me, like that was all the explanation I needed. I hadn't understood it at six, although the shame of being caught had been enough to prevent me from trying again.

I appreciated the words more now, as I stood between my mother's and sister's shadows. I had known Evie from her very first day. She had never existed in a world that did not contain me. I could barely remember a world that did not contain her, even when our corners of it rarely overlapped. We had been witnesses to each other's lives through every season. We belonged to each other. I wanted to wrap my fingers in the hem of her sweatshirt and hold on to her. She seemed too small, too fragile. It would be too easy for her to vanish into the dark.

It could have been her, something inside me whispered as I stared into the trees, my heart clenching, but Evie was safe in the kitchen. That moment of relief was fleeting, replaced almost immediately with guilt, because Maddie was still gone.

CHAPTER 8
THE MISSING GIRLS

The first thing I heard was my heartbeat. The steady pulse echoed in my skull as blood traveled under my skin. My rib cage rose and lowered with every deep inhale and exhale. There was desperation in the way I sucked in each cold, damp breath. The smell of rain lingered in the air.

A breeze dusted my cheeks, sharp with cold, and the hair on my arms stood on end as a shiver worked its way up my spine. My palms were pressed flat against the ground. As I flexed my fingers, my nails dug into the earth, and small granules of dirt clung to my fingertips.

My eyes felt too heavy to open, but I could sense the trees around me. I knew that if I could peel my eyelids open, I'd see their branches blotting out the sky.

The hum of the trees moved through me. It was a lullaby in a language I didn't understand but recognized anyway. It was electric and warm in my veins, like sunlight pumping through my body.

I heard a distant voice, the words barely distinguishable over my heartbeat: "There she is."

I slipped under the surface of sleep.

CHAPTER 9

I don't think anyone slept that night. The rest of the evening had been full of phone calls and conversations with police, where Evie painstakingly combed through every aspect of her day, looking for anything that might have been out of the ordinary. The police officers' resignation grew with every detail that failed to provide any clue about where Maddie could be. Her disappearance followed a pattern they had seen before. When the evening had started, Maddie had been a bright spot of laughter stretched across our living room floor, working through her homework while giggling with her best friend. A girl with thousands of tomorrows lined up and waiting. But now, only a few hours later, she had become just another name added to the list of missing girls.

Our parents sent Evie and me upstairs a few hours after midnight. It was comforting to be sent to bed like a child. It was another decision I didn't have to make, a gentle reminder that I didn't have to be in charge here, that someone else would take care of me. Several officers took to the woods, the beams of their bright flashlights bouncing between the trees long after I had gone to bed. Despite the fact I knew they were just looking for Maddie, their presence felt intrusive, as if they were searching through something private, something that didn't belong to them. It made it hard to sleep, and I worried I would wake up to the news that the trees had swallowed them too.

But the next morning, as soon as the sun started leaking through my curtains, I was wide awake, even though I had barely slept. I had already emailed Cerise, letting her know I would be offline for the day, but I couldn't stand the thought of being in my bed any longer. I expected to find the kitchen empty—I wanted to grab a cup of coffee and head back up to my room to endlessly scroll Instagram while I waited for someone to tell me what to do next—but my mom was sitting at the table, her laptop and a yellow legal pad sitting in front of her.

She smiled when I turned the corner before her eyes returned to her screen. She looked tired. It was a rarity to see my mom in anything less than pristine condition, so her makeup-free face, complete with dark bags puddled under her eyes, was a surprise. But her hair was still done, swept into a low bun without a bit of frizz or a single flyaway.

I started on my coffee, the machine whirring to life before I turned back to her. "What time did you finally get to bed?" I asked.

My mom looked up at me over her computer, taking a long inhale before answering. "The police were here until about an hour ago, and it seemed pointless to go to bed," she said, sipping from her mug of coffee. "Did you manage to get a bit of sleep? I hope we weren't too loud down here." Under the thin lacquer of exhaustion, my mom was still calm and composed. She was usually even-tempered, but I had anticipated an anxious edge to her mood this morning, something to indicate the horror of the night before.

"A couple of hours," I said.

She nodded, and then her eyes returned to her computer, fingers flying over the keyboard, and we fell into silence again as I finished making my coffee. I leaned against the counter, looking out the window, my mug warm between my palms. I couldn't help but scan the branches for any sign of Maddie. A part of me—an irrationally optimistic part—imagined her breaking through the trees, covered with scratches and twigs in her hair, as if she had gotten turned around in the dark but found her way back in the daylight. But the branches remained still, beyond the birds beginning to wake and flit between them.

"Ophelia," my mom said, pulling me from my distant imaginings. She waited until I turned back to her. "We've set up a search of the woods this morning with some parents and other community members."

"I thought the police searched the woods last night." Not that they would ever be able to search everything. Our house sat on a few acres, but the edge of our property butted right up against the state forest, which stretched for miles. Even now, in the light of day, it would be impossible to cover it all.

"They did. But it was dark out, and they were looking for Maddie in case she had gotten lost or hurt. Today, we're looking for anything we can find that might hint at what happened to her."

I nodded. That made sense, but it felt strange that this responsibility fell on us.

"You don't have to help search. Evangeline is going over to a friend's house. No one should be inside if you need to get work done."

"Evie doesn't want to help search?"

"I'm sure she would want to help. But I don't want her to." She swallowed and focused on me. "We don't know what we're going to find today. I don't want her or any of her friends having to see…" My mom trailed off, unable to finish her sentence, but I knew what came next: *a body*. There was a possibility that if we found Maddie today, she wouldn't be alive, that it wouldn't be a rescue but the prelude to a funeral.

"I want to help."

"Okay. Then nine thirty. Dress in layers. It's supposed to be chilly today and it's always colder once you get in the trees. And maybe put on some blush. You're looking a little pale." She tapped her cheek. My mother's phone buzzed beside her, and she gave me a weak smile, a polite dismissal, before picking it up. I grabbed my coffee cup, still half full, and headed back up to my bedroom.

When I returned downstairs, my mom was already on the front porch with a few other parents. The sky was cloudless, a vibrant blue that seemed to mock the bleakness of this morning. She had a large map of the woods stretched out in front of her and was pointing out something to a woman in long sleeves and a hot-pink puffer vest. My mom had put on makeup since

I'd last seen her—not much, but the circles under her eyes were no longer tinged purple.

I joined my mom's side, and all eyes landed on me. "Ophelia!" someone said as I approached. I recognized her immediately as Lydia Robins, a friend of my mom's. "How are you? Elizabeth was just telling me that you're back in town."

I forced a smile. "Just for the next few months. How are the kids?" I had babysat them a few times while I was home for summers in college, and I was eager to shift the conversation away from my return.

"They're doing well. You wouldn't believe how big they both are. You should come by the house sometime. I'm sure they would love to see you," she said.

The last time I had seen her kids, they had been three and six months old, so I highly doubted they had any memory of me. But still, I responded with a smile. "I'd love that."

"How's your sister holding up?" she asked, her voice lowering to a more appropriately somber level.

"She's doing okay, given the circumstances."

"It's just awful what happened to Maddie," said Casey Daniels, another mother from Evie's dance team, cutting into our conversation. "And just outside y'all's house. I'm sure it's left all of you shaken."

I nodded politely, but her words made me restless. We still didn't know what had happened to Maddie. She had vanished, but maybe we'd find her today, tucked under a tree, cold and scared but alive. I wasn't ready to declare her story an unspeakable tragedy.

Before another woman could offer me a lukewarm greeting,

my mother's voice rose above the chatter. "Okay, let's get started," she called, her hands cupped around her mouth.

I looked out at the crowd that had accumulated this morning. At least fifty people were milling around, chatting in small groups. My father climbed the steps and slipped an arm around my mom's waist. It took a few moments before everyone's attention was fixed on her, and she waited as they quieted.

"Thank you all so much for coming out here. As you know, Madison Rodingham disappeared from our house last night around seven. Police searched the area yesterday but were unable to locate Maddie. So today we'll be looking for anything that seems out of the ordinary and might give us an idea of what happened last night." My mom went on to explain the search process. We would be working in groups of four, each assigned a small portion of the woods. If we came across anything of note, we were to mark it on the map and then mark the area with brightly colored tape.

I was handed a roll of hot-pink tape and shoved toward a group of three: two women and a man. He had an arm draped around the waist of one of the women, clearly his wife based on their wedding bands. They turned to look up at me at the same moment, greeting me with polite nods.

The other woman was unfamiliar to me and looked slightly out of place. Her deep-red hair was tossed back in a high ponytail, the ends curled and glossy. Her face was bare, but she had skin I would kill for, barely bronzed and glassy smooth. The only imperfection was the slight darkness under her eyes, something a whisper of concealer could have erased. Her hand rested on her rounded belly, which stretched the fabric of her sweatshirt. I wouldn't have necessarily clocked her as pregnant, but her hand smoothed over the bump before resting on top, a gesture of maternal warmth that would have been hard to mistake. "I'm Kate," she said as a greeting, extending the hand that wasn't on her belly toward me. "I'm a friend of your mother's. We met briefly at the gala back in June."

"Lia," I said, taking her hand. It was warm and soft. I tried to place her in the blur of that night. Tom had been at that party. I had been too caught up with how I looked being paraded around on his arm to really pay attention to all the new faces I was introduced to throughout the night. "I'm sorry, I don't remember. It was a busy night." I braced for her to ask about Tom, already rehearsing how I'd explain that we weren't together anymore.

"It's completely fine. There were a million people there," she said with a smile.

I opened my mouth, ready to make polite small talk, but my mom interrupted.

"You four will be starting in this area." She gestured at a spot on the left side of the forest, indicating a twenty-foot stretch between two trees. She repeated the instructions she had given the whole group earlier, and we set off, Kate and I falling into step behind the other two.

"How far along are you?" I asked, gesturing to her stomach, which she was still smoothing her hand over.

She smiled back at me, her eyes crinkling up in the corners. "Twenty-six weeks."

I nodded as if I had any idea what that meant. "Do you know what you're having?" We were almost at the tree line by this point, and the ground was littered with dead leaves and branches.

"A little girl," she said. I could hear the smile in her words. When we reached the trees, we spread out a bit, only able to reach the person next to us if we both stretched out our hands. "We've got two boys at home, so my husband and I are so excited. I'm looking forward to buying all the dresses and bows I missed out on with the last two."

"That should be fun."

After that, neither of us spoke again as we started into the forest. Our eyes were firmly fixed on the ground in front of us, sweeping back and forth along the five feet we were responsible for. I felt claustrophobic as I stepped past the first trees. I could hear the crunch of leaves and low conversations on all sides. The woods shouldn't have felt dangerous with all these witnesses. It wasn't as if I could disappear unnoticed, but that didn't mean the forest felt benign. Even though it couldn't strike out and wrap its tongue around its next victim, I still sensed the leering eyes that always seemed to peek between the branches.

The summer after my freshman year of college, another girl had gone missing in these woods. I had spent the break at home. It was a strange time filled with the suffocating feeling of being a child again after spending nine months playing an adult. I had gone to a party at a high school friend's house. It was the same thing I would have done a year prior, but we felt changed, like we were all wearing clothes a size too small, the seams tugging as we spent the nights in our childhood beds dreaming of our dorm rooms. While the woods didn't surround their house, a trail behind it led to the trees. It was hard to escape them; they seemed to reach into every corner of this area, their spindly fingers stretching far into town.

I met the girl in line for the bathroom. I was already drunk after a few glasses of something that tasted like fruit punch mixed with lighter fluid. I was sure my lips were stained pink. We developed the effortless friendship of two drunk girls, shocked that we'd encountered our soulmate right there in line for the bathroom, all the while knowing it was temporary. Like Cinderella's carriage, it would transform into something forgettable in the morning, but the moment was richer for its short lifespan.

I held her face in my hands and smoothed my thumbs over her cheeks as she told me a story about a boy who didn't deserve her. Her dress hung by two tiny straps from her perfect collarbones. I wanted to run my fingers along the bones, measuring them, as if I would be able to re-create them under my own skin when I got home. Her skin was soft, and I couldn't stop touching it. It shimmered, looking like magic even in the dingy hallway lighting. I wanted to steal it. I told her as much, begging her to tell me what moisturizer she used. And she laughed, the sound twinkling above the din of voices. "I don't know," she said. "It has a blue lid." And then we were both laughing.

A week later, her face flashed across our TV screen. I had completely forgotten about her until I saw a picture of her in a graduation cap, with a broad white smile and a plastic-wrapped bouquet of white roses cradled in her arms. Her name was printed underneath, and I realized it was the first time I had heard it.

Chloe Brookfield.

She hadn't disappeared from that party. She'd gone missing a week later, as she walked home in the middle of a Friday afternoon. I never told anyone I had met her just a few nights before. What would I tell them? *I once saw that girl and held the weight of her skull in my palms. Her skin was soft, and I loved her in the way that is only possible when you're six drinks deep.*

I had shared this sort of experience with dozens of women in dirty bar bathrooms and alleys thick with cigarette smoke. I had forgotten all their faces, even the ones who had confessed their deepest shames while they fixed my smudged lipstick with their thumbs. But I would recall Chloe's face, the shape of her collarbones, and the exact shade of her skin until I died.

They never found Chloe. I searched her name once a month, carefully reading the updates her mom posted and picking through her sister's photos. It had been years. They wouldn't find her. I knew that. Still, I scanned the faces of every bathroom line at every party I ever attended as if I might find her right where I left her.

Part of me was surprised I hadn't immediately thought of Chloe when Maddie had disappeared, but as I walked through the trees, I couldn't help but picture both their faces. Perhaps they were together now. I took the slightest comfort from the idea that Maddie might not be alone.

We searched for a little over three hours before everyone cleared out of the forest, walking back down the paths we had slowly cleared. From what I gathered, no one had found anything substantive, although a few strands of brightly colored plastic peeked from between the tree branches.

I helped gather the remaining rolls of tape and thanked people for coming until most of the crowd had dispersed. After leaving the box on the porch steps, I went looking for my mom to see if she needed me to do anything else before I headed back inside.

I was surprised not to see her chatting with the remaining people as they slowly made their way to their cars. She usually would have been in the thick of things. I was just about to give up and head inside when I spotted her standing with Kate along the side of the house.

They were leaning close to each other, whispering back and forth. "I thought you—" Kate stopped abruptly when she noticed me over my mother's shoulder. Her expression briefly betrayed the feeling of being caught, but she quickly smoothed it into a practiced smile. It was the kind of smile I was sure had gotten her out of a speeding ticket or two. "Ophelia!" she said with a little more cheer than was necessary.

My mother turned around to face me, her expression more practiced than Kate's. "What do you need?" my mother asked. She reached for my face and brushed away a couple of loose strands of hair before her hand came to rest on my shoulder.

"Do you need anything else? I left all the rolls of tape in a box on the porch." I gestured back in the direction I had come from.

"That's perfect. Thank you. That should be all. Your father ran out to grab lunch. He should be back soon. Why don't you head inside?" she said. There was a tenderness in her voice that wasn't usually there, as if, beneath the words, she was also asking if I was okay. It was the tone of a mom whose cool hand had rested against my forehead countless times when I was sick and had whispered reassurances in my ear when I was crying. "I'll follow you in a minute."

With that, I was dismissed, but the women waited until I was out of earshot before returning to their whispered conversation. Their heads leaned so close that Kate's hair brushed up against my mother's arm as the breeze blew through it. I wished I could hear what they were saying, but they were talking too quietly for me to make out anything. My mother's eyes were still following me when I glanced back over my shoulder, and I couldn't shake the feeling that they were hiding something.

CHAPTER 10

I had been lying awake for hours, unable to quiet my restless thoughts. It wasn't surprising—I hadn't slept through the night since Maddie had gone missing. The days following her disappearance melted into a strange rhythm. I would end up in bed in the middle of the afternoon, only to wake several hours after sunset to the low hum of the television downstairs. There always seemed to be someone at the kitchen table. Sometimes it was Evie and a gaggle of her friends or my mom with hers. Either way, I would offer polite smiles and make a bit of small talk before drifting back upstairs.

My father went back to work the day after the search. His schedule was the only one in the whole town that seemed to be mostly uninterrupted by Maddie's disappearance. The rest of us were stuck waiting for something to happen that would give us permission to go back to our usual lives—all the while knowing that every day, every hour that passed, the odds that we'd ever find Maddie again shrank.

There was a strange isolation to this local tragedy. In town, every conversation I overheard seemed to revolve around Maddie. There were posters taped to the inside of every store window I passed with the same photo of her smiling face. She was everywhere and nowhere all at once. But if we drove twenty miles into the city, I doubted they would have even known she was gone. I thought about texting Tom more than once, my fingers hovering over the keyboard, his name pulled up in our texts, but his last message stopped me. The exchange had been brief. My message—**I'm headed out. I left my keys on the counter**—was sent from my car as I sat at the stoplight just outside the apartment complex.

His response didn't come for two and a half hours, the buildings and traffic of Los Angeles already replaced by great expanses of desert, not a single palm tree in sight out my car window. **Thank you. Have a safe trip.** No *let me know when you get there.* No *love you.* No *miss you.* I hadn't expected it. Our breakup had been rational, almost cold. I had cried only once about it, that first night in the shower, alone in Tom's apartment. If I were honest with myself, he wasn't worth crying over. I hadn't been in love with Tom, not really, but I had loved the space he had occupied in my life. I liked having a boyfriend. I liked having someone who made sure I made it home okay and always picked up more of the yogurts I liked when he went to the grocery store. I liked the way we looked together when we went out. He made me look smaller and daintier as I held on to his arm, balancing in my heels, smiling up at him. I liked the way people looked at him and then at me, as if I were made more important because I was attached to him. I had grown used to being a *we* instead of merely an *I*.

Tom probably would have called me if I had texted him and told him about Maddie. He would have made sure I was okay and offered to talk about it. He wasn't someone who liked to burn bridges. But the idea of being an obligation, something he would have to cross off his to-do list at the end of the day, felt entirely unappealing.

I tossed the blankets off and climbed out of bed, deciding that I couldn't tolerate another minute of staring up at the ceiling. Outside my room, the house was quiet and dark, except for the triangle of moonlight that spread out from the kitchen windows, coming halfway up the bottom step of the staircase. I padded toward the refrigerator when something moved in the shadows. "Fuck, Ev," I said, clutching my chest when I realized it was her.

"Sorry," she whispered. She was standing against the glass doors that led out to the back deck, wearing an oversize Mayfield High School Dance Team sweatshirt, the sleeves pulled over her hands.

Evie had been unpredictable over the last few days. Teary-eyed one minute, shouting at my mother the next, and then sprawled across the couch, placidly watching a movie a few minutes later. For the most part, we didn't comment on her hurricane of emotions. Even my mother, who would usually not have allowed this level of attitude from her daughters, was quick to let Evie's little tantrums roll over her. But honestly, I didn't know what else Evie was supposed to do. Her best friend had disappeared like a bad magic trick—there one minute and gone the next.

She turned back to stare out the window as I moved to stand

next to her. It was quiet for a moment, and I stepped back, not wanting to interrupt her solitude. "I'm making banana bread. It should be out of the oven in a few minutes if you want some," she offered. I knew it was her way of giving me permission to stay, allowing me to intrude on her quiet night.

I nodded. "That sounds good. I'm starving."

"Mom made some sort of chicken-salad thing," she said, gesturing vaguely toward the kitchen. "It's in the fridge."

I left her at the window and made myself a plate before returning to stand next to her again.

She didn't acknowledge my presence this time. The moon was a bright crescent tonight. We could see all the way to the trees but no farther. The dark pulled taut between the branches like panes of stained glass. A light breeze rolled through the yard, and the branches swayed ever so slightly, the occasional leaf tumbling onto the grass between our house and the woods.

I looked over at Evie. It was strange to understand so little about this person I had known from the day she was born. I could recite facts about her like I had memorized her résumé. She wanted to go to Vanderbilt next year. She was on the dance team but had grown up doing ballet. She couldn't stand the texture of crushed velvet. She had spent last summer working as a hostess at the Italian restaurant in town. Her favorite color was an almost-purple shade of light blue. But I didn't feel like I really knew her anymore. I had known the eleven-year-old her but not the seventeen-year-old version.

"So, did you have a particularly strong craving for banana bread at two in the morning?" I asked between bites of my crackers.

Evie shrugged. "It was something to do."

I understood; I also felt stuck in the cycle of not knowing what I was supposed to do with myself, even though there was nothing to do. We'd had a few searches, but they hadn't turned up anything. They felt more like a performance than a real attempt to help. It seemed irrational, impossible even, to return to our regularly scheduled to-do lists. What did any of that matter when, somewhere out there, Maddie was lost in the dark?

I nodded as I chewed another bite, too loud in the quiet kitchen. I could just barely make out our reflections in the glass. The older Evie got, the more she looked like me. We had the same round face and soft nose. Both of us were in the habit of giving it some shape with a bit of well-placed contour most days, but in the dim light, our noses seemed to melt into our faces. Even our brows matched, though it was impossible to say if that was truly a matter of genetics or a product of monthly trips to the waxing salon. Her chin was pointier than mine was, but it was pretty. It made her whole face look more delicate.

"Why don't you have any lights on?" I asked after another few minutes of silence.

"It feels creepier with the lights on down here sometimes," Evie said. Her whole body shivered.

"Feels like someone's watching you."

She nodded but didn't look in my direction. "It's the trees." She didn't explain further, but I knew what she meant. There was something about the trees themselves that felt alive, something about the noises they made when their leaves caught the wind and the way they moved. It didn't feel entirely natural. When the lights were on in here, it felt a bit like we were an exhibit in a museum, pinned to a painted background, slowly baking under a spotlight for whoever or whatever wanted to peer through the glass. Even with the lights off, it was nearly impossible for us to see past the first row of branches, but at least it leveled the playing field, all of us hiding in the dark.

"What do you think happens to them?" she asked. I knew she was no longer speaking about the trees.

I was surprised Maddie had already been lumped into the *them* that included the dozens of other girls who had disappeared into the forest. During the daytime, we talked about finding Maddie, as if she might stumble back into the yard and ask what all the commotion was about. It was strange to hear Evie say out loud what we had all been thinking as we made plans for another search party instead of a funeral. Perhaps it was just harder to pretend at night.

"I don't know." I wished I could provide her with something more hopeful than this, but I couldn't. This past week had stripped me of my ability to come up with fresh platitudes and pretty reassurances. I wasn't sure if they would have been comforting to Evie anyway. The circus of frightened parents who were constantly cycling through our house loved to assure Evie that we'd find Maddie soon, that the police were working hard and would bring her home. Even overhearing it from across the room made me want to scream. But she smiled and accepted the hugs without biting the hands that reached out to stroke her hair and tell her that everything would work out. I knew she had heard enough lies this week to last her a lifetime. So, instead, I stood next to her, our eyes fixed on the spot where her best friend had disappeared, and I reached for her hand in the dark.

CHAPTER 11
THE MISSING GIRLS

The first things I saw when I woke up were the silhouettes of two women, the details of their faces obscured by the bright light behind them. "There she is," one of them said, her voice raining down on me. "How are you feeling?"

I blinked again and again. I was no longer outside, the dirt under my palms replaced by the smooth surface of a metal table. My eyes adjusted to the lights. Her voice sounded familiar, but I couldn't place it. My memories were muddled and out of reach, a vague blur of color and sound that seemed to grow dimmer with each blink. I tried to remember where I was, how I had gotten here, but I couldn't even remember my name, the letters falling away the moment I reached for them.

"I—" My voice cracked on that first word, something in my throat breaking open like a thin layer of ice on a puddle, just cold enough to freeze. But she was patient. She didn't speak again, letting me feel the stretch of my vocal cords and the muscles of my throat working with each breath. "I feel fine." My voice sounded strange to my ears, different but not unpleasant, softer than I thought it should be. "Where am I?"

I peered past the lights at the room behind them. It was starkly bare, painted white, with pale-blue tiles that flowed from the floor halfway up the wall. A handful of machines with screens displaying numbers and graphs that meant nothing to me were seemingly the only things occupying the space. I shifted, the thin blanket that covered me moving against my skin. It was pulled high up to my collarbones.

As my eyes adjusted, I took a better look at the two women. The one who'd spoken was blond, her hair twisted up in a bun; the other's hair was dark, a brown so deep that it was nearly black, and it fell around her face, pin straight and glossy.

"Do you have pain anywhere?" the blond asked, drawing my attention back to her face.

I took inventory of my body, not moving but just feeling, searching for the dull ache of a bruise or the sharp burn of a cut, but I felt nothing. My body was cold but fresh and whole, like a crisp bill straight from the bank, uncreased and ready to spend. I shook my head.

My eyes caught on the far wall, the only one not painted bright white. This wall was open to the dirt, roots braiding through the soil. It looked entirely out of place against the white sterility of the rest of the room. As I stared, I heard a low hum. I hadn't noticed the sound before, since it had faded into the whirring and beeping of the machines around me, but now I heard it, felt it in my bones. The roots were singing. It was soothing, alleviating any fear that threatened to lick up my neck, whispering a song some part of me recognized, a song that seemed to buzz through my veins.

The blond woman beamed at me with a wide smile. "Wonderful. Isn't that just wonderful, Jane?" she said.

The other woman didn't respond. She continued to watch me, her big blue eyes blinking, and then she reached out her hand. I shivered as she trailed her finger ever so gently down the side of my cheek, her dark hair falling in a curtain over her shoulder. "Wonderful," Jane finally murmured.

"Who are you?" I asked, my voice again jarringly unfamiliar. I wouldn't have believed I was the one who had spoken the words if I hadn't felt the air moving past my lips.

"I'm Mother," the blond woman told me. A name and a title rolled into one. Something inside me fought against it, told me it wasn't true, but that whispering voice that called her a liar was quieted by her soft smile as her hand stroked my hair.

During the next few days, I didn't leave the cottage. The room where I woke up, Mother's workshop, was in the basement, but the rest of the building bore little resemblance to the sterile white room below. It was a cozy house centered around a large stone fireplace, flanked by two overstuffed floral-print chairs and a green couch. Overlooking a little garden and endless rows of trees was a big window seat, where I spent most of my time tucked under a blanket, a steaming cup of tea between my hands. A constant dread sat in my stomach for those first days, the anxious feeling that I had forgotten something important, that there was an appointment I was missing or something essential on my to-do list that I hadn't yet crossed off.

Mother always came over when she noticed me worrying. She rested her hand on the back of my head, her thumb tracing along the raised ridge of a scar that sat where my spine connected to my skull. "How are you doing, darling?" she asked.

"It feels like I'm forgetting something important."

She hummed, fingers slowly moving through my hair. "The forgetting can be hard. But you're right where you're supposed to be. You will feel better more quickly if you relax into your new life, don't push against it. The bad feelings will pass," she promised me, slipping the mug of tea from between my fingers and replacing it with a fresh cup.

It wasn't just the forgetting; my body felt strange too. My legs were thinner than they should be and stretched from my hips like pulled taffy. My arms unfurled from my shoulders like ribbons. All my limbs were lithe and graceful, a quartet of dancers I hadn't yet learned to choreograph. I crashed into things constantly. Bruises bloomed over my skin each time I bumped into the corner of a wall or the edge of a table. Mother fussed over me each time, smoothing the area with a strong-smelling cream and holding ice to each bruise.

A few days into my time at the cottage, I was allowed to venture into the garden. I misjudged the height of the front steps and fell, ripping the skin on my knee and the palms of my hands. I sat where I had fallen for a moment, the pain pulsing in time with my heartbeat. Blood bloomed from my knee, and I wiped it away with a finger before sticking it in my mouth without thinking. The red liquid was warm as it hit my tongue, salty and metallic. I looked down over my knees, the pale skin porcelain smooth except for the red patchwork still bubbling blood each time I moved. A drop fell onto the dirt below, which swallowed it instantly, hungry for a little taste of me.

I was mesmerized by the red liquid now trailing down my shin bone. This warm, living thing moved through my body with each heartbeat. At that moment, as I sat on the front steps, blood dripping down my legs, these unfamiliar limbs and beating heart felt as if they truly belonged to me. For the first time, I felt welcome in my own skin, like this sharp pinch of pain had been the last thing I needed to tie the disparate parts of my body together.

There was less tenderness from Mother this time as she dabbed away the blood with a towel, frustration slipping through her usual calm. "You need to be more careful," she told me. I nodded, tears prickling my eyes. "You don't want to scar these beautiful legs."

CHAPTER 12

A week after Maddie disappeared, we still hadn't returned to our regular lives, drifting through the house like ghosts. But our mom insisted on a family dinner, so we sat silently at the table, going through the motions.

The clink of silverware against porcelain seemed unusually loud. Our mother cleared her throat, breaking the uneasy quiet. "I've been thinking," she said carefully, "that maybe you should go back to school tomorrow."

Evie didn't look up from her plate. "Sure," she agreed.

Our mother blinked. I imagined she had expected more resistance. Evie had always been stubborn. She was decisive to a fault, unswayed by other people's opinions and whims. So, if Evie had agreed without complaint, I had to imagine that she had already thought of the idea herself and our mother was merely cosigning what Evie had already decided to do.

"Only if you feel ready," Mom amended. She had been softer with Evie, both of us really, over the last few days. She was always attentive, almost reading our minds with her ability to predict what we might need at any moment, but her usual commentary, the little nitpicks about what we should be doing better, were absent. Instead, she had been wholly focused on Evie, keeping a watchful eye on her and ensuring she was doing all right, even when Evie tried to push her away.

"I'm fine. I'll go back tomorrow," Evie said, pushing her chair back from the table. "I have to go back to school eventually, and it's not like I have anything better to do." She was right. She couldn't delay the return indefinitely, and it was becoming evident that we weren't getting a resolution anytime soon.

"Okay. Well, if you decide it's too much to handle, you can always text me and come home. I'm sure everyone at the school will understand." I knew she was already drafting the email she'd send to Evie's teachers in her head.

"I'll be fine," Evie assured her, before heading up the stairs. Our mom would have likely found it more comforting if Evie had fought her, but regardless, Evie went back to class in the morning.

Still, I wasn't expecting to find the downstairs completely empty when I finally climbed out of my bedroom a few minutes before eight. Poppy and Daisy jumped up from where they had been sleeping on their dog beds in the living room. Their claws clicked against the hardwood as they trotted over to me, and their wet noses pressed into my palm as they waited for me to pet them. I scratched behind their ears absent-mindedly, looking around for any sign of my mom.

A note was leaning against the espresso machine. I

recognized the paper. My mom ordered the same notepads year after year, edged with lilacs and the words *The Gregg Family* printed in navy blue at the top. She had written every grocery list and reminder on the paper for as long as I could remember. I grabbed the sheet and leaned back against the counter as I read the message written in her precise cursive. *Ophelia, I'm headed into town to run some errands this morning. I should be home before Evangeline gets back from school, but call me if you need anything. Love, Mom.*

I started on my morning coffee while I pondered what I wanted to do with my alone time. I really needed to use the extra hours to catch up on work. I had fallen a bit behind after all the travel followed by the recent chaos, but the thought of spending the morning updating spreadsheets was vile.

I brought my coffee upstairs. Poppy and Daisy followed me, finding spots on the floor in my room to spread out and lie down again. I opened my laptop and did a quick scan through my email. Nothing new had come in yet, which was unsurprising since it was still early in LA. I pulled up the editorial calendar and double-checked that everything was scheduled appropriately for the morning's posts. There was nothing that couldn't wait a few hours until I was officially on the clock.

I opened a new private window. No one else had access to the search history on this computer, but I wanted to keep this separate from the rest of my life. I typed *Chloe Brookfield* into the search bar. I had been thinking about Chloe a lot over the last few days. Her name hadn't been mentioned in any of the news stories I had seen about Maddie, but my mother was quick to change the channel whenever Maddie's face flashed onto the screen. I wanted to investigate further, as if perhaps Maddie's disappearance might have brought something new to the surface. Another missing girl. Another piece in the puzzle. I had waited until the house was empty, as if this were something shameful I needed to do in secret. I was anxious that I might get caught and that someone would judge me for claiming any part of this tragedy that wasn't mine. As if they would judge me for thinking about anything other than Maddie.

The first results were familiar. They were the same every time: A few links to various news articles discussing her disappearance. A headline about an unrelated Chloe in Florida who played on her high school volleyball team. Another link to the GoFundMe her family had set up to pay for the memorial. I quickly scanned through the website, looking for anything that might be different since the last time I had visited, but everything looked identical. I deleted Chloe's name and replaced it with her mother's, Sandra. Her mother's Facebook page was the first thing that popped up. I opened it for probably the hundredth time and scrolled through the posts. In the months after Chloe's disappearance, she had posted weekly updates on the search for her daughter, but eventually, the posts had become less frequent since there was nothing new to share. Now she posted once a year about Chloe, on her daughter's birthday. Usually, the posts were nothing more than a picture of Chloe as a child, her hair in braids, that same wide smile stretched across her face with a caption about how much Sandra missed her daughter, along with a note letting people know that Chloe's case was still open and providing the number to call if they had any information.

Sandra's most recent post was a collection of photos from a trip to Hawaii with her other daughter, Becca, at the beginning of the summer. I had already seen these pictures, but it was nice to see them again. I clicked through them, lingering on a photo of Sandra with her arm around Becca's waist. They were smiling at the camera, a waterfall behind them, yet I couldn't help but feel Chloe's absence in the photo. I wondered if they had heard about Maddie. If Chloe's disappearance felt sharper this week as yet another missing girl appeared on the news.

I hovered over the X in the corner of the screen, ready to leave this behind and start on my real work, when I thought of another name to type in the search bar: Elizabeth Gregg. My mother's familiar profile picture was third on the list. I didn't bother going to her posts. I wouldn't have been able to see much without logging in to my own account, and that wasn't what I was looking for anyway. I clicked over to her list of friends and skimmed through the familiar names until I found the woman I was looking for: Kate Montgomery.

Her profile picture looked like it had been taken on a summer vacation with her family snuggled in front of a blooming hydrangea bush. She had a scowling baby on her hip, his hand fisted around her hair. Her other son, a toddler with wispy blond hair, was holding her hand with a smile, eyes pointed somewhere off camera. Her husband had an arm around her waist, but I read the annoyance behind his eyes. I could almost hear his complaints about having to take this photograph.

Even among her perfect little family, Kate stood out. She was wearing a white linen dress with blue embroidery around the collar. Her hair hung in frizz-free waves just past her shoulders. Her lips were a perfect rose pink, split into a smile that looked captured mid-laugh.

I clicked through her profile, but most of it was private. There were a couple of tagged photos of her at restaurants with a gaggle of other women and another of her smiling in a baseball cap at a child's soccer game, but I couldn't see much more. I didn't know exactly what I was looking for—only that I wanted to understand her connection to my mother so I could make sense of their whispered conversation. Maybe it was nothing, but I couldn't shake the image of Kate's guilty face.

The first few things that popped up were links to her social media pages. I clicked on her Instagram. Unsurprisingly, it was private as well. All I could see was the same profile picture from Facebook. I moved on to the next link. This one opened to the town newsletter from May. There was a picture of her smiling into the camera, surrounded by a group of preschoolers in a garden. I briefly skimmed through the story about the community garden and the program she cochaired for getting children under five into nature. I scrolled past a few similar search results, clicking into each one and looking for anything out of place.

I spent almost half an hour dissecting Kate's internet presence but found nothing strange. She seemed like a great mother, active in the community, with a large group of friends. In fact, she could be a carbon copy of my own mother. Both effortlessly beautiful women living picture-perfect lives.

If her high school graduation year was correct, Kate was only five years older than me. I was closer in age to her than I was to Evie. Yet I couldn't imagine that life for myself—not even in a few years. I didn't think I'd be married in the next five years, and I certainly didn't think I'd have children yet. I wondered if my mother wished she had a daughter more like Kate—someone who seemed to have her life in perfect order.

I spent the rest of the morning sitting in meetings and working through the backlog of emails that had built up over the last week. It felt strange to be occupying both these worlds at the same time. I spoke to my coworkers about campaign goals and ROI, while I sat in my childhood bedroom, a ticket from my senior prom still pinned to the corkboard above my desk. It was exhausting to remember who I should be for these people back in Los Angeles. At best, I was getting a B- in this work version of Lia. It kept slipping off my shoulders like a too-big spaghetti strap, revealing the Ophelia who was at home here.

I was ready for a break when I heard the garage door open. I followed the dogs out of my bedroom and arrived in the kitchen as my mom stepped through the door, her arms laden with mismatched canvas bags overflowing with produce. She looked as if she had stepped out of a magazine photo shoot, dressed in a floral sundress layered over a turtleneck sweater. If I had attempted it, I would have looked confused, but on my mother, it seemed intentional. The usual rules of seasons didn't apply to her.

"Ophelia," she said with a smile as she passed. "How was your morning? I figured you might enjoy a few hours in a quiet house to get some work done, especially after the past week."

She didn't wait for my answer before she started loading things into the fridge. "I thought we might do a roast chicken for dinner. It feels like the right weather for it. And I picked up some squash from the store for soup, but I think we'll do that later this week."

It had been raining all morning, drops tapping against my windows while I talked with the team about the spring campaigns. "Sounds good," I said, my gaze drifting to the naked trees, water running down their spindly branches.

I've always had a soft spot for the rainy weather here. The warmth of our bright house seemed to taunt the gray world outside through the rain-speckled windows. Rain in college had been an inconvenience, and in LA, the rain was such a rare break from the sunshine that the whole city was immediately swept up into the novelty of the gray clouds when they finally arrived. I loved that rain here arrived without much fanfare, beckoning in a cozier afternoon with the soft, steady patter of rain on the roof.

"Have you eaten lunch yet?" my mom asked. She had finished unloading most of the groceries while I had been staring out the window.

I shook my head and settled into a barstool at the counter. I hadn't eaten anything today, beyond my morning cup of coffee. Back in California, my day had been segmented by meals I ate alone. I ate breakfast after Tom left for work but before I logged in for the day. I had lunch in front of my laptop as I scrolled on my phone or scanned through emails. Tom rarely made it home in time for dinner, so I often ate that alone too.

It was a rare event when I had a meal with someone else:

The occasional dinner with Tom at one of his favorite restaurants. Lunch on a patio with all the girls from work. Those meals felt like events. There was such a difference between those sorts of meals where conversation drifted between bites of food. They had borne little in common with the lettuce and leftover chicken I ate in Tom's house alone and barefoot with a phone in my hand as I scrolled through picture after picture.

"I was talking with Emily. Her son lives in the city. He's in finance," my mother said, feigning casualness. She pulled produce from the fridge and a cutting board from a drawer.

I didn't offer any follow-up questions, although it was clear by her pause that she hoped I would. "He's a few years older than you, so I'm not sure if you ever really met when you were in high school."

"Okay," I said as I scooped out a blob of hummus with one of the carrots she had set in front of me. I knew what she was hinting at. I would have had to be oblivious not to figure it out; still, I struggled to comprehend why she thought I would want to go on a date with some random man so soon after my breakup with Tom. I hadn't spent the last few weeks curled up in bed eating ice cream, but I also wasn't ready to jump into something new.

She started slicing a cucumber, her pale pink nails in vibrant contrast to the deep green of the peel. The knife moved through the vegetable with practiced ease, leaving a trail of almost transparent green rounds behind it. "We thought it might be nice if the two of you met up for dinner while you're both at home," she said, not looking up from the cutting board.

"I broke up with Tom less than a month ago, Mom," I said. "I don't want to date someone new yet."

"I know that, sweetheart. But there's no harm in getting back out there."

I rolled my eyes. My mom had always been able to read me. She was able to read most people. It was a talent that she had passed along to me. My mom and I were chameleons, becoming whatever the people around us wanted us to be. She was better at it than I was. She could transform from one version of herself to another so effortlessly that no one ever noticed. No one except me knew where to look for the seams.

"I just think it would be nice for you to get dinner with someone your age while you're in town. Please think about it."

I didn't bother arguing with her. She had a habit of inserting herself into my life in this way, pressuring me into the decisions that she thought would be best for my future. Sometimes, like on my move to LA, I fought her on it, acting as the driver in my life even when my choices contradicted what she wanted from me. But sometimes, like today, it was easier to fall asleep in the passenger seat than fight her for the steering wheel.

"Do you think you'll be able to make it to Pilates sometime this week? I'm sure we could squeeze something in before you need to be online, or Taylor does a great class on Saturday afternoons." She started constructing the salads in two wide bowls, portioning out two handfuls of lettuce and arranging the other vegetables.

"I don't know, Mom. I'm not sure Pilates is my thing," I said as she slid one of the bowls toward me.

I loaded a fork with lettuce and a ripe cherry tomato, then

took a bite. I looked up as I chewed, the forkful slightly too large for my mouth. My mom watched me, her fork poised above the bowl, the slightest smile on her lips. I felt almost trapped in her gaze, like an animal caught in the glow of car headlights, frozen by her observation. I was all too aware of my sweatshirt that I had stolen from the boyfriend before Tom, the collar stretched and fraying along the hem.

My hair was tossed up in a greasy bun. I should have washed it today, but I had spent the morning playing internet sleuth. It was quite the contrast to my mom, her hair freshly blown out and her face fully made up. I hadn't put on anything at all except a bit of blush and a thin layer of tinted sunscreen that served to hide a bit of my sleep-deprived dark circles.

I always wore sunscreen. It had been instilled in me from the time I was young. We didn't go to church, but my mom made skin care our religion. Sunscreen, our morning prayer. Falling asleep in our makeup, a mortal sin. Smooth, pore-less skin, a sign of the faithful. I had watched her get ready when I was little, sitting next to her at her vanity as she gave me whispered explanations of each step. *We preserve beautiful paintings; why wouldn't we take as much care to preserve ourselves?* Her voice reminded me of that every time I looked in the mirror and contemplated going to bed without washing my face.

"Okay. I just thought you might enjoy it, but you certainly don't have to go," she said. Her eyes scraped over my torso, mostly hidden by my sweatshirt, but it didn't feel like it. It felt like I was sitting naked in front of her, the bright light of an autopsy table shining down on me as she picked apart the pieces of me that she didn't like. I knew which they were without her having to say because they were the parts of me that I didn't like either. She was the one who had trained every aspect of my self-hatred.

The soft place under my chin. The lines between my eyebrows, which I tended to furrow. The bumps on the backs of my arms I got any time I skipped my three-times-a-week exfoliation and nightly full-body moisturizing. Her voice was always whispering her disapproval in my head.

"I was thinking I might pick up running again," I said. The words weren't true. Both my mom and I knew that. I had run cross-country in high school and hated every minute. I hated the feeling of being breathless as my lungs burned, begging for more oxygen. I hated the way sweat drenched my shirt and exertion painted my face bright red, as dirt coated my ankles, the line where my socks had sat distinct when I peeled off my clothes at the end of the day. I was not a pretty runner.

The corners of her lips turned up in approval. That's why I had said it. Those smiles of approval were a currency I was well-versed in. I had spent my entire childhood trying to earn them.

"It's the perfect time of year to get back into it," my mom said between bites of her salad.

I nodded. My mouth was full again. I swallowed too soon and could feel the lump slowly sliding down my throat. "Maybe I'll try to get in a run after I finish work tonight," I said, immediately regretting the words. I shouldn't have continued. I had already earned my smile for the day, but the words had slipped out, always seeking that next hit of validation.

"I'll tag along if you don't mind. It gets dark so early these days," my mom said, the little smile still lifting the apples of her cheeks. Her brow quirked up slightly, not enough to crease her forehead, but just enough to let me know she didn't entirely believe me.

"That would be great," I said, returning her smile with a fake one of my own.

CHAPTER 13

My mom was waiting at the bottom of the stairs when I came down that evening. I had dug up a pair of running shoes abandoned in the back of my closet, already stained with dirt. "You ready?" she asked as I trotted down the steps. I nodded. "I figured we'd take it easy today. A couple of miles along the trails, then head back. It's not hard to overdo it if you aren't careful." Somehow *my* run had become *her* project.

"Great," I lied.

The moment we stepped outside, I took a deep breath as a reflex. The air here in November tasted different, better than anywhere I had ever been. It was cold but not yet bitter. It felt as if I should be able to bite off a mouthful, the air crunching like the skin of a green apple as my teeth cut into it. I closed my eyes and let it wash through me like champagne bubbles. The sun was already setting, covering the world in a warm and hazy light.

My mom made off toward the tree line heading for her

favorite trail, which looped around the backside of our property and connected us to the state forest. I couldn't help but think about Maddie as we stepped into the woods.

Our mom had always encouraged us to play outside in the trees, but she had also warned us to respect the danger of this vast place. We weren't supposed to be in the forest alone after dark. And even in the day, she wanted us to stay within sight of the house. Yet despite those warnings, my earliest memories of the trees were all pleasant ones. Spending afternoons halfway up one of the oak trees, its branches wrapped around me as I read a book and imagined myself inside it. It was easier to believe in magic in these woods. Even now, it was impossible to see the trees, their branches crisscrossing and nearly bare, without feeling like something was different in the air. Like things that shouldn't have been possible happened here. But I could see that this place's magic wasn't rippling with endless possibilities of glittering new worlds and happily ever afters but something much more malicious. It was home to some sort of monster, acting as a labyrinth that drew its prey deeper, twisting and tangling around their ankles until they stumbled.

As a child, I hadn't paid much attention to her warnings. It wasn't until I was a teen, old enough to hear stories of the missing girls and the monsters that lurked within the trees, that I had learned the true danger of this place. Not to trust the quiet birdsong and the lullaby of the leaves rustling in the wind. Those stories had made me wary, but nothing had ever happened this close to our house. Part of me always believed that there was a covenant between our family and whatever haunted the trees. We had grown up in full sight of their branches; they wouldn't hurt us. But Maddie had disappeared from our back porch. It could have easily been Evie alone out there for a moment while Maddie ran inside. Would the forest have taken her instead?

Just considering that question made my chest tight. She still wasn't safe. There would be another girl who would vanish into the branches. It could be next week, or it could be three years from now, but no rule prevented that girl from being Evie. If I thought about it for more than a moment, I found it difficult to breathe properly, my lungs crushed by the weight of the what-ifs. When the house was too quiet, I imagined branches slipping in through an open bedroom window, tugging her out from under her blankets, and pulling her into the dark.

My mom broke into a jog that was barely faster than a walk. I settled into a leisurely pace alongside her, the trail wide enough to accommodate both of us. We ran in silence for a few minutes. All I could hear was my labored breathing and footsteps against the soft earth.

"How do you know Kate?" I asked. I had meant to ask her over lunch today, but I had forgotten. My voice startled both of us, breaking the silence of the forest. As I waited for her answer, the quiet seemed to settle back around us.

"Kate Montgomery?" she asked. I nodded. "We've known the Montgomerys for years. I met her shortly after she moved to town. Dad and I were the ones who set her up with her husband."

"Really? I don't remember her," I said.

"You were in college when she moved here. We don't spend

a lot of time with them these days. We're in very different stages of life. She's got young kids who keep her pretty busy. Why do you ask?" She seemed unfazed by the line of questioning and the pace that she was slowly increasing, although her breath revealed that it cost her very little to do so.

"What were you two talking about after the search party?" I asked. I knew I was pushing it with the question. I was sure she would see it as an overstep.

"That was a private conversation. Nothing you need to be concerned about," she said in a tone that indicated she was disappointed that I was even asking.

I was panting, and my words came out between shaggy exhales. "We worked together during the search. She was acting a little strange. That's why I asked," I said. That wasn't entirely true. Kate had seemed fine, but I was hoping that perhaps this might provide a little nudge for my mother to tell me more.

"It was a hard day for everyone in the community. I'm sure she was a little on edge. She's got two little boys at home and another baby due in the spring," she said. "Something like this makes you think about your own children." She glanced in my direction, her mouth pressing into a line for a moment.

I shrugged. "I know. I just thought I would mention it."

"Well, I don't think it's anything you should be worried about," she said with a squeeze to my shoulder that was meant to be reassuring. "I know this must be hard for you. You did what you could to help by answering the police's questions and by participating in the search, but we've done everything we can. Now it's time to leave the investigating to the police, Ophelia." My name was a warning not to press further.

I laughed, although I was so out of breath that it sounded more like choking. The police hadn't found a single one of the missing girls. There wasn't even a hint of where the women had disappeared to beyond the rumors whispered around bonfires and in locker rooms.

"We'll just do a mile and then head back," she said over her shoulder as she took off. "It's already starting to get dark." We were deeper in the forest now, and the path was becoming more treacherous as rocks and tree roots hid under the layer of leaves. I watched my feet instead of my mom.

The trail narrowed the farther you went into the woods, and eventually, I slipped behind my mom, no longer able to run side by side. I watched her ponytail swing back and forth in front of me. For all the warnings my mom had given, she walked through the forest without any fear. More than that, she seemed at ease under the branches that perpetually left the forest in shadow. Her head didn't jolt when a twig cracked to the side of us. The sudden burst of noise from an angry bird didn't make her jump. She didn't spare more than a glance at the tree stump that looked like it could almost be a hunched-over figure in the fading twilight.

The forest grew darker around me, night quickly swallowing the light within the trees. My eyes were glued to the ground. It was getting harder to see my own feet. My mother's footfalls slowed, and I looked up to find her standing still, facing me. Her mouth was barely open, as she breathed slightly harder than usual. I stopped next to her, and the sounds of the forest pressed in against us without the relentless pounding of our footfalls.

"You ready to head back?" she asked. I nodded. She reached into her pocket and tossed me a light. She clipped the matching one onto the waistband of her leggings so that it lit a square of forest floor.

She took off without another word. I wanted to pause and catch my breath, but I didn't want my mom to notice how much I was struggling. I followed her, my legs burning and my chest tight.

My light brightened a swath of the trail in front of me, but more than anything, it made me all too aware of the darkness that surrounded me on all sides. I could feel it behind me, licking up the exposed skin on the back of my neck, its fingers poised and ready to dig into my shoulders and pull me into the trees. I kept my eyes glued to my mother's ponytail. The gap between the two of us was growing. Somehow she kept going faster, and I couldn't force my legs to keep up. Panic clawed at the inside of my chest. It wasn't as if I could get lost. We had followed one clear path into the woods, and we were probably only five minutes from the house at this point, but I was still afraid to lose her out here.

And then it happened. She turned a curve in the path and disappeared. I couldn't see her light. I couldn't even hear her footsteps over the roaring waves of my own breathing. I was alone and could feel the branches of the trees twisting down toward me, ready to pluck me off the trail and devour me.

I forced myself to run a little faster, promising myself my mom was just around the next tree. Part of me wanted to call out to her and urge her to slow down, but it felt embarrassing, childish even, to admit I was scared. I wasn't a little girl who could scream for my mother after a nightmare and ask to sleep with the door cracked and the hall light on.

My light bounced on the trail in front of me, revealing a few more feet of the path every time I took a step forward. The feeling of eyes on the back of my neck forced me to move my legs still a bit faster, trying to outrun the trees.

The beam fell on a small mound of dirt. In the stark glow, I looked past the mound to a dark smear. I followed the stain into the shadows, twisting so my light could illuminate whatever had caused it.

A rabbit lay just off the trail. Its skin was split open in what looked like a perfect line down its back, revealing pink muscle and white ligaments, caked in a fine layer of dirt. That wasn't the strangest part—a neat row of what looked like thick black threads lined the flesh, as if it had been sewn together, before the stitches had been ripped open again. More dark liquid leaked out of the open slice of its back, still trickling through its fur and onto the ground. But that's not where most of it came from. The head was missing. Its neck was a gaping hole that oozed something so dark, it was almost black as it seeped between the leaves and into the dirt below.

I stumbled a few steps back. I was more frightened by the macabre horror in front of me than the darkness that lurked behind me. My scream tore through the quiet of the night.

Seconds later, my mom appeared, racing back toward me. "Ophelia?" she said. I couldn't see her face, hidden behind her bright light, but I could hear panic in her voice. The anxiety was unfamiliar and acidic as it wrapped around the vowels of my name. "Are you okay?" she said, panting. She took another step toward me.

I was still struggling to breathe, so instead of explaining, I pointed at the mangled rabbit.

"Oh," she said. A long exhale eased out of her. Her body softened as she recognized that I was not in danger. "Is that all?"

"The head's gone," I whispered. Silence had fallen back over the forest in the wake of my scream. I scanned the dark rows of trees, searching them for someone lurking on the other side.

"There are animals in the woods, Ophelia," my mom said. The words were a dismissal, as if she stumbled across mutilated animals every day, but there was an undercurrent of something sharper and angrier under them.

"Sh-shouldn't we t-tell someone?" I stuttered as she took another step toward the rabbit, looking down at it with her hands on her hips.

"Tell them what? That a coyote killed a rabbit?" She glanced back at me over her shoulder, her voice softening at the following words. "I know you're probably a little on edge with everything that's happened. But animals kill other animals all the time. It looks gruesome, but it's how things work out here."

"But it doesn't look like an animal did that," I said, another whispered confession. For how brutal the dead rabbit looked, the cuts weren't the ragged tears I'd expect from an animal ripping up a kill but instead the clean edges I'd expect from a knife.

"Rabbit's skin is really thin. It rips like tissue paper at the slightest tug."

"But someone tried to bury it," I whispered. I didn't know

much about animals, but I knew they didn't usually bury their dead.

"Something was digging a hole, and the rabbit ended up in it. Honestly, Ophelia, it could have even been one of our dogs. I walk the two of them out here all the time," she said. She paused for a moment, then reached out her hand to me like a mother guiding a child across a busy intersection. The gesture was familiar and reassuring, a silent promise that we could avoid any danger as long as we were connected. "Come on. We're almost back to the house."

I didn't take her hand, but I moved a little closer, feeling safer standing beside her. She started jogging again, slower this time, eyes darting over to me to ensure I was keeping up. We fell into the same cadence, our feet striking the ground simultaneously.

Within a few minutes, the glow of the house was visible through the trees. My mom slowed to a walk as we crossed the gap between the trees and the front door. I was reminded again of how much our house resembled a dollhouse at night, the rooms lit up and on display in the darkness. My father had gotten home while we had been out on the run. He was in the kitchen, illuminated by the refrigerator light, probably wondering what my mom planned to make for dinner. Evie was in the front study, papers on the desk around her as she bent over her homework.

I was eager to be back inside, still shaken from the gruesome sight of that dead rabbit. I looked over at my mom, her face visible in the blue twilight, brighter now that we were out from under the trees. As she looked at the house, her face lit with affection, unbothered by the menacing darkness of the woods at her back.

I had played in these woods for years and never encountered something quite that bloody. But I hadn't trespassed against the darkness of the forest before. My mom had. She walked these woods in the early-morning hours before the first whispers of pink lit up the horizon. If something sinister prowled these woods at night, I couldn't help but wonder if she had long since befriended it.

CHAPTER 14
THE MISSING GIRLS

Every evening after dinner, Mother asked me to stretch out on the couch. If Jane was home, I would rest my head on her lap, and she would pet my hair. The nights were getting colder now, and Mother tucked a blanket around me as I bent my knees so I could press my toes against the arm of the couch. Then she rolled down the waistband of my pants, and her fingers found the long scar that stretched from hip bone to hip bone. She pressed oils into my skin and rolled her thumb across the pink ridge. She was always gentle, her touch softening anytime I flinched. She'd spend long minutes massaging that scar before moving on to the others. The twin scars in both of my armpits. The long, thin scar that ran up my spine. The puckered scar at the back of my skull. She was always slow, careful, and methodical as she worked.

I had already fallen into the quiet rhythm of this place. My days were filled with the same simple routines. Mother was right—it was easier if I didn't try to cling to the whispers of a time before. Still, sometimes they surprised me; they snuck up and begged me to remember. A name that belonged to a face that grew blurry the more I tried to retrieve it. The smell of fabric softener that made me homesick for a place I couldn't recall. A melody that reminded me of laughing so hard, my stomach hurt. But even those whispers grew less frequent and softer with every day that passed.

I was free to fill my time however I wished, as long as I didn't leave the garden gates. Jane had been gone this morning. I spent far too long picking through the bookshelves filled with novels, mostly classics—although there were a few more modern romances that I suspected Jane had snuck in between Austen and Shelley. I landed on Jane Eyre and took the worn book to the window seat. The plot was familiar, another whisper of a life before my whole world had been shrunk to the size of the cottage.

I was halfway through the book before I grew bored and wanted some company. Mother spent much of her time in her basement workshop, the room I had woken up in. She kept the door closed, but we were usually welcome to visit her. I would watch her work, fascinated by the delicate dance of her stitches or the precision of her letters as she took notes from medical textbooks. Sometimes she told me stories while she worked. Stories of the days when it had just been Jane and her. Stories from before that, when she had been alone in the little cottage.

I didn't knock before I pulled open the doors to the basement. We weren't allowed down here alone. The basement was Mother's space, and it was where she kept dangerous things, like the gun that she kept tucked in the top desk drawer. She had pulled it out one of the first times I was down here. She told me that it was to keep us safe if anyone found our cottage and wanted to hurt us. I figured she'd meant for it to be reassuring, another layer of safety, but it made me nervous to know it was there. The whole room felt like that: a dormant danger waiting for someone to pull the trigger.

When I reached the bottom of the stairs, I was surprised to find the desk where Mother usually sat empty. All the other times I had been here, she had worked at the desk, while I had lounged on the armchair in the corner or sat on the floor, looking through her medical textbooks and her old notebooks filled with beautifully illustrated anatomical drawings labeled in her pristine print.

"I'm in here," Mother called out from the tiled room in the back of the basement.

I followed her voice through an open metal door. It was strange to be in this little room again. I hadn't been back here since waking up, yet it always loomed in the darkness, the roots humming faintly on the other side of the door.

I took in the room drenched in bright white lights. It looked exactly as I remembered it. A chill ran through me at the sight of the metal table against the back wall, but the fear didn't take hold because the hum of the trees fell on me like a heavy blanket, immediately calming me.

Mother was perched on a little stool. A pair of blue gloves were pulled halfway up to her elbows, and a bright lamp shined down on the table she was bent over. I took another step toward her before I realized what was on the table: a rabbit. Its skin was peeled away from its muscles, flayed and naked, as Mother, with metal instruments in both hands, worked in tiny stitches. All four of its legs were separated from the rest of the body, sitting in the corner of the tray in a pile. The skin where the legs had once been was now little pockets of gray fur, flat and empty.

I took several wavering steps back toward the door, bumping into the counter and knocking down a metal tray, which clanged as it hit the floor. Mother glared up at me.

"S-sorry..." I stuttered. "I didn't realize you were..."

"For goodness' sake, sit down and stop being ridiculous," Mother said, gesturing at a second stool. "You had chicken for dinner last night, and there were no dramatics about that." There was something starkly different, though, about the chicken that had sat on the table, skin golden from its time in the oven, smelling like garlic and butter, and this rabbit, who only this morning would have been hopping with her sisters in our garden.

I sat on the stool as far from the little table as I could manage, but she gestured for me to come a bit closer. "Watch," she told me.

I obeyed, palms pressed tight to my thighs as she started on a new stitch. I was surprised by how quickly I grew used to watching the needle pierce through the rabbit, pulling until the skin was taut. It wasn't bloody; it was tidy and precise. The work was detailed and almost beautiful in a strange sort of way.

"Their skin is so thin," Mother whispered as she worked. "Thinner than human skin. It tears like tissue paper at the slightest tug. It's good practice for me so I don't leave another scar like that nasty one on the back of your neck."

My fingers instinctually reached up to touch it.

Mother offered me an apologetic smile. "At least it's easy enough to hide. It's barely even noticeable through your hair."

We sat in silence as I watched her work for several long minutes until she spoke again. "Did you know I used to be a surgeon before I found the forest?" I knew she had been a doctor. Her name was printed on the inside covers of most of the medical textbooks that lined her shelves, but I hadn't ever thought about what kind of doctor she had been. "I loved it. The work was so precise, and there was an art to it, a gracefulness when it was done well." She got this wistful look on her face, staring off into the distance, imagining a version of her life where things had gone differently. She shook her head, gently dismissing whatever thoughts had drifted in. "But now I'm here, and this work"—she gestured at the rabbit and me—"is better than anything I could have accomplished at a hospital." There was something sad about her smile as she bent back down to continue her stitches. I wasn't entirely sure I believed her.

After that, Mother left for most of the afternoon, slipping out after lunch as soon as Jane returned to the cottage. I couldn't stand another moment inside—the cold of the sunless basement had seeped into my bones—so I took my book and headed into the garden instead.

I lay under the branches that reached over the fence, in a patch of dappled sunlight streaming through their leaves. I could feel the hum of the trees through the dirt. When I turned my head to the left, I could see under the fence to the rolling forest floor. A plant with a few deep-blue berries caught my eye, their glossy surfaces gleaming against the moss and shadows. Last week, on a walk with Mother, we had gathered wild blueberries and fat sun-ripened blackberries. But when we came across a plant like this one, she crouched beside it, beckoning me to kneel.

"You should never eat these berries," she said, pointing to the deep-blue globes, each suspended on its own star-shaped flower. "These berries are called *Atropa belladonna*, or deadly nightshade, and our trees have made this variety especially potent. Just one or two could be enough to kill you before you made it home to me. Even touching the leaves with your bare hands could make you sick." She held a blueberry and a blackberry in her palm, lifting them close to the nightshade to point out their differences, obvious when all three were in front of me.

They served as a little reminder that the forest was not to be underestimated. We belonged to the trees, but the forest was a vast, wild, unpredictable place. The deep-blue berries, with their deadly beauty, seemed to whisper a warning: the same force that gave life here could just as easily take it away.

I dozed between chapters, until the sun began to set and the warmth from the day was sucked out of the air. I could see Jane through the front window, working on dinner at the kitchen counter. My eyes lingered on the garden gate. I could easily get up and walk through it. Jane wasn't paying attention to me. The urge to leave pressed against my ribs. I was a prisoner after all, no matter how comfortable my prison cell was. It would be simple enough to vanish before anyone even noticed I was gone.

I sat up, eyes darting to where Jane was still absorbed in her work in the kitchen, then back to the garden gate. But before I could even stand, the branches around me moved. Their movements were subtle enough that if I hadn't been watching closely, I might have thought it was the wind, but they all reached closer to me. I suspected that if I sprang to my feet and started to run, they'd close around me like a cage, stopping me before I made it more than a few yards past the gate.

It wasn't as if the trees were creatures like me or Jane or even like the rabbits. I didn't think they felt it when branches were ripped down in a rainstorm or minded when we hammered a nail into their side to string a clothesline across the yard, but they were aware of us, especially me and Jane. Branches would bend down and comb through our hair when we sat close to their trunks. Leaves would fall in a shower around us like snow until we laughed. Roots would tuck themselves back into the ground so we didn't trip over them. They had a level of fondness for me and Jane, in whatever capacity trees had for that sort of tenderness. And they wanted us to stay here.

Now on the couch, I let my eyes drift closed as Mother's hands kneaded into my skin. The fire was warm against my face. Jane's fingers passively combed through my hair. It was lovely, and I couldn't quite remember why I had wanted to leave.

"Mother?" I asked. She hummed an affirmation. "Why am I here?"

Jane settled into the couch, satisfied that Mother's mood wasn't about to take one of its turns toward something angrier. "I made you as a gift. I picked out every inch of you, from your perfect little nose to those bright blue eyes. I stitched you together, all the best pieces, into one beautiful girl as a gift not only to the trees but to you. I wanted to give you everything I didn't have. So, one day, when you're ready, you'll go out into the world and live your own beautiful life."

I was surprised at this answer. Even though Jane often spent long swaths of time away from the cottage, I couldn't imagine Mother letting us leave her. Mother kept us close, her worry over us a cloying and constant presence. "Won't you miss us too much?" I asked.

Mother smiled, her fingers pausing for a second. "You won't go too far. This place will always be your home. But I can't keep you all to myself. That would be wasteful. I made you so you could have the lives I wasn't allowed to live. Perfect lives. For my perfect girls."

CHAPTER 15

I sat at my mom's vanity, the bathroom door hanging open and Evie lying across the foot of my parents' bed, her phone in her hand. I was surprised she was here, spending her evening with her mother and older sister, rather than out with friends or locked away in her room. But since Maddie's disappearance, she'd been sticking closer to home. I wasn't sure if it was because she was still mourning, not ready to join the usual antics of a high school social life, or if she felt like she should be close to home in case Maddie reappeared, wandering out from the trees and returning to her chair on the back patio.

My mom had spent the rest of the week wearing me down, and at some point, I had agreed to go on a date with her friend's son Matthew. I didn't know much about Matthew, just the basics my mom had conveyed to me. He worked in finance. He had graduated from the same high school three years before me. I tried to comb through my memories, hoping to find him somewhere among the rest of freshman year, but I couldn't conjure his face.

In college, first dates had been preceded by an event where half a dozen girls would pack themselves into one dorm room for at least an hour to get ready. That process was undoubtedly more hallowed than the date itself. Someone would sit with a laptop and meticulously pick through the internet for any mention of our dates, finding out how long they'd been at their current place of employment and which sports teams they'd been on in high school. We drank pink wine from a box and created a character out of the tidbits of internet facts, passing the laptop around the room if there were any pictures. I remember feeling drunker off the giggles and air of belonging than the wine we'd sipped on.

I continued the tradition on the first dates I had gone on before I met Tom, but there was something less appealing about sharing those moments via text message. And then I had settled into a long-term relationship, and those messages had stopped.

I didn't know who I would text now. I hadn't even told my college roommates that Tom and I had broken up. We rarely texted these days, and the conversations that did start on occasion quickly dissolved into silence again. I hadn't needed them while I was with Tom. I told him my stories from work, and he spent Saturday nights with me, either snuggled up on the couch or out at our favorite bars. Letting those friendships fade had been simpler than working to maintain them. My friends were behind a screen in different time zones where schedules never seemed to align. Tom was right in front of me.

But that wasn't the entirety of the problem. The bigger

reason I let most of my friendships fade was embarrassment. I wasn't nearly as happy in LA as I pretended to be. I felt like I was constantly failing at my new life and wasn't ready to admit it. It was hard to keep my friends close when I was always lying, curating a picture-perfect version of myself. Keeping up that illusion meant keeping my distance. Otherwise, they might've started to see the cracks.

"Your twenties will go by faster than you think, Ophelia," my mom said, shielding my face with her hand as she sprayed the crown of my head with hairspray.

"What?" I asked. I hadn't been paying attention to her, lost in thoughts about how quickly I had let all my friendships dissolve.

She didn't repeat herself, instead continuing her spiel. "If you want to be married in your thirties, you need to take dating seriously in your twenties."

Evie giggled from the bed as if the years wouldn't soon touch her and drag her unwillingly into adulthood, toward the guillotine of thirty, when her desirability would be sliced cleanly away. "I'm twenty-three," I said. That number had to be small enough to keep me on the right side of the line between desirable and discarded.

"I know, Ophelia, but you'll be thirty before you know it. I'm not saying you need to be engaged by the end of the week, just that you can't put your life on hold."

"Jesus, Mom. I'm going on the damn date," I said, rolling my eyes and pulling my phone out.

"Language," my mom said, without looking up from the curling iron.

I scrolled through my Instagram feed, bestowing hearts on photos whose nearly identical compositions I didn't even slow down to take in. "I'm nearly thirty. I feel like I should be able to curse."

Another round of giggles came from Evie, but my mom didn't dignify my comment with a response, tilting my chin up toward her. While I had relented and let my mom fix my hair, I had drawn the line at my makeup. I had already painted my face before I appeared in the bathroom. I had perfected the art of creating a new, better layer of skin that rested just on top of my own.

My mom nodded her approval. "You look nice," she said. Her fingers were still hugging the curve of my cheek. "What is this lipstick?" She tapped the center of my lower lip.

"Tom Ford. Sable Smoke," I told her as she tilted my face back and forth under the bathroom lights. It was the perfect nude. I hadn't found it by using any strange trick but by trying hundreds of lipsticks, swiping stick after stick of nearly identical neutral pinks along the fair skin of my forearm before selecting the top few contenders to try against my lips. This one was too dark. This one washed me out. Sable Smoke was too expensive for what it was, a colored tube of wax, but I hadn't been able to replicate the perfect shade of barely noticeable pink.

My mom's shade was Chanel's Cashmere, just a hair darker than mine. For years, all through college, I had worn that exact shade, my mother's shade, even as it washed me out in every photograph I had ever taken. I should have known better. My mom could pull off almost any color. She wore brick reds at

Christmas, deep, almost-purple berry tones for evenings out, and slipped into something peachier for summer cocktails. I was stuck in Sable Smoke, no matter the season. I looked garish in more colorful shades, like a little kid who had snuck into my mother's makeup bag and was playing pretend.

"How does it wear?" my mom asked. She had dropped my face and turned away from me, fingers running along the glass bottles lining her vanity.

"It'll smudge a bit if I'm not careful, but I'll bring the tube," I said.

My mom nodded her approval. She would have started the lecture about making sure I didn't get any on my teeth while I was eating, but suddenly Evie's face was above mine in the mirror. I was struck by how similar we looked. We had always resembled each other, but the six-year age difference had prevented us from being mistaken for each other too often. But as Evie got older, we started to look more and more like each other. Sometimes, if I looked at a photo of her too quickly, I would have to do a double take because, for a fleeting moment, I would mistake her face for my own.

My mom was a few inches taller than my sister's petite frame, and both had their heads tilted in the same direction as they appraised me. The evening cast the bedroom behind us in shadows while we were lit by the vanity, our skin bright against the surrounding darkness. We looked almost like a baroque portrait, our faces framed in the mirror. *Three Women Getting Ready*, lipstick on canvas.

"Pretty," Evie said, her eyes still making their way along my features.

"Thank you." Her approval lit the same place in my chest that my mother's had minutes earlier. I wondered when I had started to care what my little sister thought of me. Sometime in the last few years, she had grown into a proper teenager, sitting atop her social hierarchy. And the part of me that still felt seventeen desperately sought her approval, wanting to be charming enough, cool enough, to earn her favor.

"That's fascinating," I said as I sliced off another sliver of chicken from my plate and brought the fork to my mouth. Matthew had spent the last hour explaining to me, in excruciating detail, how he had gotten from lacrosse captain at his Division III university to his current job at a bank.

A candle flickered on the table between us. The lights in the restaurant were turned down low enough that everyone looked a little better under their dim glow. Though Matthew didn't need help to look handsome. He had a bright smile and smattering of stubble that added enough grit to his otherwise-crisp appearance to make him interesting, although I couldn't help but think about how it would chafe my face if he leaned in for a kiss.

"I think, for me, growing up in sports taught me more than all the internships combined," he said. We had already gone through his list of prestigious internships earlier in the evening. I hadn't responded with a list of my own, despite the fact they had been just as challenging and likely more competitive than his.

Matthew was nice. He had asked questions, and I had

given appropriate answers. But I could see how his eyes glazed over when I talked about my work. For him, the equation was simple: My work consisted of making pretty pictures for people to scroll through mindlessly on their cell phones. My audience was almost entirely women. Therefore, my work was vapid. I didn't feel the need to correct him. I didn't need to tell him I had already executed seven figures of brand deals this year. That I regularly collaborated with Fortune 500 companies. That my work was responsible for shaping the shopping habits of 1.3 million people and, therefore, was worth hundreds of millions of dollars every year. I knew he would understand that—after all, he was a self-proclaimed *"numbers guy"*—but I felt no need to impress him.

Relationships felt easier when men dismissed the nuances of my life as uninteresting. Rather than make room for the complexities of my personality, my thoughts, and my beliefs, we would pretend they didn't exist, that I was a blank slate from which they could craft whatever version of a woman they needed. Tonight, I was an impressed audience, a stand-in for the academic validation he had clearly been desperate for in the years since he had graduated.

I found it incredibly easy to remake myself for each person I met. I'd never understood the advice to "be yourself." Who was I? Where did I look to find it? How could I peel away the expectations and priorities of the people around me to discover who I was underneath it all? It was a fool's mission, the idea of this immutable individual self—a lie. I was a product of everyone around me. It was impossible to be myself because there was no such thing.

Matthew launched into another long story, this time about how he'd spent a week in Ibiza last summer with a gaggle of his lacrosse friends for a bachelor party. I half listened, waiting for the moment to murmur my admiration and ask follow-up questions.

My phone buzzed from where I had tucked it in my bag behind me. "Sorry," I apologized as I stuck my hand in my bag, silencing the buzz without glancing at the screen.

"No worries," he said. "As I was saying, it was the best time of year to go. The weather was perfect, but nothing was too crowded...."

The buzzing started up again. "I'm so sorry." I reached into my bag and pulled out my phone. "Let me just check." I glanced at the screen. Two missed calls from Evie. I couldn't fathom what she would want from me. She knew where I was.

I was about to slide my phone back into my bag when a text message from her popped up on my screen: **The police found something in the woods.**

Matthew drove me back to my house, and I spent the ride apologizing for cutting the dinner short. He understood. That was the nice thing about dating someone from town. They knew the stories about the disappearing girls. Still, it was an excruciating half-hour car ride back. I stared out the window at the dark town peeking out between the trees, and he turned the radio up and mumbled along to the words.

Red and blue flashing lights were visible before we even made the last turn down the driveway, the branches casting eerie shadow puppets along the gravel. Matthew's car rolled to a stop. He looked past me through the passenger-side window, where police were winding caution tape around the tree branches. I tried to calculate exactly where they were. It was the same side of the yard I had searched with Kate just a few days before, not far from the running trail where my mom and I had found the rabbit two nights back.

"Thank you so much for the ride home," I said. His eyes refocused on me. "I'm sorry that we had to cut dinner short. I had a really nice time."

He smiled, the vague compliment enough to assuage any doubts about how tonight had gone. "Of course," he said. I unbuckled my seat belt and reached for the door, but he grabbed my arm, his fingers wrapping most of the way around my bicep. The gesture was gentle, but something was still threatening about how easily he could have bruised the thin skin. "I want to take you out again some other time, since we didn't get to enjoy dinner."

I nodded, pasting on the smile I knew he would be expecting. "I'd love that." I was mostly indifferent to the idea of seeing him again. I hadn't had a terrible time. He seemed safe and uncomplicated. If he called, I would go out again.

My mother's words returned like a ghost: *Your twenties will go by faster than you think, Ophelia.* She was always thinking about the future. The next step that would march me forward toward her best version of my life. Not knowing what I wanted made it even harder to tune out her voice. Los Angeles had been my attempt at forging my own path, but it had failed, and I was back at square one. It was impossible to plan ahead when I had no idea what I wanted that future to look like. Maybe it was time to just listen to her, to date some nice boy with a good job, get married, buy a house, have a few babies. Continue my mom's legacy by building a picture-perfect family of my own.

But a part of me worried that, in a few decades, I'd turn around and see a life shaped only by what my mother desired for me. I'd regret the dreams I'd never followed and the lives I'd never allowed myself to try.

"I'm sure this has all been so hard on you. Call me if you need anything," Matthew said. He reached over and cupped my cheek in his palm, his thumb stroking along my skin, jolting me out of my spiraling thoughts. He was thinking about kissing me. I could see it in his eyes as he weighed it against the flashing lights behind me. I would have let him.

"Thank you," I said. His hand dropped, and I stepped out of the car. We were supposed to get the first snow of the season tonight, and the cold air hit me immediately. Matthew's car continued idling behind me until I was on the first step and waved goodbye.

My mom was on the porch, arms crossed over her chest, looking out into the forest, into those flashing lights. I waited until the sound of Matthew's tires crunching on the gravel faded before I spoke. "What did they find?" I asked.

My mom startled at the sound of my voice, as if she hadn't realized I was there. She took a moment to answer, her eyes darting back to the tree line. "A shoe. How was your date with Matthew?"

I ignored the question. I didn't think she expected an

answer but felt compelled to ask anyway. I would tell her about it tomorrow, dissect the layers of conversation for her so she could judge how it went, but tonight Matthew seemed unimportant.

"Are they sure it's hers?" I asked. I couldn't bring myself to use Maddie's name, but we both knew who I was talking about. Of course, they were sure. There wouldn't have been half a dozen police officers in our yard if they weren't sure. Evie wouldn't have interrupted my date if they weren't sure.

"It has her name on it."

I could picture it now—the shoe. Evie had the same ones. All the girls on the dance team did. It was what they wore for practices and competitions. Evie's matching pair rattled around in her dance bag, her name printed in blocky letters on the tongue, a little heart after the final *e*. They weren't supposed to wear the shoes outside, but they all did, darting from practice and letting the black of the parking lot scuff the edges of their identical white shoes.

"Where did they find it?"

She didn't answer that one, just gestured toward the flashing lights. "They were doing a final pass this evening before the snow comes in."

"I can't believe no one saw it while we were searching."

My mom shrugged. Of course, it was possible to lose a shoe in those trees. We had lost an entire girl in them.

The door opened and closed again. I didn't need to turn around to know it was Evie. I stretched an arm out, and she tucked herself against my side. I wasn't sure the last time I had held her like this. We had rarely touched once she crossed the threshold from childhood to adolescence. When we were little, I held her all the time. There were countless photos of us tangled up in each other. Her baby cheeks pressed against my shoulder as we both slept with our mouths wide.

My favorite photo of the two of us came from Evie's fourth birthday party. It had been princess themed, with layers of cotton candy pink and glitter covering every surface in our house. At some point, Evie had started crying, having a meltdown over whatever had upset her delicate four-year-old feelings. I carried her upstairs to her bedroom, which was where our mom found us asleep in our glittery pink party dresses. Evie had climbed into my lap, and I had curled around her, holding her little body against my own, my head resting on her wispy hair as it escaped the pair of braids framing her face.

Now she was an inch or two taller than me, but still, she leaned against me, resting her cheek on my shoulder again. We weren't the kind of sisters who spoke regularly. When I'd lived in California, we'd talked maybe once a month. But I still loved her with a viciousness that sometimes shocked me. The same sort of violence had drawn blood on more than one occasion when she had stolen something out of my room or threatened to tell Mom about something I had done wrong. I had pulled her hair and left scratches down the back of her arms more times than I could count. But now, as she was huddled against me, I wanted to keep her here, to become a protective shell around her to keep the world from causing her any more hurt.

"How are you doing?" I asked.

She shrugged. I squeezed her in a little closer, pressing my cheek against the top of her head. I looked out into the forest, not toward the edge where the officers' flashlights bobbed between the trees but toward the dark maw that lurked on the other side of the yard. I glared into the branches, refusing to look away from the black emptiness between trees, daring it to try to take her from me.

CHAPTER 16
THE MISSING GIRLS

Tonight was the new moon, and Jane and I were in the garden that morning, gathering the last of the vegetables she needed for dinner. It would be my first new moon—well, at least the first new moon that I would experience fully awake.

I was currently peppering Jane with questions about what to expect tonight, but her answers hadn't illuminated much. "It's impossible to explain. There's nothing like it," Jane said as we walked through the gardens together. She inhaled deeply, her eyes closing, as she tilted her face up toward the branches above us. It was quiet for a long moment as she soaked in the sunlight that filtered through the leaves, and I thought that was the only answer I would get. But then she opened her eyes and looked at me. "You know how in the basement you can hear the roots humming? How you can almost feel?"

I nodded.

"It feels like that, but times ten," she explained with a smile. I tried to imagine that, the buzz under my skin amplified, but I still couldn't really picture it. I must have looked nervous because Jane reached over and squeezed my hand. "You'll love it. It's wonderful."

We spent the afternoon in the kitchen, working on dinner. It was more elaborate than usual, a celebration of tonight's sanctity. Jane had several dishes bubbling on the stove, the whole house smelling warm and delicious. She tasked me with slicing the mushrooms she had gathered earlier in the day while she worked on a strawberry cobbler at the other end of the counter.

We whispered back and forth while we worked, careful not to disturb Mother, who was reading in the living room. A record player in the corner played a jazz album, and the whole house was filled with music. Mother had a book open in her lap, her reading glasses sitting low on her nose, a pencil tracing along the words as she read them.

Several hours later, dinner was ready. I set the table, and Jane lit the line of taper candles in the middle. We had both changed a few minutes ago, trading our pants and sweaters for dresses that floated around our legs. Jane's was a deep sapphire blue, mine a pale pink. Our hair hung loose down our backs, mine in waves from the braids I had slept in the night before and Jane's in her usual slick, straight curtain. Jane had helped me stain my lips a rose pink, the first time I had put on a hint of makeup.

We all slid into our chairs around the table. "Everything looks wonderful," Mother said, gesturing at the dishes in front of us. "You've come a long way from your first attempts at cooking. Let's hope it tastes as good as it smells."

We passed around the dishes until we all had full plates, and then Jane pulled out two bottles of wine. A red for Mother and a white for Jane and me. We weren't allowed the red because it would stain our teeth, but Mother preferred the deep reds over the light, crisp whites. If I had been given the choice, perhaps I would have chosen the red, though I didn't know if that was because I would have genuinely preferred it or simply because it was something I wasn't allowed to have.

I must have looked for too long at the bottle of red because Mother caught my longing glance. "Would you rather have the red tonight?" she said.

I turned pink, embarrassed at being caught wanting something more than what I had been given. That was the biggest crime here—not being satisfied with what Mother had provided us. "No." I shook my head. "The white is perfect. Thank you."

"It's all right. It's a special occasion. Have a glass of the red," Mother continued. "You'll just need to be careful to brush thoroughly tonight before you go to bed."

I glanced at Jane, trying to get some insight from her on which answer was the right one. It was impossible to tell whether I should stick with the usual rules and deny Mother's request or accept this gift. I wasn't sure which would earn her approval. But before I could read the expression on Jane's face, Mother was already tipping the red into my glass.

"Thank you," I said.

Mother waited as I took a sip. It was delicious.

"Do you like it?" she asked.

"It's fantastic. Thank you." I would have said yes regardless, but I loved it.

"Good." Mother looked at the other end of the table, where Jane had filled her glass halfway with the bottle of white. "Jane prefers the white. Don't you?"

Jane smiled. "The red's a little too heavy for me." I wasn't sure if that was the truth or if Jane was just saying what she hoped Mother wanted to hear. It was impossible to untangle the places where we had changed ourselves to please Mother from our own wants and desires. Perhaps there wasn't really a difference. We grew into the places she'd built to hold us, like trees bending shape around the wind.

The conversation over dinner was hushed and unhurried, and we all pretended that we weren't bursting with anticipation for what would happen later that night. My leg was bouncing under the table until Mother reached over and gripped my knee, a silent admonishment. After that, I was careful not to let my body betray my impatience.

Still, the minutes seemed to tick by painfully slowly. I picked at a loose thread on the edge of my napkin. Jane was barely better at hiding her anticipation than I was, her eyes flicking to the window every few seconds, marking the setting sun.

Mother glanced up at the window. Jane and I both watched her every time she moved. I was holding my breath. "I think it's dark enough," Mother announced. She turned back to the two of us with a smile.

"Jane, will you get one of the baskets by the door?" Mother asked as she slowly pulled herself to her feet.

Jane rose and headed for the door, and I followed. The basket was covered with a towel, but I had peeked inside earlier. It was full of bones and scraps of flesh: The empty chicken bones from the dinner Jane had made from the night before. And the skins of the rabbits Mother practiced on in the basement. And bones that were far too big for rabbits or chickens. My stomach turned, and I looked away as Mother passed me a flashlight.

"Let's go."

A cold breeze swept into the cottage the moment Mother opened the door, sending a shiver up my spine. Our feet were bare, as Mother had instructed us, and I could feel the cold seeping into my soles when I stepped onto the little dirt path that led from the front door.

We followed Mother without speaking, through the garden and out the gate that led to the wide expanse of trees. The branches lifted into an arch above us, clearing a path deep into the forest. Even though we weren't talking, it was not quiet. The dark was full of the branches moving in the wind and animals that weren't awake in the day. I stayed close to Jane, ready to reach for her in case anything jumped out from between the trees.

I was so close that when Mother suddenly stopped, I almost crashed into Jane. We had come to a small clearing, the ground covered in a soft layer of moss and grass. The whole forest always felt sacred. Something ancient and powerful pulsed through its underground veins, but there was something even more sublime about this space. The hum of the trees was even louder, as if it converged here.

Mother and Jane had already begun preparing, setting our things in a pile near the trunk of a tree and grabbing two trowels. I knew I should help them, but I was too mesmerized by this place. As we stepped into the clearing, the sky opened above us—vast and endless, no longer hidden by the trees. I tipped my head back, taking in all the stars.

"Darling?" Mother called over to me, pulling my attention from the sky. "Can you shine the flashlight here?" She indicated a spot in the ground between two wide roots. I nodded.

I watched as Mother and Jane dug. They moved with practiced efficiency that told me they had done this together many times before. The hole they made wasn't very large, maybe six inches deep and just over a foot wide. It took them a couple of minutes, the ground soft with rain from earlier in the week. The two of them leaned away from the hole, dusting the dirt off their palms.

"Now what?" I whispered.

"Now," Mother said, sitting back on her heels, "we return what was taken from the forest. We complete the circle of life and death and life again."

Jane stood without being asked and grabbed both baskets, then brought them toward where Mother knelt over the hole in the ground. Together they dumped the bones and flesh into the earth. I tried not to look too closely at all those mangled pieces.

Once both baskets were empty, Jane stood and took my hand. She pulled me closer to Mother, until my bare toes were almost at the edge of the hole. My feet had gone numb a long time ago and felt heavy against the ground. Jane stood close to me, her thigh almost touching mine, as Mother covered the hole where the discarded pieces now rested.

A hush fell over the forest, everything going still as Mother finished and rose, wiping her hands against her pants. The trees leaned in toward us, branches sweeping down to almost brush against our cheeks. Jane gripped my hand tighter as we both felt it begin.

There was no speech or spell; there didn't need to be. The trees didn't speak in words but in the rustle of leaves, the scrape of branches against each other, and the hum that poured from their roots into our bare soles.

At first it was a little buzz, a faint tingle under my skin, a pleasant warmth that felt a bit like a bath after a morning spent in the snow. But then it grew even stronger as Mother reached for my open hand. I shivered as it rolled through me, painting every corner of my body with something that felt like sunlight, even as a cold breeze brushed against my bare skin.

After it was over, as the warmth faded and the buzz quieted in my blood, we walked home without speaking, as if we, like the trees, found speech superfluous. Our cheeks were flushed from the cold, our hair tangled by the wind, and our feet still flecked with dirt as we climbed into our beds and dreamed of endless leaves and branches.

CHAPTER 17

When I woke up the next morning, the house was empty, missing even my mother's usual note on the counter. The snow that had fallen overnight was already melting, the sky a bright blue and the sun sparkling off the stretches of white. Even through the windows, I could hear the slow drip of water off the branches around our house. The police cars were gone. They had left not long after I had arrived home the prior evening, once it had become clear that they weren't going to find anything else in the dark. Yellow police tape still roped off a section of trees, although a long strand had broken loose and was now waving in the breeze.

Despite the snow, the sun felt nice as it poured through the windows. *I should go for a walk.* I wanted fresh air and had no other plans until this evening.

I hadn't been back in the forest since that run with my mother, where we had encountered the bloody rabbit, and even thinking about it made my stomach turn. But it was daylight now, the forest bright as sunlight pierced through the leafless branches.

I wouldn't go far. I had walked through the trees a million times before, and nothing had ever happened to me. But that wasn't a promise of safety. Still, I refused to let my fear keep me trapped in the house. I had inherited a stubborn streak from my mother. Once I decided I should do something, I would follow through, even when, like now, something inside me whispered it was a bad idea.

I changed into pants I wouldn't mind getting a little muddy and headed downstairs, the dogs following on my heels. I put them on leashes, not entirely trusting Daisy to stick by my side, and walked out the back door. I headed in the opposite direction of the police tape, both leashes going taut as the dogs pulled away from the house, leaving a trail of paw prints behind them in the melting snow. I scanned the branches and then stepped into the woods.

There was something soothing about the trees, a magnetic hum that settled into my bones when the blue sky disappeared behind crisscrossing branches. I was still on edge in the forest, bracing at every sound like something or someone might jump out from behind a trunk. Yes, it was full of potential danger, but it was also quiet, undemanding, requiring nothing from me. I didn't need to become some other version of myself to exist here. I could just be.

I closed my eyes for a breath as a gentle breeze brushed against my face. Perhaps it was all a trick, a luring sort of calm that sought to put me at ease before the forest swallowed me whole. But despite myself, my breaths grew a little deeper, and my heart rate slowed as my house disappeared behind me.

The dogs were eager to be out, their paws quickly growing muddy as they darted between the trees, sniffing the ground. This morning, the forest was full of the sound of melting ice dripping off the branches all around me. Now that I was deeper in, there was less snow on the ground.

I followed a narrow trail through the forest, letting the dogs wander as far as the leashes would go, untangling them as they wrapped themselves around tree trunks. The soft sounds of the woods fell over me like a blanket as we walked. I let my mind wander, picking through thoughts about Tom, about my job, about what I wanted to do next.

I didn't want to stay with Cerise's company forever. It was small. There weren't really many positions for me to grow into, and I wanted something more challenging or at least new. I had been playing with the idea for at least a year now, but since I was no longer in the city, maybe it made sense to try to make the jump somewhere else. I didn't think I wanted to live in another big city again. There were too many people packed too tightly. It was easier to breathe out here, where there was space to exist without any eyes on me. I took a deep breath, the air cold and a little damp.

I had missed this place, the quiet, the fresh air. It almost seemed to sing, settling in my bones. I had missed my sister. I wasn't sure I'd want to be so far from her again, seeing her for only a few days once or twice a year.

After a while, the cold morning air that at first felt invigorating slipped past my jacket and started to make my fingers ache. It was time to head home and eat something warm for breakfast. "Come on, ladies," I called to the dogs. They both immediately returned to my side, tails wagging and tongues hanging out of their mouths.

I turned around and started back the way I had come, leashes loose in my hand. The ground was slicker than usual, a layer of rotting leaves coated in the melting snow, making each step precarious. Mud caked the bottom of my shoes. I was so focused on not slipping that it took me longer than it should have to notice that the trail was gone.

I stopped, expecting to find the trail a few feet away, thinking I might have taken a couple of steps off course to avoid a tree root. But there was no path—just a densely wooded patch of the forest, surrounded by branches. A bit of snow and mud shouldn't have been enough to camouflage the trail completely. And even if the snow had covered the path here, I should have been able to see my footsteps in the mud. I made a slow circle, the dogs' leashes tangling around me.

Daisy, deciding this was some new game, barked at me, wagging her tail excitedly.

"Shh." I tugged her a little closer to my side. My heart was in my throat. The woods sounded as they should—birds chirped, the wind rattled through tree branches, and melted ice dripped onto the forest floor—but I listened for anything out of place, suddenly feeling like I wasn't entirely alone out here. I took a tentative step in the direction I thought the house might be, eyes glued to the ground, looking for any sign of where we had come from. We hadn't walked that far. I should've been able to see some recognizable landmarks.

A cloud rolled in front of the sun, making the whole place fall into shadows. I shouldn't have been able to get too lost. I would stumble across another house or a trail soon enough, but even as I thought the words, I knew they weren't entirely true. The forest was huge. It could so easily make me disappear.

The dogs didn't seem to realize anything was wrong, still bopping alongside me happily. I pulled them to a stop. "Go home," I told them, voice shaking, as if they were bloodhounds instead of goldendoodles and could lead me back to our house by scent. Poppy stared at me, her tongue lolling out of her mouth, and Daisy nudged my hands, asking to be pet. "Go," I encouraged them again, but they continued to stare at me, neither wanting to lead us anywhere.

A twig cracked somewhere in the forest, and I shrieked. All three of us whipped our heads toward the noise. Daisy's ears flattened, and a low growl started in her chest. My breaths came faster as I scanned the forest, looking for the source of the sound. Everything looked the same, but it felt different, like the trees had shifted closer, slowly moving to cage me in.

I pulled my phone out of my pocket. It didn't have a signal. Even back at the house, service was spotty, and it completely vanished at the tree line. Regardless, I tried pulling up the map, hoping my phone might figure out where I was, but it wouldn't load. It stayed zoomed out, showing a wide swath of green forest, my house in the middle of the screen.

I knew I should stay in one place if I was lost so it was easier for people to find me, but I couldn't help but continue forward. The forest seemed to lean in toward me. I stumbled a few times as the ground became more uneven. I needed to get out of here to reach the safety of the house. I was running at this point, the dogs keeping pace alongside me. The trees around me didn't look familiar, but I wasn't sure if I would have recognized them. Everything looked the same.

I nearly crashed into a fallen tree. I hadn't noticed it until I was on top of it, but I wasn't sure how I had missed something so big. The trunk was massive, almost reaching my hip, even though it lay horizontally across the forest floor. The edges of the bark had rotted away, leaving hunks of it caving in on itself. This had been here for a long time, likely decades, yet I had never seen it. I would have remembered this giant. I was in a new section of the forest, somewhere I had never explored before.

I reached out to touch the thick layer of moss that ran up the side, obscuring where the tree met the ground. It was pillowy, denser than I expected, and still damp from the snow that must have melted away this morning. A family of black beetles emerged from a crack disturbed by my presence. I stepped back, rounding the tree.

A little clearing sat on the other side of the log. It wasn't huge, maybe twenty feet across, in what looked like a near-perfect circle. It was covered in a thin layer of grass and moss that was unnaturally green under the bleak, bare branches of the trees, as if this spot were reaching into spring while the rest of the woods slipped into winter. I walked into the clearing, moving along the edge.

Someone had carved something into one of the trees that lined the clearing. Moss had crept up the trunk, nearly obscuring the name that must have been carved decades earlier. I traced my fingers over the four letters: MARY. A heart was etched below Mary's name. I imagined a boy chipping away at the bark to add the name to the tree, trying to impress the girl he was seeing. There was something sweet about it. I was comforted by the thought that someone had been here before me, hopeful that it meant I wasn't too far from one of the trails that cut through here.

I ran my fingers over the letters again when both dogs jumped back, pulling against the leashes in my hands. "What?" I asked, following their gazes to the ground. A red-and-white snake moved through the grass inches from my feet. I stumbled back a few steps, and Daisy pulled at her leash, wanting to put even more distance between her and the snake. Taking that as my cue to leave, I stepped away from the strange patch of green.

Back in the forest, I hoped to hear the distant hum of cars or maybe even the footsteps of a hiker on some nearby trail, but the woods were silent. Even the earlier sounds of nature had fallen away, leaving only an unnatural stillness. Daisy clung to me, her warm body pressed against my leg. Poppy wasn't far either, both eyeing the grass warily where we had seen the snake. The birds had stopped singing. No breeze rustled the last of the dried leaves. It was silent.

The momentary distraction of the strange clearing fell away as quickly as it had arrived. I was no closer to finding my way out of this than before. I didn't know where I was or in which direction I needed to move. A restless fear crept up my spine, pushing me to keep going. It looked like there might have once been a trail to my left, although it could have been a trick of the forest floor. I decided to follow it anyway.

Clouds rolled through, each blocking the sun for a few seconds as they passed. I pulled out my phone, hoping for a signal, but there was still none. Even a weak one might be enough to text my mom or sister. I stared down at my phone as I walked, waiting for a single bar to appear in the corner of my screen.

I kept moving, faster now, my steps lengthening to cover more ground with each movement. All the earlier comfort I had felt at the peaceful morning evaporated. The quiet felt foreboding now as the shadows grew darker, the branches drooping lower, snagging at the edges of my clothes.

"Ophelia?"

My name cut through the silence. I jolted at the sound, catching myself against a branch as I turned toward the voice. My mother emerged from behind a tree as if pulled from its shadow. Relief washed over me as she cleared the distance between us. "What are you doing out here?" she asked.

I was still bracing myself against the tree, trying to catch my breath, my heart pounding. "I was walking the dogs, and I got turned around. I lost the trail," I said. Tears threatened at the corners of my eyes.

My mother grabbed the leashes from my hand without asking, and both dogs happily joined her. "You're not far from the house," she said, gesturing in a direction slightly to the left of the way I had been walking. "It's a few minutes that way."

I must have looked as terrible as I felt. I was sure the stress from the last hour wandering around out here was clear on my face.

"Are you okay?" she asked.

"I'm fine," I said with a deep inhale. "Just got a little freaked out when I couldn't figure out where I was."

She reached over and squeezed my hand, where it hung limply at my side. "I've got you now. Let's get you home." She started forward, glancing over her shoulder to make sure I was behind her.

Her blond ponytail bounced ahead of me as I followed her out of the woods, and a flood of memories rushed in–walking these same trails nearly every day of my childhood, no matter the weather. I remembered trudging through the trees with rain jackets pulled tight around our heads during a downpour and wading through icy creek water during the hottest days of the summer. The forest air was good for us, she'd say, cracking open our windows at night when we started to come down with a cold. Part of me had believed her, believed in whatever sort of magic the trees possessed. I'd always felt better after a day spent in the woods.

In high school, when the stories of the missing girls made me afraid of the forest, I still wanted to believe in my mother's version of it, where its branches were filled with comfort and safety, at least when my mom acted as my guide. Even now, the trees that moments ago had felt menacing as I raced through them felt still and peaceful as I walked behind my mother.

She was a few steps ahead of me, frequently glancing back over her shoulder to check on me. She wasn't dressed for an afternoon in the woods. It wasn't the sweater or jeans that stood out as particularly abnormal but her choice of shoes—not her running shoes or her snow boots, but a pair of pale leather flats, completely out of place against the mud. "Why were you out there?" I asked.

"Oh, I was just coming home from Jane's," she answered over her shoulder. Her best friend, Jane, lived less than half a mile from our house, if you cut through the trees, and my mother often made the trip on foot.

I didn't have time to ask follow-up questions. The trees suddenly thinned, and the blue sky was bright on the other side of the branches, dotted with a few fluffy white clouds. Gravel crunched under my feet as I stepped into the driveway. I had never been so excited to see the white columns of our front porch. I stood there for a moment, catching my breath. A flash of bright yellow stood out, waving gently in the wind next to me. The police tape.

Somehow, I had ended up on the complete opposite side of the yard from where I had started. I shouldn't have been able to reach this side of the house without either crossing the driveway out front or the creek in the back, neither of which I had even seen. I turned back as I reached the porch steps, studying the trees behind me, looking for something that could explain how I'd ended up so lost, but the trees looked as they always did, revealing no secrets.

CHAPTER 18

I spent the rest of the day replaying the morning in my mind, trying to find some rational explanation for what had happened. I even went so far as to pull up a map to re-create my route, although I didn't have much to go on and abandoned the project soon after I started it. It was possible that I had gotten turned around or wandered off the trail. But it seemed impossible that I would have gotten so lost, so completely disorientated by the forest that I would have crossed the creek or even another trail without noticing. Yet I had no other explanation for where my mother had found me.

I was still thinking about the impossibility of the situation when my mother emerged from upstairs, sliding an earring into her ear as she walked toward me. "Are you ready?" she asked.

I nodded and stood, pressing the nonexistent wrinkles out of my pants with my hands. After trying and discarding most of the items in my closet, I landed on something simple: a sweater and black pants. I was comforted to see that my mom had picked something similar, although I couldn't help but notice hers was just slightly better, her pants obviously more expensive, her sweater the perfect shade of emerald. I stood still as her eyes skimmed over me. She reached out and tugged at the hem of my sweater, fingers rubbing over the fabric. "This is pilling a bit," she said.

"Should I change?" I asked.

Just then, Evie's footsteps started down the stairs. She entered the living room, sparing us a quick glance before continuing to the garage door.

"We don't have time. But leave it out for me when we get back; I'll take care of it," my mom said as she followed Evie. Now that my mother had pointed it out, all I could see was her disappointed expression at the speckles that dotted the entire sweater. I thought about dashing upstairs to switch into something else, but my mother looked back at me as her hand landed on the doorknob. "Let's go," she said.

When we arrived at the high school, the parking lot was already full of cars. The drive had been quiet except for the low hum of the radio, none of us in the mood for polite conversation. But as soon as we stepped out of the car, we were swarmed by other parents eager to speak with our mother.

They whispered as they talked to her, trying to shield us from whatever new bits of information they had learned about Maddie's case. "Elizabeth, have you heard anything else? I know the police were at your house again last night," someone said in a low voice, with a darting glance in our direction.

"I heard they found evidence that there was a struggle," someone else said, before my mother could answer.

"Police did another search yesterday. They just wanted to make sure they didn't miss anything with the snow we got last night," my mother said, completely ignoring the comment from the second woman.

"Did they find anything?"

"The police are still investigating," my mother said with an apologetic smile. "I don't feel comfortable discussing anything that isn't publicly available information. We don't want to do anything that could disrupt their work." Her eyes darted over to Evie, an unspoken second reason hidden in the glance: *I'm not going to discuss anything more in front of my daughter.* The other mothers reluctantly nodded. Even in this brief interaction, it was clear that my mother was the one in control, everyone else following her lead.

"How are you all holding up?" another woman asked. A small cluster of parents had formed an audience for my mother at this point.

"We are just doing everything we can to support the Rodinghams right now. I can't even imagine what they are going through," my mom said, shifting the conversation away from our family in a way that spoke only of her empathy.

Chatter started among the other parents about starting a meal train, and my mom took the opportunity to excuse herself from the group. "I'm going to get the girls settled and see if anyone needs help with the setup," my mom said. She reached over and set her hand on Evie's back, guiding us toward the football field.

We had made it halfway across the parking lot when my mom's hand landed on my arm. "I'm going to talk with Jane for a minute," she said, gesturing vaguely toward a gaggle of parents. "I'll find you when I'm done."

I nodded. Evie hadn't stopped, and I had to walk quickly to catch up with her. A few girls came up and hugged her, their eyes already leaking tears, as soon as our mom was no longer at our side. I expected her to join one of their groups. If anything, she moved another inch toward me every time she stepped out of the embrace of another classmate, answering their questions in as few words as possible. It was such a contrast from the way our mother had just played the whole crowd, treating the other parents like they were reporters at her press conference. Evie had her shields up and wasn't interested in performing for anyone.

By the time we reached the field, her shoulder was bumping into mine as we walked. The sun had almost disappeared below the horizon, the last streaks of golden color fading from the sky. We found a spot near the front, where someone had rolled a makeshift stage onto the track. It was only a few feet high, the sort of thing used for graduations. Maddie wouldn't get to walk across the stage at graduation. That realization was enough to make my throat tighten.

Evie pulled her phone out of her pocket and started scrolling, while I searched the crowd at the edge of the field for my mother. She was now standing off to the side of things, leaning in close to talk with Jane. Evie and I were way too far away to hear what they were talking about, but even from this distance, I could tell my mother was upset, all her composure from a few minutes before gone. She spoke forcefully, her words punctuated with sharp hand movements, and her face was an unmistakable scowl. I watched her for a long moment as Jane spoke, her head ducked low, speaking rapidly in what looked like an attempt to calm my mother. Mom looked up and found me watching her. Her face immediately softened into her usual practiced smile as she caught my eyes, holding up a finger and mouthing that she needed another minute.

A microphone squealed to life, pulling my attention back to the front of the field. The principal took the stage. "Thank you, everyone, for coming tonight. Before we get started, we will hear from Officer Bodell."

A uniformed brunette officer in her mid-thirties took the microphone from the principal. She had been one of the officers asking questions the night Maddie disappeared. I wondered if she had daughters. If she lost sleep at the thought of them going missing. She repeated the exact words I'd heard at least a dozen times at this point, promising that they were doing everything they could to bring Maddie home and urging anyone with information to come forward. They didn't say what I knew to be true: They weren't going to bring her home. They didn't have any idea where she was. They had nothing.

The update, if you could call it that, lasted less than a minute before she passed the microphone back. The principal gave instructions from the podium, gesturing at the boxes of candles being distributed through the crowd. I grabbed two white candles, then silently gave one to Evie. The principal waited until it seemed like most people had gotten one before speaking again.

"Madison Rodingham was a friend to so many of you, and I know she's deeply missed. But tonight we come together as a community to support each other, not in grief but in hope. We light these candles to illuminate Maddie's way home."

Flames slowly twinkled to life as the crowd lit their candles, until half the field was golden with flickering light. A stranger lit my candle, and I turned to pass the flame to Evie, her hand coming up to shield our candles until hers caught.

The gesture felt painfully hollow. What was a field full of candlelight supposed to do for Maddie? For all the missing girls who had gone before her? For the girls who might go after her? I was angry. I could feel the rage bubbling in every corner of my body, pushing against my skin, fighting to break free. I wanted to scream. I didn't want to be here, pretending this mattered. We should have turned our candles into torches, marched to the forest, and burned the trees to the ground. Instead, we'd stand out here for an hour while the marching band played a sad song, and by this time next week, half the town would have forgotten all about Maddie.

I watched Evie, the light catching her expression as she sucked her bottom lip into her mouth. Her eyes were glassy as she held back tears, the flame dancing on the candle in her hands. As I watched her, I had a hard time distinguishing where my fear ended and my anger began. They bled into each other.

I was angry that these girls kept disappearing, and no one seemed to be able to do anything to stop it. We cared for a few weeks, the girls' faces and names impossible to escape, but then a month or two would pass. We'd let the girls vanish from our collective consciousness, another drop in a bucket. We let these memories of the missing girls fade because remembering was too frightening. How were we supposed to live in a world where girls disappeared from backyards and on walks home from school? So it would happen again. Maddie would not be the last. The forest would swallow another and another, its appetite never satisfied.

On the stage, Maddie's mother had replaced the principal at the microphone. "Maddie—" Mrs. Rodingham's voice was shaky as she almost whispered her daughter's name. She cleared her throat and started again. "Maddie, if you are watching somewhere"—her words were directed entirely to the news cameras—"we love you and will do anything we can to get you home safe." The audience members held their breath, waiting for her to continue, but what else could she say? Her daughter was missing, and she wanted her home. Nothing else really mattered.

She stepped back from the microphone, and a rickety projector started playing a slideshow of pictures of Maddie as the marching band played a somber melody. Hot wax dripped onto my fingers as the candle burned down, and an image of Maddie as a little girl at the beach faded into one with her face painted at a football game, surrounded by a group of other girls, Evie right next to her.

Evie didn't move, staring straight ahead at the screen. She wasn't crying, but I saw the way her breath hitched, a quiet stutter that didn't quite make a sound but seemed to echo in the space around us. It was like the air thickened with her sorrow, taking on weight, wrapping itself around her.

Mom chose that moment to reappear. I wanted to ask what

she had been talking about, but she took one look at Evie and passed me her candle. She wrapped her arms around my sister from behind, resting her cheek against the back of Evie's head. Mom started to sway, rocking gently back and forth, her arms crossed over Evie's chest. They moved together like branches catching a breeze, bending and swaying to the rhythm of Evie's grief. My sister curled one hand around our mom's forearm, holding her there.

The rest of the vigil continued in much the same way. A few more people spoke. Evie had been asked, but she had refused, saying she didn't think she could do it. More photos. More music. My mom didn't move from her position wrapped around Evie until the last song finished and the crowd dispersed back to the parking lot.

"Lia?" someone called out from a group gathered along the edge of the field.

All three of us whipped around at my name. I immediately recognized Kiera, who had broken away from her friends and was walking quickly in our direction. "I heard you were back in town," she said when she got closer.

I didn't have time to formulate my answer before she hugged me. "I'm so sorry," she said as she held me for a long moment, and tears welled up in the corners of my eyes. I refused to cry. Evie hadn't cried tonight, so I wouldn't either. But I wanted to. I wanted to sob for Maddie being gone, for Evie being without her best friend, and for me being alone. It was too much, and even the gentle kindness of this hug threatened to break my carefully constructed walls.

Kiera leaned back, although her hands still lingered on my

shoulders, and addressed her next words to my whole family. "Please let me know if you need anything. I can't even imagine what you all are going through."

"Thank you, Kiera," my mom said. "We appreciate that."

"I won't keep you. I just wanted to say hello." She took a step back but paused before turning to leave. "You should come over sometime. I'd love to catch up."

I was ready to thank her for her offer without meaning it when Evie spoke for the first time since the vigil had started. "You should do that," she said in my direction, although it was clear that the words were for both me and Kiera. "Lia was just talking about how she wanted to catch up with you now that she's back in town."

Kiera broke into a smile. "Perfect. Do you have my number? It's the same as it was in high school."

I nodded and looked back at Evie, who had already pulled her phone out of her pocket, acting like this was nothing. I recognized Evie's comment as a sign of her care, a small gift. Even tonight, on what had to be one of the worst nights of her life, she was thinking of me, somehow knowing I might need a friend.

"Please text me, and we'll do something. I mean, if you want to," Kiera said.

"I will." And I was a bit surprised to realize I meant it. After everything that had happened over the last few days, the idea of restarting our friendship was surprisingly alluring.

CHAPTER 19
THE MISSING GIRLS

Evenings together were my favorite part of this new life in the cottage. Jane twisted my hair back into a pair of French braids while we talked. I would tell her about whatever book I was currently reading, and she would tell me stories about her boyfriend, Frank. All the while, Mother worked, shaking her head at our giggles, her legs stretched out in front of her, a notebook in her lap as she sketched her next project. If someone had glanced through our windows, it would have looked like a scene from a fairy tale, the cottage filled with laughter and happiness under the glow of a roaring fire.

Tonight, Jane and I headed to bed like usual, while Mother, who always stayed up a few hours later than us, continued to work in the corner. My bed had quickly become one of my favorite spaces in the cottage. Recently, Jane had replaced the old quilt with a duvet in my favorite color, a sky blue, and had even embroidered my name onto the pillowcase in a matching thread. I slipped under the covers and quickly fell asleep.

It couldn't have been much later when our front door opened with a crash, jolting me from sleep. A desperate scream tore through the house, and I knew I'd hear it in my head for years. I sat up in my bed, throwing back the blankets before I even realized what I was doing. I felt the dread in my bones; they ached with it. My heart thumped hard in my chest, trying to break free of my rib cage. My skin felt too tight to contain all of me, as if my scars might split open and my insides might spill onto the quilt.

I screamed too, our voices braiding together into a pained melody. Although I could no longer remember the details—what had happened to me and how—I recognized the fear. My body remembered it.

And then Jane's arms were wrapped around me, pinning my arms to my side. "Shh..." she hushed in my ear. "It's okay." She squeezed me tightly as the screaming continued. Something was knocked over in the main room, glass shattering across the wood floors, and the screaming went quiet.

I tried to break out of Jane's grip to help whoever's screams still echoed through my mind. Tears streaked my cheeks, and my chest heaved with sobs, but she wouldn't let me go. "We're okay," she promised me, her voice softer than I had ever heard it. There were tears in her voice, and I knew if I turned around, her cheeks would be wet.

Her arms loosened, but she didn't let go of me. "What was that?" I asked, although I suspected I knew the answer.

"It's over now," she said with an exhale. I tried to believe her as my fingers went to the scar along the back of my neck, tracing along my seams.

CHAPTER 20

I woke up in the middle of the night to find my room lit by a glow leaking past my curtains. I slipped out of bed and padded to the window. Snow was falling in a slow trickle from the sky, not yet coating the ground in white.

I reached for my phone in the dark. The impulse to share a photo of this strange and magical thing grabbed me even through my sleep-addled brain, but my charger was empty. My bag still sat on the chair where I had tossed it last night, but my phone wasn't inside. I grimaced, realizing I must have left it downstairs. I considered leaving it until the morning, but now that I knew it was missing, I wouldn't be able to sleep until I found it.

I threw on a sweatshirt and my slippers before slowly peeling open my door. The house was quiet. I moved through it carefully, not wanting to wake anyone. My mom was a notoriously light sleeper and would check the house at the slightest noise. The main floor glowed with falling snow, the soft light pouring in from all the windows, making our house look like something from a dream.

I watched the snow fall through the glass as I tiptoed across the main floor. It was stunning, the way the snow drifted down through the air, slowly starting to cling to the naked branches at the edge of the forest. It was unfair how someplace so dangerous could look so beautiful.

My phone was sitting in the middle of the kitchen island, but before I could reach for it, a slow click sounded from upstairs, a door opening so quietly that I almost missed it. I tucked myself into the corner, hoping it was dark enough that my mom wouldn't notice me. But to my surprise, it wasn't my mom who came down the stairs a minute later but Evie. She was dressed for the weather, with a puffer jacket pulled on over her pajama pants and snow boots in her hand as she tiptoed across the room, following the same path I had. She barely even looked in my direction as she entered the kitchen. Her eyes darted back up toward the stairs, listening intently for anyone following her. Then she slid her feet into her boots and opened the back door.

I reached out and grabbed her wrist. She let out a gasping inhale before covering her mouth with her hand, as if to quiet her own scream, eyes wide. "What the fuck!" she whispered, slapping my arm with her other hand. "Why are you hiding down here?"

"Ow," I whispered. It hadn't really hurt, the sting barely noticeable through my sweatshirt, but I dropped her wrist anyway. "I left this in the kitchen." I grabbed my phone off the counter and waved it in front of her. "What are you doing?" I asked, keeping my voice as quiet as I possibly could.

"There's someone out there," she whispered.

I looked past her toward the trees. Even though it was bright out tonight thanks to the falling snow, it was still impossible to see past the first few rows of branches. "Where?" I whispered back. Snow was blowing in the open door, my bare ankles already freezing.

"There are people walking in the trees. I saw them out my window."

"And you're just planning to go out there by yourself?"

She shrugged, stepping out the open door.

"Are you stupid?" I asked, leaning over the threshold. The snow melted as soon as it hit the kitchen floor, already creating a little puddle at the edge of the doorframe.

"What if Maddie's out there?" Evie asked. She watched me in silence for a moment, daring me to stop her, before she started into the yard. I hesitated for only a second before following her.

Unlike Evie, I hadn't dressed for a walk in the snow. The moment I was outside, the wind cut through my sweatshirt, sending shivers up my spine. I was grateful for my rubber-soled slippers, despite the fact snow was already sliding in the sides.

Evie tiptoed to the spot where her bedroom window looked out over the trees, clinging tight to the house, and I walked close behind her. We both paused when we reached the corner. Evie peered around it and then turned to nod at me. "Right over here," she mouthed.

The night was eerily silent. I could hear my breath in my

ears as we tried to move without making a sound. Evie stayed within arm's reach of me, her head whipping around every few feet to make sure I was still with her. When we reached the next corner, right under Evie's bedroom window, she pointed out at the trees. "I thought I saw someone here," she whispered, leaning in so her mouth was almost touching my ear. We both stared into the darkness between the trees, trying to make something appear between branches. As we waited, I reached up and wrapped my hand around Evie's elbow, worried that if we weren't physically anchored to each other, one of us could just disappear.

"I don't see anything," I whispered, after what felt like several minutes of waiting, neither of us moving or making a sound.

Evie nodded. I thought she might ask to go into the forest. Watching from the safety of the yard felt like one thing, but wandering through the dark would have been too dangerous. I would have dragged her back into the house kicking and screaming if necessary.

But she didn't ask to go into the trees. "I must have been imagining things," she whispered. Her voice wavered with barely restrained tears. For a few minutes, she had been able to hope that Maddie might come stumbling out of the woods, or at the very least we'd find a clue about where she might be. Instead, Evie was right back where she'd started her evening, steeped in grief and despair.

"Or it's already gone?" I offered. I didn't know if it was true. I hadn't seen anything, but there was something about the way Evie spoke that made me want to leave her with a little hope.

She just shrugged in response.

"Ready to go back inside?" I asked. I was frozen at this point, eager to dash up the stairs, peel off my wet clothes, and climb back into my bed. Evie nodded.

We started back along the house, still careful not to make too much noise. The snow muffled our footsteps, and all I could really hear was the shallow sound of my breath, each exhale creating a little cloud that caught the light. We were about to round the corner that would land us at the back door when I heard voices from across the snow-covered yard.

"She promised she would be done after Kate."

I would have recognized my mother's voice anywhere. I turned to look at Evie, a finger pressed against my lips. She nodded, both of us clinging even tighter to the shadows. My mind immediately turned to Kate Montgomery, the only Kate I could think of at the moment. Perhaps I'd finally learn what they had been talking about that day after the search party.

Another voice joined hers, slightly deeper and without the lightness that seemed to permeate my mother's every word. "There's no such thing as 'done' with this. You know that." I took another step forward and peered around the corner, hoping the shadows would hide me. A pair of women trudged up from the trees. I recognized my mom in her black coat and snow boots in an instant. It took me a moment longer to identify Jane. She, too, was dressed in black, her long dark hair pulled into a ponytail at the base of her neck.

What were they doing out here so late? My mother was known for taking walks in the woods, but it was the middle of the night and snowing.

"I thought we'd have longer," my mom said with a hiss.

"Lizzy," Jane said. I had never heard anyone call my mom by a nickname without being promptly corrected. She had always been Elizabeth or Mrs. Gregg. *Lizzy* didn't seem to fit her; it was too small to contain her. Lizzy was a third grader with freckles and overalls. Elizabeth was the name of a queen. "She needs another project. I don't know what you expected." I was desperate to know who they were talking about.

"She took her from my back porch," my mom hissed. Evie reached for my hand, her nails digging into my palm. They were talking about Maddie. "Evangeline was gone for minutes; if she had returned just a few seconds earlier..."

"Don't be ridiculous," Jane said impatiently. "If Evangeline had been out there, nothing would have happened."

"I don't know if that's true anymore. Mother's being reckless," my mom snapped back. I never heard her speak like this outside the house—and rarely inside. She was measured and patient to a fault. I was almost more shocked by her tone than anything else about the conversation. But I also wondered who they were talking about. Whose mother? It couldn't be our mom's mother. Our grandmother had been dead for decades. She had died years before I was born. My mom rarely spoke about her.

"No more than she always has been," Jane said. "You only care now because it's affected you."

"I've always cared," my mother argued. "It's just... Evangeline is devastated."

"They've always had families, Liz. There have always been some devastated parents out there."

"This is different," my mom protested.

"It's not," Jane said, this time louder than she should, given the hour. My mother didn't say anything in response to that, but I heard her huff indignantly. "I'm not saying I've done any better than you," Jane continued. "But you can't pretend there is anything fundamentally different about this girl. We all close our eyes and act like we don't know where the girls come from."

They both fell quiet, and if it hadn't been for their steady footsteps still making their way toward the back door, I would have imagined they had vanished into the night.

"How is Evangeline doing?" Jane asked. Their footsteps had stopped. I assumed they were standing on the back porch.

"She's been having nightmares about it, so she's barely sleeping. She doesn't want to hang out with her friends. She's not herself. I don't know what to do," my mother admitted. She sounded tired, almost defeated.

I turned to Evie. I didn't know she had been having nightmares. I met her eyes for a second. She shrugged, an acknowledgment of the truth and a dismissal. I reached toward her, wanting to offer her a little bit of comfort, but she waved me off and gestured for me to turn around and keep listening.

"Give it time. It'll get better."

My mother sighed. "You should get going," she said. "It's cold out tonight." I heard the shifting of coats and then footsteps again.

"Good night," Jane called, her voice already growing distant.

"Be careful. It's getting slick out there," my mom warned. "Text me when you get home."

Jane agreed, and soon enough, I heard the back door open and close again.

"Wait," I mouthed to my sister as she took a step toward me. We stood around the corner for a few minutes. My toes had gone painfully cold. The snow had fallen over the edge of my slippers, soaking the lining with ice water.

"What were they talking about?" Evie whispered, after Jane's footsteps had faded and the air was once again still.

"I don't know."

"Do you think Mom knows what happened to Maddie?"

"No," I responded immediately. There had to be another explanation for what they were saying. I couldn't fathom a world in which my mom was complicit in Maddie's disappearance. "Why would she keep that a secret?" I knew the answer to my own question before I even finished it. If she was somehow involved, somehow connected to whoever had Maddie, of course she'd want to keep it a secret.

"Let's head inside. I'm freezing," I whispered before Evie could ask anything else. I peeked around the corner. The backyard was empty except for the trail of footsteps, two sets heading toward the house and one set leading away, disappearing into the tree line as they reached the yard's edge.

The doorknob turned easily, and I breathed a sigh of relief, grateful that my mom hadn't locked the back door. I eased the door open and stepped through it, pulling off my slippers as soon as I was inside. Evie followed, pulling the door silently closed behind her.

The kitchen light flicked on. Both of us froze when we saw our mom standing at the counter. She had taken off her coat and was wearing a thick sweater, cheeks still flushed from the cold. "I thought you might be out there. You left a puddle by the door."

I felt trapped as she looked us over, waiting for our explanation. She leaned against the counter, her chin resting on her fist. There was no evidence that she felt caught, even though she had been sneaking through the snow minutes earlier. I tried to find some excuse for us being outside, but there was no rational reason to be out there so late.

Evie's solution was to go on the offensive. "What were you doing out there?" she asked in a voice that felt too loud for the house at this hour.

"Shh," our mom said, turning toward a cabinet and pulling three mugs down from the shelves. "Don't wake your father." Her voice was low, but she did not whisper as she pulled the kettle from its shelf and filled it with water. "I couldn't sleep. I was texting Jane, and she was awake too, so we decided to meet up and take a walk."

"It's an odd hour to go walking," Evie said, accusation lacing through every word.

"I could say the same thing to you. I think all our schedules have been a little strange these last few weeks." Something was off about her cool responses to our questions. I looked for any crack in her armor, some clue that she was nervous about what we might have overheard, but she was icily calm.

"Who were you talking about?" Evie asked, interrupting my mother's fixed gaze on me.

"We were talking about Maddie." My mother softened substantially as she talked to my sister, speaking with the careful tenderness of someone cleaning a wound. "I wish I had done something sooner. Jane and I were just saying we should have done everything differently. We could have been more involved in the search when the other girls went missing. Maybe then..." I finished her sentence for her in my head: *Maybe then Maddie would still be here.* She shook her head. "Anyway, do you both want a cup of tea? I need one to warm up before I go to bed."

Evie nodded and pulled out a stool. I did the same, happy to follow her lead. Our mom's story didn't quite make sense, didn't entirely fit the words we had overheard in the yard. I turned to look at Evie to see if she was still unconvinced, but her grief had swallowed her again, smothering any suspicions. She looked exhausted. I didn't know how I had missed the dark circles under her eyes, but now that I was paying attention, she seemed frail.

We fell into silence as our mom put a tea bag in each mug. I thought back to the conversation we had overheard, but it was late, and my memory was already growing fuzzy as I tried to recall the specific words Jane and our mom had used, which sentences seemed out of place. "Whose mother were you talking about?" I asked.

Her face scrunched up, my mom clearly surprised by my question. "What?"

"Outside with Jane. You said something about someone's mother being reckless?"

"Oh, um." She paused, the first flicker of nervousness crossing her face. "I'm not sure. Maybe all of us, like the mothers in town. I don't entirely remember."

"That's not what you said," I pressed. I hadn't planned on the words coming out, but I couldn't help it. It didn't make sense, not really. "You didn't say 'all the mothers' or someone specific like 'Maddie's mother.' It was just '*Mother*,' but your mom passed away a long time ago." Both my mother's parents had passed away when she was quite young, before she had even met my dad.

Her hand went to the back of her neck, her fingers massaging the tendons there. Her hair was piled on top of her head tonight. She rarely wore it up when she was out of the house, but tonight she hadn't thought we'd see her. She turned to the counter to check on the hot water, fingers still on the back of her neck, tracing along the scar that sat there. It was barely noticeable in most lights, but now, in the bright white light of the kitchen, I could make out the slightly puckered scar that started at her hairline and disappeared under her collar. "I don't know, Ophelia."

CHAPTER 21
THE MISSING GIRLS

"Good morning, Jane. Good morning, Elizabeth," Mother greeted us, as if nothing had happened the night before. As if the vase that had held a bouquet of wildflowers I'd picked yesterday weren't missing from the center of the table. As if last night, after the screams, I hadn't heard something heavy being dragged down the stairs to the basement. We ate in silence, a few pleasantries exchanged, but mostly the air was filled with spoons clinking against the sides of our bowls or the thump of Mother setting her mug back onto the wooden table.

I had lived here, in the cottage with Jane and Mother, for nine months. Now I moved with a lithe grace that made Mother smile as the last of my bruises and whispers of my old life faded. My world had grown a little bigger. I was allowed to leave the garden gates now. I could spend the afternoon walking through the trails that seemed to loop endlessly around us, though the trees would never let me get too far without delivering me back to the cottage door. Sometimes Jane even took me on short trips into town to the grocery store or the coffee shop, driving me in her little red car.

At night, when we were all curled up in front of the fire, Jane would tell stories about her day. While I got only a small taste of the world beyond the trees, she had friends, a boyfriend, and a whole other life in town. This information was doled out slowly, little crumbs sprinkled into stories. Sometimes I asked questions, hungry for more details about what Jane was doing in the world away from this forest. Often, Jane wouldn't answer, her eyes flashing to Mother for a moment before she shook her head at me. But, despite my world getting larger by inches, no one except Mother, Jane, and I had ever come to the cottage, until the girl who'd screamed last night.

"Did you girls sleep well?" Mother asked. I didn't miss the slight smile she tried to hide behind her mug of Earl Grey.

Jane was opening her mouth to answer with what I was sure would be some polite agreement, the response that had been trained into us. Mother never touched us, although sometimes I could almost taste her desire for violence, her hand clenched tight against the impulse to hit us. I didn't think it was for our benefit but hers. She'd spent too long working on us to damage our perfect bodies. Instead, her favorite punishment was simply not allowing us to eat. Meals were a privilege we earned when we behaved. But, sometimes, she deemed a few skipped meals weren't enough. Last week, I had been locked in the hall closet overnight when I had laughed after she had tripped over the doorframe, spilling a whole basket of cherries. The tiny space was pitch-dark, and I was sure it was home to several families of spiders. When she let me out, my eyes were puffy and red from a sleepless night of crying. I spent the morning getting lectured on not being careful as Mother tended to my bruises from slamming my shoulder against the doorframe and my broken nails from when I had tried to pry open the edges of the door.

So I should have known better, but the words tumbled out of me regardless. "What was that last night?" I asked, even though my too-long limbs already knew the answer. I knew the rabbits were only practice. The screams were what came after the rabbits.

Jane flashed a warning glance in my direction, but Mother was already smiling down at me. "I'm starting work on making you a sister."

"I don't want a sister," I said, my voice even and level. "I have Jane. I have you. I don't need anyone else."

"Jane's getting married soon. The house will be too quiet without her," Mother said with a soft smile in Jane's direction.

"I'll still be here," I said, as if I could convince her to unwind time and take back last night.

"Well, I've already started. I've mastered some new techniques to help with the scarring." Mother's eyes flicked to my throat as if she could see through me to where the scar sat at the base of my neck. "I think she'll be perfect this time."

I looked down into my yogurt, stirring it without taking a bite as Mother stood, pressing a kiss to the top of my head. "Maybe your new sister won't be so self-centered. Clearly, I've gone wrong somewhere since you are so ungrateful for everything I've given you," she said in a teasing voice. She was in a good mood this morning, but the words were a warning.

I couldn't help the tears that pooled in the corners of my eyes as the screams from the night before replayed in my head.

"I know last night was unexpected, perhaps even frightening, but it was necessary," Mother said, noticing my tears and smoothing a hand over my hair. I wasn't sure I would have called the previous evening *frightening*. That didn't seem to be quite the right word. *Frightening* implied that I had been afraid for myself. But I knew nothing was going to happen to me—I was safe in my bed—but that girl's screams had ripped at the places in me where I could still feel the seams.

Mother must have decided that my silence meant I needed more convincing. She ran her fingers through my hair, which had fallen into soft waves overnight thanks to the braids Jane had given me the evening before. "You're happy, right?"

I nodded. I enjoyed our lives in the cottage for the most part. I enjoyed the company of Jane and Mother. I liked having the time to read books and wander through the gardens. "I'm giving that girl a gift," Mother said. She reached down and tilted my chin up so I was forced to look her in the eyes. "She gets to be part of something beautiful."

She smiled at me, and I knew she wouldn't release my face until I returned the gesture, so I smiled back. She let go of my chin and ran her fingers over my face, fingertips pressing against my cheeks and at the corners of my eyes. We were her perfect dolls, Jane and I, and she was already worried about what we'd look like in a decade or two. She often smoothed over my skin in the moments after I had wrinkled up my face, as if she could convince my skin to remain pristine, unmarred by the creases that told the story of a life. She kissed the top of my head and disappeared down into the basement.

That afternoon, Mother sent me and Jane into town. I suspected she just wanted us out of her hair so she could start work on the newest girl. We went to the grocery store and stopped by Jane's favorite café for a few minutes, but then we headed home. I let my cheek rest against the cool glass, already dreading my return to the cottage. How long would I need to wait before Mother let me leave again? Perhaps this would be the start of regular outings, and soon enough, I would build a life in the world like Jane had.

I also couldn't help but think about the girl now in that white room in the basement. The screams hadn't stopped replaying in my head, haunting the few hours of sleep I had gotten the night before. Had she found some sort of peace in her sleep, or was she still afraid even in her dreams? Did her family know she was missing yet? Had I passed by someone who knew her in the grocery store?

Jane patted my leg as we pulled out of town and back toward the forest. "Are you okay? You're being quiet. Did you have a nice time?"

"I had a wonderful time," I said with a sigh. "But I'm thinking about that girl from last night. I can't keep myself from picturing what Mother is doing with her down in that room." An involuntary shiver rolled through me, and I pictured the rabbits I had seen her working on.

"You can't think about it. Box it up, and put it on a shelf in the back of your mind," Jane said. "There's nothing you can do about it."

"We could have stopped her. There's two of us and only one of her," I said, imagining what it would have looked like if instead of cowering in our room last night, Jane and I had gone out into the living room to free the screaming girl.

"She's giving that girl a gift." The words were an echo of what Mother had said this morning. "I'm grateful for what Mother has given me, aren't you?"

I shrugged in the passenger seat.

Jane continued, when it became clear I wasn't going to respond. "I remember feeling the same way when Mother started gathering the girls to make you. It feels so gruesome and terrible to have those girls in the basement, but Mother makes sure they don't feel a thing. They don't usually scream. Most of the time, I didn't even wake up when Mother brought another one home. And just think of how wonderful it will be to have another sister."

After that, Jane let the car fall into silence. She turned on the radio, and we listened to music as the buildings and people slowly turned back into trees.

"I don't want to get locked back up in the house again," I complained as Jane turned onto the long dirt road that connected the highway to our cottage.

"I'm sure you'll be spending a lot more time in town now," Jane said.

I huffed. I didn't want to wait weeks to spend only a few hours in town. I wanted to visit like Jane did, for days at a time, building myself a life. She looked in my direction and must have noticed my sour mood because she pinched me through the sleeve of my sweater.

"Ouch! What was that for?" I asked, swatting at her.

"Lizzy, soon enough, I won't live at the cottage anymore. Then it will be just you and Mother, and it will be your job to take care of her."

"What do you mean?" Perhaps I shouldn't have been so surprised by this announcement, with Jane rarely home at night already, but the words caught me off guard. We belonged to the forest. It felt strange, almost impossible, that she would make her home somewhere else.

"When I marry Frank, I'll have to live with him, of course," she stated. There was no waver in her words, no room for some chance that it might not happen. She was sure of it and seemed unmoved by the idea of getting married and starting her life with him. I must have given away my nervousness because she tried to soften the blow of the previous statement. "I spend so many nights at his house anyway, it won't make a tremendous difference."

But it felt like a tremendous difference. Even though Jane wasn't around as much as she used to be, the cottage was still her home. I knew that, eventually, she would need to return, even if it was just for a few hours to do laundry. Tears welled up and spilled out of my eyes. Jane glanced in my direction. "Oh, Lizzy." She reached out, found my hand in my lap, and squeezed my fingers. "It's not like I'll be gone forever. I'll still visit all the time, and when Frank travels for work, I'll come and have sleepovers."

"It won't be the same." I pouted. I knew I was acting childish. It was the sort of behavior Mother would have reprimanded me for, but Jane was more indulgent than her, and she would fuss over me instead.

"Soon enough, you will find some handsome young man of your own, and you'll be the one moving out," Jane promised me.

I glared out the window, letting angry tears streak down my cheeks as we drove in silence for a while. "Can I meet him?" I finally asked.

"I don't know. Probably not. Not yet, at least," Jane hedged. I had suspected that would be the answer. She didn't have to explain further. I knew our lives were strange, a secret we shared among the three of us.

"Then tell me about him." It wasn't as if Jane hadn't shared stories of Frank over the months, telling me and Mother about their dinners out and the brief weekend trip they'd taken to the coast, but she'd rarely talked about Frank himself.

Jane painted him with broad strokes. Talking about his smile and his laugh. How he'd taken her to a movie and brought her flowers. I had expected more emotion as she spoke about the handsome, kind man with whom she spent most of her time when she wasn't with me, but she spoke evenly.

I gathered myself, wiping away any traces of my tears as we drove down the narrow dirt road to our cottage. I held it together when Mother helped us carry groceries and asked how the trip went. I kept a smile on my face while Mother cooked dinner, and I relayed every aspect of our journey in explicit detail. But after dinner, after Mother had gone through her nightly ritual of smoothing oil over my skin and I had washed my face and climbed into bed, the tears came again.

I cried not just at the idea of losing Jane, although that had been the impetus for the tears, or even for the girl in the basement, who would be spending another night cold and alone. I cried mostly for myself. I couldn't remember exactly what had come before the cottage and Mother, but pieces of my body remembered. My ribs remembered hugs that squeezed my torso, almost too tightly, but instead of feeling trapped, I had felt safe. My neck remembered the feeling of breath as someone whispered secrets in my ear and promised me friendship. My feet remembered dancing, spinning, and twirling, their path guided by someone else who very occasionally stepped on my toes. And my thighs remembered lips that had kissed them, tenderly skating up the skin, eliciting goose bumps and shivers. I couldn't remember their faces or their names, but I missed them, the people who had loved all the pieces of this body.

The next few days were strange. On the surface, they were the same as they always were; I spent my days reading and doing chores upstairs while Mother worked in her basement. Yet I couldn't help but think about what she was doing. Different versions of the girl haunted my dreams every night. Her face always changed, but I recognized her screams and the terror in her voice. I imagined I could hear the snapping of bone and the zippering of flesh being pulled away from skin.

I watched the door over my book as footsteps climbed the stairs on the other side. I shouldn't have been surprised to see

Mother as the door swung open, since it was nearly lunchtime, but still, I jumped as her face appeared. "Did I startle you?" she said with a chuckle as she made her way to the refrigerator. I inspected her clothes for traces of blood, but she looked pristine as always. She had been in a particularly chipper mood for the last several days, obviously delighting in her new project.

"Sorry. I lost track of time," I said. I stood, made my way to the counter, and started pulling out plates for lunch as she gathered ingredients for a salad.

"No worries, my darling," she said, brushing a hand against my arm. "I was thinking you could come downstairs and meet your sister this afternoon."

I froze. I had known this day would come. Mother had spoken about it each night at dinner as she explained the work she had been doing. I wasn't sure if seeing the girl's face would make the nightmares better or worse. Perhaps she would haunt me less if she were less of a mystery. But, regardless of whether my curiosity or horror would win out, I didn't have a choice.

I didn't taste my lunch, just chewing and swallowing by muscle memory, and then dishes were loaded into the dishwasher, and it was time to follow Mother downstairs. My heart raced, thrumming against my rib cage, as I descended the stairs. I imagined the girl's body pulled open, innards on display, her eyes staring unseeingly at the ceiling while her mouth hung open, trapped in that perpetual scream. I should have known better. Mother liked to keep things tidy.

When I got downstairs, the large worktable in the center of the room was covered with a sheet. The girl was underneath. I could see the mountain peaks of her toes pointed toward the sky and the valley where the sheet dipped before skimming over her face.

"Elizabeth..." Mother said. She took a couple of steps toward the table, fingers curling into the sheet. "She's going to look a little pale, a little odd. You have to remember that she's not all put together yet. It's a process."

I nodded, then leaned back against the wall, feeling woozy. I had seen dozens of rabbits at this point, their fragile bodies naked of skin, muscles on display, veins and arteries crisscrossing their tiny skeletons. This could not be significantly worse than that. Mother pulled the sheet back, exposing the girl to just below her collarbone.

Her eyes were closed, her body moving ever so slightly, just the occasional rise and fall of the sheet as she breathed. Wires and tubes looped under the sheet connected to a whole host of ports and needles that kept the girl's organs alive. This girl wasn't really my sister, not yet, at least. She was just the foundation. Mother had explained the process to me over the last few months as I watched her stitch together bits of rabbits, perfecting her technique for this next project.

This first girl would be most of the skeleton and the muscles for my new sister. Mother liked her petite frame. Even with her lying down, I could tell she would be much smaller than me. But her features were too sharp and bony for Mother's liking, so a different girl would be selected for the structure of her face, her skull added to the bones already in place. Another girl might be needed to replace hips or finger bones, making sure each element of my new sister was perfectly proportioned. A different girl would be used for her eyes and maybe a jawbone or a bit of extra muscle along her arms. Another girl would provide the skin. Unlike the bones, the skin needed to be from one girl so that the color perfectly matched when Mother zipped my new sister into it, hiding lines of nearly invisible stitches at the seams. Knowing how many girls Mother would need to complete this project was impossible. She'd work until my new sister was perfect.

Below the sheet, she was peeling the skin away from the girl's muscles and bones, examining the structure of the skeleton. The state of the organs was challenging to judge from the outside, so the healthiest ones from all the girls would be given to my sister. So, this week, Mother had been doing the work of deciding which pieces she wanted to keep and which she'd replace with something better.

All the girls would be spliced into one. A new life would be breathed into the pieces, but my sister wouldn't be any of them. Not really. She would be a new creation—blood, bones, muscles, and skin stitched together to create something entirely new. Nothing would be wasted. The parts Mother didn't use would be given to the trees to continue the cycle that sustained us.

A tear slipped down my cheek. I quickly wiped it away, but Mother noticed anyway, squeezed me against her, and kissed my forehead. "I know it feels cruel and a little scary, but I promise it's the beginning of something beautiful."

I took a deep breath, trying to ignore the smell of antiseptic tinged with the faint twist of moss and oak. "She looks dead," I said, my voice barely louder than a whisper, as I worried it might wake her from her slumber.

"I know, but she isn't. It looks frightening, but only because we're in the space between." I must have looked unconvinced because she continued. "She can't feel anything right now. It's like she's sleeping," Mother explained. "And when she wakes up, she'll be something new and beautiful. We're creating something wonderful."

I didn't like being included in this *we*. I had done nothing. If given the choice, I wouldn't have brought this screaming girl into our peaceful little cottage.

I took another step forward to look at the girl's face. She was pale like Mother had warned, but it wasn't a result of fairness, although she would have been fair even on an average day. It was the complete lack of color in her expression. There was no blush to her cheeks. I was sure if there had been a mirror down here, my cheeks would have been pink, flushing in the cold. Even her lips, thin and flat, seemed to lack any tint.

Her face was dainty and fair with sharp features that fit well on her tiny frame. She was pretty at first glance, but as I looked a little longer, it was easy enough to pick out flaws. Her cheeks were covered in a thin layer of freckles. I knew Mother would hate that, eventually peeling that skin away and replacing it with something new. Her nose was too pointy, the left nostril slightly larger than the right. But those little defects wouldn't last long. Mother would fix her; she would smooth over every imperfection, like a sculptor with wet clay.

I couldn't help but compare the girl's face to my own, to measuring each feature to those of mine that Mother praised. I found no category in which she bested me. I took a malicious sort of delight in that. Then I immediately regretted the feeling, her screams once again echoing through my memories. She looked peaceful now, as she lay there, and I hoped she wasn't afraid. That perhaps she was dreaming of somewhere warm and safe far away from this white room.

"Look at those clavicles. Great musculature. There's too much fat on her arms, but that's easy enough to fix. She's a little shorter than you"—Mother took a step back and compared me to the girl lying on the table—"but I think that's for the best. It took you so long to adjust to those long limbs. They're gorgeous, but I think someone more delicate might be nice."

"How long will she be like this?" I asked.

Mother turned toward me to respond, but she kept her hand on the girl's cheek, thumb still stroking the skin. "It'll be a long time until Mary wakes up, as I still have much to do, but it will go by faster than you think. Soon enough, you'll have another sister."

CHAPTER 22

I had slept in far later than usual. Evie was already at school, and I expected the house to be quiet, but my mom was still here, her laptop open and her reading glasses on. Given the strangeness of the night before, I wasn't sure how this morning would unfold. Part of me would have almost believed last night was a dream if I hadn't seen the pile of damp clothes in the corner of my bathroom this morning. But my mother seemed unbothered by it, happy to pretend whatever had happened under the falling snow last night had vanished, melting away in the morning light.

"Good morning. How did you sleep?" she asked, not looking up from her computer as I fumbled with the coffee machine.

"Fine. How about you?" Surprisingly, that part wasn't a lie. I had showered after we had come inside, slowly letting the water warm my half-frozen skin. But I was fast asleep as soon as I hit the pillow, as if the night air had been drugged with something.

"I slept wonderfully. Thank you. A late-night walk always makes me sleep a little deeper. There's something about the cold, I think. It clears the mind," she said.

I nodded as I went through the motions of making a cup of coffee.

"Your father and I are supposed to be gone this weekend. He's driving out to Chicago for work for a few weeks, and I was planning on going with him to help him get settled," she continued while the machine whirred behind me. "We're supposed to leave tomorrow, but then I'll be back on Monday. Will you and your sister be okay? I can stay back if you think it would be better. Your father can make the drive alone."

"I'm sure we'll be fine," I replied more sharply than intended. "I've been living on my own for years, so I think I can handle two nights."

"It's not really you that I'm worried about."

"I'm sure Evie will be okay for a few nights. I'll keep an eye on her," I said. I thought back to what I had overheard the night before. I hadn't realized it had gotten so bad, although maybe I should have suspected it. Evie had lost her best friend. That was sure to leave a mark. "She's been having nightmares?"

My mother nodded, slipping her glasses up to the top of her head. "Almost every night. Honestly, I'm surprised you haven't heard her. It's been a tough few weeks." I could see how much this pained my mother. Part of me wanted to comfort her, even though I was still wary after the night before.

Last night, while I showered, I had turned over the snatches of the conversation I had overheard, replaying them again and again, trying to piece together the version that made the most sense. I spun wilder possibilities every time I tried to rearrange the facts. The only thing I was sure of was that my mother knew far more about the missing girls than she was letting on.

Before I could find a tactful way to bring up what I had heard the previous night, my mother spoke. "You can ask me," she said. She had always been so easily able to read my face.

I swallowed. Even with permission, it felt ridiculous to be asking, to be accusing my mother of being involved in something so dark, but I needed to know what she was hiding, who she was protecting. "What were you really talking about last night? Do you know what happened to Maddie?"

She ignored the first question, which was fine with me. I suspected she would have just recited her answer from the night before again. "Of course not," she said. "I've known that girl since she was four years old. And you've seen how it's been destroying Evie. Do you think I'd do that to her?"

"Maybe," I said. Perhaps I should have lied. She didn't like that answer, and her spine stiffened at the word. I could see the betrayal and hurt on her face. "I think you'd do anything necessary to keep up appearances. If what happened to Maddie had the potential to make you look bad, I think you'd do whatever you needed to keep it hidden."

"Do you really think so little of me?" she asked, clasping her hands on the table in front of her. She was staring at me, refusing to break my gaze. My mom's eyes are this bright blue. They're incredible. It's really a shame that neither Evie nor I inherited the color, both stuck with a very ordinary brown. But right now, as they pinned me in place, I was a bit frightened of them. I may not have always liked my mother, but I had never been afraid of her. I knew she loved me. I didn't think she would've intentionally hurt me or Evie, but there was something vicious under her gaze.

Maybe I should have brushed it off and allowed her to keep her secrets, but something, that stubborn piece of me I had gotten from her, wanted me to dig deeper. I shrugged. "You were always more interested in making a good impression than anything else. It's always been your top priority. That we all looked perfect so that we reflected well on you."

She laughed. The sound was somehow worse than the sharp silence that had preceded it. "Ophelia." She said my name slowly, her mouth carefully shaping each letter. "Everything I've ever done has been for your own good. I want you to be the best version of yourself. I set high standards because I see your potential. You should be grateful for that—for someone who believes you are capable of so much."

Now it was my turn to laugh, but even that couldn't drown out the voice in my head, the one that always sounded just like my mother. *She would love you more if you were better and had your life together.* Tears threatened in the corners of my eyes, but crying would be admitting defeat, so I instead let my voice go colder, sharper, finding the mean place inside me that was never far where my mother was concerned. "I wish I had a mother who cared about me and not just what I had the potential to be."

"I love you and your sister more than I can express," my mother was quick to say. There wasn't tenderness to the words, well practiced, the edges worn with the number of times she had said something similar. "Everything I have done since you were born has been to make your lives better. I've given you so much. I don't know what else you want from me, Ophelia."

"The truth," I said. "You know something about what happened to Maddie. About what happens in that forest."

There was a long silence. For a moment, I thought she might actually confess everything she knew to me and invite me into whatever mess she was trying to hide, but then she shook her head. "I'm trying to keep you and your sister safe. Leave it alone," my mother whispered, almost hissing. She never raised her voice, but she didn't require volume to be intimidating. There was something menacing about the words.

"What do you know?" I asked again. I leaned closer to her.

"Nothing," she lied. "Please, leave it alone." She straightened, and her voice leveled out. "Anyway," she said, spinning on her heel and turning to unload the dishwasher, "I can stay. Your dad will be fine without me."

I stood there, blinking at her, jarred by the sudden change in topic. It was clear that she wasn't going to say anything else. I pushed away from the counter, leaving my coffee mug, which was still sitting next to the machine. "I can't be in this house anymore."

I was halfway out of the room when my mom said, "Then it's settled—I'll stay."

I spun back around to glare at her. "Go. I'll take care of my sister."

Thirty minutes later, I was in line at a local coffee shop, fighting a headache caused by some combination of the argument with my mother and the lack of caffeine in my system. After leaving the kitchen, I had promptly gone upstairs, thrown my laptop in a bag, and left the house. I hadn't paid much attention to my appearance—my hair was tossed into a ponytail with a scrunchie I had found in the center console of my car, and my outfit consisted of a pair of leggings and an oversize hoodie.

Which was why, when I heard my name from behind me in line, I flinched.

"Lia?" I recognized the voice immediately and turned slowly to find Kiera standing behind me. She looked effortlessly put together, especially in comparison to me.

"Hi, Kiera. How are you?"

"Good! Actually, I'm so glad I bumped into you again. I meant to text you. I'm having a movie night next weekend at my place and wanted to invite you! It's going to be very casual, like five or six girls. You know Millie from high school?"

I nodded, vaguely remembering the name, although I couldn't quite conjure a face.

"Well, she'll be there. And I'm not sure if you'll know anyone else, but everyone is very nice. You should come!"

"Um…" I paused, thinking of a way to decline the invite without seeming rude.

"I'm sure things are up in the air right now," she said, lowering her voice. "But if you feel up to it, I'd love to have you. I'll text you the details."

"Okay, thanks," I said. I was relieved it was my turn to order, sparing me from continuing the conversation.

But Kiera joined me again a minute later while we waited

for our drinks. "How are you doing?" she asked. I could tell her question was genuine, not just an attempt at polite small talk.

I blew out a long breath. "I don't know," I said with a tired laugh. That was the truth. I didn't know, not really. So much had happened in such a short time that I didn't know where to begin sorting through it all.

She nodded. "I totally get that." She started to say something but hesitated before finally asking, "Do you have a few minutes? I know we haven't really kept in touch, but I'd love to talk." I could tell she was a little nervous to ask. "Only if you aren't busy," she added, holding up her hands and waving away any obligation.

My initial impulse was to think up some excuse about why I couldn't stay, but I had been planning on camping out with my laptop and getting some work done. And beyond that, it would be nice to have someone to talk to. "Sure."

We found a table with a pair of chairs in the corner a little more tucked away from the rest of the room. We settled in with some small talk about the weather and the first few snows of the year when I realized it was odd that she was here right now. It was a weekday in the middle of the morning, and she taught elementary school. "Shouldn't you be at work?" I asked.

"I have the day off," she said with a smile. "I had a dentist appointment this morning and decided to give myself the rest of the day as a mental health day. Honestly, I'm not saying this competes at all with what your family has been going through"—she reached across the table and set her hand on my arm—"but I've been having a hard time with all the news around Maddie going missing. It's been bringing up a lot for me. Do you remember when we were in high school and Krista McNeil went missing?"

I nodded. Of course I remembered.

"I went to church with Krista, and this just feels so similar. It's bringing up a lot of memories."

"I didn't realize you guys had been close," I said.

"I mean, not *close*."

I recognized that impulse to appropriately weigh your connection to these tragedies as if grieving were a line and you didn't want to cut in front of someone who had experienced a "real" loss. But if Chloe and Maddie had taught me anything, it was that sorrow wasn't limited. There was always enough for everyone. "But close enough to remember," I added softly.

She nodded. "Almost everyone in the town has a connection to at least one girl who's gone missing. Or at least it feels like that."

"It's weird, right?" I said. "So many girls from this area go missing. It feels like there's at least one every few years."

"Yeah, it feels like it," Kiera agreed. "But I guess stuff happens. Maybe it's because the town is small; it feels like a bigger deal. I'm sure in cities people go missing every day."

"Maybe we just notice it more," I said.

She nodded in agreement. "I don't know what makes me feel worse, that there might be some guy out there who's been taking girls for decades or that it's just random." Kiera shivered and shook her head. "What brings you back to town anyway?" she asked, shifting the conversation to a lighter topic.

I considered lying, pretending it was the next step in some grand plan. But the truth was easier. "I broke up with my boyfriend, and I was living with him. I probably could have found another place out there, but I kind of hated LA."

"Really?" Kiera seemed completely shocked, mouth wide. "It seems so nice, the beaches and the weather. So much better than this place."

"The weather got old. I strangely missed the snow and rain, and I literally went to the beach maybe five times in the two years I lived there. I just don't think it was for me."

"And the breakup, how are we feeling about that? Are we crushed?" she asked.

I liked that she talked about it in terms of *we*, as if we were in this together, she and I. I was grateful to have a partner in this, even if only for a minute. "Not really," I admitted. "But I think I should be. We were together for almost a year and a half, but I was weirdly relieved it was over." It was the first time I had said it out loud. It felt almost too honest. I wasn't sure I had even fully admitted that to myself. "Does that make me a monster?"

"No way. It's easy to get stuck in a bad relationship, especially if you're living together. Sometimes, we need a little shove to get us in the right direction."

"I don't know if it's the right direction. I'm not sure if I'm going in any direction. I don't have any idea what I want to do next."

"You'll figure it out," Kiera said with a confidence that I wished I felt.

We ended up talking for almost an hour. We talked about what she'd been up to for the last few years, and I told her the best stories from my time in California. I recounted everything that had happened with Maddie, except the stuff with my mother. That felt too unknown to unpack with her.

By the time she got up from the table, leaving me with a hug, I had agreed to the movie night and planned another lunch for next week. I felt better than I had since the breakup, lighter. As if sharing a bit of my mess made it feel less shameful because I wasn't alone in it.

CHAPTER 23
THE MISSING GIRLS

Jane was getting married this afternoon. She was already at the church, preparing with her fiancé's family. I was sad that I couldn't be there with her, that she had to pretend her family didn't exist.

Mother spent the day helping me get ready at the cottage. You would have almost thought I was the one getting married with the care she took in applying a thin layer of makeup to my face and pinning back my hair. "I was in love once," she said as she slid another hairpin into the twist covering the scar at the nape of my neck. "I thought we were going to get married one day."

Mother had told me the story dozens of times before, but I knew better than to mention that. She liked to tell it. "I was twenty-seven, still in medical school. When I wasn't at the hospital, I was reading everything I could get my hands on about the advancements in the field, and I kept encountering this name again and again in my research: Dr. Paul Harvey. He was pioneering cutting-edge techniques that allowed him to construct entirely new faces for his patients. I was in awe of what he was doing, so I sent him a letter letting him know how much I admired his work.

"I didn't think anything would come of it, since I was sure he got dozens of these sorts of letters every week, but he wrote back, and we started a correspondence that quickly turned into phone calls. A few months later, I was talking with Paul every night I had off from the hospital. A little over a year after that, I had fallen completely in love with him, and when he asked me to move out here, I said yes without hesitating. It was so easy to imagine the life we'd have together: Dr. Wolston and her brilliant husband, Dr. Harvey, changing the world, side by side.

"I was leaving in the middle of my residency program, but I wasn't worried about it. Paul had connections with hospitals. I thought I would be able to jump into a program out here once we were married. Yet, from the moment he picked me up at the airport, I knew he was disappointed in me. We tried for a few months, but I wasn't pretty enough to hold his attention. It didn't matter that we had so much in common or that he had told me I was the smartest girl he'd ever met—he wanted someone who would look good on his arm at parties. How awful is that? I had given up my whole life for that man, and he didn't even have the human decency to try to make things work."

One of the first times I had heard this story, I interrupted Mother at this part. "I think you're beautiful," I said. It wasn't the same kind of beauty Jane and I shared, built on symmetry and perfectly carved features, but I had grown fond of her sunspots and crooked nose. I found Mother beautiful in the same way as the smell of lilacs in the summer and tulips peeking out from the last snowfall of spring, a reminder of the passage of time and the familiar comforts of home.

"No need to lie to me," Mother said with a laugh. "I was never under any impressions that I was some great beauty. I had just been foolish enough to believe it wouldn't matter." She had leaned in closer to me and whispered this next part, as if it were some great secret: "The truth is, it always matters. People love to pretend it doesn't, but as a woman, so many more doors are open to you if you look like you do."

I didn't interrupt her this time. I let her get to the moment that had changed everything and brought both of us here.

"I'm not proud of this part of the story," Mother continued. "But you have to remember, I was all alone out here, without a career, without anything to go back home to, and now without him. I had nothing." She'd always give this little disclaimer when telling this story, as if it made what came next less horrible. "I was so angry with him. I was cooking in his kitchen, making him dinner, when he told me he wanted to end things. I was using one of those big, heavy cast-iron pans, and something came over me. One minute I was standing at the stove, and the next, he was on the ground, head bleeding, and I was above him, holding the empty pan."

I always pictured the scene too vividly. I couldn't help myself. Sometimes I imagined chili running down the side of the cabinet, while he lay there in a pristine white button-down. Other times it would be two chicken breasts sitting next to his body on the floor, his tie askew, shirt stained with a splatter of oil. Or perhaps green beans fanned out in a halo around his head. I had never been brave enough to ask what she had been making.

"I knew people would be looking for him, so I drove him to the woods. I buried him where he wouldn't be found. It took longer than I expected to dig the hole. By the time I finished, it was completely dark out. It was a new moon, and I immediately felt the holiness of this place. The trees were hungry. They had been deprived, forced to live on the scraps of what they could gather themselves for too long. Still, they gave back.

"Not long after the hum of the trees began, a rabbit with blood still coating its fur hopped over to me. The forest had brought it back from the cusp of death. It not only healed that rabbit but also something in me. I think it was all meant to happen the way it did. I was called to this place to become its caretaker, an acolyte of the forest. That night the trees adopted me as one of their own. I needed someplace to go, and the trees showed me this cottage. It wasn't as nice as it is now, but I spent months fixing it up, making it a home. I built myself a life in the forest while I learned about our trees, what they need and what they can give back. It took many years, but then I made my own family out here, starting with Jane and then you.

"The love I have for you, the daughters I have created, is so much greater than what I lost. I hope you have daughters someday so you experience that same joy I have."

I knew better than to say it, but I thought that her relationship to us didn't feel particularly joyful. In fact, it often felt less like love and more like ownership, a possessive pride over having made us.

She reached down and squeezed my shoulder. "I promised myself that I would give my daughters a better life than I had. I would make you beautiful enough that no doors would be closed to you. You would have perfect lives. Do all the things I never got to do. And now Jane's getting married. Soon, you will too. Although I hope you pick a better man than Jane. There's nothing wrong with Frank, but you could do so much better."

I nodded. Tonight wasn't the first time I had heard this from Mother. Over the last few weeks, she had frequently talked about the types of men whose affections I should seek. "Tonight," she continued, "might be a good opportunity to meet someone suitable. Frank comes from a good family and attended a prestigious school. I'm sure he has some friends of the appropriate caliber." The implication hung in the air, heavy and unmistakable. "Don't squander this opportunity, Elizabeth."

At the wedding, I sat alone in the back corner of the church, at the end of a pew, disappearing into the crowd. It was the first time I would actually meet Frank. *Meet* may have been too strong a word. I didn't exchange more than a few words with the man, but at least now I had seen him in real life rather than in the photos Jane had ferried back to the cottage.

The reality of Frank was underwhelming. He was exceedingly dull. Theirs wasn't a love story like in the books I'd read. He was sweaty as he stood at the altar, waiting for Jane to walk down the aisle. As she walked toward him, I pried my eyes away from her to look at him, eager to see the awe on his face. But he looked at her like she was ordinary, like it was an average Tuesday and she was the woman on the other side of the bank counter. But, in the end, marriage wasn't all about romance, as Mother had told me more than once; in fact, according to her, love was far down the list of priorities. We should select men who promised stability, a solid foundation from which we could build a life. Frank would do that for Jane.

Jane was always beautiful. For the wedding, she had swept her hair back into a low twist that showcased the long lines of her neck. Pearl earrings hung from her ears, a gift from Mother. Her dress was simple, a bright white silk with clean lines that nipped in at the waist. Mother had steered her away from anything too gaudy or trendy. She wanted Jane to look classic. Timeless.

Jane pulled me into the bathroom a few hours into the reception. "How are you doing?" she asked.

"I'm fine. It's been a beautiful wedding so far," I said, trying not to betray my nervousness at the crowds and making sure I made a good impression on every person I encountered.

Jane smiled softly at me as I stood there chewing on my cheek. "Ignore Mother. I'm sure she told you that you need to use tonight to snag some rich man. You don't, Lizzy. Go have fun." I stared at her, wide-eyed, surprised at the suggestion that I should abandon my goal for the night. "Have a drink. Dance. Eat a piece of cake. Don't worry about trying to be perfect tonight. Mother isn't here. Enjoy it."

My version of enjoying the evening, it turned out, was hiding in a corner of the room and watching the dance floor. I wasn't ready to face the oscillating mass of bodies, so I instead observed from the back, a sweaty glass of champagne in hand.

"Are you hiding?" The words made me jump, and I spun to face the voice, which belonged to a man with a mass of curly light-brown hair that he had twisted back into a ponytail. He didn't have a tie or a jacket, and he had unbuttoned the top three buttons on his shirt.

"No..." I answered. He tilted his head and raised his eyebrow as he smiled at me, unbelieving. "Maybe," I admitted.

The minute the word was out of my mouth, he laughed. "I'm Josh," he said, his smile still lingering. He stuck his hand out. It was rough, the skin tanned and callused.

"Elizabeth," I offered. He let go of my hand after a moment, but he didn't drop his gaze..

"Well, Elizabeth, I can leave you to your hiding spot if you'd like, but I'd love to dance with you if you're willing." He dipped a little at the waist and offered his hand again.

I nodded and slipped my hand into his.

He led me to the dance floor and spun me toward him as we started to move to the music. His hand slowly moved to my waist. "So, Elizabeth"—I liked how he said my name, a smile turning up the corners of his lips—"how did you end up at this wedding alone?"

"I'm an old friend of Jane's. From high school," I repeated the answer I had given at least a dozen times over the night.

"Sure, and I'm Frank's cousin, but why are you alone? Certainly, a girl like you has men lined up around your house, desperate for the chance to take you out."

I shrugged. "Haven't found the right guy yet?" I said it like a question, as if I wanted him to answer.

"Hmm, that makes sense. A girl like you gets to be picky."

"What do you mean?"

"Elizabeth."

I swallowed as he said my name again. I couldn't help it. It made my stomach flutter.

He noticed; his gaze dipped to my throat as it bobbed before coming back to land on my lips. "I'm sure you're aware that you are one of the most beautiful creatures I've ever seen."

I laughed. I knew I was beautiful. Our features, Jane's and mine, were a product of carefully measured ratios and proportions, masterpieces crafted from hours and hours of delicately shaving jawbones and slipping skin over perfectly laid fat and muscle. I was a testament to the golden ratio. My beauty was a mathematical reality confirmed by everyone who saw me.

"Have I told you I'm an artist?" he said. My body had moved closer to his, almost touching him. I shook my head. "I could spend a lifetime painting you and never grow tired of it."

My cheeks flushed, and I turned my head so he couldn't see my smile. The music slowed, and his hand moved to my lower back, pulling me closer to him until I melted against his chest, swaying.

I spent the rest of the evening with him. Songs bled into each other, and we danced and talked and laughed. It was simple. It didn't feel like a game where I needed to think three steps ahead. I knew other eyes were on me, but I felt only his gaze, his breath against my cheek, his whispered words tickling my ear.

At some point, Jane came over. She rested her hand on my shoulder. "Can I steal her for a minute?" she said with a smile in Josh's direction.

"Be my guest," he said as he released me, his hand trailing down my arm like he wanted to delay our separation for another moment. I felt colder without his body against me. I missed the heat of him already.

Jane ushered me toward the back of the room, guiding me to the door. "Did you have a nice time?" She was smiling like she already knew the answer.

"I did," I said. "Thank you."

"I'm glad. Mother will be here soon. You should go," she said. I scrunched up my nose. I wasn't ready for the night to be over, but I knew Mother would be upset if I was late. I looked back over my shoulder at Josh, but Jane stopped me with a hand on my wrist. "It might be easier if you just go."

Josh had gotten swept up into a conversation with someone else on the dance floor. His head was tossed back as he laughed. The line of his neck was beautiful, though not in the mathematical way someone could measure. I wanted to run my lips over it. To be the reason he was laughing. It was beautiful because it was him, and joy fit him well. I nodded. "Yeah, probably," I said. I turned back to Jane. "Love you. Congratulations. I'll see you next week." I hugged her quickly and left through the back door.

The morning after the wedding, I was still yawning at the breakfast table even though I had slept later than usual. "Did you have a nice time last night?" Mother asked.

I nodded. "It was very nice. Jane looked stunning."

"Did you talk with anyone interesting?" she asked. I should

have expected this question and planned my answer, but I had been so caught up with the buzz of the night before that I hadn't considered it.

"Ummm…a few of Frank's cousins, his younger brother, a bunch of his family, really," I mumbled. "But nothing came of it. Most people were drinking too much to be interested in a conversation."

"So, what did you do?" Mother had already eaten and was working on something in one of her leather notebooks, but she looked up at me over her reading glasses, her eyebrows rising.

"Danced a bit," I said with a shrug, swallowing another spoonful of yogurt.

She put her pen down. "With anyone in particular?"

"A man named Josh. One of Frank's cousins."

She slid her glasses off her face and set them on the table next to her pen so she could lean toward me as she asked the next question. "What does Josh do?" I knew this was where her interests lay. She wanted to know if the boy I had spent the night dancing with was worth my time.

"He's an artist," I said into my yogurt.

Her sudden burst of laughter took me by surprise. It was loud, thumping up against me with its cruelty. "An artist. Could you have picked anyone worse?"

I had known she would disapprove, but still, it hurt to see her flicking him away like a bug trying to crawl over the threshold. I hadn't seen anything Josh had painted, but I wanted to defend him anyway. Perhaps he was a brilliant artist who sold his paintings for millions of dollars each. She couldn't know anything about his work. And more than that, what if I didn't care if he was good at painting? I liked the way he made me feel.

"What good is your beauty if you're going to squander it?" Her chair scraped against the floor loudly as she stood. "I made you beautiful because I want you to have a great life. Not a life where you have to wait to see if you can make rent on your shitty apartment because your artist hasn't sold a painting in months."

"I know," I mumbled. "It's not like I'm trying to marry him. I just wanted to have a fun night."

"Elizabeth, I have given you everything I can. But even I cannot give you time. Every day, you get a little older, and your skin gets a little closer to wrinkling, and your hair gets a little thinner, a little closer to getting gray. Last night was an opportunity to find a man of value, and you squandered it."

I rolled my eyes. "It's not that serious."

"Do you think Jane found a suitable husband because she was running around with any man who spared her a glance? Good lives don't happen by accident, Elizabeth."

Mother stepped toward me, and I flinched. I could feel the anger rolling off her. I thought of Paul, the man she had killed with a frying pan. It would be easy for her to hurt me. I had seen her brutality, heard it that night when the girl lying in the basement had been screaming in our living room.

She held my chin in her fingers and tilted my face up to hers. She didn't pinch or press too firmly. There would be no bruises on my skin tomorrow, no marks to mar my perfectly proportioned face, but the gesture was still mean. "What will that artist do for you? In twenty years, you will no longer be the most beautiful girl in the room, and he will move on to someone younger and prettier than you, and where will that leave you?"

Hot tears threatened as she continued.

"Do you really think he would have been so enamored with you if he knew what you are? You were just the pretty thing he wanted to fuck." She held my face for another long second before dropping it and heading for the door to the basement.

I was still sitting at the table when Mother returned upstairs a few minutes later, a file folder in her hand. "I need your help. Clean up breakfast, quickly please," she said in a voice that left no room for negotiation.

When I joined her in the living room, she had fanned out three photos on the coffee table. "I want you to see the process I go through when selecting the girls I use to build you and your sisters. Today, I need to figure out where I'm going to get Mary's skull from. It's probably one of the most important pieces." She gestured toward the three faces in the photos in front of us. "All these girls are good matches. We just need to make decisions on the bone structure," she said.

I looked at the pictures. Mother had zoomed in on their necks and faces, but I could tell the first photo had been a group shot, the shoulder of the man next to her just visible in the frame. Mother pointed to that one first. "I like her proportions, but I'm worried her head is too large. Mary is just so much smaller than you or Jane. She's going to have a tiny waist. That's partially due to bone structure, but I will be careful with fat distribution. When you gain a few pounds, you immediately lose your waist, and I'm hoping to spare her that." At that, Mother turned and pinched an inch of skin on my stomach.

She didn't squeeze hard; she didn't need to leave a bruise to hurt me.

We spent the next two hours drawing lines and measuring distances on these girls' faces. Mother did calculations on a sheet of paper, explaining the details of the face she could change and those that were harder to alter. She could remake noses and shave down jawbones, but adding to them was much more challenging, so we prioritized cheekbones and head shape.

Soon, the girls, with their wide smiles and bright eyes, disappeared under notes and calculations until Mother selected the one she wanted: a girl with big doe eyes and a heart-shaped face that looked so delicate, I imagined I could crush it between my fingers.

I breathed a sigh of relief as Mother tucked away the girls we wouldn't be using to build Mary. I hoped they would stay safe, unaware of how close they had come to vanishing. The screams from the first girl played in my head. "I'll be collecting her sometime this week," Mother said. "I know it was quite upsetting for you last time, so I wanted to warn you."

"Jane won't be here," I said. Jane was going to the beach with Frank this week for their honeymoon, but even when she came back, she wouldn't be coming back to the cottage. She didn't live here anymore. The thought made my chest ache.

"You'll be okay. You might even sleep through it. They aren't all screamers," she said. "Stay in your room. It will be over before you know it."

CHAPTER 24

All the snow had melted yesterday, and the trees glistened under a blue sky. I remembered how relaxed my mother and Jane had been while walking through those trees in the middle of the night, yet I had gotten twisted up and lost in them on a bright, sunny morning. A chill ran up my spine at the memory of being trapped in the labyrinth of branches, feeling that I might never find my way back home.

I blinked away the thought and sat down at the kitchen counter, my laptop open in front of me. I was supposed to be making a list of all the places where I needed to change my address, but I kept getting distracted by the world out the window. Yesterday, I had arrived home, hoping to avoid my mother, but unfortunately, she and Evie had been in the kitchen. Part of me had expected my mother to pick up our argument again, but instead, it seemed she was pretending it hadn't happened.

Today Evie was stretched out across the couch in the living

room. A teen drama was playing on the TV while she sat with her math homework in her lap, a pencil in her hand, despite the fact her eyes were firmly glued to the screen. I was grateful for her quiet company, but I couldn't stop thinking about what we had heard the other day with Mom in the snow. I wanted to talk to Evie about it, to understand what she thought, but that wasn't a conversation I wanted to have with our mother lurking around.

"Where's Mom?" I asked.

"She's upstairs," Evie said without looking up from her show. "I think she's packing." Last night, over dinner, my mother had once again brought up the idea of staying home, but Evie had agreed with me that we would be fine without her, so now she and our dad were planning on leaving sometime this afternoon.

As if she had heard us talking about her, Mom appeared on the stairs, followed closely by both dogs. She first went to the living room, scooping up a glass and plate covered in crumbs from the coffee table.

"Thanks," Evie mumbled.

"Is any actual homework getting done, or is your math book just keeping you company?" she asked Evie, gesturing at the open notebook on my sister's lap.

"I'm working," Evie protested, her pencil touching the paper in front of her for the first time since I had been downstairs. "I've already seen this show. It's just background noise."

My mom looked unconvinced by this, rolling her eyes over my sister's head, but she didn't press the issue. She moved into the kitchen, adding my sister's dishes to the sink before turning to me.

"I wanted to talk to you before your father and I left," she said, waiting until she had my attention before continuing. "I think it might be best if you and your sister both stay out of the woods while we're gone. You got turned around on the trails the other day, and neither of you should be out there at night. You can take the dogs out, but don't go too far from the house."

I resisted the temptation to ask her why it was okay for her to be out there at night but not for us. "I wasn't really planning on it."

I wasn't eager to make a return trip through the trees after my incident earlier in the week. Even the thought of getting lost in those trees again made my stomach turn.

"Okay, just be careful." She raised her voice so Evie could hear from the couch. "Evangeline? Did you hear what I just told Ophelia? Stay out of the woods while we're gone."

Evie lifted a thumbs-up from where she sat on the couch, not even turning in our direction.

"We'll stay out of the trees," I assured Mom, although I couldn't help but wonder if it was worry for our safety or worry that we'd find something that prompted her to make that request.

A few hours later, I had made a substantial dent in my to-do list, still working at the kitchen counter while the rest of the house buzzed around me. My dad finished packing up the car while my mother darted through the house, trying to make sure everything was in order before she left.

She had just finished going through instructions about the dogs, which she gave me both verbally and had printed out to sit on the counter. She had already gone over the mile-long list of numbers on the fridge that included everything from the vet to an aunt who lived in the next state over. Mom always got a little anxious when she was spending time away from the house, even if it was just for a few days.

"We'll be fine, Mom," I said.

"Jane knows we're gone and can help if you need something," she said, ignoring me. "Her number is on the fridge."

"I know. You already told me that."

She was moving over to Evie, who had migrated to the kitchen table around lunchtime, schoolwork spread around her. "I love you," Mom said as she kissed the top of Evie's head.

"Love you," Evie mumbled, barely glancing up from her chemistry textbook.

My mother came over to where I sat at the counter. "Love you," she said. A waft of her perfume hit me as she leaned down to kiss my temple. It was familiar. The same scent she had worn since I was little, and it always reminded me of home.

"Love you too," I said. It wasn't a lie. I did love my mother, even if her words from yesterday morning still hovered in the back of my mind, even if I thought she was hiding something.

"Call if you need anything," she said, making her way to the garage door, where my dad had stuck his head out, likely wondering what was taking so long.

"We'll be fine," I assured her.

"They'll be fine," my dad echoed. "Be good, girls."

"Take care of each other," my mom yelled over her shoulder, my dad's hand on her lower back as he urged her out the door.

The garage door rumbled open and then closed. The house fell quiet again, and I returned to my computer screen as the sound of their car on the gravel driveway faded. Evie shot up from her chair, abandoning her headphones on the table, still leaking muffled music into the kitchen. She went over to the front window and peered through the glass. I watched her as she opened the garage door and stuck her head inside.

"What are you doing?" I asked.

"Checking to make sure they're gone," she announced. "I want to go out into the forest to where Mom and Jane were walking."

"What?" I asked.

She was back at the kitchen table, closing her books and stacking everything. She had spent the day yawning and languidly moving through her work, but now she moved with purpose. "I want to see what Mom and Jane were doing." She stared at me, her arms crossed over her chest, daring me to challenge her.

Part of me was glad she shared my suspicions, but I didn't relish the idea of going back into the woods again. "What do you think we're going to find?" I asked.

"I don't know—that's why we're looking."

"Mom asked us not to go out there." I didn't really care about Mom's prohibition, and I doubted Evie would either, but it seemed like my responsibility as the older sister to at least remind her that we would be breaking the only real rule our mom had set for us.

"That was really weird, right? Mom has never tried to stop us from going into the woods. Honestly, I was a little suspicious after we saw her the other night, but then when she was like, 'Don't go out there,' I knew she must be hiding something."

"I mean, I did get lost in the woods earlier this week," I told her, then explained the whole story of how I'd somehow left the path and ended up on the complete other side of the forest.

She listened intently, but I couldn't tell if she believed my story. "You wandered off the trail. We'll pay closer attention."

"No, Ev, I didn't wander off the trail. I swear, the trail just disappeared." The moment I'd turned around to find the trail gone replayed in my head, the hairs on my arms rising at the memory.

"That's not possible," she said, but she sucked her bottom lip into her mouth—the same nervous tell our mother had.

"I know, but it happened."

"We'll be careful." She didn't deny it this time. Both of us knew, although I wasn't sure either of us was willing to admit it, that there was something unexplainable and maybe even impossible about those woods.

"We've got only a couple of hours until it gets dark," I said. I didn't think it would discourage her, but I had to try anyway.

"So we'd better get going."

"Or we could go tomorrow?" I offered. Maybe Evie wouldn't be so keen on the idea by tomorrow, and we could skip it entirely.

"I'm going today, and I'll go by myself if I have to."

It was a trap, albeit a pretty transparent one. I doubted she'd really go far alone, but she knew there was no way I would let her go into the forest by herself. "Okay, let me get changed."

CHAPTER 25
THE MISSING GIRLS

Over the next year, we fell into a new rhythm in which Jane no longer played a consistent part. Her life was separate from ours, even though she stopped by the cottage most days for long lunches or afternoons spent chatting with Mother while she worked. But still, at night, I was alone in the room we'd shared, her bed always empty. I spent those lonely nights thinking about Mary, her body split open as Mother worked on the careful stitches to pull her together, not quite ready yet in the cold basement. I wondered what she'd be like when she finally woke.

My nights were spent alone, but my days were filled with new people.

With Jane gone, Mother's attention was all focused on helping me find a husband. During the day, I was often sent into town to try to find someone who would make a suitable match. Mother didn't accompany me on these outings, but I would recount them to her when I returned, getting her approval and notes for next time.

But today, Jane and I were both at the cottage. Tonight was the new moon. I could hardly eat the plate of food in front of me because I was so excited. I had spent the day walking in the woods, listening to the whispers passed among trees. They were excited for tonight too.

Mary was finished. It was time to wake her up.

Mother spent much of the dinner reminding me that *awake* didn't mean *ready*. It could be a few days before she opened her eyes and could talk with us, for the energy from the forest to reach every corner of the body Mother had carefully crafted for her.

After night fell, the three of us headed for the line of trees at the back of the garden. It was cold out, but the trees were budding. It was time for the slow unfurling of new life. Mother carried Mary out the front door, her arms wrapped around the still-lifeless body after unhooking her from the bevy of machines that whirred in the basement's background all the time.

Mother was a strong woman, but I didn't think she would have needed to be particularly strong to carry Mary. Mary was tiny, each of her limbs thin and birdlike. The only thing large about her was her eyes. She had giant doe eyes, a golden brown ringed with green.

We made the journey to the clearing where we gathered on each new moon. Mother laid Mary on the ground, making sure as much of her naked skin as possible pressed against the earth. I searched her skin for imperfections by the lantern light, for the little pink scars like mine that had faded over the years, but Mother's new techniques must have worked—Mary was flawless.

Jane had brought a blanket out with us that night, and as soon as Mary was settled on the ground, Mother spread the blanket over her so that only her face was visible. I carried over the basket that contained our offering for the trees, overflowing with bones and pieces of flesh. Some of them came from the kitchen, like the leftover chicken bones and the scaly skin of a fish, but much of it came from the basement, the pieces Mother hadn't used of the girls. Our basket was always filled with crooked noses, jutting elbows, and bumpy skin. We gave the trees scraps of the dead, and in return, they filled us with life. Mother had already prepared the hole and dumped the contents in, and then we waited.

Jane reached for my hand. I intertwined my fingers with hers, the little squeezes we shared, our wordless language of reassurance. I could feel the forest waking up, the low buzz tickling the soles of my feet. I gripped Jane's hand tighter but didn't pull my eyes away from Mary and her still body. We waited, quiet and motionless, for Mary to take her first breath.

Then, as the minutes ticked by, unmeasured under the stars, a long, slow inhale filled her chest, raising the blanket before letting it fall. No one moved for another breath as Mary shifted, her arm stirring under the blanket. Tears blurred my vision as Mother dropped to her knees and ran her fingers along her newest daughter's face. "Hello, Mary," she whispered before turning to us. "Come, girls, say hello to your sister."

I bent down, close enough so that I could see Mary's lashes fluttering against her cheeks. Her eyes didn't open, but there was life behind them. I couldn't hold my tears anymore, and I let them drip onto this beautiful new girl. In total, five girls had gone into making Mary, and as I held my younger sister's hand, their sacrifices felt worth it. The song of the forest thrummed under her skin. The familiar melody echoed in my own blood. I looked up at Jane and found her face lit with the same intoxicating delight as she leaned over Mary.

Even Mother, the woman who had created us, who had channeled the energy of this place into us, didn't know what it was like to have the hum of the woods flowing through her veins. She didn't know what it was like to be a creature made of parts. We were death and broken pieces formed into life again. And Mary was ours, the third in our circle, another sister to share the weight of our secrets, to understand.

I had imagined what my first words to my new sister might be for weeks, but none of them felt right, so instead, I whispered what I would have wanted to hear when I woke up in darkness. "Don't be afraid. We'll take care of you."

CHAPTER 26

Fifteen minutes later, both of us were dressed in jackets and standing on the back porch. I had a roll of fluorescent-pink tape left over from the search party for Maddie. I figured we could mark some of the trees along the trail so we'd have something to help us if we got turned around.

"One hour. Then we head home. That should give us plenty of time to get back to the house before sunset," I said, checking the time and then looking up at Evie. "We can always go back out tomorrow, but we do not want to be wandering around out there after dark."

Evie nodded.

"And we stay together, no matter what."

"Obviously," she said, rolling her eyes. "I know that."

I knew she was smart enough to know better, but maybe too brave for her own good. "I'm serious, Ev. If you so much as think about running off, I will drag you home and call Mom. Got it?" The thought of turning around and Evie being gone, like the trail had been a few days before, made my chest ache.

"I'm not going to run off," Evie said. "I don't have a death wish; I just want to find Maddie."

"Okay, then let's go."

We headed for the trees.

"The other night, Mom and Jane were coming from that direction." Evie pointed toward the trail where we'd seen them.

I nodded and gestured for her to lead the way.

She hesitated for a moment at the edge of the trees, turning around to make sure I was still with her even though we had gone only a few steps. The shadows were heavy, the sun already at a lower angle than I would like. This felt like an incredibly bad idea.

I didn't know what we would find or what we would face out there, but we owed it to all the girls who had vanished into those branches to try. For Krista. For Chloe. For Maddie. And for the girls whose names we didn't know. A familiar frustration bubbled up under my skin. They were owed answers. They were owed more than a shallow investigation that petered out in a few weeks. If no one else would give them that, we would. Borrowing a bit of my sister's bravery, I followed her into the forest so that maybe we could stop adding names to the list of missing girls.

Evie started down the little dirt trail that cut between the trees. It was still damp along the forest floor, though not as muddy as the day before, but the leaves were a bit slippery underfoot. Evie walked slowly, taking in the forest around her, looking for anything out of place. Everything seemed normal, pleasant even. Birds sang, a gentle breeze blew through the branches, and it was chilly but not cold. Familiar comfort slipped over me like a blanket. I knew better than to trust it today; I was wary at every turn.

At first, we walked in silence and fell into a comfortable cadence. Evie was the first to speak. "How long do you think you'll stay here?" she asked.

"Why? Are you sick of me already?" I said as I followed her around a low-slung tree branch.

"No," she said with an eye roll. "I like having you around. It's nice to have someone to split Mom's attention with. It takes some of the pressure off me, since she's got you to manage too."

"Mom has always been a little high-strung." It felt weird to make this joke about our mom when both of us were still so suspicious of her. I had thought I knew my own mother, but she clearly had secrets. And even though we didn't know what those secrets were, their existence was enough to make me question everything.

"Do you think she's connected to all this somehow?" Evie asked, as if she could read my mind.

"I don't know." She knew more than she was saying—that seemed almost incontrovertible at this point—but her being tangibly tied to the girls' disappearances seemed too horrific to even consider.

Evie let my answer hang in the quiet for a moment, our footsteps audible even against the soft forest floor. "You're probably ready to get out of here," Evie said.

I shrugged. "Not really. Despite everything, it's been nice to be home for a bit. What about you? Is college still the plan?

I don't think anyone would blame you if you wanted to take some time off."

"I'm positive Mom would murder me if I tried to take a gap year. But no, I'm ready to be away from here for a while. Take some space."

"Space is good."

"But you? How long are you staying?" Evie asked again.

I had avoided directly answering because I wasn't entirely sure. "I think I'm going to hang around for a while, maybe a few months, until you go to college. Then I don't know. I don't think I'm a city person, but I don't want to stay here. Maybe somewhere closer, though, like driving distance. I missed home more than I realized when I was gone. I missed you." I bumped her with my shoulder, and she rolled her eyes again, but the soft smile that spread across her face told me that she'd missed me too, although she'd never admit it.

I didn't really know why I continued, except that I needed her to hear about my mistakes so, hopefully, I would save her from making the same ones. "I never really stopped to think about what I wanted to do with my life. I went to LA because I thought a good career meant I needed to be in a big city. And I started dating Tom because he seemed like the kind of guy I should be dating. I was so worried about what I was supposed to do that I forgot to actually take stock of what was happening around me. Then, when I finally looked up, I realized I was sort of miserable. So I think maybe I'd like to spend some time figuring out what I want my life to look like. Let things be a little messy for a while. I don't know how long I'll stay and what I'll do next. And I'm trying not to let that freak me out."

"Well, I like having you around. I'd be happy to have you for a few months," Evie said.

I would have hugged Evie if I hadn't thought she'd use it as an opportunity to shove me into the mud, so I just smiled and followed behind her.

We got quiet again as we continued walking. The forest was getting denser as we got farther from the house. After walking for about twenty minutes, I turned to Evie. "What are we looking for?" I asked her, my voice close to a whisper. I wasn't sure what we were expecting. A hidden bunker or some caged monster? The police had already extensively searched these woods. They wouldn't have missed something so obvious.

Evie shook her head. "We'll know it when we find it."

"If Mom has hidden something, and that's a big *if*, how the hell do you think we're supposed to find it? This forest is fucking huge." I recognized the words for what they were as soon as they were out of my mouth. I was being too sharp with her. My anger was just a disguise for my fear.

Evie didn't respond. She waited for me while I tied another piece of pink tape to a tree, her eyes darting over the forest around us. I was trying to space them out so we would be able to spot one ribbon of pink from the next, but it was hard because the trees were so dense that we'd lose sight of the bright spot of pink after a few steps.

We continued in silence for a while, with me checking my phone every few minutes to make sure we still had time, while Evie continued ahead of me, never more than a couple of steps away. I should have been scanning the forest around us, but I didn't take my eyes off her ponytail bouncing against her black jacket. I was afraid that if I looked away, even just for a second, I would turn back to find only empty space where my sister had been a moment before.

It was already getting dark, and I was about to suggest we head home, when Evie stopped suddenly in the middle of the trail. "Lia, look," she said.

I followed her finger past the rows of spindly branches toward the sky, where a thin pillar of white smoke rose from the forest. It was difficult to judge the distance, but it seemed to be close.

I took another step closer to Evie. "It could be a campfire or something?" I whispered.

Evie shook her head. "There's no campground over there or even any houses in that direction," she said, her volume matching my own.

Neither of us said anything as we watched the smoke, a white finger reaching into the sky, for a long moment. I knew the calculations we were running in our heads—we would need to leave the trail and climb a hill dense with trees and undergrowth to reach the smoke.

"It's probably nothing," I said, although I didn't believe that. It felt important–the only real clue we'd encountered today about where our mother might have been.

"Probably," Evie agreed. "But we've come this far, so we should check."

I nodded. "Okay, but we're only looking," I said, suddenly nervous about what we might find. If there was a fire, there was likely someone who'd lit it. And if they had any connection to

Maddie's disappearance, we had to stay far away from them. "We see what we can see, and then we leave. We're not going to do anything stupid, right?"

"Yeah."

I turned to look at Evie. She looked nervous, her eyes wide as she chewed her bottom lip. I was sure that the fear must have been evident on my face too.

I led once we left the path, a bright pink piece of tape tied to a tree at the edge of the trail as we stepped into the tightly packed branches. I moved slowly, making sure Evie was never more than a step behind me.

The ground started to get steeper, and our feet threatened to slip out from underneath us on the rotting leaves underfoot. I grabbed thick branches, their bark scraping across my palms as I struggled to stay upright. Neither of us spoke as we climbed. I could smell the smoke now, the warm wood rising above the scent of the damp forest around us.

We were nearly to the top when I froze.

"What is it?" Evie whispered, slightly out of breath, as she stopped next to me.

I pointed at the tree a few yards in front of us and the pink ribbon that stood out so dramatically against the deep browns of the trees around it, flapping in the breeze.

"That can't be ours. We were walking in a straight line up that hill," she said between pants, pointing back at where we'd come from.

"It's either ours or someone else has been marking the trees out here with that same pink tape." I wasn't sure which option was more frightening.

"Maybe it was from the search party?" she offered. We both knew that made little sense. The search hadn't gone this deep into the forest.

"We must have looped around somehow." I didn't know how it was possible, but I didn't have a better explanation.

We climbed the rest of the way up the hill, only a few more steep steps toward the tree with the tape tied around one of the branches. The pink tape was almost certainly mine. It was an exact match to the roll in my pocket and clearly hadn't been out here very long, unaffected by the weather. But the area at the top of the hill was unfamiliar, the mud and leaves around the base of the trunk undisturbed, as if the tree had dug its roots out of the earth and replanted itself here.

"We haven't been here before," Evie said, looking around. "This place doesn't look familiar."

"It's probably just the light. We don't recognize it because it's getting darker," I lied.

Evie nodded, although I didn't think she actually believed me.

I leaned in to look at the pink tape. It wasn't knotted onto the branch, just tangled around it. Maybe the wind had blown it over here.

"Lia," Evie called.

I swung around and found her about fifteen feet behind me. I didn't like how far apart we were, and I started to close the distance when she gestured past where she was standing.

"Look at this."

There was a perfectly round clearing on the other side of the trees. I recognized it immediately. The large fallen tree would have been hard to miss.

Evie had already started into the open space. "This place is so weird. I can't believe I haven't seen it before."

"Ev, be careful. I don't know if we should be here," I said, a shiver rolling through me. Something about this place made my skin crawl.

"It's fine," Evie said, barely looking back over her shoulder at me as she approached one of the trees at the perimeter.

I followed her to where she stopped, her finger tracing over the familiar carving in the tree trunk. "Mary," my sister read the name aloud. "Do you think she's one of the missing girls?"

CHAPTER 27
THE MISSING GIRLS

Months passed, but Mary never seemed to fully acclimate to her new body. She startled at every noise and rarely left the cottage. And she was so exhausted all the time. She had taken over Jane's bed, and it was not uncommon to see her little body curled under the sheets at all hours of the day.

I tried to become what Jane had been to me: an older sister, a mentor, and a guide—someone to help Mary navigate this new world. I'd offer to go on walks together in the garden or sit with her while she gazed out the windows, but she rarely wanted company.

Mother was devastated by Mary's inability to adjust, but she tried not to let us see it. She had made two nearly perfect girls. It was unclear why Mary was struggling so much more than either of us had. "Give her time, Elizabeth," Mother said. "It's an overwhelming transition." But I could see that even as she said those things to me, she didn't believe them.

It wasn't just that Mary was listless but that she was also

defiant. She didn't listen to Mother when asked to help set the table or when it was time to come in from outside. She'd spit at us as we tried to brush through her hair and kick at our shins when we tried to make her sit with us at the dinner table. She was hostile to every element of this place.

Mother was frustrated that nothing she did seemed to get through to Mary. She had used all her usual methods. Mary was regularly sent to bed without dinner, but that hardly seemed to impact her; she was often reluctant to eat regardless. She had spent a few nights in the closet too, but she seemed unbothered by all that darkness that made my skin crawl. No matter what Mother did or threatened, Mary's disposition never changed.

One afternoon, months after Mary had woken up, I found her sitting in the window seat. She had always been small, but now she had withered to something skeletal. She barely ate, refusing most meals. Her skin was papery, like she might melt if she went out in the rain. Her cheeks were sunken. Her eyes rested in two deep hollows.

It was snowing softly, and she watched the flakes cover the world in white. As I approached her, she turned to me, her big eyes filled with anger, and said, "Leave me alone. I don't want you here."

I settled into the cushions next to her. "The snow is beautiful. Isn't it?" I said, pretending I hadn't heard. She stood and headed for the bedroom. "Mary, wait," I called after her. "Please just sit with me for a while."

She turned back around, and I thought for a moment that she might return to the seat next to me, that maybe she was softening. But she didn't sit in the window seat. "How can you stand it?" she asked.

"Stand what?"

"The feeling that your skin is too tight and your limbs don't belong to you. The whispers of memories of before. I feel broken," she said. She fisted a handful of her hair and pulled it away from her scalp. Clumps of the dark strands clung to her fingers, some drifting to the floor around her.

"Oh, Mary," I said. I rose to give her a hug. I remembered that feeling; it was difficult, but she had to let herself forget. She would never be happy here until she learned how to let the ghosts and memories of before disappear.

She shoved me hard. I stumbled back, crashing into the wall behind me.

"You are no better than she is," Mary said through clenched teeth. "You leave this house every day and do nothing to stop it. It would be so easy for you to tell someone, anyone. She's going to do it again. She's going to make more monsters like you, like us."

Mother hadn't begun on the next girl yet, too busy worrying about Mary, but she had started talking about it. I was surprised when she first mentioned it. I thought Mary would be the last, our family complete. But Mother wasn't satisfied with how Mary had turned out. She needed another girl to perfect her process—at least that's what she claimed. Jane and I suspected that wasn't the whole truth. We didn't think her pursuit of perfection would end with just one more sister. She'd always want another doll in her collection. There would always be something she could do a bit better. She'd never be entirely satisfied with any of us.

I tried to soothe Mary, but she was too upset. She kept

getting louder and louder, her hands shaking as she pointed at me. "You are all monsters," she shouted. "I am a monster."

She raked her fingernails down her cheeks, drawing blood. She was screaming now, no longer words but an endless wail. I reached for her, tried to pry her hands away from her face, but she lashed out at me instead, clawing at my skin. I was screaming too, shouting at her to stop.

I didn't hear Mother come up the stairs from the basement, but suddenly she was there, pulling Mary off me. Mother grabbed her by the hair and yanked, tossing Mary aside before I could react. Her head cracked against the wall, the sound sickeningly loud. Mary crumpled in a heap on the ground with a pained groan.

I flinched at the noise, and then Mother's hands were on me, tenderly assessing the cuts on my cheek. I could only look at Mary's hair splayed around her head in a halo, a bruise already blooming on the side of her face. Hours later, after Mother had spread ointment against my cheek and dosed Mary with a sedative, I tiptoed into our bedroom and found her asleep under the blankets, sunlight streaming through the window. It was difficult to understand how so much fury could live inside her tiny frame.

I watched her sleep as I thought about what she called me: *monster*. It wasn't as if I hadn't considered the same thing. How could I not? I was unnatural, formed from the unwilling sacrifice of others. Like Frankenstein's monster, I was a creature composed of parts. But Frankenstein's monster was driven to violence not because he had been made, but because he was alone. I had never been alone. I had been wanted and loved even before the forest had breathed life into my chest. Mary didn't have to be alone either. I wanted nothing more than to love her, if she'd only let me.

Mary tried to run a few days later, breaking out through the front door while I had my back turned, washing dishes in the sink. Within a few days, she had recovered from our scuffle and got back to staring out the window and glaring at anyone who dared approach her. If anything, she had been a bit quieter in the days after the incident. I didn't expect her to try something so dramatic. I hadn't heard the front door open over the sound of the water, but when I turned around, she was gone from the window seat and the door was open.

I raced to the door, but she had already made her way through the garden and was slipping out the gate. By the time I reached the edge of the trees, she was nowhere to be seen, already disappearing into the crisscrossing branches. I tried searching for her, but within a few minutes, I realized the pointlessness of my hunt. She could have gone anywhere.

I went downstairs and tearfully told Mother what had happened.

She shouted at me: "Elizabeth, do you know what you've done? What if she tells someone about us? What if she makes it to the road and leads people back to us? Everything I've built out here is at risk because you didn't keep an eye on her." She held me by the shoulders and shouted so close to my face that I could feel her hot breath.

"The trees will bring her back home," I said, a little confused at her anger. The trees had never failed to return me right back to the cottage's door; surely they'd do the same for Mary.

"You better hope so," she said, looking past me into the forest, an uneasy fury on her face.

We spent the afternoon in the garden, waiting, both of us scanning the tree line around the house for Mary. It was cold, and despite my coat and hat, I was still freezing. I hoped Mary, who was out there in just a sweater, was okay.

It was almost sunset when Mary stumbled back through the trees. Mother had been anxiously pacing along the perimeter of the garden when I spotted her.

She was confused, her skin icy, as I led her through the garden and back into the house. She rambled, none of the words making any sense. I tucked her in front of the fireplace, wrapped a blanket around her shoulders, and went to the kitchen to make her something warm to drink.

Mother had followed us inside but stood against the far wall.

"You should check on Mary," I whispered to her. "I think she might be sick, and it looks like she hurt herself." Her palms were scraped up and bloody, but I was mostly worried about how cold she had gotten out there.

"I don't know what to do with her," Mother said. "She's becoming a danger to all of us."

I wanted to disagree and protest that Mary just needed more time, but we had given her time. Nothing seemed to make her better; if anything, she was getting worse. "What are you going to do?" I asked in a low whisper. "Can't you fix her?"

Mother nodded. "I'll take care of it."

CHAPTER 28

Evie still hadn't looked away from the name carved into the tree. Her pointer finger traced the heart again.

"I don't know who Mary is, but I think we need to leave," I said. I looked over my shoulder. "Doesn't this place feel creepy to you?"

She seemed unbothered, but I couldn't shake the feeling that there was something more to this place. The air felt thick, humming with a strange, electric energy. "It's pretty," she said. "Peaceful, sort of."

I didn't have time to argue with her. We could easily see the sky here, and the clouds were already turning pink and gold in the fading sun. "Let's go. We need to get back soon." As it was, I was worried that we wouldn't make it out of the trees before it got dark.

Evie started to follow me out of the clearing but froze before we were back between the trees. "I can't see the smoke," Evie said, searching the sky. I followed her gaze, looking for that distinctive white cloud we had spotted only a few minutes earlier. I searched the entire visible swath of sky. She was right; the smoke was gone.

"What do we do now?" she asked as I pulled out my phone. It was later than I had realized, ten minutes past the hour mark, when we said we'd turn around.

"We need to go back. We can figure out where the smoke was coming from on a map and try to get there tomorrow." Like usual, the corner of my phone indicated I had no service.

Evie nodded. I looked down the hill, trying to spot the pink tape I had tied to a branch at the bottom, but it was too far to see. We started making our way back down, with me again in the lead, checking every few feet to make sure she was still behind me, even though I could hear her breathing. It was getting dimmer. It wasn't dark yet, but the shadows were longer. There were no more patches of sunlight on the forest floor.

Going down was even slower than climbing up, as we slipped every few feet, both of us clinging to trees to prevent ourselves from sliding down the hill. But when we reached the bottom, a bright pink strand of tape awaited us. I bent, bracing myself on my knees, with a massive exhale of relief.

Evie was next to me a minute later. "Where's the trail?" she asked.

"What?" I looked up. The trail should have been just on the other side of the tree. It wasn't. There was nothing but tight clusters of trees and undergrowth.

"It's fine. It's probably just hard to spot because it's getting darker. I'm sure it's right up here," I lied. I took a few steps forward, searching for anything that would indicate where we were or which direction we should be going.

We had gone only a few steps when it became clear that there was no path to follow, no trail, or any of the pink markers I had diligently left along our journey. "I'm sorry." Evie's voice had lost all its earlier enthusiasm. Instead, anxiety bled into every word. "I shouldn't have made us come out here. Now we don't know how to get back home, and nobody knows where we are. No one will even know to look for us until Mom gets home."

"We're not lost," I lied again.

"Then where are we?" she asked, her voice halfway to a sob.

"We're a little turned around, but we'll find our way back to the trail soon or end up somewhere along the road. We haven't been out here that long. We couldn't have gone too far." I looked around again, hoping I would spot something that might lead us back home, but the trees around me didn't offer anything helpful.

"So the plan is to keep walking? We could be going in the completely wrong direction."

"Do you have a better plan?" I snapped back. I knew we could be going the wrong way, but I didn't think we had much choice.

"Maybe we should just stay here?"

"You already said it—no one will know we're missing for days. I didn't dress to spend the night out here." It wasn't that cold now, but it would get down to freezing tonight, and I didn't think my coat or Evie's would be enough to keep us warm. Not to mention that these woods were home to many things that might not appreciate overnight guests.

"We're just going to wander around and hope we stumble home?" Evie's tone was more forceful now, and her frustration was evident in her words.

"Again, Ev, I am happy to do something else if you have a better plan. But the only options I see are to spend the night out here or keep walking, so I think we should keep walking." I tried to keep my tone civil, but I was scared too.

"Whatever. Let's go."

She tried to hide the slight tremor in the last word, but I still heard it, even as she rolled her eyes and stomped off.

I turned to follow her and almost ran right into a massive oak tree. It hadn't been there a minute before. There hadn't been any trees close to me when we had stopped. I glanced at Evie to see if she had noticed, but she was already a few steps ahead.

The light was fading to a deep blue. If the sun hadn't entirely disappeared behind the horizon line, it would soon. The forest was coming alive with the sounds of night, birdsong quieting, replaced with the occasional distant howl from a coyote. I tried not to jump at animals shuffling in the dead leaves on either side of us. As the trees got closer together, Evie moved behind me. We didn't talk, but I could hear her footsteps echoing mine as we trudged through the trees.

Then there were only my footsteps. I whipped around, expecting to find Evie stopped a few feet behind me, but she was gone. "Ev?" I said, looking around to see if she had ducked behind one of the many trees. No one was there. "Evie!" I shouted loud enough that I felt a pinch in my throat.

It was silent in the wake of her name. The forest was holding its breath with me.

"Lia?" Her voice came from somewhere behind me.

I spun toward the sound. "Ev, where are you?" She didn't sound close.

"Lia?" she called again.

"Ev!" I shouted, my voice echoing around me, before I spotted her pale-blue jacket between the branches. She was standing on the other side of a clearing, the same perfectly round clearing we had left fifteen minutes before. A chill crept up my spine as I realized we had somehow returned to this place, though we had been walking in the other direction.

As soon as Evie saw me, we raced toward each other, then met in the middle of the perfect circle. The trees seemed more sinister now, their shadows stretching long and spindly, as if reaching for us. "What were you doing? How are we back here?" I asked, gripping both her arms, my heartbeat thrumming in my ears.

She looked confused and a little frightened. "I was right behind you, and then I looked away, and when I turned back, you were gone." She scanned the forest around me as if it might offer some clue as to how, within a few seconds, we had ended up in entirely different places.

"It's okay," I reassured her. I was beginning to think the forest was amorphous, changing around us, shifting the moment our backs were turned. "We're fine." I could see the tree with Mary's name carved into it just over Evie's left shoulder.

"How the fuck are we back here?" she asked in a whisper.

It seemed impossible that we'd circled back without realizing it. It was even more impossible that Evie and I had gotten separated and ended up on opposite ends of this clearing.

"I don't know, but we need to keep moving. I don't think we should stay in this place." I didn't want us to dwell too long on what it meant, how we might not be able to find our way home again. Evie grabbed my hand, squeezing it so tightly that each fingernail left a crescent moon in my skin.

We kept walking hand in hand through the forest. Roots seemed to sprout out of the ground to trip us. Branches swung down to catch strands of our hair and to leave scratches along our cheeks. The night was still; it wasn't the wind moving the branches.

All the light was nearly gone. It was getting harder to see the ground in front of us. We might need to give up soon and find a place to sleep for the night. I didn't like the idea of sleeping in this forest that didn't seem to follow the rules of the natural world, but I wasn't sure we'd have a choice. I was about to suggest it to Evie when she tugged on my hand, her head jolting to the left. "Do you hear that?"

"What?"

"Water," she said. She didn't wait for my response, pulling me toward the sound.

Then I heard it too: the soft gurgling of a stream. Only one stream ran through the woods here, meandering through the forest and crossing under the road at the North Creek Bridge. Evie and I picked up our pace and then raced to find it. We cut through another row of trees and landed on a well-maintained running trail.

A laugh snaked out of my chest, relief bubbling to fill my lungs as Evie dropped my hand. We still had to find our way to the highway and then home, but until a minute ago, I hadn't been entirely convinced we would ever find our way out of the trees.

We stood there for a minute, catching our breaths, before I turned to my sister. "We should get going. I'm not sure how far we have to walk." We started down the trail, and I glanced over at Evie; she had twigs and bits of leaves in her hair, and I was sure I wasn't in much better shape.

We hadn't been walking long when we noticed we weren't alone on the trail anymore. Footsteps echoed behind us. Evie flashed me a glance, and for a moment, I thought about ducking back into the trees, weighing the dangers of an unknown stranger against the forest itself.

"Hello?" I called out. Evie inched closer to me, and we both tensed and were ready to run if needed.

Just then, two women dressed in brightly colored leggings and sweatshirts rounded the bend. I exhaled, immediately recognizing the pair: Lydia Robins and Kate Montgomery. Kate had raised her hand to wave at us but then stopped short, taking in our appearance.

"Are you both okay? What happened?" Lydia asked, her face filled with concern. Both women were standing within arm's reach now. Lydia smoothed a hand over Evie's back and picked one of the large leaves from her hair.

"We got lost," Evie confessed.

"Where were you coming from?" Lydia asked.

"We left our house and were planning on taking the North

Creek Trail, but somehow, we got turned around and ended up off the trail entirely," Evie said. I was glad Evie had left out large chunks of the story. It wasn't that I didn't trust these women, although I wasn't entirely sure I should, but I wanted to avoid the lecture I was sure would come if they knew we were looking into Maddie's disappearance.

"Well, you're on North Creek Trail, but you're pretty far from home. I think we're less than a quarter mile from the parking lot off the highway," Lydia said.

"Let us drive you home," Kate cut in. "It's getting late, and I don't feel comfortable with you walking alone in the dark."

"Thank you," my sister said.

They were right. The parking lot was only a few minutes down the trail, and soon enough, Evie and I were both in the back seat of Lydia's minivan. Evie leaned against the window and let her eyes drift closed.

As soon as we were back on the road and out from under the dense canopy of trees, my phone buzzed with dozens of messages and missed calls. I bumped Evie with my shoulder and gestured toward her phone. She pulled it out of her pocket, and her eyes went wide. I was sure her phone contained a matching screen full of missed calls and texts from our mom. "We'll call her when we get home," I whispered. "Don't text her back until we can talk to her."

Evie nodded.

"Can I ask you both a favor?" I said, loud enough so I was sure I would be heard in the front. Kate turned around in the passenger seat, and Lydia's eyes darted to the rearview mirror.

"Of course," Kate said.

"Our mom is out of town this weekend with our dad. As you can imagine, she's had a hard couple of weeks, and I really want her to relax this weekend. Would you mind not telling her about this?"

Lydia and Kate looked at each other. "I'm not sure we can do that. If it were my kids, I'd want to know," Lydia said.

"Just until Monday. We're not trying to hide it from her," Evie said, although that was exactly what we were trying to do. "We want her to enjoy her weekend. We made it home safely. There's nothing to worry her about."

"We can wait until Monday," Kate said, although Lydia shot her a glare that said she wasn't too pleased with the decision.

We were less than a ten-minute drive from the house, and I didn't think I had ever been so grateful to come rolling down our long driveway. The familiar crunch of the gravel under the tires reassured me that we were nearly home, but it wasn't until we passed the final bend in the drive and the house's warm glow cut through the darkness that I let myself finally exhale.

After thanking both women and getting reassurance that they'd keep this quiet for the weekend, Evie and I climbed out of the car and walked through the front door. Both dogs greeted us when we stepped into the house, tails wagging. Evie crouched down and pressed her face against Daisy's head.

My phone screen lit up again. "Let's get this over with," I said, flashing my phone toward Evie. Unless Lydia and Kate had called our mother the minute we were out of the car, there was no way she could know we'd been in the woods. Still, I hesitated before answering. She had always had a sixth sense about what happened to Evie and me, especially if it happened in the forest.

"Where have you been?" Mom asked as soon as she answered, her annoyance edging toward panic.

"Sorry," I said. "Evie and I both had our phones off so we could get some work done. I just turned mine on and noticed all your messages."

"Where's Evangeline?" she asked.

"I'm here," Evie said. She stood next to me, leaning against the kitchen counter, typing on her phone.

"Phones stay on the rest of the weekend," my mom said. The anxious edge hadn't left her voice.

"Of course, sorry," I apologized again. "We didn't mean to scare you. How's the drive been so far?" I glanced up at the clock. It had only been a few hours since they had left.

"It was fine. We hit some traffic on the highway but made it to the hotel."

"That's good." Evie had left my side and pulled her laptop onto the kitchen counter, sliding onto one of the barstools.

"What are your plans for the night?" our mom asked.

"I think a quiet night in. Maybe a movie," I said. I looked over at Evie, but she was too absorbed in whatever was on her computer screen to contribute to the conversation. "Do you guys have plans to do anything exciting?"

"Probably just dinner once we're settled," she said, before quickly switching topics. "Please be careful this weekend. Don't do anything reckless." It felt strange that she was insistent on this point, almost like she was aware that we had been doing the opposite.

"We will, Mom." There was a pause on the other end of the line. "Is there any reason you called?" I was surprised to hear from her so soon after she'd left. I'd expected her to wait until later tonight before checking in.

"Oh, um…" She paused. "I just wanted to make sure you knew there's a lasagna in the freezer if you're looking for dinner. I got a little panicked when I couldn't get a hold of either of you."

"Okay, thanks. Love you, Mom. Have fun with Dad this weekend."

"Love you. Be safe," she said.

I waved my arms to get Evie's attention and mouthed, "Say goodbye."

"Love you. Bye," Evie said, and I hung up the phone.

I waited a few seconds after the call ended, then turned toward Evie. "What are you doing?" I asked.

She spun the laptop toward me, a map of the trail system and the forest pulled up on her screen. "I'm trying to figure out where the fuck that clearing was and how the hell we got so lost." She leaned over so she could see around the device. "Here's our house," she said, pointing at a spot on the map. "This is the trail we were following initially." She traced along a familiar path that led northwest away from our house, slowly curving toward the highway. "So I think the smoke was coming from somewhere over here." She pointed out an area of the forest that was blank on the map. There were no campgrounds or roads. Not even a hiking trail seemed to cut through that swath of trees.

"There's nothing there."

"Right, but that's not the weirdest part." She looked at the map and then pointed out a spot a good distance away from our house and where we'd seen smoke. "This is the parking lot where we ended up."

"How far is that?" It was hard to judge distances on the map—a wide swath of green forest, crisscrossed with trails and intersected by the blue ribbon of North Creek.

"It's about four miles west of where we left the trail. But I can't see a way for us to get there from here"—she pointed at the spot on the trail near the smoke before moving to the trail directly next to the parking lot—"without us running into the creek or the trail way sooner than we did. It really doesn't make sense."

A shiver ran up my spine as I looked over my sister's shoulder at the trees surrounding us. "There's a lot that doesn't make sense about that forest."

CHAPTER 29

Evie and I spent at least an hour poring over trail maps and talking through scenarios that could have led us to travel miles in the wrong direction without realizing it. By the time we gave up and turned on some brightly colored rom-com to fill the silence of the house, we were even more convinced that the route we had traveled was impossible. We fell asleep in the living room sometime long after midnight. There was something comforting in being able to reach over and touch my sister, her body curled up under a blanket on the other end of the couch. I didn't think either of us wanted to sleep alone, even if sleeping down here meant we were in full sight of the trees peering in the window.

In the morning, I braced for Evie to bring up the idea of going out there again. But neither of us mentioned it. It felt too dangerous. The impossibility of those trees was too big and frightening to tackle, even in the daylight.

Instead, Evie made plans to work on a history project at her friend's house. I was happy that she was going to spend time with a friend, even if it was just an excuse to get away from the forest for the day. I left soon after she did, deciding that this was the perfect opportunity to head into town to run all the errands I had been putting off. I wasted as many hours as I could slowly wandering, popping in and out of stores I had no reason to visit, but eventually, I had to return to the house.

It was late afternoon by the time I got back, but it was cloudy and already getting dark. I parked my car in the driveway and walked as quickly as I could to the front porch, hating the sensation of the trees at my back. It felt like they were waiting, ready to pull me back into the maze of branches we had been lost in yesterday. I felt nominally better once the front door was closed and locked behind me.

I wasn't entirely sure what to do with myself in the quiet emptiness of this big house. I skimmed through the books on the bookshelf in the living room, plucking a pink book with a familiar title from the shelf before settling myself into the couch. After a bit of prompting, the dogs jumped up to join me. My mother didn't allow them on the furniture, but I found the weight of their warm bodies comforting. We were all breaking the rules this weekend.

It took me twice as long as it should have to get through the first chapter. I couldn't focus on any of the pages. It felt like someone was watching me through the window every time I looked down to read the next paragraph. Still, I kept trying, although I barely absorbed any of the words, too busy listening for a twig snapping or a floorboard creaking.

My phone buzzed from the coffee table and startled me.

The screen lit up with a message from Evie: **I might spend the night at Sarah's. I already texted Mom and she said it's fine.**

The house felt even darker, the trees on either side pressing in closer. As glad as I was that Evie was enjoying time with her friends, I was dreading being alone in the house tonight. Regardless, I couldn't put that on Evie. **Have fun!**

Her message back to me was almost instant: **Will you be okay home alone?**

I'll be fine.

Are you sure? I can skip it if you'd rather.

I appreciated the thought, but I really did want Evie to have fun. I'd stay safely locked inside, and nothing would happen. **I'm good. I'm not planning on going on any midnight strolls through the forest. I can handle a night home alone.**

Text me if you change your mind.

I'll be fine, I sent again, then tossed the phone back on the table when I finished.

The house was too quiet. I had been so eager to be rid of my parents for the weekend, to luxuriate in the house without my mom's eyes constantly following me, but now that I was alone, I wished she were here. The forest felt less threatening when she acted as a mediator between us and the trees.

An instant later, I decided to leave, a plan formed in my head. I needed the company of strangers. I wanted to put on makeup and nice clothes and slip into the costume of the girl I had pretended to be in LA. I texted Matt before I could think better of it, already starting up the stairs to change. I wanted to let him take me out to dinner, tell me about his life, and shower me with surface-level compliments.

Are you busy tonight? I'd love to grab dinner again to make up for cutting things short last time. I sent it without the usual number of rereads I would have applied to a text like this. I considered a shower but decided against it, instead plugging in my curling iron and settling for a few waves.

I was halfway through my hair when my phone buzzed—the response from Matt. **You were great and I had a nice time, but I'm not feeling a spark. I think we would be better as friends. Hope you and your family are well!**

I laughed aloud as I read his message. The sharp bite of rejection stung. I wasn't really interested in pursuing something long term with Matt. Still, it left me without plans for the evening.

I thought about texting Kiera, but the fear that she might not want to hang out either prevented me from reaching for my phone. I didn't think I could tolerate another rejection, no matter how small. But I didn't need anyone; I could go out by myself.

I dug through the makeup bag that had spilled onto the counter over the last several days, going through a quick version of my normal routine. It was messier than I usually would have allowed, but I tried to embrace it. Maybe this would be the start of something bigger; the little rebellion of smudgy black eyeliner felt like coloring outside the lines of how I'd usually present myself. It was uncomfortable because it was unfamiliar, but the girl in the mirror was a fiercer, braver version of me, one who wouldn't still be preoccupied with the reasons behind Matt not wanting a second date.

I held my usual nude lipstick up. The shiny black-and-gold tube stood in stark contrast to my unpainted nails. I capped the tube without applying any and slipped out of my room, then down the hall to my parents'. Their bed was neatly made, corners crisp, and pillows evenly creased in the middle. Their bathroom sat perfectly undisturbed. I moved to my mother's vanity. I didn't bother taking a seat, instead lifting the lid and running my finger over the vast array of lipsticks she had tucked into an organizer. I pulled one at random. Something from the back. Something she didn't wear every day. I smiled as I pulled off the cap. It was a deep, glossy red that almost looked purple in the vanity lights.

I traced it across my mouth, careful of the edges, and watched it drain the color out of my face. I didn't care. It was the kind of hue that would almost certainly leave stains on every glass I drank from tonight and leave its mark on the necks of anyone I kissed, like a bruise. I blotted my lips against a tissue and then smiled in the mirror.

I'd spent many nights at the bar in town when I was home on breaks from college, but I had never been here alone. It was early, so most of the seats still sat empty. There was one large group in the corner booth, a bunch of people who looked like they could have been in high school, and their laughter filled the space. I felt so much older than them, despite the fact only a year or two likely separated us.

I wondered what they thought of me. If they saw me alone on a Saturday night and felt sad for me. The twenty-one-year-old version of myself would have been embarrassed to find me here two years later, back in my hometown bar alone, because

I couldn't even get a second date with a boy my mother had set me up with.

No version of Lia fit here. Not the high school version of myself, who had spent too many nights like this one at basement parties with warm cans of cheap beer. Not the LA version of myself, who far preferred a twenty-dollar cocktail. Not this girl in messy lipstick, who would go home tonight and sleep in her childhood bed. I thought briefly about turning around and leaving, but I caught the eye of the bartender and felt too embarrassed to slip out the door.

He greeted me with a nod as I settled onto a stool in the middle of the bar, rolling through the same niceties he spouted dozens of times every night. I ordered a shot of tequila, needing something that would soothe my self-consciousness quickly, and leaned into the blue light of my phone screen.

When the bartender returned, I accepted the shot with a slight smile but waited until he disappeared to the other end of the bar before I tilted my head back and swallowed. I felt the warmth of the liquor slip down my throat and into my cheeks. I contemplated whether I should order another shot or switch to something more palatable to sip when a man sat beside me. "Anyone sitting here?" he asked, his ass already firmly settled into the stool, hands resting on the edge of the bar. He was shorter than Tom, but he still had a couple of inches on me.

"You are," I said, gesturing at the seat he now occupied. It wasn't an original line, but he smiled anyway. It was a good smile, a fan of wrinkles sprouting up on both sides of his eyes. I had always liked that feature in men. A sign that they smiled enough for their face to remember the motion.

When the bartender circled back toward us, I ordered a Paloma, the effects of the shot still buzzing through my system. He ordered a beer. As I turned toward him, I let my body go soft and slouchy against the bar. "So, what brings you out on this fine evening?" I asked.

He smiled at me and started talking. He was friendly, telling stories littered with little jokes that required nothing from me. I was grateful for the shallow conversation. I wanted the company but didn't want to carry the weight of pushing a conversation along by asking questions and sharing bits of my own life. I wanted to drift through tonight, forget about the tangled mess back home with the trees and the secrets they hid.

We must have sat at the bar for at least an hour, but I couldn't recall anything he had told me, beyond his name: Ryan. If I had told him anything about myself, I had also forgotten that. I wasn't sure how many drinks I had gone through. Three or maybe four. By the end of the hour, my knees were pressed to his, and my fingers had found themselves rubbing against the worn denim of his jacket.

"I'm going to head to the bathroom," I said. I felt giddy, a little warm, not quite drunk, but right on the edge. Far past being able to drive, but not far enough where I felt out of control. I swayed as I stood, perhaps slightly drunker than I realized.

"I'll be right here when you get back," Ryan assured me.

The bar had filled up while we had been drinking, and there was a line outside the single-stall bathroom door. I found a spot at the end and leaned against the wall. I hadn't been paying close attention to the other women in line, but as the person directly in front of me shifted, I saw the girl in front of her. I could see only the back of her head, but the dark curls were familiar. It was impossible, but plenty of impossible things had happened over the last few days. Maybe I could hope for one good thing.

"Chloe?" I said, raising my voice over the din of the bar. Overlapping conversations and laughter filled the space, but my voice cut through it all, and several faces turned toward me at the sound. The girl with curly hair turned half a second later, her brow raised in the same confused expression everyone had. It wasn't Chloe. Her nose was too small, her skin a few shades too pale. For a minute it was like I was back in front of my TV screen, Chloe's picture on the evening news, the shock of hearing she had disappeared fresh once again.

"Sorry," I said, my voice too small in this place. "I thought you were someone I knew."

She nodded, already looking away.

When I returned from the bathroom a few minutes later, Ryan was waiting for me. "Do you want to get out of here?" he asked. I leaned against him, letting my head rest against his shoulder. I was still shaken by that girl who had looked so much like Chloe, but I tried not to let it show.

I nodded. "Will you take me home?"

"Your chariot awaits," he said with a chuckle. He walked behind me out of the bar with both hands on my waist. It felt nice to be held by him, grounded by something I knew was real.

We hadn't made it very far into the parking lot when an older woman approached us. "Ophelia," she called out. I wasn't entirely surprised she knew my name, even though I didn't recognize her. My mother knew everyone in this town—so by proxy, they knew me.

"Who's that?" Ryan whispered to me.

I shrugged. Even if I had known, there wouldn't have been much time to explain. She was in front of us in an instant.

She was a few inches taller than me and stocky, her gray hair tied back in a tight bun. "What do you think you're doing?" she asked Ryan, whose hands were still on my waist.

"I was just going to take her home," he said. He held up his arms in surrender, taking a step back.

"She's drunk. I don't know what your plans were, but I will be driving her home," the woman said. She yanked on my wrist, and I stumbled forward a few steps. Ryan caught me before I fell.

"I don't even know who you are?" Ryan said, looking at me as if I might illuminate things.

I shrugged again.

"Dr. Wolston. I'm a friend of her mother's," the old woman clarified. It was too dark in the parking lot to make out the details of her features, but there was something familiar about her, some distant memory I couldn't quite recall. "Time for you to go. I'll take her from here."

CHAPTER 30
THE MISSING GIRLS

Nothing seemed to really change in the week between Mary running away and the next new moon. I kept waiting for Mother to say something to Mary—perhaps give her one of her usual lectures or, worse, take her back into the basement and switch out a few pieces for something more compliant. But the days passed in silence, as if we were all pretending her failed escape hadn't happened. The only real difference was that Mary had been quieter, sleeping more than usual. I suspected Mother had been putting something in her breakfast, sedating her so she was more docile. It didn't feel like a long-term solution, but for now, things were much more peaceful in the house.

Mother was cooking tonight, a rare treat. It was pasta, and the house smelled of garlic and red wine all afternoon. Jane was already over. We had both offered to help, but Mother had shooed us away. It was a little strange, since it was rare that she didn't want to share the work, but Jane and I took the opportunity to talk. Jane told me all about her life. She was taking classes at the local college, slowly working on a degree. She was decorating their house. And she had joined a book club with the women on her street. I was happy to hear her life was full of so many things that brought her joy. Still, a quiet unease seemed to linger in the cottage. It hovered over Mother's dinner preparations in the space between the soft clatter of dishes and our hushed conversation.

Our voices dropped to a whisper as she told me that they still hadn't managed to get pregnant. She and her husband had been trying for almost a year. It wasn't a secret. Jane had told Mother when the problem initially arose, but any further conversation always descended into an argument. Mother was frustrated that Jane's body wasn't working how it should. And Jane felt it was Mother's fault, that Mother had failed and broken Jane somehow. Regardless of why it was happening, I squeezed Jane's hand and wished I could take away a little of her heartbreak.

Mother called us to the round table at the edge of the kitchen, where four plates piled high with steaming red sauce waited for us. A white tablecloth covered the old, worn table, and a pair of candles sat in the middle, already lit and flickering. Mary had emerged from the bedroom and was perched on her seat. She was yawning despite having woken up only a few minutes before. I took my usual seat between Jane and Mary.

The sun was setting outside. We were in the part of late fall that existed in between the bright leaves of October and the first snow. The world outside felt like it was bracing for the cold to take over. Inside, it was no different. We were waiting too, steeling ourselves for whatever storm would come next.

Mother, Jane, and I made polite conversation for a few minutes. Mother's eyes kept darting over to Mary, who was silently picking at her salad. "We're thinking of painting the house white or maybe a pale gray," Jane said. She'd been updating us all on the renovations they were planning for the following year.

"You're going to paint the brick? It will look terrible," Mother said. Her tone was sharp and dismissive, as if Jane having an opinion about her own home was frivolous and irritating. Mother hadn't loved the little house Jane and her husband had purchased after their wedding. She thought it was too small and too old, and she seemed to hate everything Jane did to the place, even though I thought it looked quite lovely. "And once you paint brick, it's impossible to undo."

"We just thought it might brighten the exterior a bit," Jane said, her shoulders sagging under the weight of Mother's criticisms.

Mother shook her head but didn't offer a reply. The table fell into silence; the only sound was our forks clinking against our plates for a moment.

"Dinner is delicious," I said, offering Mother a compliment that I hoped would lighten the awkwardness that had fallen.

"Thank you, darling," Mother said. She turned to Mary. "Have you tried the pasta yet? I think you'll like it."

Mary looked up, almost startled at being spoken to. She didn't say anything, but she pinched a strand of spaghetti with her fingers. I winced, waiting for Mother's reproach, but she didn't say anything. The strand waved loosely, leaving a trail of red against Mary's wrist. Then Mary lifted it to her mouth. She slurped it past her lips. The sound was wet and almost vulgar, as sauce dripped from Mary's fingers onto her white dress, speckling it with red.

Again, I waited for Mother to say something, to offer a familiar lecture about manners, but she just sat there watching. Her gaze was steady, unreadable, but the smallest smirk raised the corners of her lips.

Mary did it again, taunting Mother by scooping up a cluster of strands. The mushrooms and red sauce clung to the noodles and splattered against the tablecloth as she chewed them with an open mouth.

Everyone at the table stared at her in stunned silence as she reached for another handful. Then she started laughing. It was frightening, uncontrolled and too loud coming from her small frame, as her hand rose again and again, carrying a mess of long noodles dripping sauce from the plate to her mouth. Her eyes looked strange, the pupils swallowing her irises until only the slimmest ring of green lined the black.

I looked to Jane, who just stared back at me. Then I turned to Mother, who was seemingly unbothered by Mary's behavior, as she took a slow, deliberate sip of wine.

Mary's laughter abruptly stopped, cut off by a jagged cough, and then replaced by a desperate wheezing inhale as she struggled for breath. She scrambled for her glass of water. The coughing got more violent, a ragged sound that clawed its way out of her throat.

Jane rose.

"Sit down," Mother demanded, but Jane didn't listen, walking behind my chair to get to Mary. Panic flickered in Jane's eyes.

"I think she's choking on something," Jane said, patting Mary on the back.

Mother remained in her chair, wineglass raised to her lips, still wearing that same smirk. In that moment, I knew this was not an accident.

"You put something in her food," I whispered, eyes locked with Mother's. My voice was barely audible, and I trembled as the realization settled over me.

I had known Mother was dangerous. But there had been some line that I imagined she'd never cross. We were hers, which meant we had to listen to her, but it also meant we were supposed to be safe from her. This, whatever she had done to Mary, was firmly on the other side of the line. She had made each of us, spent months poring over each of our features, carving us from muscle and bone, stitching us together. We were her creations.

I hadn't considered she could just as easily unmake us.

Mary's coughing had moved to wheezing now, and her hands clawed at her throat as she tried to get air, eyes unfocused as she stared up at the ceiling. Jane stood next to Mary, panicking now, shouting at Mother to do something. But Mother seemed to ignore the chaos at the other end of the table. "I promised to keep you girls safe," she said to me. Then she rose and calmly walked over to Jane, who was kneeling on the floor next to Mary.

"She's not breathing." Jane was crying now, tears streaming

down both cheeks. Mary had fallen out of her chair and was in a heap on the ground. Jane leaned over her. "She needs help. We need to call someone!"

Mother knelt next to Jane. "There's nothing you can do. It's too late."

"What did you do?" Jane asked, a tearful accusation. It was bolder than Jane usually allowed herself to be, but the shock of the evening had worn away her usual restraint.

"The nightshade berries," I said in a whisper. I was the only one still sitting at the table, but I didn't move from my seat. I watched a drip of white wax trail down the candle. The deep-blue berries Mother had warned us were too dangerous to even touch. She had mixed them into Mary's meal and poisoned her at our dining table.

I wasn't sure if Jane had heard me, but Mother nodded. "She was becoming a danger to us all. We'll give her back to the trees," Mother said softly, a hand running over Jane's head as if this would comfort her.

Jane was still crying as she held Mary's head in her lap. I blinked back tears of my own. My relationship with Mary had borne little resemblance to my relationship with Jane, but still, I had tried my best to love her. She was difficult and miserable and dangerous, but she was one of us. She had belonged to our little family, and now she was gone.

The rest of the night was quiet. Mother took Mary's body downstairs while Jane and I cleaned up dinner in silence. What was there to say? Mary had been here this afternoon, and now she was dead in the basement. Jane would go home in the morning, back to her husband and her life, and I would stay here with Mother. The woman who had made and then killed my sister. "Maybe you should come home with me," Jane whispered as we scraped the plates into the trash.

I shook my head. There was no point. Mother would bring me back here. We couldn't leave this place, not really, not for long, not far enough to escape Mother's grasp. We were connected to the forest. Jane knew that better than I did. She'd told me about how miserable it was to no longer live in the woods. She felt the loss of the trees like an itch under her skin, this constant tug that pulled her back to the forest again and again. She couldn't go more than a few days, maybe a week, without returning to spend a few hours breathing the crisp air and feeling the hum of the roots beneath the ground.

We buried Mary on the new moon, returning her body to the forest so the trees could feed us new life. By the time we laid her to rest, she was in pieces, ripped apart at the seams. Mother had kept me out of the basement while she worked, but I had seen the aftermath, the wheelbarrow of limbs that we carted into the trees. Mother had taken her apart to see what had gone wrong, as if she were a vacuum cleaner or an old clock. If she had found some broken belt or rusted gear inside Mary, she had never told us.

After she was buried, we didn't speak of Mary again. We all pretended she hadn't existed at all.

CHAPTER 31

Dr. Wolston stared at me, waiting for me to respond. Something about the way she looked at me made me nervous, even though she was an older woman who really didn't pose much of a threat. She seemed determined. I could already imagine the phone call from my mother.

"It's fine. She can take me home," I said to Ryan. He looked reluctant, but I knew that if I didn't go with this woman, I would never hear the end of it. I was already dreading the stern lecture that would come when my mother found out I had drunk too much to drive home. He hesitated until I said it again. "It's fine. I promise."

Dr. Wolston waited until he turned and headed for his car before she directed me toward her own. It was an older car, but the inside was tidy. "Watch your head, darling," she said as she loaded me into the passenger seat.

We were pulling out of the bar parking lot when she turned to me and said, "You should be grateful I found you when I did." The implication was clear: Letting a strange man take me home was dangerous. Thoughtless. Irresponsible. I didn't think Ryan would have hurt me, but he easily could have. He could have done anything he wanted to me. *How could you be so reckless?* I could almost hear my mother saying.

"He was a nice guy," I said. I felt the urge to defend Ryan, despite barely knowing him. I wouldn't admit it out loud, but being in this woman's car, knowing she was a friend of my mother's, felt safer than going home with him. *I shouldn't be hopping into strangers' cars when girls are going missing.*

"A nice boy would have made you switch to water three drinks ago," Dr. Wolston said.

I rolled my eyes, letting my head rest against the window. "You're one of my mom's friends? I don't recognize you." While I couldn't name all the people in my mother's circles, usually their faces were familiar, but I couldn't place her.

"I've known her for a long time. Since before you were born," she said.

"Do you need directions to my house?"

"No, I know the way."

I let my eyes close as I leaned against the window, feeling the car move and turn underneath me. I must have drifted off because the next thing I remembered was turning onto the driveway—the familiar sound of gravel woke me.

I sat up with a yawn as the car's headlights illuminated the trees in front of us. "Did you have a nice nap?" Dr. Wolston asked. I detected a sneer in her voice, but I deserved it. I shouldn't have drunk as much as I had.

"Sorry. It's been a long couple of days," I said.

She nodded. I assumed she knew about Maddie's disappearance. The whole town did. "What were you doing out there tonight anyway? Was your plan always to drink too much and then go home with a strange boy?"

"I didn't want to be home alone." That felt embarrassing to admit, but it was the truth. I hadn't had much more of a plan than that.

"Where's your sister tonight?" she asked as the porch lights came into view.

"Friend's house." I was confessing too much to this woman who was essentially a stranger to me, but I was too tipsy to really care. The car rolled to a stop at the end of the driveway. "Well, thank you for the ride. I'll be sure to let my mom know you said hello."

I opened my car door and was surprised to see Dr. Wolston also getting out as well.

"Thank you," I said again. "But I think I can find my own way to the front door."

"Your mother will have my head if I don't make sure you get inside and drink a glass of water," Dr. Wolston said, heading for the porch. I followed her because what else was I supposed to do? She was the kind of woman who spoke with an innate authority that made it difficult to question her instructions.

She paused, turning to look at the trees. "I think our forest at night is absolutely beautiful," she said. I walked past her, climbing the porch steps with my keys in my hand. "Don't you?"

"I think the forest at night is terrifying." After the last few weeks, I found the woods frightening even in the daytime, but the way the dark clung to the branches, obscuring everything beyond the trees, made me shiver.

"You're just feeling how powerful it is. Power is scary only if you get on its bad side," she said while I turned the key in the lock.

I wasn't sure what she meant by that, but I nodded as if I did. "I guess that's one way to look at it."

The dogs ran up to us as soon as we crossed the doorframe. "Daisy's usually a little nervous with strangers," I warned as Dr. Wolston reached for her blond head, but Daisy was already pressed against her, tail wagging.

"Daisy and I aren't strangers," she said, with another pat on Daisy's head. I stopped to lean down and scratch behind Poppy's ear, but Dr. Wolston had already walked past me and was halfway to the kitchen.

I followed her and flicked on the kitchen light. She paid me no attention, walking over to the window and peering through the dark glass. I grabbed a cup from the cabinet and filled it in the sink. Then I took a large gulp and looked over to the kitchen table, where she had already settled herself in a chair.

"That lipstick looks terrible on you; it completely washes you out. It's a shame you didn't inherit your mother's coloring," she said. I was caught off guard by the insult and just stared back at her, not sure what I was supposed to say in response. "You should offer me a drink. Has your mother taught you no manners?"

I was growing uncomfortable with the way her attitude had shifted into something mean. "I didn't think you'd be staying. You've delivered me home safely and watched me drink a glass of water. I'm sure my mother will be grateful."

She ignored my comments. "I would love a cup of tea," she said. "Then I will get out of your hair."

I thought about insisting that she leave immediately, but it seemed easier to acquiesce to her demands. I put on the kettle while she made herself at home, looking out over the trees.

She tapped her fingers across the table, and I noticed the bracelet around her wrist. I immediately recognized it as the same charm bracelet I had found in the forest a few weeks ago. "I'm glad my mom got that back to you," I said, gesturing toward her wrist. "I found it out in the trees."

"It must have fallen off during a walk," Dr. Wolston said, running her fingers over the charms. "I love walking out here with your mother."

"I didn't realize you guys were close." I didn't think I had ever seen this woman or heard her name before, but she spoke like she frequented our house.

She just nodded, smiling politely.

"What are the letters for?" I asked, gesturing again to the bracelet.

"My daughters. I've got four of them. They're all grown now, but I like to keep them close to me."

"That's nice." The kitchen fell silent as we waited for the kettle to go off. I was sure it didn't usually take this long.

"You all have the most gorgeous view," she said, after a few awkward moments. I willed the kettle to boil faster.

"I guess." I watched her as she stared out the window.

"Although I would bet anyone could see inside at night. There could be someone out there right now watching us, and you wouldn't be able to see them unless you knew where to look." Something about her statement felt threatening. This woman, despite her supposed connection to my mother, was as much a stranger as Ryan had been. I couldn't believe I had been careless enough to let her in my home. I was alone here. The nearest house was a quarter mile away. No one would be close enough to hear my screams for help. There was nowhere to run. Where would I go? Into the trees that seemed impossible to navigate even in the daylight?

"How did you find me tonight?" I asked, before considering that I wasn't sure I wanted to hear the answer. I didn't think she had been in the bar, although it was possible I had missed her. She seemed to have just appeared in the parking lot.

"I know your mother's out of town, and I've been keeping an eye on you and your sister," she said. The answer made my skin crawl; she had been watching us. We both turned our heads at the sound of a car rolling down the driveway. Had she called someone? I would be outnumbered. "I know you have been up to things you shouldn't, sticking your nose into things that don't concern you," she said. The car door slammed outside, and Dr. Wolston rose from her chair. I pressed my back against the counter, trying to stay as far away from her as possible. Had she seen us in the forest yesterday?

"Your mother is like family to me. Do not make things difficult for her," she said.

"I won't," I promised, my voice smaller than I would have liked. The front door opened, and I closed my eyes, bracing myself for whoever might come around that corner.

"Lia?" My sister's voice filled the front hall. "Whose car is that?" She appeared a minute later, her face immediately betraying her confusion as she took in the sight of Dr. Wolston. "Sorry—I didn't realize you had people over."

"I was just leaving," Dr. Wolston said. She started toward the front door, then paused at the counter across from me. "Remember what I said: powerful things are only scary if provoked. Don't give me a reason to make you an enemy."

She didn't wait for a reply before continuing to the front door. "You've grown into such a beautiful young lady, Evangeline. Lovely skin," Dr. Wolston said, pausing as she passed Evie.

"Thank you?" Evie said, looking over at me as if I could explain what was going on.

I waited until the front door had closed before racing from my spot at the counter to lock it behind Dr. Wolston.

"Who was that?" Evie asked.

I stared out the front window and waited for the car to disappear back down the long driveway. "Apparently, a friend of Mom's," I said, without turning around.

"She gave me the creeps," Evie said, with a dramatic shiver.

"I didn't love her either. What are you doing home? I thought you were spending the night at Sarah's."

"I got worried about you being here all by yourself," she admitted. "Apparently for good reason, since you were inviting creepy old ladies into our house."

Dr. Wolston finally pulled out of our driveway, and I turned back to Evie with an exhale of relief.

"Ew. You smell like a bad margarita."

Evie and I had headed upstairs not long after Dr. Wolston left. I had already washed my face, letting the bright lipstick and eyeliner wash down the drain. Now I was in bed, Evie's shower audible through the wall as I mindlessly scrolled through my phone to keep the dread pooling in my stomach at bay.

I had checked the locks on all the doors and windows at least three times before coming upstairs, but part of me wanted to go back downstairs and check again. Dr. Wolston had rattled me. Even though she was gone now, I still felt unsafe.

The shower stopped on the other side of the wall. I took that as my signal to turn off the lamp by my bed and try to get some sleep. I plugged in my phone and stared out the window. I could see the barest outlines of branches in the gap between the curtains. Sleep wasn't coming quickly; my brain was too busy sorting through the last several days to let me drift off.

I wasn't sure how long I had been lying there when a soft knock on my door made me jump. I sat up in my bed, my heart thumping a little faster. The door slowly creaked open, the hall light falling across my bedroom floor. "Lia?" Evie whispered from the doorframe.

"What?" I whispered back, even though there was no one in the house we could have woken up by speaking at a normal volume.

"Are you still awake?" she asked.

"Obviously."

"Can I sleep in here tonight?" She was already moving toward my bed.

I didn't bother with a reply, but I scooted toward the edge

and tossed the comforter back so she could crawl in next to me. The mattress dipped as she settled on the other pillow.

"Don't steal all the blankets," I chided as she pulled them over herself. She laughed in response. When we'd been little, my mom would let us have sleepovers on the weekends where Evie would crawl into my bed. At the time, I pretended that I was too cool to really want a sleepover with my little sister, allowing it because Evie was desperate. But even at ten, I couldn't help the way my chest ached when I heard her breathing while she slept; those long, open-mouthed exhales had cracked my heart wide open.

I could imagine every version of her asleep next to me on the other pillow. I'd loved her back when she'd worn princess dresses and cried during thunderstorms. I loved her now with her fierce stubbornness and laugh that I would recognize in a lineup of a thousand other girls. I wished I could reach into her chest and carve out the grief that I knew sat there like a rock.

I could still see the branches in the window, Evie's face silhouetted against the curtains. Her breathing was already slowing. I'd keep her safe, I promised myself, no matter what.

CHAPTER 32
THE MISSING GIRLS

Things changed quickly after Mary died. It was as if Mother needed my life to move faster to make up for the girl who was now gone. I went along with it without complaint, always eager to appease Mother, whose mood was even more tempestuous these days. I was engaged before the end of the year, married the following summer, and pregnant a few months later.

Ophelia was born in the middle of the night, two days before her due date. When I delivered her, I almost felt the pressure might be enough to rip me at the seams. I could practically feel the pieces of me splitting, my fingers pulling apart from my skin. My rib cage bursting open and my organs spilling from my chest. My bright blue eyes popping free from the skull they hadn't always belonged to.

I'd thought I might be like blown glass dropped on a concrete floor. Perhaps I would shatter into a million pieces, leaving my daughter in the center of it all, as the bits of me fell around her like confetti.

"She looks like you," I said to David, wrapping my hands around my daughter out of instinct. And she did. She had her father's nose. Her face was already scrunched like she was thinking about something bigger than herself. I couldn't find an inch of her that looked like me. I didn't know where her chin or the curve of her lip came from. Perhaps the chin belonged to a grandfather she'd never meet and the lips to an aunt who wouldn't even know she existed.

I looked nothing like my daughter. I had never hated my face before, but as I looked at my new baby, her face a stranger to mine, I hated every inch.

Jane had been at the hospital when Ophelia was born and had already met my daughter, but Mother had yet to meet her. Once David was back at work, I loaded Ophelia into the car.

It had snowed a few days earlier, and the last piles of heavy snow were still visible in the forest's shadows. As I got closer to the cottage, I felt the familiar hum of the trees. They seemed to lean toward the windows of my car to catch a glimpse of the baby.

Mother was waiting at the open cottage door as I unloaded the car seat. "How are you doing?" she asked, her eyes going to my belly, still swollen and soft, under the loose maternity dress I was wearing under a sweater. I squirmed under her exacting gaze. I knew exactly which parts of me she saw and found wanting.

"I'm feeling fine, just sore and tired, but nothing that a few weeks won't fix." I tried to reassure her with a smile. I sank into the couch, grateful to be sitting. I hadn't lied to Mother. I was sore, and carrying the car seat the short distance from the car had made my whole body ache.

Ophelia had fallen asleep in her car seat on the way here and somehow managed to sleep through being brought inside. I watched her momentarily, her mittened hands curling under her chin. "Do you want to hold her?" I asked.

"Sure," Mother said.

I carefully extracted my daughter from the buckles of her car seat. Ophelia stirred a bit as I lifted her, a little grumble of discontent slipping from her lips even though her eyes didn't open. I passed her into Mother's waiting arms.

Mother bounced her momentarily, settling her back to sleep as she snuggled against her chest. She ran a finger down my daughter's cheek. "It's a shame she doesn't look more like you."

Rage twisted in my gut, and I had to resist the urge to slap her. My daughter looked exactly as she was supposed to. The implication that Mother wished she looked different—that perhaps she could take my tiny, flawless little girl to the basement and carve her face into something else—made me want to scream.

I wanted to snatch my daughter back and storm out of the cottage, but years of pretending allowed me to stay in my seat and smile. "She's perfect."

Mother didn't say anything in return but made a noncommittal noise in her throat. It was clear that she didn't think so. She continued looking at Ophelia, but her words were directed at me. "I've started on your sister." My stomach dropped, the familiar screaming that had haunted my dreams for years now echoing around my skull. "Do you want a new auntie?" she said, her words higher and directed at the sleeping Ophelia.

"I didn't know if you would make another after Mary."

"Of course. I had always planned on it. You and Jane turned out beautifully. I think some of the girls I used with Mary didn't have a great disposition. I won't make the same mistakes again."

"Aren't Jane and I enough?"

"Elizabeth. Just because I'll have another daughter doesn't mean I'll love you any less," she cooed in my direction, as if my complaints were based on jealousy. I stared blankly back at her and could almost feel the blood that must permanently stain the bottom of Mother's fingernails seeping onto my daughter.

"We're both mothers now," she said, turning toward me. "I thought you would understand."

David and I bought a house in the forest a few years after Ophelia's birth. I had insisted on buying a place in the woods. There was a restlessness that constantly gnawed at me when I wasn't surrounded by the trees. Every time I drove back toward the cottage and the trees began to block out the blue bowl of the sky, it felt like I could finally breathe again. I wanted to fall asleep every night to the whispers of their branches. I wanted my daughter to grow up playing beneath their canopy, bathed in sunlight as it filtered through their leaves. I wanted to be able to slip out my back door on nights when I couldn't sleep and walk until the forest carried me home.

Mother was happy to have me back so close to her. The

cottage was a little more than a mile if you went straight through the forest. There was no trail, but the trees never let me get lost.

By that point, Mother had already started working on Lydia. Her progress with this newest sister seemed to be faster than ever before. I wasn't sure if it was eagerness to be done or fear that perhaps the slow pace had caused some of Mary's discontent. Each time I came to the cottage, she seemed to have some new development to show me in the basement. One day, it would be a heart beating without a rib cage on top, a sight that seemed almost too fragile to be possible. A week later, she'd be working on braiding Lydia's muscles and ligaments, attaching the long, sinewy fibers to the bones. By the following Friday, she'd be doing the careful work of sculpting a face, a little cloud of bone dust hovering around her as she shaved down Lydia's brow. The final step in Lydia's construction was the delicate stitches that would pull her together. This was the longest part of the process. It took weeks of working under the bright fluorescents of the basement to hide rows of tidy seams in her skin so they'd vanish.

Less than a year later, Lydia was ready to wake up.

Jane and I were quiet and almost somber as we walked to the cottage for tonight's full moon. We weren't giddy or excited like we had been when waking Mary. There was a gravity to tonight that made us both nervous.

Jane had bought a house less than half a mile down the same road from me at the end of last year, so we walked together to the cottage. With the moon's light unable to pass through the trees, the darkness hung around us like a thick blanket, making it impossible to see anything, but Jane and I knew the paths by heart. It was one of the last nights of summer, but the beginnings of fall had already settled into the night air.

Back home, I had left Ophelia asleep in her room and David asleep in ours. I would only need to be gone for a few hours, but still, part of me longed to be nestled back in my bed, with my daughter just down the hall. I felt a similar restlessness being away from my daughter as when I was away from the forest. It wasn't unbearable, but it was an insistent tug to be with her, a reminder that she was waiting for me.

These days, I had to do the strange but necessary work of severing myself into disparate pieces. One version of me belonged to this world, to the trees and the cottage. Where bodies were built in Mother's basement, carved piece by piece into girls, where the roots of my trees hummed ancient melodies into my bones. This version of me was a daughter and a sister. The other version of me lived in a big white house with my little family. Where I rocked a crying baby through the night and then fell asleep on the pillow next to my husband. Where I was a wife and a mother. Those two versions of me had never felt as if they could exist inside me at the same time; in each moment, I had to choose who was more important.

"How are you feeling?" I whispered to Jane. "About tonight."

She shrugged. I couldn't see the motion but heard how her jacket crinkled around her shoulders. "I don't know. I hope it goes well. Or maybe I hope it doesn't," she said. She didn't need to explain the contradiction. We had been discussing Lydia and all the possible outcomes for weeks, spreading the options between us like a deck of cards. Possibility one: It went terribly. Lydia never woke up. Mother tried again and again until she got it right. Possibility two: It went wonderfully. Lydia was beautiful and charming and lovely. And Mother shaped her into the kind of woman who would fit in perfectly at the table between Jane and me. Mother would be satisfied for a few years, until she inevitably got bored and needed a new project again. Mother always thought she could do better. This version of a sister would be the best only until Mother thought of something that could be improved. Possibility three: Lydia woke up but was never quite right. Maybe she would be like Mary, marred by an anger and discontent that constantly boiled under the surface, or perhaps there would be some new vice. Mother would be forced to return her to the trees and try again.

There was no scenario in which this ended.

I wasn't sure if it was selfish that Jane and I wanted Mother to stop. We were so charmed and in love with our little lives, both of us with our houses in the trees and me with my daughter. Was it selfish to rob someone else of that same happiness? But it also felt selfish to want another sister to sit with us at the table. Despite Jane's and my reluctance to invite another sister into our home, I desperately wanted to have another woman who understood, with whom we could peel back the layers of pretense and not fear that she'd look at us with horror.

The rhythm of the evening was familiar: Mother stood at the cottage's open door. Dinner was already on the table, candles illuminating the whole house. Lydia waited in the living room. Her body was sprawled across the couch, unmoving, muscles slack and loose. Mother had draped a blanket over her, but her shoulders were bare, peeking over the edge.

We ate while discussing Mother's plans for the garden this spring and things she needed Jane to pick up for her next time she was in town.

But finally, it was time.

Mother passed me a lantern and leaned down to scoop Lydia into her arms. The blanket slipped as Mother picked up her limp body and tucked Lydia's head under her chin. Even Mother had taken on a slightly more somber tone tonight, reminders of Mary loud even in her absence. "Let's go," she said as she headed out the open door.

Jane picked up the blanket that had fallen to the floor and followed Mother. I held the lantern, its gold glow barely touching the dark, but it was enough to illuminate the path in front of us.

We moved slowly, as Mother's pace was tempered by the weight of Lydia's body, but eventually, we got to our little clearing.

I let my fingers brush against the tree trunk carved with Mary's name. Mother had never commented on it, but I was sure she had noticed. Jane and I had come out here the morning after we'd buried Mary and carved it. It wasn't anything substantial, but it felt important to make some tangible mark that she had been here. She had existed. Her life, even if it had been short and miserable, had mattered.

Mother stopped and settled Lydia on the ground, her naked body nestled in the dirt and fallen leaves. We all formed a half circle around Lydia, Jane's hand instinctively reaching for mine in the dark. I wasn't sure how long we stood out here. The wind kissed my cheeks and caressed my hair as I felt the forest hum through me. We waited, eyes sweeping over her skin in the dim lantern light. We looked at her as if studying a marble statue in a museum, trying to comprehend the magic of creating life from something so cold and still. My eyes darted over the curves of her thighs, the arch of each foot, and her chestnut waves as they curled against the smooth skin of her neck, taking in each perfection. But she was not made of marble.

Her chest rose with a little gasp as her eyes fluttered open.

CHAPTER 33

Sunday passed in a quiet blur. We stayed close to home, neither of us acknowledging why we were wary to leave the house. When it was time for bed, Evie followed me into my room again without a word.

By the time I woke up the next morning, she was already gone. The other pillow was empty and the blankets folded back into place as if she had never been there. A headache threatened at my temples, so I climbed out of bed, hoping a cup of coffee would stave it off before I needed to start work in a few hours.

The house was unsurprisingly empty. Evie would have left for school hours ago. As I came down the stairs, the dogs barely lifted their heads from where they were stretched out in a square of morning sun. The kitchen was a bit of a mess, and I started cleaning it while the coffee machine warmed up. My mom would be back sometime this afternoon.

I grabbed Evie's breakfast dishes from where they sat on the kitchen table and went to add them to the small pile that we'd abandoned in the sink over the weekend. I paused, staring at the mug still waiting on the corner of the counter.

I never had gotten Dr. Wolston that cup of tea. Evie had arrived before the water had finished boiling. The reminder of that strange woman's presence made me shiver. Her odd behavior, the things she'd said, the way she'd invited herself into our house, and her insistence that she drive me home now felt even more menacing.

I wiped down the counters, still thinking through the events of the weekend. I couldn't find a reasonable explanation for anything. But I had a feeling that if only I could look at things from another angle, I would find something that connected it all. If I laid out the contents of my mind on the kitchen counter in front of me, there would be pictures and maps, gold bracelets and whispered conversations—my mother somehow in the middle of it all. I had been wiping circles around the same spot on the counter for a while, long after it was already clean, staring out the window at the trees beyond as they cast long shadows in the morning light.

I abandoned the kitchen, taking my coffee up to my desk. I spent the day working until I heard a car driving down the gravel driveway. I knew it was my mother arriving in her Uber from the airport. She had texted Evie and me a little while ago that she had landed.

I closed the project I was working on and went to meet her. As I came down the stairs, she walked through the front door, rolling a little suitcase behind her. "Ophelia," she said with a smile as she spotted me. Both dogs were pressed against her, tails swinging as they pushed each other out of the way, eager for some attention. She was clearly sizing up what kind of conversation this would be. Tensions between us lingered from our fight a few days earlier. We treated each other with a bit of apprehension.

"Welcome home," I said. I had no desire to put her in a bad mood before explaining what Evie and I had been up to this weekend. "How was your flight?"

My mother smiled wider. "Not too bad," she said. Her eyes darted all over the house, immediately assessing if anything had changed since she'd been gone.

"Was the drive okay?" I asked.

She left her suitcase by the front door and continued into the house toward the kitchen. "It was fine. Your father did most of the driving. I'm sorry, I'm starved," she said, pulling an orange out of the fridge. "How were you girls?"

"We were fine," I said. The question seemed genuine, which made me think Kate and Lydia hadn't yet told her what Evie and I had been up to Saturday night. We would need to tell her about it before they got the chance, but I'd wait until Evie got home.

My mom nodded, a small pile of orange peel collecting on the counter. "How's Evie doing?" she whispered, mouthing the words more than speaking them, as if afraid of being overheard.

"She seems fine. She spent most of Saturday at Sarah's house, working on a project for school or something."

"Where is she?" she asked, keeping her voice low.

"She's still at school." I glanced at the clock over my

mother's shoulder. It was just after four. "And I think she mentioned staying after for practice today, so I don't expect her home for another hour at least."

"Oh," my mother said, her brow furrowing. "Her car's here. I saw it as I was coming in."

I paused for a second, surprised. I hadn't been outside today. Evie's car was parked to the right of the garage, barely visible from any window unless you pressed your face to the glass. "Maybe a friend picked her up?"

"Probably," my mother said, trying to reassure me with a smile. "Did you see her this morning?"

"No. When I woke up, she was already gone. But she fed the dogs before she left, and her breakfast dishes were on the counter."

"I'm sure she got picked up by someone. You mentioned she had a project with Sarah. They probably just needed to finish it up before school."

"Yeah," I agreed, although I wasn't wholly convinced.

"Did you get up to anything else this weekend?"

Part of me wondered if Dr. Wolston had already called to tell her about driving me home from the bar. If so, my mother was hiding it well. But, even if she hadn't had the chance yet, I was sure my mother would hear about it soon. "I went to a bar in town on Saturday," I confessed.

"With who?" my mom asked. I was sure she thought it had been a second date with Matt. She would be disappointed to find out he had turned me down.

"Just me. I wanted to get out of the house for a while, but I actually bumped into one of your friends."

"Oh, really?" My mother was leaning against the counter, eating a section of orange.

"Yeah, she gave me a ride home. I drank a little more than I thought, and obviously, I wasn't going to drive. This guy I met was going to give me a ride, but she saw me in the parking lot and offered."

"Who was it? Rebecca from book club?"

"Dr. Wolston."

My mom's eyes went wide, and she inhaled sharply, immediately coughing as she breathed in some of the orange. The shock was evident on her face, and it took her several long seconds to smooth it away as she grabbed a glass and filled it with water.

"Are you okay?" I asked as she took a long drink.

"I'm fine. Sorry. I was just surprised. She doesn't get out much, so it's a little unexpected, but I'm glad you got home safe."

"She said she was keeping an eye on us since you were out of town," I said. I tried to read her face, searching for what had caused such a big reaction from my mother, but she had already put on her mask again.

"Of course. That was nice of her. I'll have to thank her." She threw the rest of the orange in the trash. "I imagine you still have work to do, so I won't keep you. I'm going to unpack and rest for a little bit in my room. We'll figure out dinner when Evie gets home, okay?"

"Okay," I agreed, still slightly confused, but my mother was already out of the kitchen.

Before I went back upstairs, I stopped to look for Evie's car out the front window. Sure enough, it was still sitting on the far side of the driveway. She could have gotten a ride from a friend this morning, but she hadn't mentioned anything about it the night before. Maybe she had just forgotten to say something, but it felt weird.

I sent a text to Evie—**What time will you be home?**—and then waited, hopeful for a quick response. I knew that if she was at practice, chances were she wouldn't have her phone on her, but I just needed some indication she was okay. After a few minutes with no reply, I couldn't wait any longer. The feeling that something was wrong was too strong to ignore. My mom could call the school just to confirm Evie had been there. It might be an overreaction, but I would feel better if we knew for sure she had made it to class that morning.

I rose from my desk and opened my bedroom door. My parents' room was at the other end of the hall. The door was closed, but I could hear my mother talking with someone on the phone. The words were too muffled for me to hear what she was saying. While I waited for my mom to finish her call, I crossed the hall into Evie's room. The bed was still crisply made, her closet hanging open, clothes piled on the floor, spilling off a few hangers. There was nothing unusual there. I moved to her desk, where papers were stacked in a few haphazard piles. I skimmed the surface, but there was nothing written on the calendar for today, nothing to hint at where she might be.

I looked out her window at the trees, and my mouth fell open with a worst-case scenario I hadn't considered until that moment. What if she had decided to go back out there?

I immediately tried to rationalize it away. Evie wouldn't have gone alone. She would have woken me, and we would have gone out together. She knew it was too dangerous.

Unless she was worried that I wouldn't agree to come. Unless she saw something and didn't have time to wake me before she ran after it.

I was already in the hallway, my fist poised to knock on my mother's door. If Evie was in the forest alone… I didn't want to contemplate the possibility.

My mother opened the door as soon as I knocked, only halfway, keeping the rest of her body hidden behind it. "What do you need?" she asked, her voice edged with something that made me hesitate.

"I was thinking that maybe you should call the school to check that Evie was there today. I'm sure it's nothing, but just in case." I didn't want her to think I was overreacting, but a pounding anxiety seemed to demand that I do something.

"I think it's fine, Ophelia. I'm sure she'll be home soon. Besides, the front office is already closed." She tried to reassure me with a smile, but something was too tense and forced about it.

"Can you call her coach, then?"

"Ophelia, it's fine," she said, a bit of annoyance leaching into her tone. "I'm feeling pretty tired from traveling today. I'm going to lie down for a bit, and if Evie doesn't get home in the next hour, we'll call, okay?"

"Okay," I agreed. It was a reasonable request, but there was something about the way my mother was talking to me that made me nervous. She had been too quick to dismiss me, as if she wanted to get this conversation over with as quickly as possible.

She smiled at me one last time before closing her door again. I didn't move for a second, just stared at the white door. She was probably right. It was nothing. I was overreacting. I should have returned to my desk, to my work, and to the last few items on my to-do list, but instead, I headed down the stairs.

I tiptoed through the house. I pulled open the front door, then was careful to silently close it behind me as I stepped onto the front porch, not wanting the sound to draw my mother's attention.

I crossed to where Evie's car sat. How had I missed this? Her car had just been there for hours while I was oblivious inside. I crept closer, as if the car were a wild animal that I didn't want to frighten away.

Outside the car, nothing looked awry, but the moment I got near enough to see through the windows, all the blood drained from my face. Her backpack sat on the back seat, her dance bag on the floor next to it. I leaned in close enough that my breath fogged up the window. Her phone was sitting face down on the passenger seat.

I couldn't breathe. Evie had never made it to school. While I was sleeping, something had happened to her. I stood there staring at the car for a second in shock. The night Maddie disappeared replayed in my head. The phone calls. The police. The questions. The reporters. But this time, my sister's face would be the one in the corner of the TV screen. Her name would be the one whispered in the school hallways, and girls would tell stories of how they'd known her.

Then the back door opened on the other side of the house. I could barely hear it from over here, but I recognized the slight creak as the door opened and the subtle sound of it clicking closed. Someone was trying to sneak inside. I crept along the yard, under the living room windows, careful not to make a sound, hoping to catch whoever had slipped through the door.

The moment I peeked around the corner, I saw my mother. She was off the porch and nearly to the trees by the time I spotted her. She looked back up at the house over her shoulder, her eyes going first to my window and then to Evie's, checking to make sure she wasn't being watched. She took a few more steps, and then she was swallowed by the trees.

I waited for one breath and then another before I followed her.

CHAPTER 34
THE MISSING GIRLS

After Lydia joined the family, Jane and I developed the habit of journeying to the cottage as often as possible. When Ophelia began kindergarten, we made the trip most mornings. It wasn't a long walk, but I looked forward to the time with Jane. She was the only person in the world who knew the whole me, the monstrous parts butted right up alongside the beautiful ones.

My hand strayed to my belly as we walked. My stomach was still flat, but I was pregnant again. Jane knew—she had been with me when I had taken the test—but I had yet to tell Mother. I hadn't told David yet either. He would be glad. He had wanted Ophelia to have a sibling for a while now, reminding me about how close he was with his brother and sister. But I had enjoyed having Ophelia all to myself for those years. I wanted to soak up every minute that she was tiny and perfect without the interruption of another baby.

"How are you feeling?" Jane said. Her voice was quiet, not

quite a whisper but close, as if the full volume of our voices would shatter the magic of this place.

"Fine. A little more tired than usual, but nothing too terrible."

"Are you going to tell her soon?" Jane didn't need to clarify who she meant.

"Not yet."

She nodded in understanding. The moment I told Mother, the pregnancy would become about her, about how my body, which she primarily viewed as her work, would hold up against a second pregnancy. She would obsess about how my skin stretched and my bones shifted, always equally impressed with herself and worried that I would be ruined by the changes. So I'd keep this thing growing inside me secret for a few weeks, letting it be something that belonged to just me for a while.

The cottage seemed to have some of its joy back now that Lydia was here. I hadn't realized how bleak things had gotten with Mary and in the months after her death. With Lydia here, our cottage regained some of the simple charm it had lost. Lydia was joyful and lovely. She was precisely the kind of girl Mother had dreamed of. She was beautiful and always smiling. Mother had kept Lydia home longer than she had Jane or me. It took nearly two years before she let Lydia go into town alone, without Jane or me to accompany her. I think Mother relished having someone with her in the cottage. But recently, Lydia had gotten serious with a man from town, and soon enough, she'd be engaged and gone.

Mother equally hated and loved these engagements. On the one hand, they were everything she had worked for. She had made us to have the life she'd missed out on. She wanted us to find husbands and have children. Her work would have been wasted if Lydia had stayed with her and grown old in the cottage. But letting us go into the world was also a loss. No longer would we be across the table at every meal, sleeping just down the hall.

As Jane and I approached the cottage, singing poured through an open window. Lydia's voice wasn't well trained or particularly powerful. It was light and airy, the sort of singing voice that felt right at home among the spring wildflowers littering the hillside. Jane smiled as the sound reached us.

Lydia ushered us inside, and within a couple of minutes, all four of us were in the living room with cups of warm tea in our hands. We had been chatting for a few minutes, talking about our life updates and what Lydia needed to work on in the garden this afternoon as they started to prep for the first frost, when Mother put a halt to our conversation. "Girls," she said, "I've decided to start on another sister for you."

I should have known this was coming with Lydia leaving soon. She needed another girl, another project to occupy her time. "Another one?" I whispered, and my stomach dropped. "Aren't the three of us enough?"

"Elizabeth, I'll be all alone once Lydia is married. And I think I've finally perfected the process. It should be easy this time," she said. When I still didn't look convinced, she continued. "What I give those girls is a gift, Elizabeth. Look at you and Lydia and Jane. You are all so happy. Your lives are better than anything you could have ever had before. You know that."

"What about their families?"

"Don't get sentimental on me just because you have a daughter now. Some sacrifices need to be made, but it's always worth it," she said. Neither Lydia nor Jane said anything, but I could feel the weight of what this meant sitting on them too.

Sometimes, when the wind cut through the trees just right, I could hear the screams of the first girl Mother had brought home. Could still feel the press of Jane's arms holding me to her chest as that girl's fierce terror sliced through the walls of the cottage.

Mother was back to her usual rhythm with this new project, making each choice with deliberate slowness and patience. Each layer of this latest sister was handled with meticulous reverence, as if Mother could create perfection itself if she just took enough time. The years passed while she worked. Evangeline was born. Lydia was engaged and then married. All the while Mother was slowly building her latest creation.

I'd become good at avoiding the cottage on the nights she brought the girls home. But even back in my bed with my husband beside me, I could imagine the sounds. The thump of their limp bodies as Mother dragged them across the floor, their feet snagging on the edge of the rugs. The desperate cries that haunted my nightmares.

Tonight, I wouldn't need to imagine. All three of us went over for dinner. When I arrived, Jane was already there cooking. Lydia was freshly back from her honeymoon, her wedding band sparkling on her ring finger. Mother had left an hour or so before, out on some sort of errand. We didn't ask questions about where she was going; we were too happy to be together to care. We didn't think much of it, enjoying each others company and hearing Lydia's updates as the roast finished in the oven.

Lydia darted to the front door at the sound of the car. "Oh!" she said, in a little chirp as she stared out the open door. Jane and I rose and stood behind Lydia, watching as Mother opened the back seat of her car to reveal a slumped-over young woman, her head lolling loosely against her chest.

"Darlings," Mother called back to us, "hold the door for me."

I stepped out of the door frame and blinked back the tears that threatened to fall.

Jane stepped next to me, while Lydia stayed by the door, holding it open as Mother had requested. "Are you okay?" Jane asked.

I had never actually witnessed Mother bringing one of the girls home. I had heard, of course, like the first girl with her screams, but I hadn't seen them. More often than not, they just appeared in the basement. It was easier that way. To pretend that they weren't girls Mother snatched out of their lives to serve as pieces and parts for her next project, as if they existed only in that basement, existed only as the next ingredients Mother needed. Watching her pull that limp girl from the back seat shattered that illusion.

"I'll be fine. I'm just surprised." I tried to put on a convincing smile, but I knew Jane didn't buy it.

Suddenly, there was shouting from outside. Jane and I jumped to the door. I wasn't sure what was happening, except

Mother was screaming, shouting for me to "catch her." Lydia was still holding the door, frozen in place, eyes wide. I followed Mother's finger toward the tree line.

I turned just in time to see the girl disappearing into the forest. For another moment, I didn't move. I hoped the trees would send her back to the road, absolve me of my involvement, and allow us to pretend this hadn't happened.

"Get her. She can't get away!" Mother shouted at me.

I didn't know what the girl had witnessed. Had she seen Mother's face? Could she recount the route she had taken to get to the cottage? Had she seen me standing in the doorway? She could ruin everything if she made it back to the main road, so I started running after her. By all metrics, she should have outrun me. Her legs were much longer than mine, and she had a head start. But she didn't know the trees like I did, and more importantly, they didn't know her like they knew me.

Roots reached out and grabbed for her ankles while branches swung low, trying to catch her arms. The ground seemed to push into me at every step, lengthening my strides and making me move faster. I was gaining on her. She spun to look at me, and fear was painted across her face.

Something about the expression made her look so much like Ophelia, a determination behind her terror that reminded me of my daughter. The resemblance startled me. For a moment, I couldn't move. The girl kept running, tearing through the trees.

A branch whipped in front of her, and she couldn't slow fast enough. She fell backward, her head striking hard against the ground.

I rushed toward her. The girl was so still that, for a moment, I thought the blow to her head had killed her. But as I dug my fingers into the side of her neck, I could feel her pulse racing from her sprint through the forest.

Jane's running footsteps broke through the trees a moment later. "Is she okay?" she asked, breathing hard.

I nodded and gestured for her to help me lift the girl. We carried her back to the cottage in silence, one of her arms slung around each of us, her feet dragging through the leaves.

"What did you do?" Mother said as we approached.

"She fell and hit her head," I said. We passed Mother and dumped the girl on the couch. Her body crumpled, almost falling onto the floor.

"I cannot believe you two were so careless with her! I really hope she didn't fracture her skull. That would be incredibly wasteful," Mother shouted at me, but I looked past her to where Jane was leaning against the wall. Her eyes had the same glazed expression I was sure was present on my own face.

"Will you walk home with me?" I asked Jane, even though Mother was still yelling.

Jane nodded and followed me to the front door.

"Elizabeth! Jane! Get back here. You can't just leave. I'm talking to you. We haven't had dinner yet." Mother's voice followed us as we walked toward the trees.

The walk home was silent. Neither of us spoke, even as we broke through the trees at the back of my house. I knew we would talk through everything that'd happened, eventually, look at it from every angle, but for tonight, we were in too much shock to do more than stumble back into our other lives.

David was alone downstairs when I came in. He was sprawled on the couch, watching a trio of men recapping a sporting event on the television.

"Did you have a nice time?" he asked, sparing only a quick glance in my direction. He thought my evening had been spent at book club at Jane's, not looking up long enough to notice my tangled hair or the dirt under my fingernails.

"Yeah, I'm tired. I think I'm going to head to bed early."

"Okay. Good night." he said, his attention already back on the screen.

I climbed the stairs, my feet like lead blocks underneath me, but I didn't head toward my bedroom. I opened Evangeline's door first. She was stretched out on her back, her arms and legs spread wide like a starfish. I watched her chest rise and fall a few times before I was satisfied.

Ophelia's door was only a few feet down the hall. I was surprised to find a little book light glowing over the hardcover she had checked out from the school library. For a moment, I thought she was awake, but her eyes were closed, and as I listened, I heard the slow cadence of her breathing. She had fallen asleep reading. I tiptoed inside the room and gently pulled the book from her fingers, then flicked off the light and rested its spine on her nightstand so I didn't lose her place. Ophelia shifted a bit but didn't wake. I kissed her forehead and left her room, closing the door quietly behind me.

I headed straight for my shower, peeling off my clothes and leaving them in a heap by the door. I turned the water blisteringly hot and stepped under the stream, letting it turn my skin red as I wept.

Jane, Lydia, and I watched Mother gather all the girls she needed for our newest sister. It got easier, almost routine, until the last girl: Krista McNeil. She was young. Fifteen. Younger than the girls Mother usually used, but she had become obsessed with the girl's waist-length auburn hair. She was the same age as Ophelia, though she went to a different school. It wasn't as if I had ever seen her before. But perhaps Ophelia had. Maybe they had sat across the bleachers from each other at a football game or they had been shopping in the same store at the mall, hands brushing as they both grabbed for the same pair of jeans. She felt too close to Ophelia.

This girl had grown into herself in a way my daughter had yet to do. Ophelia was still lingering firmly in the awkwardness of her teenage years, her limbs too long for the rest of her frame, her forehead dotted with acne. This girl had already grown past that, or perhaps she hadn't ever had an awkward phase. But I couldn't help seeing my own daughter's face transposed over Krista's. On my way home, after seeing her body in the basement, I had to yell at Jane to stop the car so I could throw up on the side of the road.

"Maybe we should tell someone," I said to Jane as I finished, my hair still held back in her fist.

"Who? The police?" Jane asked me. It wasn't the first time we'd had the conversation. We often talked about turning Mother in on nights when the guilt was too immense to bury deep inside ourselves like we usually did. "We can't."

She didn't need to explain more. We'd been through it

before. If we told the police what we knew, we'd be implicating ourselves too. We'd be revealed as monsters who had been complicit in everything. We would be studied and poked and prodded and pulled apart again. I had nightmares about it, dreams in which the families of the girls who had made me ripped me apart, each taking the pieces of me that were owed to them. We would lose our safe place—the cottage, the forest, and each other.

Even barring that, I didn't know if I really could have brought myself to betray Mother. Despite everything she had done, she was nevertheless the person who'd made me and raised me. I felt I owed her something for that. And a part of me still loved her.

So we stayed quiet.

Now we stood as we always did, in a little half-moon around the still body that would soon become our newest sister, Kate. I couldn't peel my eyes away from her hair, a bright red streak against the forest floor, as we waited for the trees to give her a first breath.

CHAPTER 35

It didn't take long before I was swallowed up by the trees, the house disappearing behind me. The world sounded different out here; noises moved strangely, echoing as if someone had cupped their hands over my ears. I listened for any sign of my mom, as if her presence would have left behind ripples in its wake. But the forest seemed unchanged.

I slowed, carefully considering each step. I had followed her without a real plan, which wasn't logical. Given that the only thing I knew for sure about the forest was how dangerous it could be, I should've hesitated before coming out here alone. I should have called for my mother, told her about Evie's things left in the back seat of her car, and waited at the kitchen counter while she called the police.

But I couldn't trust her. The thought throbbed under my skin like a bruise. The real reason I was out here was my mother and her secrets. I couldn't risk that she was somehow connected to Evie's disappearance. It seemed impossible, but still, the what-if had prevented me from yelling for her when I found Evie's things. Because I wasn't willing to take the chance.

Out here in the trees, the recklessness of my choice was clear. There was no sign of my mother, and I had no idea where to begin my search. I turned and scanned the dense forest all around me, realizing it wasn't just a matter of not knowing where to go—I wasn't sure I could even find my way back home.

The same dread filled me as it had just a few days ago when Evie and I had gotten lost out here. But under that feeling was a hum in my bones, a gentle urging to keep moving forward, as if the trees themselves were whispering to me. It felt dangerous to listen, but I wasn't sure I had a choice. I picked up the pace again, my walking turning into jogging, as if I were being pulled on an invisible string.

I took the path of least resistance, pretending there was a trail to follow. But branches arched out of my way, bending out of my route. The ground was clear of roots, and the way forward was smooth.

I looked for any sign that my mom had come this way, but I did not know what to look for. The ground was wet but too thickly covered by a layer of leaves to make any mud in which I might find footprints. The trees had always been good at hiding things that did not want to be found.

The deeper I went, the more my determination overshadowed my fear. Evie was out here. She had been gone for hours without me even knowing. I pushed down the aching guilt that this knowledge stirred in my chest. I couldn't undo it, but I could find her. I *would* find her.

I was so focused that when a hand grabbed my shoulder, I jolted back and let out a little gasp. A second hand clamped over my mouth as I tried to scream. "Ophelia!" My mom's voice was instantly familiar, even as a whisper. "What are you doing out here?" Her blue eyes were wide as they met mine, immediately darting around to search the trees for anyone who might have heard me.

She waited half a breath, eyes meeting mine again, asking silently for me not to be too loud, before she removed her hand from my mouth.

"I could ask you the same question," I said. My heart pounded against my rib cage, the shock of being grabbed still working its way through my system.

"Ophelia, not right now," she said, worry lining her face as she bit her lower lip.

"I'm looking for Evie. Where is she?" I asked her. "Her backpack and phone are still in her car. She never made it to school." Saying that out loud made tears well in my eyes as I felt the enormity of my fear.

My mom didn't look surprised. "I'm not sure," she whispered.

I shook my head, struggling to keep my voice steady. "Why are you still lying?"

My mother's mouth pinched tight as she let out a long exhale through her nose. Her face was serious, eyebrows furrowing with thought, but she appeared calm. She looked past me into the forest. I tried to see what she saw between the trees, but all I could make out was row after row of branches, the gray sky barely visible. The forest chattered around us: birds singing, squirrels hopping from tree to tree, and rabbits darting across the open spaces. She didn't meet my eyes, staring into the branches above my head, as she said, "I think I know where she is...and who took her."

I waited for her to explain, but she was silent and unwilling to meet my gaze. "Who?" I breathed, barely audible, over the sounds of the trees.

"It's an incredibly long story. But it will be fine." She finally met my eyes again, and a forced smile was on her lips. "I'm going to go get Evangeline, and I'll be home soon."

"Where is she? Why did they take her?"

She was still searching the forest behind me. "Do you think you could find your way back to the house from here?" she asked.

"I'm coming with you." I didn't answer her question, but the truth was I had no idea where I'd ended up. I turned around and saw that the path I had followed to get here seemed to have been swallowed up behind me. I would almost certainly get lost.

My mom didn't immediately respond, but I could tell she didn't want to argue. "Fine. But if you come with me, I need you to listen to everything I say without question."

"Okay," I agreed, although I wasn't sure I meant it. If the situation came to it, I would do whatever it took to get Evie back.

"Let's go," she said, turning toward me. "It's probably another half mile from here."

My mom talked to me in a low voice as we started moving. "I'm not sure what we'll be walking into," she said, her voice softer than a whisper. "I need you to stay calm, no matter what happens, what anyone says. I can't have you panicking. Do you understand?"

I nodded.

"I promise you, I'm going to get you and your sister out safely, but I need you to trust me," she said.

"Okay," I agreed.

We continued in silence for several more minutes. The forest looked unfamiliar to me, but my mom easily picked through the trees as if she were navigating the hallways of her own home. I wasn't sure how she moved so quickly without anything around to guide her path, but she was sure of each step. When Evie and I had traveled through here a few days earlier, the branches had seemed to reach down to tangle themselves in our hair and scratch our skin while roots had sprung up out of nowhere to trip us. Now the opposite seemed to happen, with branches bending away from my mom, making room to clear her path, roots melting away underfoot. The trees knew her; she was a welcome guest in this place.

My mom stopped. She leaned down toward the base of a tree and started carefully picking small deep-blue berries nestled in a low bush at the base of the trunk. There weren't many left at this point in the season, but she carefully combed through the leaves, hands covered with the edges of her shirt as she plucked the berries and tucked them into her pockets.

"What are you doing?" I asked. I recognized the berries, each one hanging from a star-shaped flower, as nightshade. My mother had taught me the difference between the nightshade berries and the blueberries that grew here that we'd eat by the handful on summer days until the tips of our fingers were stained purple. We were warned again and again about the deadly berries, their poison so potent that we shouldn't even touch the plants.

"Hopefully we won't need them," she said, by way of explanation. I wanted to ask her what she planned on doing with a handful of deadly berries, but she was already moving again. "We're almost there," she added, glancing over her shoulder.

I scanned the forest around us, trying to spot anything different, but it all looked the same as it had before. It was getting dark, the light coming through the branches dimmer than it had been even minutes before.

"Just at the top of this hill is a house. That's where we're going," my mom said. I nodded and tried to take another step forward, but she pulled me back. "I need you to listen to me before we go in there. I love you and your sister more than anything. No matter what you hear. No matter what I say, know that is true." She watched me for a minute, fear evident on her face, waiting for my reaction. "If you and your sister get out without me, I want you to call Jane and tell her *exactly* what happened. Do you understand? Don't worry about me. Just go home and call Jane. Do not open the door for anyone else."

I nodded, and she smiled softly, but her eyes were sad, heavy with a weight I didn't yet understand. "It'll be okay. I promise I will bring your sister home," she said.

I didn't know if I should believe her.

CHAPTER 36
THE MISSING GIRLS

The night Maddie went missing, the moment I could get away from the police and my daughters, I called Mother. I knew she had been involved. She had been working slowly on this new project, Emma, collecting pieces over the course of years, but I had never expected her to take someone so close to my girls. She didn't answer my phone call.

I called again, twice more throughout the night, each of my calls directed straight to voicemail. I stopped calling after that. I didn't want to risk unwanted suspicion if the police decided to peek at my phone records. It was clear Mother wasn't going to answer anyway. She knew I would be angry not only about her callous disregard for how this would affect Evangeline, but also about the risk of taking someone so connected to my family. It was the kind of thing that might eventually tie back to me or any of my sisters and bring people knocking on the cottage's front door.

Perhaps I should have started distrusting Mother sooner.

Looking back, her frequent little cruelties, the ease with which she took all those girls without remorse, and the way she was never satisfied with any of us seemed apparent. But despite all the moments that had made me wary and hesitant, the cottage was the place in the world where I felt most at home.

It took me two days after Maddie's disappearance to make it out to the cottage. My place was a revolving door of police officers, other parents, and Evangeline's friends. I couldn't leave for a few hours without explaining where I was going. I had expected Mother to call me at some point to justify herself, but my phone never rang. Kate and Lydia were shocked when I came to them furious, asking what had happened. They were apologetic. Mother had told them I knew the plan. Jane hadn't known. She would have called me the moment she heard.

When I arrived at the cottage, everyone was in the living room, waiting for me. I didn't knock, storming in through the front door, letting the handle slam against the wall.

Lydia and Kate winced, both sinking deeper into the couch. Jane flashed me a warning glance to remind me to keep my emotions in check. This situation was treacherous; I needed to be careful where I stepped. It was a test.

Mother looked over her reading glasses, as if she had barely noticed my entry.

"You didn't answer my calls," I said, trying to bite down on the anger I had held in for two days.

"I was busy," Mother said, already looking back down at the book in her lap. Those words confirmed my suspicions. It was too late to stop this. I was sure Maddie was already in parts in the basement. Mother was efficient.

"Why, Mother? Of all the girls in this town, why my daughter's best friend?" I took a few steps forward until I stood right in front of her. Her posture didn't waver as she turned another page.

When it became clear I didn't intend to back down, she closed her book with a huff, annoyed that I was interrupting her nightly reading time. The sound echoed around the room, and Kate flinched in her chair. "Why not?" she said with a shrug, like taking Maddie was as small as picking up a different type of cereal from the grocery store. "I needed her. She was convenient."

I knew that wasn't the real explanation. It didn't make sense. It was too messy to be the most convenient option, and Mother liked to keep things tidy.

I felt the familiar click of the closet door as it locked, trapping me inside once again. This was a punishment. I had grown complacent lately. I was tired of the constant upkeep of this perfect facade. My marriage was fine. My daughters were nearly grown. When did I get to be done with the performance? So I had started to let things slip, missing Pilates classes, running errands without makeup. There were nights when I canceled plans and stayed home instead of going out to be seen. They were small things. No one else even really noticed, but Mother did. I knew she hated it. She didn't make a secret of it, telling me each time I violated the guidelines she had tied me up with for the last two and a half decades. So taking Maddie was a penalty for deciding that I could choose those sorts of things for myself. Or maybe it was just a reminder that Mother controlled everything. Even the aspects of my life that I thought were mine alone could be ruined in an instant if she felt like it.

"I should tell the police it was you," I said through my teeth. It was an empty threat, and Mother knew it.

She smiled a wide, mean grin. "If you do that, you'll damn yourself and your sisters as well as me. Do you want Kate to give birth in jail? She was there that night."

Kate had already confessed this to me. She had watched my daughters search from the safety of the forest, Maddie's limp body in her arms. We were all tangled up in this.

"I don't care," I lied.

"Please, Elizabeth, don't be ridiculous. You aren't going to do anything."

"What if I did? Would you kill me like you killed Mary?" That made Mother angry. We didn't talk about Mary.

"No, I wouldn't do that," she said, her face hard.

"Wouldn't you? To keep the rest of the family safe?" I pressed her. That had been her excuse for killing Mary, after all. Her death had been for the greater good.

"Evangeline has gorgeous lines. Ophelia too. Her face is a little too round, but it's nothing I can't fix." The threat was evident in her words, even though she didn't spell it out. Still, I believed she wouldn't dare hurt them. They were an extension of me. There was a clear line in the sand she wouldn't cross.

Jane cut in for the first time. "That's enough, Mother."

"Why, Jane? She's threatening all of us. I thought I might remind her that I can hurt something she actually cares about since it's clear she doesn't love *this* family," Mother said. The words were directed at Jane, but Mother stared at me as she said them.

"Lizzy didn't mean that," Jane said, trying to defuse the situation. "It's been a hard week for her."

Mother ignored Jane's attempts at placation. "It's all mine. Your lives are mine. I made you. Without me, you wouldn't exist. You owe me everything. So don't threaten me because I made your week a little more difficult. I don't have the patience for it, Elizabeth."

I couldn't be in this place anymore. I turned to Jane. "Will you drive me home?"

Jane nodded, looping her arm around my shoulders.

"I'll see you both soon," Mother called as we walked through the open door into the night air.

After that night, I should have taken my daughters far away from here, but I didn't. Even then, I trusted Mother enough to believe that my girls were safe, that hurting them would be a complete violation of everything I had held to be true. They would be safe because I loved them, and she cared enough about me to respect that. Even her threat that night hadn't been enough to get me to stop trusting her.

I looked nothing like Mother. There was no reason I would, but sometimes I'd catch myself in a mirror moving like her. The way we both read with a pencil pinched between our index finger and thumb, always moving, flicking back and forth as our eyes scanned the page. The little sound we both made in the back of our throat when we were delighted by something, like the first flower of spring or a particularly good sentence in a book, like an exhale cloaked in a laugh. She was wound through every aspect of me. She might not have been tied into my DNA, but she had been written into my bones.

If I let myself admit that she would take my girls—because really, what difference was there between them and the other nameless bodies that came in through our front door and left in pieces?—I would have had to sift through myself to find the shards of her lodged inside me. The pieces of me that were too sharp and too ugly to face. The pieces I pretended didn't exist.

So, instead, I pretended the line that protected my girls was a canyon hundreds of feet deep and wide, the kind of place you could drop a stone and count to three before it hit the bottom, something she wouldn't even attempt to cross. But it was just a line in the sand, and it was already being washed away by the tide, even though I refused to look down.

CHAPTER 37

We had to walk for only a few more minutes before the ground in front of me turned from damp leaves to stone. A little house stood at the end of the path. I had anticipated something twisted and gnarled, a gingerbread house from some sort of dark fairy tale, but the house was strikingly ordinary. It was worn but not neglected. It looked like it had been here for years, longer than I had. The wood shingles were littered with the last leaves of fall, the trees reaching toward the house like they were bending down to whisper secrets past the gray shutters. The whole thing was painted a pale green that I was sure made it almost disappear in the springtime when the trees and bushes were green and bright, but as the first whispers of winter had already ravaged the branches here, it sat in contrast to the naked trees behind it.

My mom didn't pause at the edge of the yard. She opened the garden gate without looking and walked ahead of me with determined steps, passing the empty garden beds on her way to the house. I blinked back my surprise. I had assumed we would sneak in the back or slip in a window, but my mom walked straight up to the front door. Fear cramped my chest, and I had the urge to run off into the forest. She turned back to look at me, faltering for a second when she realized I hadn't followed her. "We'll be okay," she promised me, waving me forward.

I gave her a small nod. I didn't have a choice. There was nowhere else to go. I could hear someone moving on the other side of the door. The low murmur of voices. The scrape of a chair sliding back on hard floors. The soft patter of footsteps.

I recognized Lydia the moment she opened the door. I stumbled back a step at the sight of her face. I had babysat for her family and seen her countless times at summer barbeques and family parties. I watched her with my mouth hanging open, shocked to find her here. She didn't even glance in my direction, her smile nervous as she stared at my mom. "Lizzy," she said. Again, I was struck with the familiarity of this nickname that I hadn't heard anyone use with my mom until recently. I waited for her to flinch against it or correct Lydia, but she didn't even seem to notice.

"Hi, Lydia," my mom returned, her politeness a thin, transparent layer over her simmering anger.

"I'm sorry," Lydia mouthed.

My mom just shook her head, a barely perceptible motion. They stood in the doorway for one second and then another, neither one wanting to be the first to blink. They might have stayed there forever if a voice past Lydia's shoulder hadn't called out.

"Don't just stand in the doorway letting all the heat out of the house. Let your sister in." The voice was gravelly, tired, like even the act of calling across the room was a strain. It stood in stark contrast to the bewitching musicality of Lydia's voice and the practiced precision of my mother's.

My mom pushed past Lydia and pulled me into the house. It was small and cozy, not the dark place I had been anticipating. The main room was a similar size to the front room at my parents' house, but it contained a kitchen along the back wall, plus a round table lined with wooden chairs.

"Where is she?" my mom asked as soon as we were through the door. Her voice was quieter than I had expected. It wasn't a demand but rather a polite question that seemed completely divorced from the reality of our situation.

No one answered, but we didn't need them to. We both spotted Evie at the same moment. She was curled up on the corner of the couch, a blanket tucked around her, the rise and fall of her chest visible from here. I moved toward her without thinking, needing to confirm that she was really here. My mom somehow beat me to her. She stroked Evie's cheek. "I'm going to take you home, okay?" she whispered. Even though it was clear Evie couldn't hear.

I reached for Evie's hand, squeezing her limp fingers. The moment I'd realized Evie had vanished, part of me—a part I tried desperately to ignore—had reminded me that when girls went missing around here, they weren't found. But Evie was here, and she was alive. Relief washed through me, even though I knew we weren't safe yet. Tension was palpable in the air, everyone in the room bracing for the next blow.

"Is she hurt?" my mom asked.

"She's okay. Mother gave her a sedative. She's just sleeping," someone answered, closer than I expected. My head jolted in that direction. Kate was sitting in an armchair a few feet away, not glancing up from her phone, as if she hadn't even noticed our arrival. She wore a dress that stretched over her pregnant belly.

"You took her?" I said, words slipping out before I had a chance to consider them. I still hadn't recovered from seeing Lydia here. Despite the fact I'd had my suspicions about Kate, it was still difficult to reconcile this sweet pregnant woman, only a few years older than me, with her role as a kidnapper.

"Ophelia," my mother said. She shook her head. It was a warning. I needed to be careful. Now was not the time to ask questions; that would come later. "You stay here with Kate and your sister. Give me just a minute."

She walked toward another woman I had missed at first. She was leaning up against the wall, almost dissolving into it. It was Dr. Wolston, the woman who had driven me home from the bar. Maybe, at this point, I should've ceased to be shocked by how many familiar faces filled this room, but the sight of her in this context was jarring. My mom leaned in to hug her and kiss her cheek.

The hug lingered, and they gripped each other's forearms like they weren't quite ready to let go. It was a comforting gesture, the kind of thing you shared with someone you knew well. "Why is Evangeline here?" my mom asked, trying to keep her voice low and calm.

Dr. Wolston gestured for my mom to follow her into another room, a bedroom based on what I could see from where I was sitting. My mom followed but didn't shut the door behind her.

Lydia stood in front of me, blocking my view for a moment. "Do you want anything to drink?" she asked, as if I were a houseguest and my sister weren't unconscious on the couch next to me. I shook my head, and Lydia gave me a strained smile before settling into the other open chair.

My mom and Dr. Wolston were talking in low voices, but they were both sharp and angry, venom leaking into their quiet words. "Your daughters were getting too nosy. They nearly found the cottage the other day. It's clear you have very little control over your girls, and it's putting your sisters at risk. I can't stand for it, Elizabeth," Dr. Wolston said.

"You shouldn't have taken Maddie," my mother responded. "Of course, my girls are going to want to look into things. You took Evangeline's best friend."

My mom's eyes darted to where I was sitting for less than a second, guilt etched into the glance. She'd known what had happened to Maddie all along. I'd suspected she had, but getting confirmation was painful. It made it hard to breathe, the air in my lungs suddenly heavier. I waited for the punch line, for the moment when my mother would reveal that this was all some elaborate joke. Maddie would pop in the front door, and Evie would sit up. Together, they'd tell me that they got me. They'd point to the hidden cameras and laugh that I had believed it. My mother's willing participation felt more absurd than that.

"And since when do you get to decide which girls I use to make your sisters?" Dr. Wolston said. Her voice lingered in the space between amusement and malice.

"You took her from my house, Mother," my mom shouted. Again, I flinched at the word she used. *Mother.* Another familial tie to this place and these people. "You could have anyone. Why her?"

"Because I can. She had what I needed for Emma, and I took her. That's how this works. You know that."

My mother took a deep breath. "Okay," she said, giving in more easily than I had ever seen. "I understand. My girls won't say anything. Let me take them home. They won't be a problem, I promise you." I suspected my mom was only saying that to get us out of here, but I hated it anyway. We couldn't leave this place and just return to our regular lives. Lydia shot me a warning glance, urging me to stay quiet.

"Evangeline isn't going home with you."

"Mother, please—"

Dr. Wolston cut her off with a stern look. "Evangeline is going to become part of something beautiful. I'm giving her a gift, just like all the other girls, just like you."

"You can't have her," my mom said, each word firm and distinct.

Dr. Wolston laughed. The sound bounced around the house, hollow and too loud for the space. Kate, still sitting on the couch, scrolling through her phone, flinched when she heard it.

"Elizabeth, I'd appreciate it if you didn't take that tone with me," the older woman said with a crisp firmness that indicated this was the end of the discussion.

Dr. Wolston stepped out of the bedroom, leaving my mom behind, and came to stand in front of me. "Hello, Ophelia," she said. The skin of her face wobbled as she spoke. "Since you're here, you're welcome to stay for dinner."

My mother had followed her and was now standing a few feet behind Dr. Wolston. I kept my eyes on my mom, waiting for her to convey some plan, but she looked stoic, almost indifferent. The only sign that something was going on was how she chewed on the inside of her cheek. The room was quiet. It wasn't the sort of silence you could settle into. It was filled with tension; everyone was waiting, muscles braced and ready to spring into action.

I stared at them, not sure what I was expected to do. My sister was lying unconscious next to me. I had just learned that these people, a group of my mother's friends, had been responsible for Maddie's disappearance. And now this woman was asking me to dinner.

"I think it would be better if I just took the girls home," my mom said, saving me from having to come up with a response.

"Evangeline isn't leaving," Dr. Wolston reminded my mother. "But you're welcome to take Ophelia home before dinner."

"I promise I will be better, so can we skip this ridiculous punishment? Can I take Evangeline with me?" my mom asked timidly as if already braced for the slap of an answer.

"No. There are real consequences to your choices. I hope you reevaluate your actions moving forward and make your sisters and me a priority." From the hook next to the door, Dr. Wolston picked up a car key jangling with an oversize pink bobble key chain. "Do you want to borrow the car?"

"I'm not leaving without both my daughters," my mom

said. She turned the full force of her glare on Dr. Wolston, her feet planted firmly, her hands clenched into fists at her sides. There was something almost childish about the way she stood, like a toddler testing the boundaries of her own agency.

"How are you going to manage that, Elizabeth?" Dr. Wolston said with a shrug, not fazed by my mother's wordless threat.

My mom didn't bother responding, instead turning and moving with deliberateness toward my sister. "Ophelia, let's go," she said. She reached toward Evangeline, trying and struggling to lift her limp body. Evie wasn't particularly heavy but was only an inch or two shorter than my mother. I tried to help her, jumping to my feet to grab Evie's legs. We'd carry her out of here together.

I was so focused on lifting Evie that I didn't notice Kate moving from where she had been sitting. "Mom!" I shouted, trying to warn her, but Kate lodged a needle into my mother's neck.

"Sorry, Lizzy," Kate said softly as my mom collapsed in her arms. Evie's body flopped back onto the couch, with me holding her ankles.

I froze, unsure what to do next. My eyes darted to the door, where Dr. Wolston still stood with a set of car keys in her hand. "Your mother always did have a flair for the dramatic," she said with a roll of her eyes.

CHAPTER 38

"Wh-what do you w-want from us?" I stuttered, still surrounded by monsters dressed as suburban moms. It was cliché, a line probably stolen from some forgettable movie, but I didn't know what else I was supposed to do. I was alone in this house in the middle of the woods, outnumbered, both my sister and mom unconscious. I waited for the terror to hit me, the heart-racing feeling of adrenaline, but the burst I had gotten while following my mom through the trees had vanished.

Kate carefully set my mom on the couch, in the spot I had just vacated. Her body curled against Evie's, her head lolled against Evie's shoulder, her arm tossed across Evie's lap as if she were protecting her, even as she slept.

Dr. Wolston hesitated momentarily, looking at my mom and sister before her eyes returned to me. "I'll show you," she said.

She moved across the room toward a closed door in the corner. "Lydia, you come with us," she said as she breezed past me. Dr. Wolston wasn't careless enough to take me anywhere alone, where I might be able to overpower her. "Kate, you stay upstairs with your sister. And please, let me know if the girl starts waking up."

Lydia joined us, following a half step behind me as Dr. Wolston led us to the closed door.

"Now, Ophelia, I'm trusting you not to make a fuss. There is very expensive and fragile equipment down here, and I don't want you to break anything. I'd rather not sedate you like I had to with Elizabeth and your sister, but I will if it becomes necessary. Can you manage to control yourself?"

I nodded. It wasn't like it would do me much good to start fighting them now.

"Wonderful," she said. She pulled open the door and then waited for me and Lydia to walk through before locking us in.

A set of stairs led down to what must have been the basement, although anything past the first few steps was in complete darkness. As we descended, I braced myself for a room out of my worst nightmares—someplace covered in mold and full of rusted cages housing shivering, grime-covered girls.

Dr. Wolston walked a few steps ahead of us, and before we could reach the black hole beneath, she flicked on a light.

I was surprised by how bright the room was. There weren't any windows down here, but I hardly noticed. A large overhead fixture lit most of the space, but lamps tucked into corners added a warm glow softening what would've been long shadows. There were several tall bookcases filled mostly with what looked to be medical textbooks.

The room itself wasn't large. A desk stood against the far

wall, taking up most of the space. A computer sat on the center, alongside a cup full of pens, pencils, and a handful of pastel sticky notes. A large photograph hung above the desk in a wooden frame, the kind of photo found on a holiday card. Four women crouched in front of a Christmas tree, their arms looping around each other, bodies pulled close, smiles on each of their faces. Mom, Jane, Lydia, and Kate.

Jane's face in the photo was a bit of a surprise, since she hadn't been present in the room upstairs, but maybe I should have suspected her involvement. It seemed like at least half the women in my mom's life weren't really friends but rather accomplices to whatever terrible things happened in these woods. Her white-picket-fence life with her Pilates class and her PTA meetings was merely a thin facade for something far more monstrous.

"That was Christmas two years ago," Dr. Wolston said, following my gaze.

I nodded. Dr. Wolston kept moving toward another door on the far side of the room. I followed close behind her. The moment she opened it, I heard the whirring and humming of machines. Nothing obscenely loud. It could have easily been the sound of a dishwasher running, but it contrasted with the quiet of the other room. An overhead light flicked on, flooding the room with a bright white glow.

This room was not cozy. It was colder than the rest of the house, and my arms were immediately covered in goose bumps. It looked sterile. Most of the surfaces were white tile or metal, except one wall, where the tile gave way to dirt, as if the space were some sort of dollhouse, the fourth wall missing.

The soil wall went from floor to ceiling, broken by roots that peeked through, twisting around themselves. They were throbbing with some sort of energy. I wanted to touch them, to feel the hum against my palm, to sink into them, to let them twist around me and tuck me into the soil. If the trees and their branches whispered, these roots sang.

"Can you hear them?" Dr. Wolston asked.

"What?"

"The trees. Can you hear them?" she asked again.

I wasn't sure how to answer her question because I wasn't precisely hearing, but I could feel them. Their song stirred something inside my chest.

Dr. Wolston didn't wait for an answer, taking my stunned silence as confirmation. "Fascinating. Although I suppose it makes sense that you inherited a bit of Elizabeth's connection to the forest."

I finally pulled my eyes away from the roots and took in the rest of the room. The machines caught my attention first. They looked like things you might find in a hospital, numbers that I couldn't interpret flashing across their screens. I followed the tubes and wires as they disappeared under a blanket draped over a lumpy mass on the table. And that was when the terror came.

My stomach turned, bile rising in my throat as I stumbled back a couple of steps, Lydia's body the only thing preventing me from falling onto the floor. I wanted to scream, but I couldn't get enough air.

Dr. Wolston approached the table and pulled back the blanket, not all the way but enough to expose a head. I had expected to see Maddie's face, but the girl was unfamiliar. I let out an exhale of relief. I shouldn't have been relieved, though; that face still belonged to someone.

"Who is that?" I asked.

"This is Emma," Dr. Wolston said as she ran her fingers along the girl's lifeless face, pushing a few strands of hair off her forehead. That's when I realized it was Maddie's hair. I wouldn't have thought I could recognize her hair without the context of the rest of Maddie, but her waves cascaded in a waterfall off the end of the table, the loose brown waves tinged with caramel highlights. Maddie had always kept her hair long; it had fallen past her waist ever since she was a little girl. My breath caught in my throat in an awful choked gasp.

"Lydia, put Ophelia in a chair. She's looking a bit pale," Dr. Wolston said, sliding a stool in our direction. My knees shook in the two stumbling steps it took for me to collapse onto it. Lydia was gentle with me, ensuring I was situated before releasing her grip.

I choked out a "thank you," my manners still running on instinct.

I couldn't peel my eyes away from that hair, Maddie's hair, attached so seamlessly to some other girl's forehead. My eyes drifted over her face again, but this time they stopped on the birthmark on the girl's cheek. Maddie had that same little mark. It sat higher on this girl's cheekbone, her face shaped differently, sharper than Maddie's had ever been, but it was the same. This face was both hers and not.

I dropped my head toward my knees, taking long, slow

breaths, trying to push back the black that was tunneling my vision.

"If you feel the need to vomit, please make sure to do it in the trash can," Dr. Wolston said, a metal can scraping across the floor in my direction.

I looked up as Dr. Wolston adjusted the blanket, which slipped lower, exposing a few more inches of the girl's pale skin. Her neck and collarbone were now fully visible. She still had some color, a faint pink tinge that seemed to indicate life, even though she wasn't moving. There was no strong smell either, not of rotting flesh nor of something strong enough to cover it. The air smelled clean, with only the faintest hint of something chemical.

My eyes drifted back up to the girl's face, no longer feeling like I might faint at any moment. Even under the skin, something about her looked familiar. I recognized the almost-pixie shape of her face and her collarbones. Her face was several shades too pale, but I knew her features. I knew what she would look like with a broad smile spread across her lips.

"Chloe Brookfield," I said. The name was not a question but a statement. Under the skin that had belonged to Maddie lay the bones that had once belonged to Chloe. I wondered if Chloe could feel this new skin stretched too tight across her bones.

"What an eye for detail you have," Dr. Wolston said. "Yes, most of Emma's skeletal structure is from Chloe. Gorgeous bones. I barely had to do any shaping on her face. It was already near perfection."

I didn't linger on her words. The thought of Chloe being

reduced to nothing more than bones made what was left in my stomach churn. "How many girls?" I asked, pointing at the motionless body in front of me.

"Four," she said, knowing exactly what I was asking. "Five, if you include Evangeline."

I had to brace myself against the sound of my sister's name in this place. The thought of her being taken apart in this room made my insides twist.

I turned to Lydia, who hadn't said a single word since we had come downstairs. She leaned against the far wall, looking bored with this conversation. "How can you let this happen? How can you help her take these girls and turn them into whatever deranged art project this is?" I asked, my voice shaky with rage and fear.

Lydia glanced up at me but then turned her attention to Dr. Wolston. "Mother?" Her voice was small, wary. Like my mom, she seemed transformed by this place into something meek and docile.

Mother. Sister. The Christmas tree photo. The easy way the women moved around each other. It was all too unguarded for them to be merely accomplices to this strange crime. They were family, their relationships innate, carved into the foundations of who they were. I had grown up thinking my mom had no family. An only child. Her parents dead before she'd met my father. But obviously that had been a lie, her family—sisters, a mother—always just a short walk through the trees.

But I didn't get to linger for long on this realization. I couldn't pull it apart and trace its implications down through the web of lies that had woven through my own childhood because Dr. Wolston spoke, answering the question I had posed to Lydia. "Lydia and her sisters help me with my work because they know what a gift it is to be made."

"Made?" I asked. "What do you mean?"

Dr. Wolston didn't respond. She just let me sit there and watch the girl lying on the table in front of us. The girl wasn't dead, although she wasn't moving. She was in stasis, a sort of in-between, as though if I leaned down and whispered in her ear, she might wake, eyes popping wide in surprise to find herself here. She was beautiful, like Sleeping Beauty ripped straight out of her fairy tale and plopped in the wrong sort of cottage.

My eyes drifted to Lydia, who also possessed that same ethereal beauty. The kind of woman who attracted stares because of the improbability of witnessing something that perfect in such an ordinary setting, a Botticelli drifting through the grocery store.

"That's impossible," I whispered under my breath as I watched the body under the sheet in front of me. *Made.*

Dr. Wolston only smiled in response, a snide, slippery sort of smile that made me shiver.

"My mom too?" The question slipped from my mouth unbidden, too quiet to be heard above the whirring machines, but Dr. Wolston must have been waiting for it because she answered anyway.

"Of course."

Memories of my mom flooded through my brain, moving too fast for me to hold on to any singular moment, each immediately replaced by the next. I thought about all the times her hand had wrapped around mine as we crossed a busy intersection, warm and comforting. The way her body had folded around mine in a teary hug at the airport last Christmas. The photos of her that I had seen so many times, I could re-create them from memory: The picture at my kindergarten graduation where I stood next to her, a smile on my face, missing one of my front teeth, while she stood beside me, hugely pregnant with Evie. The photo that hung in the hallway at the top of the stairs of her and my father on their wedding day, the decades wiped away, almost as young as I was now. I knew my mom, could have picked her out of a room even if I was blindfolded. I knew the shape of her nose and the length of her fingers.

I also knew that she had a scar hidden by her hair at the back of her head. I'd found it as a child one afternoon when I'd asked her to sit on the floor so I could play hair salon, my tiny fingers combing through her silky blond strands. I remembered the summer she had broken her foot playing tennis and been surprised when the doctor pointed out an old break from her childhood. She told a story at the reminder, something about falling off a playground, but even then, it felt strange. I had brushed it aside as a symptom of a stressful day, but it had been more. Her bones held a history that she didn't entirely know.

"What do you need Evie for?"

"The muscles and bones in her hands, and probably a few of her organs. I imagine she has a good set of lungs and a strong heart, but I won't know for sure until I get in there. Perhaps even her eyes, although I've always found brown eyes to be a bit boring. Anyway, she has gorgeous long fingers, and her fine muscles are likely incredibly well developed from all those years of dancing. I was hoping to use Madison's hands, but a few of her fingers are quite crooked, and I don't love the look of such prominent knuckles."

Dr. Wolston pulled the blanket back farther and uncovered an arm. The skin was cut open and pulled apart with silver clamps. I could see rows of pink muscle braided around the bone in clusters up to the wrist, but that's where the bone stopped. It wasn't the bloody mess I would have expected from a cut like that. Where the fingers should have been was empty skin laid flat on the table, like a glove without a hand inside. It was tidy.

I threw up into the trash can at my feet.

CHAPTER 39

We went back upstairs shortly after that, Lydia once again following just behind me. I felt differently about her now, knowing that she wasn't just a woman from my mom's book club whose child I'd babysat. She was made up of stolen parts. I felt like if I leaned in close enough, I might hear those girls screaming just under her skin.

Dr. Wolston followed us, waiting until we were halfway up the stairs before flicking off the light in the lab and dipping the basement back into the dark. I wanted to urge Dr. Wolston to leave the light on or, at the very least, plug in a nightlight, in case the girls were afraid of the dark. But we didn't stop, continuing up the stairs and leaving the girls behind.

When we emerged from the basement, my mom and Evangeline were exactly where we had left them, still crumpled into each other. Kate looked up as we entered but immediately looked back down at her phone, her foot bouncing on the floor in front of her.

Jane stood in the middle of the room, her arms crossed over her chest and her face set in an unmistakable scowl, the last of the sisters from the picture downstairs. "Where's Mother?" she asked.

Lydia ignored the question, pointing me toward one of the armchairs. My mother had instructed me to call Jane if I got out of here without her, but I wasn't sure if that meant I could trust her. I wasn't sure I could trust anything in this house. Even my own thoughts felt distorted, as if I were watching everything through a kaleidoscope.

"I'm right here," Dr. Wolston said, emerging from the basement. "What are you doing here, Jane? We weren't expecting you for a few more hours."

"Elizabeth texted me and said that you had her daughter. And I arrived to find not only Evangeline but also Elizabeth unconscious on your couch. What is going on?"

"Jane, dear," Dr. Wolston said, looking entirely unruffled by yet another person entering this situation. "Please stop. Elizabeth is already being dramatic enough without adding you into the mix."

Jane ignored Dr. Wolston, her voice escalating to a shout. "You took Elizabeth's daughter. Of course she is going to be upset."

The two women continued to argue over my head, paying no attention to me.

I looked down at my mom and my sister. There was no possible way that I could get them out of here, even if Jane was willing to help me, and I wasn't entirely sure she was. I would need to get my mom's and my sister's unconscious bodies to Jane's car, and then what? I couldn't take them home. Dr. Wolston knew where we lived. She'd take them right back into the trees.

I was so lost in my schemes that I almost missed it: my mother's fingers fluttered—just the smallest twitch. I could have imagined it, but then it came again. Her index finger tapped against her thigh in a deliberate pattern. She was trying to let me know she was awake.

I glanced up at Kate, hoping she hadn't noticed. Instead, she was staring at me. I flinched as she swallowed, her tongue coming out to nervously lick her lips as her eyes darted to my mom's hand and then back to me. My mom's finger once again tapped its message.

My mom was awake, and Kate knew. And more than that, she wanted me to know.

"Wait," Kate mouthed, her eyes holding mine for a second before returning to her phone.

Jane and Dr. Wolston were still arguing, but Lydia had joined the fight, her voice rising above Jane's from behind me. In my peripheral vision, I could see her hand curled around the back of my chair, but I didn't dare turn to check, not wanting to pull Lydia's attention toward my mom.

Kate stood then, a hand dropping to her belly. "Lyd, can you take over for me?" she said, gesturing at the couch. My mother's fingers were entirely still now. "I need to pee."

"I'm watching Ophelia," Lydia said. "Those two are unconscious. I hardly think they need a babysitter within six inches."

"Someone needs to be watching them in case they wake up," Kate said, her voice almost whiny.

"Kate, just go. We're all standing in the same room. I don't think any of them could make it to the door before we caught them," Lydia said.

"Lydia, go sit on the couch," Dr. Wolston said. "You can keep an eye on Ophelia from there."

Lydia grumbled something under her breath as she rounded the chairs and plopped onto the couch, arms crossed over her chest, as Kate headed for one of the doors at the back of the room.

I flinched as a hand landed on my shoulder. "What are we going to do with you?" Dr. Wolston said, digging her fingers into my skin. I couldn't help but think she was somehow measuring my bones, trying to feel through the layers of flesh and muscle to see if something underneath was usable.

A sudden blur of motion snapped our attention to the couch as my mom lunged at Lydia. Lydia shrieked, shoving her away with the heel of her hand. Although my mom was in shape, she wasn't a fighter. Her movements were vicious but unpracticed. Her fingers dug into Lydia's arm, her other hand yanking back a fistful of Lydia's hair. I had never seen her like this. My mother—who had always seemed to be in control, who could charm a room with a simple smile—was now unrecognizable, consumed by a desperate rage.

Lydia's nails raked down my mother's cheek, drawing blood in streaks, and there was another animalistic shriek. I was frozen, startled by the shocking display of violence unfolding in front of me. Before I could react, I heard a loud huff behind me—the distinct groan of someone who had been surprised by a punch to the stomach.

I flipped around to find Jane had wrapped her arms tightly around Dr. Wolston's waist, trying to pull her away from me. Dr. Wolston clung to the back of the chair, and suddenly it flipped, my body tumbling over itself. I blinked upside down momentarily as Jane was slammed into the back wall, still holding Dr. Wolston.

I climbed up from the floor, unsure whether I should help my mom or Jane, but then a scream from the couch pulled my attention in that direction. My mom had a hand cupped over her nose, but blood trailed down her forearm. Lydia had stopped fighting, her hands fluttering above my mom. I didn't think she'd meant to hurt her.

"Stop." Dr. Wolston's voice rang through the room, and everyone fell silent. I turned and found myself looking down the barrel of a gun. The chaos of the moment before lingered in the air, but now everything was eerily still. Dr. Wolston was breathing hard, yet her hands were steady as she aimed the small black gun. Jane stood against the wall, her hands raised, a little dribble of blood leaking from her lip. I mirrored the posture, fear twisting in my stomach as my eyes locked on the barrel.

"Thank you," Dr. Wolston said. The only noises were the short pants from the women who had just been fighting. "We're done now."

Dr. Wolston turned to Lydia and my mom. "Are you both okay?" I wanted to follow her eyes to the couch, but I couldn't look away from the gun, the black metal still pointed at me.

"Fine." Lydia's voice was soft, almost repentant. "I think I broke Lizzy's nose."

My mom said nothing, but her labored breaths filled the room.

"Kate, darling, you can come out," Dr. Wolston said. I could make out the door at the back of the room slowly creeping open. Kate sheepishly emerged from the bathroom where she had been hiding. She chewed on the edge of her lip, eyes lingering on the ground.

"Please get Elizabeth some ice," Dr. Wolston said, gesturing with her gun. "Jane too, actually. I caught her in the face."

Kate nodded and headed for the freezer without speaking.

"Mother, please," my mom begged, desperation evident in her words.

"Here's what's going to happen," Dr. Wolston said, the gun pointed at my head. "Elizabeth, you and Ophelia will stay for dinner. Then you will take her home before the new moon. Evangeline stays here."

"Use me instead," my mom announced.

"That's a lovely sentiment, Elizabeth, but you're too old, you know that, and I would prefer not to take apart my own work. There will be no negotiating," she said.

"Mother, please," my mom begged again, her voice keening.

"Enough whining, Elizabeth," Dr. Wolston said. "You can leave here with one daughter or none tonight. I would prefer not to be wasteful, but the choice is yours."

The room fell silent, and I turned toward my mom, although the gun remained pointed at the side of my head. She looked at me and then at Evie. Her eyes lingered on my sister's unmoving body.

"Fine." That single word from my mom echoed through the little house.

"No," I said. I crossed the short distance to my sister's motionless body, no longer caring about the gun pointed at me. I knelt in front of her, my hands trembling when I reached for her shoulder. "Evie, wake up," I said, my voice breaking as I shook her. Her chest rose and fell slowly, indifferent to the chaos around us. I grabbed her hand. It was warm, even though it sat limply in mine. I wouldn't leave her here.

My mother wrapped her arm around me.

"She can't have her," I said through sobs as tears streamed down my cheeks. But even as I said it, a cold uncertainty settled in—I didn't know how we would get her out the door with us tonight.

I fought my mom as she pulled me against her. "I know. I'm sorry." She swayed back and forth as she held me, some instinct left over from when she had rocked me as a baby, trying to settle me, even as I pushed away. "Trust me," she whispered into my ear. "What did I promise?"

That she would get Evie home.

I sat up, glaring at her. I didn't believe her. But she stared at me, her eyes pleading for a sliver of trust. Maybe I was making a mistake, but separating the mother who had always taken care of us, despite her flaws, from the truth I had learned today felt impossible. She had sat by for decades and allowed whatever was happening in the basement to continue. She'd done nothing as countless girls had been taken, even when she could have stopped it. But still, I knew she loved us.

I gave her a tiny nod, so small that I knew only she would see it.

She returned the gesture. Then she took a step back,

smoothing on one of her perfect masks. "Ophelia, we're going to stay for dinner. Then we'll head home. Can you manage that?" she asked me.

I nodded, this time big enough so everyone could see.

"Wonderful," Dr. Wolston said from behind us. "Jane, since you're here, will you start on dinner?"

"I'll help," my mother volunteered. "Just let me get cleaned up first."

Dr. Wolston nodded her approval and then gestured for me to sit back down in the armchair, which Lydia was working on flipping back into place. "You'll sit with me over here, and we can chat."

CHAPTER 40

My mother looked more put together when she returned from the bathroom. Her hair had been smoothed down and pinned back into a low bun. She had changed into a crisp white dress, replacing the shirt stained with blood. Still, her face was covered with the evidence of her scuffle with Lydia. She held a bag of ice to her nose, her eyes purpling a bit. A few bright welts littered her cheeks.

Lydia looked apologetic from where she sat on the couch next to my sister as she glanced up at my mother. A bruise was forming on her jaw. Evie still slept soundly; none of the commotion had been enough to rouse her.

My mom quietly joined Jane at the kitchen counter. I could still see her from where I was sitting, but the distance between us made me wary. Kate sat next to Lydia on the far end of the couch, and she seemed nervous, fidgeting and refusing to look up from the floor.

"Kate," Dr. Wolston said. Kate looked up at the sound of

her name, lips pulled into a tight line, waiting for her reprimand. "Could you please explain why Elizabeth is currently awake? She should have been asleep for at least an hour with the dose in that syringe. So, unless she's suddenly developed superhuman resistance to sedatives, you did not do as I asked."

"I'm sorry," Kate immediately said, the words jumping out the moment Dr. Wolston finished. "I didn't actually inject her with much. I didn't want to hurt her. I thought if I could just talk to her, I would be able to reason with her and she would calm down." Kate was crying now, but I couldn't tell if the tears slipping down her cheeks were of remorse or fear.

"And then, while we were in the basement, you and your sister decided to cook up a little plot to overpower me?" Dr. Wolston asked, as if we hadn't all been here while precisely that had happened.

Jane cut in from the kitchen. "That was me. Kate didn't want anything to do with it. When I got here, Kate was trying to reason with Elizabeth and convince her that leaving Evie here was for the best."

They should have just taken Evie home the moment Jane had arrived. They could have loaded her into the car and gotten her out of here before Dr. Wolston and I had come back upstairs.

"I suspected as much. Kate wouldn't have been so bold," Dr. Wolston said. "But, Kate, that doesn't mean you're innocent in all this. You still participated. We'll talk about the consequences of that later."

It was strange to hear an adult woman scolded as if she were a child.

"I'm sorry," Kate apologized again, looking even smaller as she curled around herself.

"What are we going to do with you?" Dr. Wolston said, her attention shifting over to me.

I didn't know how to answer, so I blinked back at her as she continued.

"I don't have any particular use for you with Emma, and I hate to be wasteful. But I also know it is foolish to think that you won't start talking about this place as soon as you're out of here." I knew too much. There was no way she'd let me leave alive.

"I won't say anything," I lied. "I don't want anything to happen to my mom. If I tell people about you, they'll know she's connected to all this too."

"I don't believe you."

My mother paused chopping in the kitchen, like she was about to say something, but then her knife picked up the rhythm from before.

I tried to devise a way to convince Dr. Wolston that I was no threat to her or anyone here. It was the only way I could fathom getting myself and Evie home. But before I could come up with reasons she should trust me, Dr. Wolston started talking again. "You're just wasting your life anyway. Wasting your time. Wasting your brain. Wasting your youth. I'd be doing you a favor by making you something better."

The words cut because I could feel the kernels of truth in them. While I was hesitant to brush aside everything I had done over the last few years as a complete waste, there were many times I had just been waiting for the next thing to happen while the weeks slipped between my fingers. But it was my life to waste; she couldn't have it.

Dr. Wolston looked at me, assessing my form from my feet to my head. "I'm sure I could find some use for a bit of you. Your liver, your spleen, something."

"Why did you take Evie, then?" I asked, desperate to keep her talking. She felt less dangerous during her lengthy, drawn-out speeches rather than the silence that sat heavy with the weight of her plans. "Evie still has so much potential. She's got her whole life ahead of her."

"For one, it was easier. She was just out there all alone this morning. But I mostly wanted her because she's better for my purposes than you. She's prettier than you. I'm betting she likely has healthier organs since she's younger and more active, although it's impossible to know for sure until I see them."

Dr. Wolston's eyes drifted over to Evie now, and her words were becoming quieter. She was mostly talking to herself at this point. Then her eyes shot back to me. "Are you going to offer the same trade your mother did? Yourself instead of Evangeline?"

I shook my head. "I don't think you'd take it."

"Smart girl." She turned to address this next part to my mom in the kitchen. "Elizabeth, your daughter may be trouble, but she's not an idiot. She could probably make something of herself if she had a bit more work ethic." My mom didn't flinch at the words, continuing whatever she was doing at the counter. Dr. Wolston turned back toward the rest of us. "Kate, learn from your sister. When raising your daughter, make sure she isn't so lazy."

My mother continued to work quietly in the kitchen next to Jane, as if nothing were out of the ordinary. I watched her as much as I dared without drawing attention to her, part of me worried that she had already accepted Evie's fate. I was growing impatient, waiting for her to do something, anything. But all she did was chop vegetables, her hands steady, while we stood on the precipice of something terrible. The longer I waited, the more my anxiety grew. How could she remain so calm while everything unraveled?

CHAPTER 41
THE MISSING GIRLS

I tried not to flinch as Mother talked to my daughter. It wouldn't do anyone any good to get upset at her. In fact, it might ruin things and make her too wary. I needed Mother to believe I had given in or, at the very least, that I was playing along for tonight. Still, it took everything in me not to spring from the counter as she told Ophelia that her life was a waste.

I should never have brought her here. I should have taken her home when I spotted her in the forest, dragged her back, and locked her in her room. But I hadn't wanted to waste time. Every moment that I wasn't here was a moment Evangeline was alone with Mother. Another few minutes during which my daughter could be reduced to pieces and parts. But all I had done by bringing Ophelia with me was put them both at risk. Both my daughters were sitting in this room inches from a monster who wanted to rip them up to prove a point.

Jane glanced over at me, silently checking in. We had decades of practice with these sorts of conversations, the unspoken language of sisters. We moved in a familiar dance as we made dinner. Jane took the lead. She'd always been a better cook than me.

Soon enough, she had a chicken simmering in a mushroom sauce on the stove, stirring things gently while I worked on the salad. The conversation on the other side of the room had shifted. Mother went on some lecture about what she felt was the problem with Ophelia's generation. I knew she was still paying attention to Jane and me. She was too smart to disregard the two of us completely. She was suspicious, watching us out of the corner of her eye.

I glanced back at them. Ophelia was sitting perfectly straight, hands folded in her lap, but anxiety was evident on every inch of her face. I wanted to go over, kiss her on the forehead, and assure her that everything would be fine. I didn't know if she trusted me or if she thought that I had given up. I wished I could whisper my plans in her ear, but she was safer not knowing. Soon enough, she'd be home with her sister.

"Elizabeth," Mother called out. I spun toward her, my breath hitching as if I had been caught. "Could you open the bottle of red for me? I want it to have time to breathe before dinner."

"Sure," I managed to say before returning to the counter. My hands were shaking.

Jane passed me our decanter before reaching over to squeeze my hand. "You okay?" she asked.

I didn't bother answering. She knew. How could I be okay right now? I leaned closer, pretending to reach across her for the corkscrew. "Get them out of here," I whispered.

"Elizabeth," Mother called again. This time, I wasn't as startled to hear it, and I turned with a careful smile on my face. "Did you notice that I got your favorite tonight? I thought you might want a glass too."

I glanced back at the bottle. I recognized the label, although I couldn't remember ever claiming it was my favorite. "Thank you," I said. "That's so thoughtful." It was the required response, but it tasted even more bitter with both my daughters trapped in the room with us.

"We'll figure it out," Jane whispered back.

I shook my head. "Get them out." I mouthed each word, making sure she caught the motion of my lips as I worked to pour out half the bottle, watching as the red liquid swirled around the glass decanter.

"How much longer until dinner?" Mother questioned.

This time, Jane answered: "Not much longer. Maybe ten minutes?"

"Do you want Lydia to come set the table?" Mother asked.

I glanced up, hoping Jane would read the no in my eyes.

"No, that's okay. I've got it. I'm about to pull the chicken, and I'll set the table while it rests," she said.

"Let me know if you girls need any help."

"We will."

Jane turned back toward the counter, grabbing a platter from the cupboard. I pulled the berries out of my pocket and set them on the corner of the cutting board, carefully angling my body so no one on the other side of the room could see them. Jane's breath caught in her throat as she noticed, but she steadied herself quickly.

Her stare was sharp, filled with both worry and reprimand. I tried to communicate my plan without words, hoping that decades of silent conversations between us would be enough. She didn't need to understand the details, only to make sure my girls were safe, no matter what it took.

"Elizabeth," she breathed.

"Get them out," I mouthed again—an answer to her unspoken question. I couldn't see another way through. I would do whatever I needed to do to keep my daughters safe.

A glimmer of grief was visible through the understanding in Jane's eyes as she nodded.

CHAPTER 42

"Dinner's ready," my mom said. I hadn't noticed, but at some point, she had slipped off her shoes, and now her bare feet brushed up against the edge of the worn rug. She felt at home here. I could tell by the way she moved through the room, reaching over to adjust how a framed picture sat on a shelf.

The table had been set on top of a cream crochet tablecloth. A trio of taper candles sat at the center, flickering and already dripping wax onto the candleholder. Six wooden chairs had been placed around the table. It was clear one of the chairs didn't match, likely pulled from one of the closed rooms in the back hallway. I was directed to sit in that one, making it clear, as if it weren't already, that I was a guest in the space.

The women took their seats, except Jane, who was still finishing up in the kitchen. I sat between Lydia and Dr. Wolston with my mother seated directly across from me. Dr. Wolston placed the gun, which hadn't left her side since she had pulled it out, on the table between her empty wineglass and her plate. She said nothing about it, but the threat was clear anyway.

A big green salad and a basket of sliced bread already waited in the middle of the table. My stomach turned at the thought of trying to eat anything while my sister lay unconscious ten feet away from us.

"Everything looks lovely, Elizabeth," Dr. Wolston said, complimenting my mother as she reached for the basket of bread.

Kate and Lydia nodded their agreement as food was passed around. I still couldn't figure out why we were going along with this charade, pretending like nothing was wrong. I looked up and caught my mother's eye. She smiled tightly as Lydia nudged me with the basket of bread.

"Try to eat a little something," my mom said.

Jane arrived with the final platter of chicken covered in some sort of dark sauce, still steaming. She assessed the table. With my additional place setting, it was too crowded to add the platter to the mix. My mother popped up from her seat to help Jane. "We'll serve everyone, and then we can leave the rest over on the counter," she announced as she pulled the serving fork from Jane's hand.

Jane seemed a little flustered, but she nodded and stepped toward the table. My mother started with Dr. Wolston, sliding one of the chicken breasts onto her plate.

"No, no," Dr. Wolston said. "I don't want that one."

My mother seemed to falter for a second. "Are you sure? It's the biggest piece."

"I'm not all that hungry. Give it to Kate. I'm sure she's

starved." Dr. Wolston smiled and pointed to a different piece, which my mother served her, the sauce clinging to the meat. Everyone was quiet, conversation halting as Jane and my mom served everyone.

"It looks delicious," Lydia said. "Thank you."

"Of course," Jane said, returning with a bottle of white wine and the decanter filled with red. "Does anyone want wine?"

"None for Ophelia," Dr. Wolston said, before Jane had even had a chance to set the bottle down. "She had enough to drink over the weekend."

My cheeks heated at the mention of Saturday night, embarrassed even now. I looked up to see my mother's reaction to the reprimand, but she didn't seem to notice me at all.

Jane passed the decanter to Dr. Wolston before filling her own glass with the bottle of white. My mother watched closely as Dr. Wolston added red wine to her glass. A pitcher of water was passed to me.

"I think I'll try the red wine tonight," Lydia said, reaching across me for the decanter as Dr. Wolston finished. "Since it's Lizzy's favorite."

"You hate red wine," my mother said. She stood, reaching across the table to grab the decanter. "It'll stain your teeth, and you won't even enjoy it." Though Lydia was visibly shocked at my mother's outburst, she hadn't let go.

Dr. Wolston's laugh surprised me, pulling my attention from the disagreement. "Elizabeth, don't be mean. Your sister can have some if she wants. There will still be plenty for you."

My mom and Lydia held each other's gaze for a long

minute, having a silent conversation I wasn't privy to. Then Lydia released the decanter. "No, Elizabeth's right. My teeth are already looking a little yellow lately. I should be careful."

My mother sat back in her chair, pouring an inch of red wine into the bottom of her glass before setting the decanter down between her and Jane, out of Lydia's reach.

"That's probably for the best," Dr. Wolston said. The women all began eating quietly. I pushed my food around my plate, stealing glances at my mother, waiting for her grand plan to be revealed.

She wasn't eating much either, darting sneaky glances at Dr. Wolston every few seconds instead of ever bringing the fork to her mouth.

"Eat something, Elizabeth," Dr. Wolston said, noticing that my mother hadn't actually taken a bite of anything yet. "I didn't buy this food for it to go to waste."

"Sorry, just a bit distracted," Mom said before sliding a forkful of chicken into her mouth.

"It's good, isn't it?" Dr. Wolston said with another one of those slippery, malice-filled smiles.

"Delicious."

Dr. Wolston picked up her glass of wine, clearing her throat. The rest of the table seemed familiar with this behavior, setting down their forks and picking up their glasses. I followed suit, grabbing my own glass as Dr. Wolston began. "I know it's been a challenging day," she started, as if she had experienced an inconvenience at the post office rather than kidnapped my sister, "but I'm so grateful to be sharing a meal with my beautiful daughters." She lifted her glass, and the rest of the table did the same. "A toast to the new moon. To endings and new beginnings."

Lydia's glass clinked against mine, and then Dr. Wolston echoed the gesture, even though I hadn't moved.

"It's bad luck if you don't take a drink," Dr. Wolston said, tilting her glass toward mine, which was still raised in my hand.

I swallowed a mouthful of water as she stared at me over her wineglass, mirroring me and taking a long drink of her own.

My mother, too, took a sip of her wine. The room felt like it was starting to close around me. Maybe there was no getting out. Perhaps this dinner was just prolonging the inevitable. Maybe my mother was already resigned to leaving her daughters to be swallowed by this place. She licked her lips, already stained by the wine.

"Now, Elizabeth," Dr. Wolston said, "I've given it some thought and am willing to let you take your girls home. I will need to have much more of a say in how you're raising them. Clearly, what you've done so far hasn't resulted in them making the best choices, but they have potential."

I loosed an exhale. I barely even listened to the rest of what Dr. Wolston said. It didn't matter. She was going to let us go. We'd figure out the rest later.

"Thank you," my mother said. Her voice was tight, filled with emotions.

"Of course. I'm not an unreasonable woman. However, you'll need to help me replace Evangeline." I flinched at that, but my mother seemed unfazed by the idea of kidnapping another girl. "Let's talk details. First of all, Ophelia, we need to get you a proper job for a young woman of your abilities. What you do and who you date reflect directly on your mother, and it's important to make the most of what you've been given." Dr. Wolston took another big swallow of her wine. "This wine has more sediment than usual," she said, wrinkling her nose and holding out her glass. I could see it; there was a swirl of debris around the bottom, catching the candlelight. "Anyway." Dr. Wolston nodded and returned to her explanations. "We'll need to talk about where Evangeline is going to school in the fall…"

I looked up. My mother had been quiet during this conversation. Her face was unnaturally pale, her pupils so big that they seemed to swallow her eyes. Her gaze wandered aimlessly, unable to focus on anything in the room, while her lips pressed into a tense, thin line.

"Mom?" I interrupted Dr. Wolston, who was still talking about the prestige of Evie's various college options. "Are you okay?"

All the eyes on the table turned toward my mother as she let out a desperate gasp for air.

CHAPTER 43
THE MISSING GIRLS

The moment after Mother said she'd let Evangeline go, I almost regretted it. I nearly knocked the glass from her hand and confessed everything. But the thought disappeared just as quickly, when I realized that Mother letting my daughters go wasn't a surrender but a strategy.

She knew if she hurt one of my girls, it would be over. I would be done. If my worst fears came true, everything else would become significantly less frightening in comparison. She wouldn't be able to control me anymore. Instead, Mother would add my daughters to her web, a few new dolls in her collection. But their lives weren't hers to play with. They weren't even mine to trade away. Their lives belonged to them. Still, I managed to choke out a "thank you."

I watched as Mother took another sip of her wine. I couldn't risk poisoning my daughter or my sisters, so I had put the berries in the decanter of red wine—the wine that only she'd drink. Except I would have to drink it too. I knew I couldn't refuse it. I couldn't rouse any suspicion that something was off. I had squeezed the berries into the decanter, pinching each one I until their juice had run down the sides. I felt every spot where their residue had touched my skin—my fingertips burning, red patches of irritation blooming across my hands. I pulled my sleeves down, hoping no one else would notice. I didn't know much about the poison, about how large a dose would be needed to kill her or, at the very least, incapacitate her for a while, but I hoped it would be enough.

I tried my best not to drink the wine, to only let it touch my lips without looking suspicious, as Mother watched me closely. I knew she suspected that Jane and I were plotting something, but I didn't think she would suspect this. I didn't think she'd believe we'd go as far as to poison her.

"Of course. I'm not an unreasonable woman. However, you'll need to help me replace Evangeline," Mother said. But if tonight went as planned, no more girls would vanish here.

Mother continued talking, listing her plans for my daughters, but I wasn't listening anymore. It happened quickly; my face felt hot, and my throat tightened. Relief washed over me at the same moment the panic did. If I couldn't breathe, there had been enough of the berries in the wine. Mother would follow me soon. She had already drunk more than me. I held in the cough that threatened to escape. I didn't want to draw attention to myself. I wanted Mother to keep drinking, another few swallows, another few sips of poison.

I looked at my sisters around the table. We all loved Mother in the way we had been instructed to. It was the debt we owed. It was a love primarily based on obligation. But we turned to each other at night, sharing whispers and giggles between the beds in that second bedroom, two of us jammed in each bed on nights when we slept over. We danced at each other's weddings. We cried together when our skin didn't feel like it fit right. We told each other stories of the first boys we'd kissed. We watched each other's children grow up. We were each other's longest and deepest friendships. I hoped Kate and Lydia would forgive me for this, that they'd understand I had no choice. After tonight, they would be free too.

My breaths were getting more difficult, and panic was rising. It felt like I was drowning, desperate for air.

"Mom?" Ophelia interrupted. "Are you okay?" Ophelia, my brave, smart, resilient girl, I knew she would take good care of her sister for me. I was so proud of her, and I wished I could tell her that one more time. But I couldn't breathe.

The world was going dark around me as I clutched at my throat. Jane jumped to her feet and was kneeling next to me a moment later. I could hear shouting from the other side of the table, but I wasn't listening. Jane held my hand as tears dripped down her cheeks. "I'll take care of them," she promised.

I felt each of the girls who made me. I had never learned their names. But I remembered them, the pieces of all the girls who had come before me. I felt each of them fighting to keep me alive. *Breathe*, they whispered inside me. But I couldn't. My vision tunneled, the edges fading to darkness as Jane held my hand, her voice growing distant.

The moment everything went black, Mary's face flashed through my mind. I wondered what she would think about this. She had been the only one brave enough to be honest about what we were, what Mother was.

My sisters would no longer be Mother's dolls. They could live a life they could be proud of without Mother hovering over every decision, waiting for the moment when she asked them to take the next screaming girl. My daughters could walk through the forest without being afraid.

They would all be free.

CHAPTER 44

The moment my mother started coughing, the table broke into chaos. Her face turned red as she desperately gasped for air. Was this part of her plan? Some sort of distraction I was supposed to use to get Evie out? I looked at my mom and then at Jane, hoping one of them would reveal what I was supposed to do next.

"Jane, what did you do? What did she do?" Dr. Wolston yelled. She stood so quickly that her chair fell over behind her, clattering against the floor.

Jane didn't answer, instead climbing out of her chair to kneel beside my mother, who wasn't coughing anymore. She clutched at her throat, taking in loud wheezing inhales, fighting for each gasping breath. The sound was terrible, but I couldn't look away. Her hands clutched at Jane. I felt frozen, panic holding my limbs in place. This wasn't a distraction. Something was wrong.

"Jane, tell me," Dr. Wolston demanded, her voice getting frantic.

Then Dr. Wolston started coughing too. The same desperate wheezing coughs that had emerged from my mother only a moment earlier. She clawed at her throat as I watched, the only one still in my seat. Lydia and Kate had both pushed away from the table to stand beside Jane and my mother.

Dr. Wolston lurched back toward the table as she coughed. She was frenzied, her hand dipping directly into the chicken on her plate, leaving a streak of sauce that trailed up her sleeve. She knocked into her wineglass next, the red bleeding into the white tablecloth. She was still shouting at Jane and the rest of them, focused on them, not looking where she was reaching.

Her fingers continued to move clumsily across the table. Suddenly, I realized she was looking for the gun. Just as her fingers brushed the cold metal barrel, I grabbed it, springing to my feet and pointing it straight at her.

"Ophelia," Dr. Wolston warned between coughs. She lifted her hands, showing me her palms as she took a step back. That was enough to attract the attention of the women around my mother. Lydia gasped as she noticed, but none of them moved toward me. The room was eerily quiet now, except for Dr. Wolston's rattling breaths.

The gun was shaking in my hands as I continued to point it at Dr. Wolston. She took another step backward. "Stop moving," I said, my voice steadier than I felt.

She froze, lifting her hands higher. "Ophelia," she said, with another wheezing breath. "You don't want to do that."

But I did. She was a monster. I didn't know how many girls she had taken down to her basement and pulled apart over the decades, but it was too many. And she wasn't finished. If I let her, she would take more.

A loud clatter from the other side of the table drew my attention for a moment. My mother had passed out and was now slumped over on Jane's shoulder. "Help me lay her on the floor," Jane told Lydia.

I saw Dr. Wolston move out of the corner of my eye. "Stop," I said, turning back to her. Her mouth was wide open, almost panting, as she tried to suck in another inhale. She leaned against the back of a chair.

"Put the gun down, darling," Dr. Wolston said, the words difficult for her to force out.

I shook my head.

"Jane!" Dr. Wolston said with more volume than I thought possible, given how labored her breaths had become. "What did she do? Was it the belladonna?"

I couldn't see my mother anymore; the women had laid her down on the other side of the table. But Jane was still kneeling in the same spot, tears streaking down her cheeks. She nodded. "In the wine."

"Thank you, Jane," Dr. Wolston said before turning back to me. Her words were slurred, even as she tried to carefully articulate each one. "I know how to help your mom. But we don't have a lot of time. Put the gun down. I promise I will let you and your sister go."

I waited for a breath and then another before lowering the gun, letting it hang loosely at my side, the metal resting heavily against my thigh.

"Thank you," she said, each word difficult. "Lydia," she

said. Lydia's head popped up from behind the table. She was crying too, her chest rising with shaky inhales. "Go to the basement and get the physostigmine," Dr. Wolston instructed. She had to pause every few words to suck in more air. "It should be a white box, on the second shelf in the cabinet closest to the door. Bring everything we have. And some syringes."

Lydia jumped to her feet and started for the basement door.

By the time Dr. Wolston finished her instruction, I could tell she was close to passing out. She was leaning most of her weight against the back of the chair, both hands gripping it so tightly, her knuckles were going white. Her eyes closed as she bent forward, focusing on trying to breathe.

I didn't think she was thinking very clearly either. Her brain must have been working slower with the lack of oxygen. Otherwise, she would have demanded the gun.

I raised the barrel again, and before anyone even had time to notice, I pulled the trigger. For Chloe. For Maddie. For Krista McNeil and all the girls whose names had been forgotten. For their families and the people who had loved and grieved them, who had never forgotten their names and faces. For taking and threatening my sister. Dr. Wolston had said we could leave. But how long would that have lasted? We'd leave today, but if this monster remained here, we'd never feel safe.

And maybe even for my mother. There was still so much I didn't know about her, a whole life she'd lived in secret, so much more complicated than I could have imagined, monstrous and rotting under the beautiful, perfect exterior.

I was surprised by how strong the kickback was, jolting me back a step. I closed my eyes in the instant after the gun went off. There was a second of silence after the loud bang of the gunshot before the screaming started. Lydia let out a piercing wail from where she stood by the basement door. Kate repeated, "Oh my god. Oh my god," through her sobs.

I stood there with my eyes closed, still holding the gun out in front of me.

"I'm coming up behind you," Jane said softly as the other women continued to sob and scream. She put her hand on my back, her palm warm through my shirt as it rested against my spine. "You're safe now. I've got you."

I opened my eyes. Dr. Wolston was lying on the floor in a growing puddle of blood. So much blood. My stomach turned, and I worried I might throw up.

"Hey, look at me," Jane said. I looked away from the crumpled, lifeless heap of Dr. Wolston's body and met Jane's eyes. Mascara had smudged along her lashes. She had a scratch on her cheek from earlier this evening. "Can I have the gun?"

She slowly reached for the barrel when I didn't say anything. She pulled it out of my hand and exhaled deeply once she had it safely out of my palm.

"I'm sorry," I whispered. I wasn't sure what I was apologizing for. The mess? The dramatics? Maybe it was just the instinct of manners still working even though the rest of me was frozen. I wasn't sorry I had done it. Even as the shock of having killed someone rolled through me, I knew I had made the right choice.

"Don't apologize. You did what needed to be done," Jane said. She led me away from the table and had me sit on the couch next to my sister, where I couldn't see the body anymore.

Evangeline was still out cold, her chest moving with the long, lazy breaths of sleep. "Stay here for a minute, okay?"

I nodded, and Jane headed toward Lydia, whose screams had turned to ragged sobs as she leaned forward, hands braced against her knees.

"I need you to go downstairs to get the white box on the second shelf in the cabinet closest to the door, plus the syringes," Jane said, gripping Lydia's shoulder as she repeated Dr. Wolston's instructions. "Hurry. Elizabeth needs it."

Lydia nodded, wiping her face with both hands before righting herself and stepping through the basement door.

CHAPTER 45

The women hovered over my mother in the corner. Lydia returned from the basement with her arms full of little boxes. I was only half paying attention to what they were doing. I couldn't focus on anything as images from the last few hours reeled through my mind like a movie montage: A few seconds of that body lying in the basement. Dr. Wolston's back bent over the chair a moment before the gun went off. My mother's face as she gasped for air.

I avoided any thoughts of the body that lay across the room. From where I was sitting, I could just barely make out the edge of the puddle of blood, slowly spreading across the floor. I had shot her. I had killed her. There was so much blood.

"It's not working," Lydia whispered from next to my mom.

Jane wiped her face with her forearm, rising onto her knees. "We just need to keep her heart pumping," she said as she started chest compressions.

I reached for Evie's hand. Her fingers were limp but warm. I used my other hand to curl her fingers around mine. Our mom was dying. The thought made me feel incredibly small, like a child who had gotten lost in a busy shopping mall. I wanted my mom. I wished she were here, rubbing circles on my back like she would when we were sick as kids, staying next to us until we fell asleep.

She had watched and said nothing as countless girls had been taken down to the basement and pulled apart, but she had also raised me and my sister, kissing scraped knees and packing peanut butter sandwiches. She was controlling and sometimes even mean, but she was the first person I called when something in my life went wrong. She was broken and messy, and I hated her for what she had participated in, but I loved her too. She had known what she was doing today from the moment she picked those berries in the forest. She had been willing to die to save us.

Jane rose, and Lydia took over the same rhythm of compressions on my mother's chest, a silent drumbeat that filled the room. "Hey," Jane said, pulling my attention from my mother. "Lydia and I need to move the body. Are you okay to stay here?"

I got stuck on that word: *body*. It felt strange that Jane hadn't called Dr. Wolston by her name, as if she had ceased to be someone when she stopped breathing. Was my mother a body yet?

"Should we call an ambulance?" I wondered aloud.

Jane shook her head. "No. We can take care of her here."

I wasn't sure if I believed her, but Jane didn't give me a

chance to protest. She stood and left me sitting there. Lydia's hands were replaced by Kate's on my mother's chest.

"Don't touch her mouth," Jane instructed as the other two women moved to where Dr. Wolston's body lay. They whispered back and forth for a few minutes, not loud enough for me to make out what they were saying.

As soon as they bent to pick her up, I turned away, staring at a blank spot on the wall across from me. I could hear the shuffling of their feet as they carried her out of the room. Kate let out a single choked wail as they took Dr. Wolston's body out the front door. I waited until the door clicked closed before turning back to where Kate was pressing on my mom's chest. Tears were streaking down her cheeks. A trail of blood cut through the whole front room. It would be impossible to clean. Tonight's events had left a stain on everything.

Jane was gone for only a few minutes, then returned through the front door without Lydia. "Lyd's taking her out to the clearing in the wagon," she announced to Kate before washing her hands in the sink.

Kate nodded blankly, continuing chest compressions on my mother.

Jane knelt in front of me. Her shirt had a smear of blood across the front. "I need your help carrying Elizabeth."

"Where?" I asked, my voice strange in my own ears.

"Just through the front doors. We have a wheelbarrow we'll use from there."

"She needs to go to the hospital," I said, although she had already rejected my suggestion of calling an ambulance.

Jane shook her head, not bothering to explain. "Lydia's

already out there. And Kate can't carry anything heavy. Please, I need your help just to lift her into the wheelbarrow." I nodded. "You can come, or you can stay here. Your choice."

"What about Evie?" I asked, my sister's limp hand still clutched in mine.

"She shouldn't wake up. We won't be gone long."

I followed Jane to where my mom was stretched out on the floor. All the color was gone from her lips and cheeks, her skin taking on a bluish tinge. She looked dead. My stomach rolled as Jane slid her warm hand along my back.

"We need to move quickly. We'll only have a few minutes once we stop compressions," she said, her voice both soft and assertive.

At some point, Jane must have brought a stretcher over because now it lay next to my mother. I didn't ask questions about why they had one. I knew.

It was easier than I would have expected to get my mother's limp form onto the stretcher and then carry her through the same door we had walked through earlier that evening. As soon as we were outside, Jane lowered the stretcher to the ground, and we lifted my mom into a wheelbarrow. She barely fit, curled inside it, looking impossibly small. Jane didn't wait; the moment my mom was settled, she took off for the trees.

Kate came up behind me and took my hand in hers, giving it a silent squeeze. We followed Jane. Night had fallen while we were inside the cottage, and the dark hung over everything. Once we were in the trees, I couldn't see more than a foot in front of me. Kate and Jane seemed unbothered by the deep dark, moving quickly by instinct alone. I should've been bumping into branches and tripping over roots, but the forest seemed to morph around us, the trees bending away to create a smooth path for us to follow.

Part of me, the logical piece of my brain that was still working, warned me that I should be terrified of the darkness, but there was something almost tranquil and comforting about being here in the trees.

I wasn't expecting the clearing when I emerged into it. But I recognized it immediately—the perfect round little meadow I had visited twice before. Lydia was already here, digging a hole. It was too dark to make out the details, but I could see enough to realize that the lump on the ground next to her as Dr. Wolston's body.

The sky above us was flecked with stars. It was a new moon. Kate had paused at the edge of the clearing. She dropped my hand and took off her shoes, gesturing for me to do the same. I followed her lead without question. Something sacred hung over this place tonight. I didn't want to disturb it.

The ground was cold and wet against my soles, grass and soft moss tickling my toes. Jane had wheeled my mother close to Lydia on the other side of the clearing, and Kate walked toward her as soon as both our shoes were removed.

"Help me get her on the ground," Jane told me as soon as I was close enough for her to speak without shouting. It was even easier this time to lift my mother's body, carrying her a few feet before laying her gently on the mossy ground. In the dark, it was impossible to see the pallid details of my mom's face. She looked like she was sleeping peacefully, as if tonight had been a bad dream.

"What are we doing?" I asked in a whisper.

"You'll see," Jane replied.

Kate reached for my hand again as I stood, while Jane moved over to where Lydia was still working to dig a shallow hole. "It's deep enough," Jane said.

"I don't think so," Lydia said. She didn't stop digging. There was something frantic about her movements. Jane reached out and grabbed her shovel.

"We don't have time, Lyd. It'll be okay. The trees will take care of her," Jane said. Her voice broke on the last words. Jane carefully pulled the shovel from Lydia's hands and leaned it against the trees. "Let's get her in."

Kate and I watched as the other two women rolled Dr. Wolston's body into the shallow grave. Kate let out a little sob, her shoulders shaking, as the women rose and joined us. Kate reached for Lydia, whose hand was already in Jane's, and the four of us created a little chain around my mom.

Kate was still crying, but besides that, we stood in silence. I didn't know what we were expecting to happen. I watched the faces of the other women, waiting for them to announce the next steps. But then I felt the hum. It warmed the soles of my bare feet, moving through me, pumping into my blood and bones like summer sun. I gasped as I felt it, but the others seemed unsurprised, their eyes fixed on my mother's face.

"It's not working," Lydia whispered.

"Shh. Wait," Jane said.

The sounds of the forest at night folded in around us. It took another minute, each second slowly ticking by, before a deep, gasping inhale broke through the silence.

My mother's chest rose, and then her eyes flickered open. Jane was kneeling next to her instantly, pushing her hair away from her face. "Mother?" my mom croaked. Her voice was weak. I could barely hear it even though I was only a couple of feet from her.

"Gone," Jane assured her.

"My girls?"

"They're safe."

My mom's eyes fluttered closed again, as if those two short questions had taken all the energy she had in her, but her chest continued to rise and fall. She was alive.

CHAPTER 46

My mom woke again once we had gotten back to the cottage. Jane wanted to keep her here to make sure she recovered well, but my mom insisted we go home. She didn't want Evie to wake up here and didn't want to be away from us.

So, not long after, our feet covered in dirt, our shoes in our hands, we were sitting in the back of Jane's car. Evie was still asleep, though she seemed more restless now. She almost woke as we carried her to the car, her eyes fluttering open for a few seconds before falling closed again.

My mother sat between us, an arm wrapped around each of us, even as her eyes shut. During the short drive home, I drifted between waking and sleeping, but my body was aware of the subtle shifts of each turn in the road. At some point, I found my sister's hand across my mother's lap and held it in mine.

After a few minutes, the car slowed, the sound of gravel under the tires as familiar as my first name. I opened my eyes and watched the house emerge from the dark. I had never been more grateful to see the porch lights, beacons of a safe harbor.

My mom was still asleep, her cheek resting against Evie's head. "Mom," I whispered, shaking her shoulder. "We're home."

Jane and I helped her into the house, one of us tucked under each arm. Then we carried Evie in from the car. We laid them both on the couch, not wanting to carry them up the stairs. The dogs were grateful for our return, greeting us with wagging tails before settling down to lie on the ground next to my sister and mom.

"Will you be okay for a few hours? I'm going to head back to the cottage to help Lydia and Kate clean up," Jane whispered.

I remembered how much blood had coated the floor. I didn't think getting it all out would be possible. I didn't even want to think about the basement. The whole place felt like a terrible nightmare that I hoped would fade when I opened my eyes in the morning. But I knew it wouldn't. The weight of everything that had happened sat heavily on my chest.

Jane seemed exhausted. Her face was heavy and sad. "You did the right thing," she said again, squeezing my arm. "Your mom's going to be proud of you."

I waited for a glimmer of satisfaction to hit me, as it usually did when I did something my mother would approve of, but it never came. Tonight hadn't been about earning my mother's approval. I had done it for Evie, for all the girls who'd come before—in a smaller way, for my mother too. Not because I thought it would make her proud, but because no one deserved to be controlled by a monster. My entire life, I had measured myself against my mother's expectations, but tonight those expectations had crumbled to ash around me. It had never been real—her effortless perfection was carefully crafted, leaving a trail of casualties in its wake.

"Get some sleep. I'll let myself out," Jane said before turning for the front door.

As soon as the door closed, I pulled myself up the stairs. I was initially only going to change, but the moment I saw myself in the mirror, I knew I needed to shower. I was flecked in blood. It had splattered across my face and neck, a collection of deep-red dots sprinkled over my skin.

I rinsed myself off as quickly as possible, leaving the bathroom door open to listen in case anything happened downstairs. Every minute I didn't have eyes on my sister was painful, anxiety creeping up my spine at the thought of her being taken again. But when I returned to the living room, she was right where I'd left her, curled up on the corner of the couch.

My mom hadn't moved either, but she was awake now.

"How are you feeling?" I asked in a whisper. Evie seemed like she was sleeping deeply, but I didn't want to risk waking her up.

"Tired. How are you?" she said. She looked terrible, evidence of the night's events everywhere I looked. Her face was covered in dried blood from her fight with Lydia. Her hair was clinging to her head in a damp, tangled clump, dirt streaking along the edges of her scalp. Three scratches stretched from her temple to her chin. They looked deep enough to scar.

"Exhausted," I said.

My mom just nodded. "Is she really gone? Did it work?"

"She's dead." A lump rose in my throat as I readied myself to say the next part. "I shot her."

"What?" Her brow crinkled in confusion.

"After you passed out…" I began, my voice breaking. I cleared my throat and started again. "After you passed out, she was having trouble breathing. When she figured out what you had done, she tried to grab the gun. But I got it first."

"I'm sorry. You shouldn't have had to do that," she whispered.

Fat tears rolled down my cheeks as I looked over my mother's head. I couldn't hold back a sob. She lifted the edge of her blanket and gestured for me to sit next to her. I climbed on the couch, tucking myself under her arm. Everything felt so complicated, but for now, I was grateful that she was alive.

"I'm so sorry, Lia," she said again, this time whispering the words against my hair. "I will never be able to apologize enough for the danger I put you and your sister in tonight. For what you had to do."

I wasn't ready to forgive her. I wasn't sure I ever would be. Still, I was grateful for the apology. I had so many questions, but one felt more important than the rest, at least for tonight: "Did you know she was planning to take Maddie?"

"No." The answer was short but clear. I didn't think she was lying.

"But you knew about the other girls?"

She nodded but didn't offer any excuses. I didn't know how to feel about it. In so many ways, I knew she was a victim in all this too. But she had known and done nothing to stop it. The blood of those girls was on her hands. I didn't know where it left us, but I was too tired to figure it out tonight.

How much of my life had been spent pretending to measure up to her expectations, striving for the perfection she prized? For the first time, I understood that her beauty, her relentless pursuit of control, had been carved into her, stitched into every piece of my mother. Her beauty had been created from violence, shaped by the very forces that confined her. She had spent years hiding the truth of what she was and where she came from, pretending she had control when, in reality, she had been as trapped as any of us. Bound by the same rigid rules she enforced—the only ones she had ever known.

She wrapped an arm around me as I slid closer to her. I rested my head against her chest as her fingers rubbed circles on my back, and she pressed a kiss to my crown. I let my eyes fall closed as I sank against her, her stolen heartbeat echoing in my ear. Maybe I would forgive her one day. Maybe I wouldn't. But tonight, I could rest in the uncertainty, knowing that I had a future ahead of me—one shaped by my own desires, not hers. I didn't know what the future held, but for once, my life would be mine, not to pretend but to actually live.

EPILOGUE
THE MISSING GIRLS

The next few weeks were difficult. It took me a while to recover, my body aching and exhausted for a long time after the new moon. Lia and I had many long conversations—the first truly honest ones I had ever had with anyone besides my sisters—about my life and my choices. That night had changed Lia. It had hardened her, grown her up in a way that made me a little sad. I wished I had protected her from what she had been forced to do.

We decided not to tell Evangeline the truth. She didn't remember anything from that night. In the end, Lia and I decided that telling her everything would cause her pain without offering any real closure.

I cried with my sisters more than I was willing to admit. Grieved harder for Mother than I had for all the girls whose lives she had stolen. I felt guilty. It was impossible to mourn the woman who had raised us without also mourning the monster who had made us.

Lydia and Kate apologized for their roles in Evangeline's kidnapping, but I couldn't hold them responsible. How many girls had I helped take over the years? How many mothers had I ripped daughters from? Why had I imagined my own daughters would be safe?

We were all guilty. It was impossible to draw a line between our crimes and Mother's. We had been both her hostages and her accomplices. We were afraid of her. She made us feel like we owed her our very lives, a debt we could never repay. We had been told what we were doing was a gift, although I didn't know if I'd ever really believed that.

I could make excuses for days, tell my version of the story in a way where I wasn't an active participant, merely another victim of Mother's crimes. But it wouldn't have been true.

I had looked into Christie's eyes and told her I would do whatever I could to find Maddie, while I knew her daughter sat less than a mile away. I had lied to my own daughter, watched as she grieved her best friend, and then watched Mother peel Maddie apart. There were no excuses big enough to absolve me of that.

I took some comfort in the fact that it was over now. No more girls would vanish into these woods. Maddie would be the last.

Jane and I had left what we could find of Maddie's bones on a trailhead and called in an anonymous tip to the police. At the very least, her parents could have closure. They would be holding a funeral in a few days.

We held our own funeral of sorts for Mother. Her body was gone, given back to the trees, but we carved her name under

Mary's. A small something to remember the woman who had raised us. No words were spoken, no hymns sung, and no promises made for the dead to find a better life after this one. We laid our mother to rest in silence, letting the language of the trees wrap around her memory.

There were long conversations about what to do with the girl in the basement. The four of us sat around the dining table in the cottage and discussed it, carefully weighing the merits of all options.

She was nearly done. Her heart was already pumping blood, her lungs breathing air, all with the help of the machines in the basement. It wouldn't take much to finish her. Jane had already figured out that we had enough pieces remaining. She could do it. Maybe not with Mother's level of craftsmanship, but well enough.

All it would take was the spark of the forest to wake her up.

We felt it was more of a tragedy to let all those girls' sacrifices go to waste. We would love this new sister. Take care of her. Give her a better life, a softer life than we'd had.

On the next new moon, as the hum moved through us, warming our blood, the trees leaned in closer. Our sacrifice was accepted. Jane held my hand tightly as the girl's chest rose with an inhale.

Emma was awake.

LOOKING FOR YOUR NEXT GREAT READ?

ENJOY THIS EXCERPT FROM
NO CHILD OF MINE, ANOTHER
UNFORGETTABLE STORY BY
NICHELLE GIRALDES.

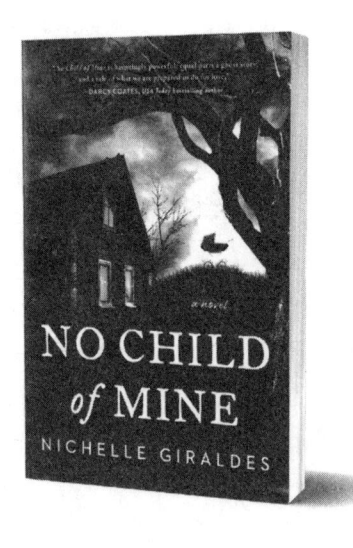

CHAPTER 1

Essie hung a white frame in the middle of an empty wall and collapsed next to her husband, avoiding the stacks of half-opened boxes that littered what would become their living room. The frame held a matchbook from a restaurant Essie and Sanjay had visited in Venice on their honeymoon. Even though it was more than four years old, it had never lived outside a box. The dinner was a long, leisurely affair with countless bottles of wine and the most divine food Essie had ever tasted. It was their last night in Italy, but the allure of calling Sanjay her "husband" had yet to wear off. They had spent the evening talking about buying a house—not this house specifically but an old house they could renovate on the weekends.

Essie gifted the framed matchbook to Sanjay on their first wedding anniversary. He had refused to hang it in the little apartment they shared. "We'll save it for that house we talked about. It'll be the first thing we hang on the walls," he promised her.

Even though the house was already full of their belongings, boxes cluttering every corner, it hadn't felt official until this frame was hanging on the wall. It looked strange in the middle of the empty room. It would have to come down before long, when the room was painted and the floors redone, but for now, it served as an official declaration that this place was theirs.

When she closed her eyes, she could imagine the room decades earlier, the wallpaper bright and crisp, and the room swirling with laughing guests. She leaned against Sanjay and stole a swallow of beer from the bottle in his hand. He kissed her temple. "You have dirt in your hair," he said. His mouth was close enough to her ear that she could feel its low, familiar rumble in her spine.

She let her head fall back against him. "I have dirt everywhere. I feel gross, and I stink." He laughed and buried his face in her shoulder. She relaxed into him, his body more familiar than her own. The line between the two of them felt blurry, as if over the years the paint had bled, and now it was impossible to tell where she began and he ended.

The house echoed. Most of their things hadn't made the move with them. Their last place, a little basement apartment, had been filled with mismatched furniture that fell apart before they could even finish putting it together. Sanjay had wanted to wait to buy real furniture until they bought a place of their own. It had sounded like a great idea at the time, but it meant that they were the proud owners of a very empty house. Despite the emptiness of these rooms, with their voices bouncing off the scratched wooden floors, it already felt like home to Essie.

Sanjay leaned into Essie's ear again. His voice rose barely

above a whisper as he pointed toward the big front window with its rippled glass, distorting the tree in the front yard into something from a fairy tale. "I think we should do built-ins around the window. And then..." He moved his hand to point to the other wall, and she shifted her body to follow without thinking. She could do this blind, follow him. "I think we should add a grand mantelpiece. Something that makes sense with the house's style but also feels a little more modern." He gestured toward the hulking fireplace that loomed on the other side of the room. The central section was in good shape. The green tiles were still intact, although quite dirty, but the surround and mantel were in disrepair. The wood had been painted countless times over the decades, and Sanjay didn't think it was salvageable.

Essie had a strange fondness for the peeling paint with its corners chipped off here and there to reveal layers of former families underneath. It wasn't something she'd usually gravitate toward. Typically, she wanted pristine lines and completed to-do lists, but here, in her new home with her husband, she would allow her world to take on some unfinished edges. She liked the idea of Sanjay and her adding their layer, their time in this house the next chapter in an ongoing story.

Sanjay had a vision for this place, and she trusted him. She would have opinions on the details—the paint colors, the furniture, the curtains—but easily drifted along to whatever new version he imagined. Her eyes slipped closed as he continued to talk about his plans for the main floor. She was still listening, but she knew these plans by heart. He had been telling her about them, making sketches and showing her pictures, since they had seen this place weeks ago. He had known immediately that it was their house. Sanjay had begun to almost drool the minute he saw the original hardwood and the central staircase and, of course, that grand fireplace. Essie had known the moment she saw his face that it was going to be theirs. She hadn't thought she would care too much about the house. She just wanted three bedrooms and a yard, but even she had gotten swept up in the magic of this place.

The moment they had gotten the keys, Essie saw herself five years from now, with a glass of wine in hand, sitting at the kitchen counter while Sanjay cooked, jazz playing from some hidden speaker. She imagined herself poring over papers in the room that would be her office, the window shaded by an old oak tree, massive wooden bookcases behind her. Essie didn't believe in fate, but there was something about this house that felt right. It felt like their home.

Sanjay shifted next to her, his neck cracking as he stretched his arms over his head. "I'm getting too old for this," he said. "Makes me wish we had kept our old couch."

"We both know that our couch wasn't much more comfortable than this floor," Essie said as she stood. "Do you want to take the first shower? I'll wait for the food."

She helped pull him up off the floor. "Or," he said, draping his arms around her neck as he stood at his full height, a few inches taller than her. "We could share the shower."

"And who would pay for the Thai food? It should be here soon."

"We'll tape an envelope to the door."

"Do you know which box the tape or envelopes are in?

Go shower," Essie said with a smile, flicking his arm. Sanjay kissed her quickly before trotting up the stairs. She listened as her husband's footsteps echoed across the bare floors into their bedroom and waited for the sound of the water turning on.

Wind swirled in through an open window, bringing with it the promise of an evening rainstorm and raising goose bumps on her sweat-dampened arms. The house made noises, creaks and whispers. She wasn't yet familiar with which noises were benign and which sounds that echoed against the peeling walls were more sinister.

ACKNOWLEDGMENTS

This book wouldn't exist without the incredible team behind it. Huge thanks to my literary agent, Claire Friedman, for her guidance and support. To my editor, Rachel Gilmer, who helped shape this book through its many transformations—your insight and patience made all the difference. Thank you to Jenna Jankowski, who also helped bring this story to life. I'm so grateful to Emily Engwall for her work in marketing and publicity, and to everyone at Sourcebooks and Poisoned Pen Press—so many hands touch a book on its journey to publication, and I'm deeply grateful for each one.

To my friends and family, who supported me through my debut novel and endured my chaos while I worked on this one—I'm so lucky to have you. Marlee Bush, thank you for reading an early draft of this story. And to Chelsea Iversen, my conversation partner for so many book events—your friendship and our discussions about writing have meant the world.

A special thank-you to Amy Lukavics and Darcy Coates,

whose generous blurbs for *No Child of Mine* helped bring my debut into the world. Finally, to the readers and reviewers of *No Child of Mine*, thank you. I'm so grateful to everyone who made time in their lives to read and share their thoughts—it means more than I can say.

ABOUT THE AUTHOR

Nichelle Giraldes is the author of *The Forest of Missing Girls* and *No Child of Mine*, a Colorado Book Award–winning horror novel. She writes Gothic, feminist horror about the tangled expectations placed on women. When she's not writing, she teaches math to middle and high school students and spends as much time as possible among the trees in Colorado.

Website: nichellegiraldes.com
Instagram: @nichellegiraldes
TikTok: @nichellegiraldes